MOLLY C

YOKED WI

MARY 'Molly' Clavering was born in Glasgow in 1900. Her father was a Glasgow businessman, and her mother's grandfather had been a doctor in Moffat, where the author would live for nearly 50 years after World War Two.

She had little interest in conventional schooling as a child, but enjoyed studying nature, and read and wrote compulsively, considering herself a 'poetess' by the age of seven.

She returned to Scotland after her school days, and published three novels in the late 1920s, as well as being active in her local girl guides and writing two scenarios for ambitious historical pageants.

In 1936, the first of four novels under the pseudonym 'B. Mollett' appeared. Molly Clavering's war service in the WRNS interrupted her writing career, and in 1947 she moved to Moffat, in the Scottish border country, where she lived alone, but was active in local community activities. She resumed writing fiction, producing seven post-war novels and numerous serialized novels and novellas in the *People's Friend* magazine.

Molly Clavering died in Moffat on February 12, 1995.

TITLES BY MOLLY CLAVERING

Fiction

Georgina and the Stairs (1927)
The Leech of Life (1928)
Wantonwalls (1929)
Susan Settles Down (1936, as 'B. Mollett')
Love Comes Home (1938, as 'B. Mollett')
Yoked with a Lamb (1938, as 'B. Mollett')
Touch Not the Nettle (1939, as 'B. Mollett')
Mrs. Lorimer's Quiet Summer (1953)
Because of Sam (1954)
Dear Hugo (1955)
Near Neighbours (1956)
Result of the Finals (1957)
Dr. Glasgow's Family (1960)
Spring Adventure (1962)

Non-Fiction

From the Border Hills (1953)

Between 1952 and 1976, Molly Clavering also serialized at least two dozen novels or novellas in the *People's Friend* under the names Marion Moffatt and Emma Munro. Some of these were reprinted as 'pocket novels' as late as 1994.

MOLLY CLAVERING

YOKED WITH A LAMB

With an introduction by
Elizabeth Crawford

DEAN STREET PRESS

A Furrowed Middlebrow Book
FM66

Published by Dean Street Press 2021

Copyright © 1938 Molly Clavering

Introduction © 2021 Elizabeth Crawford

First published in 1938 by Stanley Paul & Co

Cover by DSP
Shows detail from *Bemersyde House* (1922) by E.W. Haslehurst

ISBN 978 1 914150 47 0

www.deanstreetpress.co.uk

THIS BOOK

is dedicated with love to the
kindest and most charming of

GRANDMOTHERS

INTRODUCTION

Of *Yoked with a Lamb*, the second of Molly Clavering's novels to be published under the pseudonym of 'B. Mollett', the *Dundee Courier and Advertiser* (19 May 1938) commented, 'The intimate social atmosphere of a homey community is made wonderfully real'. However, the *Daily Mirror* (7 April 1938) was rather more incisive, recognising that what fuelled life in that 'homey community' was gossip, so that 'If an extra pigeon went stalking across the old paving stones . . . it was news in Haystoun. Tongues wagged – teacups clinked in delightful scandal-spreading.' *Yoked with a Lamb*, describing the events surrounding an attempt to repair a marriage, broken when the husband had left his wife several years earlier for another woman, was a rather audacious choice of subject. Played out in a small Scottish Border community, it did indeed allow the author plenty of scope for the creation of gossip and gossipers, as well as demonstrating that there was more to marriage than mere fidelity.

Yoked with a Lamb was, in fact, Molly Clavering's fifth novel, the first three having been issued under her own name. The pseudonym 'B. Mollett' had most likely been a whim of her new publisher, indicating neither, it would seem, any desire for privacy or change of style or genre. Whether writing as 'B. Mollett' or as herself, Molly Clavering centred her fiction on life in the Scottish countryside, with occasional forays into Edinburgh, the novels reflecting the society of the day, with characters drawn from all strata, the plots driven, as we have noted, by small-town gossip, rendered on occasion very effectively in demotic Scots. Molly is peculiarly adept at describing, in all seasons, the scenery and atmosphere of the Borders. We have no doubt, for instance, that it is through her eyes that in *Yoked with a Lamb* Kate Heron sees 'The Lammermuirs, her own hills, looking far away and hazy in the heat . . . a long dim blue rampart against the summer sky. The very names – Bleak Law, Lammer Law, Nine Stane Rig, Crib Cleuch – rang wild in her ears as a Border ballad.'

Born in Glasgow on 23 October 1900, Molly Clavering was the eldest child of John Mollett Clavering (1858-1936) and his wife, Esther (1874-1943). Named 'Mary' for her paternal grandmother, she was always known by the diminutive, 'Molly'. Her brother, Alan, was born in 1903 and her sister, Esther, in 1907. Although John Clavering, as his father before him, worked from an office in central Glasgow, brokering both iron and grain, by 1911 the family had moved to the Stirlingshire countryside eleven miles north of the city, to Alreoch House outside the village of Blanefield. In an autobiographical article Molly Clavering later commented, 'I was brought up in the country, and until I went to school ran wild more or less'. She was taught by her father 'to know the birds and flowers, the weather and the hills round our house' and from this ability to observe were to spring the descriptions of the countryside that give readers of her novels such pleasure.

By the age of seven Molly was sufficiently confident in her literary attainment to consider herself a 'poetess', a view with which her father enthusiastically concurred. Happily, her mother, while entirely supportive, balanced paternal adulation with a perhaps necessary element of gentle criticism. In these early years Molly was probably educated at home, reading 'everything I could lay hands on (we were never restricted in our reading)' and having little 'time for orthodox lessons, though I liked history and Latin'. She was later sent away to boarding school, to Mortimer House in Clifton, Bristol, the choice perhaps dictated by the reputation of its founder and principal, Mrs Meyrick Heath, whom Molly later described as 'a woman of wide culture and great character [who] influenced all the girls who went there'. However, despite a congenial environment, life at Mortimer House was so different from the freedom she enjoyed at home that Molly 'found the society of girls and the regular hours very difficult at first'. Although she later admitted that she preferred devoting time and effort to her own writing rather than school-work, she did sufficiently well academically to be offered a place at Oxford. Her parents, however, ruled against this, perhaps for reasons of finance. It is noticeable that in her novels Molly makes little mention of the education of her heroines, although they do demonstrate a close and loving knowledge of Dickens, Thackeray, Trollope, and, as shown in the choice of title for *Yoked with a Lamb*, Shakespeare.

After leaving school Molly returned home to Arleoch House and, with no need to take paid employment, was able to concentrate on her writing, publishing her first novel in 1927. Always sociable, she took an active interest in local activities, particularly in the Girl Guides, with which her sister Esther, until her tragically early death in 1926, was also involved. During these years Molly not only acted as an officer for the Guides but was able to put her literary talents to fund-raising effect for them by writing scenarios for two ambitious Scottish history pageants. The first, in which she took the pivotal part of 'Fate', was staged in Stirlingshire in 1929, with a cast of 500. However, for the second in 1930 she moved south and wrote the 'Border Historical Pageant' in aid of the Roxburgh Girl Guides. Performed at Minto House, Roxburghshire, in the presence of royalty, this pageant featured a large choir and a cast of 700, with Molly in the leading part as 'The Spirit of Borderland Legend'. For Molly was already devoted to the Border country, often visiting the area to stay with relations and attending, on occasion, a hunt ball.

Molly Clavering published a further two novels as 'B. Mollett' before, on the outbreak of the Second World War, joining the Women's Royal Naval Service, based for the duration at Greenock, then an important and frenetic naval station. Serving in the Signals Cypher Branch, she eventually achieved the rank of second officer. Although there was no obvious family connection to the Navy, it is noticeable that even in her pre-war novels many of the most attractive male characters, such as 'Robin Anstruther' in *Yoked with a Lamb*, are associated with the Senior Service.

After she was demobbed Molly moved to the Borders, setting up home in Moffat, the Dumfriesshire town in which her great-grandfather had been a doctor. She shared 'Clover Cottage' with a series of black standard poodles, one of them a present from D.E. Stevenson, another of the town's novelists, whom she had known since the 1930s. The latter's granddaughter, Penny Kent, remembers how 'Molly used to breeze and bluster into North Park (my Grandmother's house) a rush of fresh air, gaberdine flapping, grey hair flying with her large, bouncy black poodles, Ham and Pam (and later Bramble), shaking, dripping and muddy from some wild walk through Tank Wood or over Gallow Hill'. Her love of the area was made evident in her only non-fiction book, *From the Border Hills* (1953).

During these post-war years Molly Clavering continued her work with the Girl Guides, serving for nine years as County Commissioner, was president of the local Scottish Country Dance Association, and active in the Women's Rural Institute. She was a member of Moffat town council, 1951-60, and for three years from 1957 was the town's first and only woman magistrate. She continued writing, publishing seven further novels, as well as a steady stream of the stories she referred to as her 'bread and butter', issued, under a variety of pseudonyms, by that very popular women's magazine, the *People's Friend*.

Molly Clavering's long and fruitful life finally ended on 12 February 1995. Describing in her the very characteristics to be found in the novels, Wendy Simpson, another of D.E. Stevenson's granddaughters, remembered Molly as 'A convivial and warm human being who enjoyed the company of friends, especially young people, with her entertaining wit and a sense of fun allied to a robustness to stand up for what she believed in.'.

Elizabeth Crawford

CHAPTER ONE

1

Miss Flora Milligan, tripping westwards through the royal burgh of Haystoun with a bowl of her famous potted head, decently shrouded from vulgar gaze by a snowy napkin, in a neat basket, was the first person of any social standing to notice that the 'To Sell or Let' board had been taken down from the Soonhope entrance. This discovery, deliciously exciting though it was, put her in a quandary. Her immediate impulse, born of inclination and duty alike, was to turn back and carry the news red-hot to her mother. As everyone knows, news, like a boiled egg, is only worth having when it is absolutely fresh. On the other hand, it was Miss Milligan's proud boast that every dish of potted head made by her for the Parish Church Fancye Fayre was always sold before the sale was even opened; and if she went home now, she would not have time to deliver the very last consignment, and would thus break her proud record, for this was the day of the Fayre. Apart altogether from that, there was a danger that Mrs. Anstruther, who would be sure to hear that all Miss Milligan's other clients had already received their orders, might feel slighted if hers did not arrive this morning, and refuse to take it at all, out of pure malice. Miss Milligan shuddered at the thought. She had no wish to be left with even one shape of potted head on her hands.

Excellent though it was, the concocting of this dainty in bulk left its maker with strangely little appetite for it. Miss Milligan saw quite clearly that she must go on her way, and trust that Mamma would not hear the news from another source in the meantime. The chance that she might meet someone who could give her a few additional facts to add to the bare statement of the notice-board's disappearance lent lightness to her feet, and she proceeded at a brisk pact towards Mrs. Anstruther's red-roofed villa beyond the railway station, at the very west end of the town.

Miss Milligan had the reputation of being the most kindly and amiable woman in Haystoun, though in fact she was more cowed by her mother than anything else, but she felt a trifle displeased with Providence as she pushed open the green gate of The Anchorage.

She had not met a soul of whom she could ask information about Soonhope without loss of dignity, and while she agreed in theory that virtue was its own reward, in practice she preferred something a little more substantial. So, although she saw Mrs. Anstruther waving a hand from behind the zareba of ferns which filled her drawing-room window, she pretended a wilful blindness, and marched up to the front door, where she rang the bell with greater vigour than usual.

"Well, Flora. You look very flustered, and surely you're getting short-sighted?" was a greeting not calculated to soothe her as she entered the drawing-room. "What's that rubbish in your basket, eh?"

"The potted head you ordered, Mrs. Anstruther," said Miss Milligan with restraint. Really, Mrs. Anstruther, sitting there in her arm-chair by the window, where she could peer through her ferns at everything that passed, was becoming daily more difficult to bear with. So knotted with rheumatism that she could barely move, dependent on the kindness of such of her friends as owned cars for her rare outings—for that nephew of hers up at Pennymuir did little enough for her—alone save for the elderly grenadier of a maid who looked after her with grim devotion, she should have aroused only gentle feelings of pity and sympathy in others. Yet how often, thought Miss Milligan, unpacking her basket with hands quivering with annoyance and flurry, was one conscious not of pity but of exasperation. It was all wrong.

"Stop fumbling with that paper," said Mrs. Anstruther suddenly. "There's no hurry to unpack the stuff. How many years, Flora Milligan, have you been making potted head for the Fancye Fayre? (It used to be a plain church sale in the days when I had a stall, but I suppose Haystoun is too grand for that nowadays!) How many years have I been buying it?"

"I—I don't quite know," Miss Milligan was confused by this unexpected question. "It must be quite a long time now."

"What an object in life! The making of potted head which nobody really wants to buy!" Mrs. Anstruther uttered a sudden scoffing hoot of laughter. "And yet I suppose you consider that you lead a useful life, eh, Flora?"

Really, Mrs. Anstruther was worse than usual to-day. Poor Miss Milligan, drawing herself up, answered with tremulous dignity. "I have always *tried* to lead a useful life in my own small way."

"Small way. Yes, our ways are certainly pretty small. I wonder if they count for anything in the scheme of the universe? There, Flora!"—as a small sniffing sound came from her visitor. "I am only being cantankerous, as usual, and speaking my mind for once. Always a mistake. It is, fortunately, too expensive a luxury to indulge in often. You must allow me a little license, my dear. Remember that if you are the best-natured woman in the burgh—though that isn't saying much in a place so overflowing with scandal—I am well known to be the worst. Now I'll try to make amends. You'll have a glass of elderberry wine with me, and I'll give you a piece of news to take home to your mother."

Miss Milligan, inwardly telling herself that it was only for Mamma's sake, blew her nose and listened.

"Of course you saw on your way here that Soonhope is no longer to let." This was a statement rather than a question, but Mrs. Anstruther did not hurry. Indeed, she paused for so long that her listener almost danced with impatience. Finally, when Miss Milligan had decided that flesh and blood could not bear the suspense another moment, she said with careful casualness: "The Lockharts are coming back, and about time too."

"The Lockharts?" gasped Miss Milligan, her faint resentment forgotten. This was news with a vengeance. Virtue had received a reward so much greater than she looked lor that she felt humbly grateful. "But—surely you can't mean the *Lockharts*?"

"I do mean the Lockharts. After all, Andrew Lockhart owns Soonhope, and has neglected his duties far too long as it is."

"But—the *scandal*!" whispered Miss Milligan, her thin face flushing a delicate shade of mauve. "What will people say?"

"If people have any sense they'll say nothing," Mrs. Anstruther answered grimly, and touched the handbell at her side to summon the grenadier, who presently marched in carrying a tray with elderberry wine in tiny thistle glasses, and a plate of crisp, wafer-thin home-made wheaten biscuits.

Not until the two ladies had tasted this refreshment did Miss Milligan pluck up courage to ask: "Is Mrs. Lockhart coming too? And the children?"

"Well," said Mrs. Anstruther, most regrettably smacking her lips over her elderberry wine, "if you mean, is Andrew Lockhart bringing the woman he ran away with, to Soonhope, I must disappoint you. Lucy Lockhart and the children—the girl is grown-up now, by the way—are coming back also. When I said the Lockharts, of course I meant the whole family."

In moments of stress Miss Milligan's nose quivered like a rabbit's, and it now became violently agitated. "Since you have brought up that—that very painful subject, Mrs. Anstruther, I must say I think it shows a want of proper feeling on Andrew Lockhart's part to come back to the place which he left in such disgraceful circumstances," she said.

"For goodness' sake, Flora, if you want to talk about things, why can't you call them by their names? Everyone in Haystoun—everyone in the county knows that Andrew ran off with Colonel Fardell's wife, but it's an old story now. *I* think it shows a good deal of courage to come back, knowing how much unkind gossip there will be," said Mrs. Anstruther. "I had a feeling that he'd have to come back sooner or later to his own place, and the best thing we can do is to forget what is past, and try to help the Lockharts to forget it too."

"We look at it from such different points of view," said Miss Milligan gently, for to the purveyor of news like this much could be forgiven. Not Mrs. Anstruther's next remark, though. When that lady rejoined, "Yes, thank God!" with fervour, her guest rose to go, feeling that even the most Christian forbearance could not be expected to remain proof against this sort of thing.

"Oh, are you going?" asked Mrs. Anstruther, setting her empty glass on the tray and fumbling in the depths of a capacious black bag which permanently occupied her lap. "Well, you want the money for the potted head, eh? One-and-fourpence and the dish back, isn't it? Now hurry home to your mother with the news. It ought to keep her in conversation for to-day at least. Good morning, Flora."

Miss Milligan, empty basket over one arm, and a shilling, a threepenny-bit, and a penny clasped in the grey fabric palm of her other hand, closed the gate of The Anchorage, looking like a small ruffled bird. Really, poor Mrs. Anstruther!

But as she pattered quickly on her homeward way, indignation gave place to other feelings. Excitement over the thought of Mrs. Lockhart's return and the family reunion which was to be staged at Soonhope was one. The other, as she saw the noble square tower of the Parish Church rising above a huddle of roofs on the low ground sloping to the river, was a gush of modest joy in her share of the restoration work towards which the Fancye Fayre laboured yearly to acquire funds. Certainly a part of it, however humble, would be built on a solid foundation of potted head.

When Miss Milligan reached the little house in Old Pettycraw Street where she had spent almost the whole of her life, she decided to give herself the pleasure of adding the last one-and-fourpence to the sum already in her cash-box before going up to Mamma with her news. The discovery that the grand total reached was twenty-three and eightpence, quite an advance on the previous year's harvest, was doubly delightful, and she took the steep dark stairs almost without noticing them. Outside Mamma's door she paused for a moment to regain her breath and compose herself to a more decorous frame of mind. Dear Mamma, being an invalid, disliked any suspicion of excitement, undue gaiety or acute distress. In her presence all emotions had to be muted to subdued half-tones, and her daughter surrounded her with an almost visible haze of tender solicitude. Before meeting Mrs. Milligan, strangers pictured her as a tiny, fragile creature, a delicate edition of her daughter, and were apt when they saw her to experience a rude shock. For Miss Milligan, hovering over her parent with unending care, was as improbable and ludicrous as a small, elderly linnet ministering to a barn-owl. Immense, billowing over a double bed which looked too small for her, her outlines made fluffier by a mass of soft shawls, old Mrs. Milligan's resemblance to an owl was increased by a hooked nose projecting from a round white face, and a pair of eyes magnified by horn-rimmed spectacles. These eyes, as her daughter entered, were skimming the Births, Marriages and Deaths column of *The Scotsman*, nor did she look up, though she said in a faintly suffering tone: "You've been a long time, Flora."

"I know, Mamma," said Miss Milligan apologetically. "Jean Anstruther would have nothing new, I suppose?" asked Mrs. Milligan, her sharp eyes leaving the newspaper for long enough to dart to her daughter's face.

"We—ell," began Miss Milligan with caution, for she knew better than to rush things. "I wouldn't say that, Mamma. I believe Mrs. Anstruther had a letter from Mrs. Lockhart."

"Ah!" exclaimed Mrs. Milligan alertly, now laying the paper aside. "From Lucy Lockhart? What had she to say for herself? Did you see the letter?"

"Well, no. But I knew it was in that black bag of hers. She kept on touching it all the time she was talking—you know how she does, Mamma."

"Then," Mrs. Milligan deduced with calm authority, "the letter wouldn't be from Lucy at all, but from Andrew Lockhart's aunt, Robina Barlas. She and Jean Anstruther have always kept up. And so there's news of the Lockharts, is there?"

The preliminary canter over safely, Miss Milligan began her recital with confidence, and was rewarded by her parent's undivided attention. Finally Mrs. Milligan leant back against her pillows with a sigh of exhausted satisfaction. "I'll take my Bovril now, Flora," she said. "Hearing the news has quite tired me. You know what excitement does to my heart."

The Bovril had been brought, tasted, and pronounced lacking in salt, and only when this defect had been remedied did Mrs. Milligan feel equal to further discussion of the engrossing topic.

2

"Oh, the whole town is bound to know about it by this time," said Mrs. Anstruther composedly. "They had to hear some time or other, and by telling Flora Milligan I've saved everybody a lot of useless speculation. But I did *not* tell her that you were coming here this afternoon, Lucy."

"You are being," said Mrs. Lockhart, "incredibly kind as well as discreet. Aunt Robina assured me that you'd be pleased to see me, but I rather discounted that. You know her sweet nature. She always expects the world to share her own large-hearted charitable views, bless her."

"I'm glad I haven't fallen below standard," Mrs. Anstruther said rather dryly. "Though I have not a reputation for kindness in Haystoun, I don't think I am quite a gorgon, and I was always fond of Andrew."

"I didn't mean to offend you, but I am rather—on edge just now," said Lucy Lockhart with a nervous laugh. "And of course everyone here will be busy raking up the old scandal, picking it to rags to see if they could possibly have missed anything. Do you think we are complete fools to come back to Soonhope? It was Andrew's doing, not mine."

"I always expected it," said Mrs. Anstruther. "The call of his own country rings very loud in the ears of a man like Andrew. 'The sun rises fair in France, and fair sets he, But he hath tint the blithe blink he had in my ain countrie.'"

Lucy Lockhart stirred restlessly, as if the cushion at her back was not comfortable, and a faint spasm of distress momentarily distorted her still pretty, skilfully made-up face. "Of course. The place," she murmured. "Andrew was always crazy about Soonhope." Then she leaned forward. "Mrs. Anstruther," she said, her eyes searching the older woman's, "what do you suppose is going to happen when we've settled down here again? Will everyone cold-shoulder us? It's going to be—awkward—especially for the children, if they do."

"You needn't be afraid of that, my dear Lucy," said Mrs. Anstruther with her grim laugh. "Everybody will flock to call on you, at least once."

"I—see." They looked at each other with complete comprehension for an instant, then, shrugging her shoulders, Lucy Lockhart sank back into her chair. "Well, we're asking for it, of course," she said resignedly. "And I suppose it doesn't much matter, after all."

"That's the proper spirit," Mrs. Anstruther approved. "Tell 'em all to go to the devil, my dear. Your friends will see that you aren't lonely, and as you say, the others don't count."

"I suppose it was stupid of me to sneak out here by bus to-day, but I did want to have one look at the house and garden all by myself, without people staring at me and asking silly questions. *You* know what Haystoun is."

"I certainly ought to," answered Mrs. Anstruther. "But you're safe enough to-day, Lucy. You couldn't have chosen a better afternoon for a stealthy visit. It's the 'Fancy Fayre'—with a lot of extra Y's and E's—for the parish Church restoration fund, and everyone is down at the Manse, where I've no doubt poor Flora is telling them all about your romantic return. You can go out at the back here and along the Loaning to the garden gate at Soonhope, and not a soul will be a penny the wiser except Hannah and me, and we don't chatter."

"I know you don't," said Lucy, with a grateful smile for the grenadier, who had just carried in the tea-tray. "That's why Aunt Robina told me to come to you."

She accepted a cup of tea, and by silent consent the talk drifted to impersonal matters, until Mrs. Anstruther said: "I don't want to hurry you, but remember that everyone will go home from the Fancye Fayre—ridiculous name for a decent sale of work!—by way of Soonhope. In fact, I'll probably have a good many unexpected visitors myself this evening. It you want to go over the place in peace, you ought to be starting now."

"I will." Mrs. Lockhart stood up, very trim in her neat brown tweeds, but, her hostess thought, far too thin, for she could remember when Lucy had been pleasantly plump as a partridge.

"Don't worry too much over what people say," she said on a sudden impulse.

"Oh—worry—!" Lucy smiled the suggestion away. "Good-bye, Mrs. Anstruther, and thank you. I won't say more, for I know you hate gush, but I am very glad indeed that Aunt Robina insisted on my coming to see you. It's done me good."

She walked quickly along the green Loaning between high hedges of thorn and wild roses. Ahead of her she could see the familiar gateway, the two stone pillars each surmounted by a moss-grown stone ball, the old walnut tree hanging its dark green leaves over the wall. So little was changed; so little—except herself and Andrew, and her world which had tumbled about her ears with a crash which still rang in them after four years. . . . The gate—it was a double door, really, its supporting pillars a part of the high garden wall— still creaked when she pushed it open after unlocking it with one of a bunch of keys which she carried, and the general appearance of the garden was unchanged. Overgrown though it was, she could still pick out well-known rose-bushes, clumps of ripening lavender. Her hand felt mechanically for the southernwood which grew in the left border just inside the door, and at once her fingers tightened on the soft, feathery leaves; she smelt their sharp, spicy fragrance as she bruised them. . . . There was the weather-stained teak seat under the big pear tree, and the arbour where earwigs lurked, to fall with a horrid plop! on to the book of anyone who sat reading in its green shade. The grass walks had been cut not long before, and the daisies which had escaped were wide open, very close to the turf, their golden eyes staring up at the sun.

Lucy Lockhart walked all round the garden slowly, remembering. Andrew had asked her to marry him, standing near the great bush of Malmaison roses, and she had been wearing a cluster of them tucked into the belt of her white piqué skirt. His Aunt Robina, Mrs. Barlas, a widow even then, had kept house for him, until he married. Lucy wondered a little if he would not have been better to remain a bachelor, looked after by Aunt Robina, but she did not really believe it. She had always been a good wife to him. Anyhow, it was too late to worry over that sort of thing now! And he had always had a good deal of freedom in spite of marriage, she thought bitterly; his eye for a pretty woman might often have led him into mischief if it had not been for her intervention. And this last affair, with Elizabeth Fardell, her own friend, as she had supposed, had been more than mischief unfortunately. Again Lucy's face contracted with that little spasm of distress. Elizabeth had been often to Soonhope, had walked here in the garden. To-day it seemed as if the place rang again with the ghost of her charming voice raised in some old song, or in careless laughter, as if no one else had ever known the garden. Would Andrew find the same thing? Or would he remember, as she usually did, all the children who had played and quarrelled, filched strawberries and been stung by wasps, within these mellow walls? Their own children, and Aunt Robina's grandchildren Kate and Grey Heron, and farther back, Andrew himself and his brothers, three of them, killed in the greedy years between 1914 and 1918, as his cousin and playmate Gavin Barlas had been.

The house itself, Lucy thought, could hardly remind her of more, and yet, when she had left the garden by the other door and stood on the lawn looking at the prim white rough-cast front, the door set back between the curves of two half-round towers roofed with purple slate, she knew that she could not go inside, could not brave that echoing hall, the untenanted rooms. She began to wonder whether she could live in it again, even after it had been restored to its former state of cheerful occupancy. It was four years since she and Andrew had met. Their reconciliation—if reconciliation was the name for an arrangement made to benefit the children and save Soonhope from neglect—had been carried out by letter. Perhaps Andrew had changed; perhaps she had, too.

It was while she was being jolted back to Edinburgh in the bus that the idea came to Lucy. Instead of meeting Andrew alone, with only the staring, interested eyes of the children to embarrass them both further, she would have a house-party at Soonhope, gathered before he came back. It would probably annoy him intensely, but he deserved that. "Yes," thought Lucy, "I'll do it. Aunt Robina, and the Herons if they'll come. I know Greystiel Heron doesn't approve of us now, but, after all, his wife is Aunt Robina's daughter and Andrew's first cousin, and Kate and young Grey came to Soonhope often enough in the past. Kate would be a tower of strength. . . . Oh!" A further idea had come to her, of such brilliance that she almost shouted aloud. "Oh! I wonder if Kate would come and look after the opening of the house, and painters and things? I believe she'd love it, and if I can only make her look on it as a job then I could give her something for her work and time I'd give almost anything in reason not to have to see Soonhope again until it's ready for us to move in. Yes, that's an idea of such beauty that I can hardly believe it came to me. If Kate will do it, she'll be the very person for the job!"

3

Old Mrs. Milligan, wreathed in Shetland shawls, lay among her pillows and luxuriated in gloomy thoughts. She was being grossly neglected by her only child. Ever since the day of the Fancye Fayre Flora had been, to use her own phrase, 'neither to hold nor to bind,' so inflated with the idea of her importance that the sharpest rebuke failed to puncture her conceit. Little did it matter to her nowadays if her poor, helpless mother's Bovril was too hot or too cold, too salt or not sufficiently seasoned. Off she jaunted to tea-parties here and bridge there, leaving the parent who should have been her first charge to the mercies of a heavy-footed peroxide blonde whose fingers were all thumbs.

Here it was, three minutes past twelve by wireless time, and no one had brought up her glass of Wincarnis, though Flora knew very well how much she depended on it to bridge the gulf between her

Bovril at eleven and one o'clock lunch. Downstairs she could hear Mima, the peroxide blonde, engaged in shrill converse with some tradesman: the butcher's boy, probably, a worthless young scoundrel whose chubby red cheeks, and black hair sleek from constant smoothing by its owner's suety hands, made him an object of admiration to every domestic in Old Pettycraw Street. Yells of laughter followed by a prolonged coquettish screech and the slamming of a door seemed to indicate that at last Mima had dismissed her swain. Mrs. Milligan prepared to stage a heart attack the moment that her bedroom door opened to admit her handmaiden with the delayed restorative. But two more minutes ticked by, and still there was no sign of Mima or the Wincarnis. Mrs. Milligan gave up the idea of the heart attack, and decided merely to turn faint if anyone should be good enough to remember her existence. After that, it was the last straw that she should be taken unawares munching a Rich Tea biscuit, book in hand, spectacles on nose, when Flora, without warning, charged—yes, *charged* was the only word for it—into the room like a mad bull.

"Mamma!" she cried excitedly, quite forgetting her usual sick-room manner, and speaking in a high voice and with what her parent considered a sickening assumption of girlishness. "What do you think? Old Mrs. Barlas was out at Soonhope yesterday afternoon. And the painters are going in next week!"

"I'll thank you to remember, Flora, that I am not deaf," responded Mrs. Milligan. "Though I soon will be if you persist in screaming at me. Perhaps that's your object? And look at the time. Six minutes past twelve, and I've never had my Wincarnis yet."

"Six minutes past—!" Miss Milligan shrank under her mother's accusing look, then tried bravely to rally. "Oh, no, Mamma, not *six* minutes past. This clock is a little fast. I heard the Town Hall strike as I came upstairs."

"Six minutes past by Big Ben. I can't help it if the Town Hall is slow. The wireless is good enough for me, and I prefer to take my nourishment by it. Perhaps, if you can *spare* the *time*, Flora"— bitterly—"you will bring me my Wincarnis at once."

This severity, Mrs. Milligan was glad to see, had its desired effect. Flora crept away, reduced to her normal mouse-like quiet. On her reappearance with the wineglass of tonic, justice was tempered with mercy, for Mrs. Milligan expressed a wish to hear the morning's news. Not out of the daily paper, she could read that for herself, but the richer, more intimate news of Haystoun, told with a wealth of minute detail and delicious conjecture, which was so much more enjoyable than anything happening in the world beyond its bounds. Finally, when she had plucked every smallest shred of interest from her daughter's account, Mrs. Milligan royally extended forgiveness in the shape of a suggestion that Flora should call on Mrs. Anstruther after lunch.

"You'll see, Flora, that Jean Anstruther will know more about Soonhope and the Lockharts than anyone in the town."

Miss Milligan demurred. She was afraid of Mrs. Anstruther's sharp tongue, and was also apt to forget, in her new character of expert on all the Soonhope affairs, that she owed her knowledge in the first place to the rheumatic owner of The Anchorage.

So: "Oh, I don't believe she does, Mamma," she protested feebly. "After all, she can't get about—"

"Jean Anstruther will know," repeated her mother inexorably. "She and Robina Barlas were great friends when they were girls, and Robina is sure to have told her all the Lockharts' plans. I wish I could go myself. It would take more than Jean Anstruther to frighten me. If you can get her to talk, she'll tell you *plenty*. But you're a poor creature, Flora, and easily daunted. No more spirit than a mouse!"

As it was easier to cope with Mrs. Anstruther, from whom at least she could escape, than to thwart Mamma, Miss Milligan put on her second-best straw hat—it had been her best the summer before, and next year would see it relegated to the humble position of shopping headgear—and set out through the length of the town towards The Anchorage.

Haystoun lay sleeping in the sun, lost in a dream of the glorious past. It had cradled kings, it had boasted a palace, besides a proud abbey outside the walls on the banks of the slow-running Alewater, it had been a bulwark against the invading English, a poet had sung of it as 'Scotland's wall.' Before the river silted up it had been a port, with the small ships sailing to the very gates of the town. The Napoleonic Wars had seen its last days of importance, when soldiers from the new barracks beyond the West Port had thronged the streets, and there had been sounds of 'revelry by night' from the

Assembly Rooms in the Town House. Very little had changed since that martial bustle died away. The barracks, fallen into ruin, had disappeared as completely as the ancient palace, though a remnant of the great abbey still stood, forming the Parish Church, and never even half-filled now of a Sunday morning.

Pigeons sidled over the rough cobbles of the High Street, where encroaching grass thrust slender green spears between the stones. They were so tame that they hardly moved as Miss Milligan passed. The tall old houses, the newest built in the early days of the Georges, rose towards the sky, their upper stories still stately above the shops which had usurped the ground floors. The gaunt stone fronts and small-paned windows smiled down with ineffable disdain even on the flaring ice-cream saloon of Signor Emilio Mazzoli opposite the Bell Inn.

The Town Hall, like a headland between two bays, separated the High Street from Crossgate Street, which ran parallel with it towards the river. West of the Town Hall was Port Street, wide and straight, the Corn Exchange midway on one side behind a row of plane trees, and on the other a few of the best shops in the burgh. Miss Milligan, passing these, came to large houses standing back from the street among gardens brilliant with summer flowers. A little farther on the street climbed a slight hill, turned a bend, and became a road, tree-lined, with the high wall of Soonhope marching along its right-hand side.

At the gates Miss Milligan did her best to peer in without seeming to do so, a difficult feat, but one which years of practice made possible. The glimpse of Soonhope from the gates, however, was always disappointing. The house lay a hundred yards back from the road, obscured by the great beeches on either side of a winding avenue which doubled the distance from lodge to door. Only the slates of the roof were visible above the heavy midsummer foliage, and though the sun had lent them the purple sheen of the feathers on a dove's breast, Miss Milligan felt cheated. A roof told you nothing, especially when all the chimneys were hidden and it was impossible to see even if they were smoking. As for the painters, an army might be at work in there, and no one the wiser. A woman came out of the lodge just inside the gates and Miss Milligan, bending down, pretended to tie a shoe-lace. Then, rising with a somewhat flushed face, she hurried on. It would never do if the Pows at the lodge were to suspect her of vulgar curiosity. Really, on the whole, it was more satisfactory to brave Mrs. Anstruther, even in a crusty mood.

Mrs. Anstruther, of course, was in, and in a surprisingly amiable frame of mind. Her manner, as she greeted her caller, might almost have been described as affable. Since affability had never been one of Mrs. Anstruther's strongest suits, a visitor more acute and less nervously flustered than Miss Milligan might have read the ironic amusement behind her welcome. For Mrs. Anstruther found this seeking after knowledge on the part of Haystoun infinitely more amusing than any book. She knew exactly why Flora Milligan had come to see her, and was prepared to give her a fresh packet of information to take home to her mother, but it was not in her nature to deny herself the dry pleasure of watching her victim's clumsy efforts to come to the point in an easy and natural manner.

At last, after Miss Milligan had made several fruitless attempts to break through a hedge of weather and garden small-talk, her hostess took pity on her. 'Poor Flora,' she thought, much more charitably than she ever spoke, 'she will get her head in her hands if she goes back to that old harridan without having found out anything.'

Aloud she said carelessly: "By the way, I saw Mrs. Barlas yesterday."

Miss Milligan was quite pathetically grateful. "Did—did you?" she stammered, striving in vain after a decent composure. "That must have been very pleasant."

"It was," said Mrs. Anstruther. "She took tea with me, and we had a long *siderent*, gossiping over old times. She came out for Lucy Lockhart, to see what papering and painting was necessary at Soonhope."

"Oh, of course, of course," said Miss Milligan, in a tone which meant, more plainly than she realized: 'Go on, go on!'

"She also brought me a letter from Lucy, who has decided, I think very wisely," continued Mrs. Anstruther, fumbling in her black bag. "... Now, where did I put my handkerchief? Ah, yes, here it is. ... Lucy has decided to keep away from Haystoun until Soonhope is ready for occupation again."

Miss Milligan was more than a little shocked. In Haystoun every workman who entered a house was stood over until his job was properly completed. Such evidence of carelessness on Mrs. Lockhart's part, however, was only to be expected. "But—the painters?" she hazarded timidly. "Do you think they will do their work if they are not looked after?"

"Personally, I fail to see why they shouldn't," said Mrs. Anstruther. "But, of course, it is just conceivable that they might do something foolish. So Lucy has arranged for someone to come and stay here until everything is in shape. Fortunately, she has persuaded Mrs. Barlas's granddaughter, the Heron girl, to do it. Kate Heron, you know. I really could not have borne with a total stranger, much as I might wish to oblige Lucy and Robina."

Miss Milligan summed all the courage of her curiosity. "But—dear Mrs. Anstruther, would it matter so much to *you* who came?"

"As she is to stay in my house—dear Flora," said Mrs. Anstruther, "I think it would. Now, Flora, you run along to your mother and tell her that Kate Heron is coming to stay with me."

Miss Milligan, too dazed to feel indignant at this summary dismissal, ran along.

4

Greystiel Heron, his son 'young Grey,' and his daughter Kate were the only survivors of an old and obstinate family which could trace back its stormy history almost without a break for five hundred years. A bend sinister on the escutcheon, dating from the time of Charles II, did not worry the Herons. In fact, they were quietly proud of their Stuart connection, and admired the ancestress whose son had borne his mother's surname, and by a king's wish had succeeded to the estates—the heirs male having proved themselves true courtiers by getting themselves killed off, one in battle against the Dutch at sea, the others less reputably in various duels and brawls. As the family clung tenaciously to the Stuart cause, and when James II had finally fled the country, continued to drink with fervour to the King over the Water, and to be deeply engaged in every Jacobite plot, fortune turned her back on them. After the '45 was over, and Charles Edward's hopes gone out like a blown candle, the only Heron left was a boy of twelve, whom his mother had taken to France just about the time when the Highland army was beginning its disastrous retreat from Derby. His father had been killed at Culloden, his only brother had died of his wounds in Carlisle Castle before he could be condemned to death. His sister had shown a prudence foreign to her family by marrying a prosperous English banker of pronounced Hanoverian sympathies, who satisfied his ambition to become a landed proprietor by buying up the confiscated Heron estates. Their eldest son assumed the name, and so started a new branch of the Herons, which his uncle in France refused to acknowledge. Exiled and penniless, he was still the head of the family, and his descendants continued to ignore their kinsmen, regarding them as robbers both of lands and name. When Charles Edward had been forgotten by the world and remained only a memory in the hearts of faithful Highlanders, a Heron came back to his own country, settled in the prosperous town of Glasgow, married, and took to business. The upstart Herons died out, house and lands were broken up and sold in small lots, but the main line persisted, and though it could hardly be said to multiply, increased the population by one or two at fairly regular intervals.

Never was a family less dependent on its material possessions to assert its individuality. The Herons carried their heritage in looks and character, they did not need the setting of the old house, the slowly gathered treasures, to mark, them for what they were. They made very little money in business, but, remembering their history, held their heads higher than ever.

And now, here was Greystiel Heron, whose proper setting was the eighteenth century, elegant even in shirt and aged kilt, slim and active as a young man at something over seventy, with his bold well-cut nose, fine forehead and beautiful sulky mouth, looking as though his white hair ought to have been long enough to club and tie with a black ribbon. He was cleaning his gun in the dining-room and waiting for his daughter Kate, who had been into Glasgow to shop.

All he said when she appeared was, "So you've got back?" but Kate was perfectly satisfied. She knew that he meant he had missed her, was glad to see her, and wanted her to stay and talk to him.

"It was disgusting in town. Everyone looked hot and sticky," she said. "Including self. But I got off with a beautiful young policeman on point duty. He held up the traffic to let me cross, and called me sweetheart. The Oxford Group movement, probably. Or don't Trenchard's lovely policemen belong to it?"

"Damn' cheek," murmured Greystiel Heron from force of habit.

"Which of us, darling? I am going to cultivate the police," said Kate. "They'd be so handy, don't you think, if I were taken up for shoplifting or something? Have you had a good day?"

Pretty fair, he answered in his curious grudging way. "Quite a decent bag."

"It must have been very hot on the hill. You're sunburnt, Paw."

"Ay." When talking to his intimates, Greystiel often relapsed quite naturally into Scots, which had been, after all, the language of gentle as well as simple only a century earlier. He held up his gun-barrels to the light, peered through them with passionate interest, and fell to work again with cleaning-rod and oily waste. Suddenly he looked at Kate, his eyes brilliant with the remembrance of past enjoyment, his caution forgotten. "We had a *rare* day, Kate. Seventy-one and a half brace."

"Isn't that a record bag for Craigdhu?" Kate was properly impressed.

"N—no. We had seventy-three in nineteen-twelve," said her father. "But it was a good day, and I shot well."

"You must be up to form for Andrew Lockhart's partridges," said Kate with guileless innocence. "I believe they're very good this year."

"H'm. They're not looking too well hereabouts. All that rain we had drowned a good many of the young birds," said Greystiel. Then he added suspiciously: "Andrew Lockhart? Who said I was shooting with him this year?"

"I did." Kate met his baleful glance serenely. "You know that he and Lucy and their offspring are to be back at Soonhope by September, and Lucy has asked us and Granny to stay there. The idea being, I gather, to take some of the cold air off their reunion."

"I don't know that I want any of you to be mixed up in the Lockharts' affairs." Greystiel's jaw set obstinately. "The fellow deserted his wife and family and behaved like a blackguard. Much better to have nothing to do with them."

"I expect the whole of Haystoun is saying that," Kate answered carelessly. "You know how they love scandal."

"Damned hole. I dare say their talk had something to do with it at the start," growled her father.

"Very likely, Paw. And of course it no one will go and stay with the Lockharts and they're left severely alone by their own relations, Haystoun will have all the more to say."

"Well, that's Lockhart's look-out."

"I know, but it's rather a pity, and Granny will be so disappointed, when she's hoping that they'll be happy again. After all, Paw, you always liked Andrew, and his private affairs are none of our business."

Greystiel Heron hesitated, torn between his liking for Andrew Lockhart as a good fellow and a sportsman, and his dislike of having himself and his family connected with a man who had run away from his wife with another woman.

"Andrew was always a fine shot," he said with apparent irrelevance, but Kate was quite able to follow his line of thought.

"Don't you remember he used to say that you were the only man he knew who could do a really hard day's walking among turnips and things?"

"They're a soft lot nowadays. I used to think nothing of shooting all day, dancing half the night, and then having to walk sixteen miles to catch a boat or a train back to Glasgow early in the morning, so that I'd be in time at the office," said Greystiel. "Well, your mother's keen for me to go, and I don't want to disappoint your grandmother—"

"We all want you to go, Paw. It would be so good for Haystoun to see that the Lockharts' friends are standing by them."

"Mind, if I do—" Greystiel put barrel and stock together with a click and shot his daughter a threatening look, "If I *do*, it'll only be to please your mother. Not because I want to. I'd far rather potter about here on my own, as you know."

"Of course, darling. It's very sweet of you. So would I," said Kate demurely, but her eyes were laughing. "I've promised to go and stay with old Mrs. Anstruther and my wary eye on the doing-up of Soonhope."

"I don't like it," Greystiel said at once.

"I know, Paw. But it's to help Lucy, who after all is the injured person—as far as we know—and Granny was so keen on it. I really couldn't wriggle out of it," said Kate.

"Well, I can't stop you—" began her father, and got no farther.

"Thank you, darling. I knew you'd see that I couldn't very well refuse," said Kate.

"It's all right, Mother. He's going, but we'll have to gang warily," said Kate, shutting the drawing-room door and sitting down on a chair near the open window.

"How did you do it?"

"Low cunning, or *haute politique*. Call it as you like it or what you will. I'm not very sure which it is, but I fear low cunning is the answer."

"Very clever of you," murmured Mrs. Heron.

She was lying on the sofa, a handsome Paisley shawl over her feet, a stack of cushions behind her head. She had been a beauty as a girl, in the days when there was a distinct line of demarcation between pretty and plain, and still bore traces of it in the straight Barlas nose, the breadth between her soft, short-sighted eyes, and the white skin that had been so striking with her black hair. It always seemed to Kate most unfair that two such well-favoured parents had not succeeded in handing down their good looks to their daughter. Grey, of course, was amazingly like his father. The Heron type was unusually well-marked and had not altered very much in the course of centuries. Kate herself was a throw-back to some more plain-featured ancestor, or so she insisted. Certainly there was a very distinct family resemblance, though her nose turned up. The rather heavy brows, the fine modelling of the mouth with its deeply cut corners, the broad low forehead and stiff chin, the setting of the eyes, could all be seen in one or two of the earlier Herons, photographs or reproductions of whose portraits were all that their direct descendants now owned.

"There they go, the old grey fishers," said Kate from her coign of vantage at the windows, as two herons flapped past, uttering their occasional harsh angry scream. "I always like to see them, I feel they're lucky to us."

"What a good thing it is that there are so many herons about," said her mother dryly. "Though, judging from the fact that we see one or more practically every day, I can't help thinking that we ought to be luckier than we are—if your feeling is correct."

"Oh, probably it isn't," said Kate cheerfully. "But aren't you pleased to know that Paw is going to Soonhope?"

"Of course I am, Kate. But I sometimes get a little tired of all the tact and care required to approach the simplest matter. After all, I'm not a member of the diplomatic corps."

"Men always ought to be handled with care, like high explosives. I'd have them labelled in large red capitals 'Dangerous. Highly Inflammable.' You should know that, Mother. You've lived with two of the most difficult men in the world for quite a time."

"Two? You make me sound like a bigamist."

"I didn't say you'd slept with two of them! I mean Daddy and Grey, oddly enough. Charming creatures, but *not* easy."

"No," said Mrs. Heron with a sigh. "Certainly not easy. Perhaps that's partly why they're charming."

"Very likely."

"There are times," confessed Mrs. Heron, "when I feel that I could do with a trifle less charm and a little more reasonableness."

"None of our family is very reasonable," said Kate.

"Kate! I'm sure I'm *always* reasonable!"

"Oh, *darling*!" said Kate reproachfully. Then: "Hullo! Here comes Grey."

Approaching the house by a narrow path across the moor was Grey Heron, his tweed kilt swinging above a pair of admirable knees and legs of whose symmetry their owner was fully aware. A fishing-rod was in his hand, a creel hung at his back. He was whistling loudly but melodiously the pipe-tune known as *Donald's Away to the War*.

Kate, leaning perilously out over the window-sill, hailed him. "Hi, Grey!"

He jumped the low wall dividing the moor from the stretch of rough grass which surrounded the house and refused all attempts to make it into a lawn, and came to stand under the drawing-room window.

"What cheer, my poppet! I've got some trout for you to cook!"

"Ugh! Nasty little things!" came in a faintly protesting voice from Mrs. Heron. Kate called cheerfully: "You'll have to degut them, then, if you want me to cook them."

"All right. Come and watch me," said Grey.

"I don't know that your invitation makes much appeal to me, my love."

"Now, Kate," said her brother. "Don't try to be a lady, for it's no use."

"Fishwives to you!" cried Kate indignantly, but she turned from the window and went downstairs.

5

The house through which she made her way to the back premises was shabby, badly in need of paper and paint, lighted by paraffin lamps in the sitting-room and kitchen, by candles in the bedrooms; but the furniture was all good, and some of it very fine. Kate hardly noticed the shabbiness of everything, for it had been like that as long as she could remember. She was so accustomed to being poor that she seldom stopped to think just what it might be like to have enough money for what most people would have considered necessities. Even Grey, who had come home after six years in India to join his father in propping up a rather shaky business, never compared the house with others he had known. It was simply home, a place by itself in his mind. Long ago he and Kate had decided that the family motto 'Hernes flee heich' was of no practical use to them in their circumstances, and proceeded to get as much amusement as they could out of everything that came their way. If the thought sometimes occurred to Grey that his sister did not have the same sort of good times as other girls he knew, if he wondered whether she had had a fair chance, living as they did, of meeting men and perhaps getting married, he kept it to himself. Kate seemed happy, perhaps she did not mind growing older without having seen much of life. Besides, he had an infantile faith in his powers of making money, as lovely and impossible as the child's belief in the hidden pot of fairy gold lying at the foot of the rainbow. One day he'd have enough money to give Kate a decent time. They might set up house together and live happily ever after. . . .

His mind occupied by bright pictures of the parties they would give, the cruises they would go—for if you dream about money you may as well dream about having a great deal of it—Grey operated on his trout with a penknife of insanitary appearance at the sink in the stone-floored scullery. As Kate joined him he said amiably: "Well, funny-face?"

"Grey, I have more than a suspicion that that knife is not surgically clean," was Kate's reply.

"Oh, that's all right. The fish have to be washed anyhow, don't they?"

"Fortunately, yes. And now, as the minion is going out to a dance in the village, and I am cook to-night, how do you want these little brutes done?"

"Split and fried with lots of oatmeal on 'em," said her brother, smacking his lips. "Abracabroccoloni says it's by far the best way to serve trout."

"Abracabroccoloni is an infernal nuisance," said Kate laughing. "If he's going to interfere in the kitchen when I'm cooking there will be no dinner to-night."

Abracabroccoloni, a mythical Italian chef invented by Grey, was almost a member of the household, but fortunately for the tempers of the Herons mother and daughter, and their trusty cook-general, only paid them flying visits. If any meal was not as Grey liked it, Abracabroccoloni was certain to be quoted. Kate knew his views on various dishes by heart and nervously waited to hear him pronounce on anything new she tried.

"You ought to be glad to have a few tips from old Abra," said his creator reproachfully.

"Well, I'm not." Kate piled the wet trout on a plate and carried them to the kitchen. "But you might put some coal on the fire, Grey. I'm sure old Abra would agree with me that a good fire is essential for successful cooking."

Grey picked up a coal-scuttle, shot a large part of its contents into the red heart of the range with considerable noise, and shouted above the din: "When you go to Soonhope, would you like me to come and keep you company for a week-end? I'm sure my exquisite taste would be of value when you're arranging the furniture and draping curtains."

"Grey, that would be lovely. My own taste is quite exquisite enough, and besides, I'll have Lucy's directions as to where everything is to go, to the last footstool, but your brawn and muscle might come in handy. Do come. I'll leave Mrs. Anstruther's and we can camp out at Soonhope."

"All right." Grey wandered out in the passage, then turned to put his head round the door. "Abracabroccoloni says that a teaspoonful of vinegar added to the water when potatoes are being boiled makes them beautifully mealy."

"*Blow* Abracabroccoloni! You're not to bring *him* to Soonhope, mind!" cried Kate. Then, as she thought of the week-end which would be so much more amusing with Grey as her companion, she added generously: "but I'll remember the vinegar. This evening all shall be exactly as Abracabroccoloni would wish it."

CHAPTER TWO

1

KATE, as the small train puffed on its leisurely way towards Haystoun from the junction, sat with the windows of her third-class compartment opened to their widest extent. Smuts flew in and settled freely on her face and ungloved hands, but she cared nothing for that as she gazed out at the country she loved. Part of its charm lay in the fact that to people who demanded a more obvious beauty of scenery it was hardly worth a second glance, and this made it peculiarly her own, a treasure shared only with the discerning few. Not to those who knew it as a county of excellent golf-courses by the coast, invaded in summer by smart society, was the secret of its glamour revealed. They plodded over the links after their little white balls, hardly noticing the sea except as a hazard to be avoided, and if they did lift up their eyes to the hills it was almost without seeing them, unless they threatened rain which might spoil the afternoon's round.

Kate Heron lifted up her eyes to them, and felt her heart lift in sympathy. The Lammermuirs, her own hills, looking far away and hazy in the heat, lay, a long dim blue rampart against the summer sky. Kindly, rounded hills they looked, after the peaks of the north and west, but Kate knew how bleak they could be, how desolate and windswept, how terrible in snow and mist. She had heard them described as tame, these miles of lonely moorland, those hidden glens and cairn-topped heights. The very names—Bleak Law, Lammer Law, Nine Stane Rig, Crib Cleuch—rang wild in her ears as a Border ballad.

The train was crawling peacefully through the wide shallow valley, where the ripening corn grew golden brown and strong, where haycocks stood in neat rows anions the green second crop. Tiny wild strawberries flourished on the railway embankments, and Kate could still see a few. She longed to jump out and pick them, staining hands and lips with the wild fruit which had a flavour, she remembered, not to be equalled in her childish estimation by the finest in the garden at Soonhope. There was a tangle of blue and yellow vetch in the hedgerows, purple crane's-bill and honeysuckle, and a few late scarlet poppies waving like flags. The tower of the Parish Church came into view, welcoming her back to Haystoun, and all in a minute the train gathered speed, dashed under a bridge, and presently thundered into the station, to stand panting and puffing as if its short row of carriages and its two cattle-trucks had been an overflowing bank-holiday excursion from London at the very least.

Kate, after making a rather unsuccessful attempt to remove the grime of her journey, groaned and sprang out on to the almost empty platform. 'It's a great pity,' she thought ruefully, 'that I am such an untidy traveller. In books there's always a tiresome heroine whose most salient feature is her band-box smartness even after a trip across the Sahara. I wonder how those fragile young women *do* it? I know what I'd look like if I had crossed even a small desert. A dilapidated sand-bag!'

The station-master, a friend of her childhood, came bustling up as she gave her ticket to the shock-headed boy who was meandering along beside the train bawling unnecessarily "Hays-toun! Hays-toun!" in his slow country voice.

"Well, Miss Heron, I'm verra glad to see ye back. No, you'll not need to order a taxi. Mrs. Anstruther's sent to meet ye."

"Oh, has she? That's very kind of her," said Kate. "And how are you, Mr. Callander?"

"Oh, I canna complain, I canna complain at all, though I'm getting no younger, Miss Heron. But that's a disease we all have to suffer from. Ay. Away you out to the car, and I'll send Peter with the luggage."

Kate obediently started down the long echoing flight of covered steps leading to the station yard, smiling a little wryly at Mr. Callander's obvious tact in refraining from any mention of the Lockharts. In the old days it had been: "Well, ye'll find them all in the best o' health at Soonhope, and Mr. Lockhart's waiting on ye outside." But she had come prepared for change, and no doubt others would not be so careful of the family pride as the station-master. She emerged, blinking a little, into the strong sunshine, and a broad-shouldered figure, black against the light, blocked her way. A man's voice said: "Are you Miss Heron? I'm Robin Anstruther. My aunt sent me to meet you."

With a final blink Kate cleared her eyes and saw him plainly. So this was Mrs. Anstruther's nephew, the retired naval officer turned farmer, this square-built solid block of a man, black-haired, harsh-featured, with two parallel lines so deeply scored across his forehead that they looked like scars. "Or tram-lines," thought Kate, unfortunately aloud, for he said: "What did you say?" sharply.

"Formidable!" thought Kate, and murmured: "How d'you do?"

Peter hove in sight, trundling her two suit-cases and the round hat-box on a barrow so large that it mocked their puny insignificance.

"The car's over there," said Robin Anstruther, and stalked beside her in silence towards a car so shiny and splendid that she could not restrain a faint squeak of astonished admiration.

"Anything wrong?" he demanded.

"Good gracious! That's not a farmer's car!" said Kate.

He uttered a short, deep-toned shout of laughter which stopped as abruptly as it had begun. "Huh! No, it isn't. It's a piece of unjustifiable extravagance. Here, Peter, stow that gear carefully, will you? That's right. Now"—to Kate—"in you get. I'll settle with the boy."

Kate protested. "Why should you?"

"Don't argue," he said coolly. "This is my show. I came to meet you, didn't I?"

"It was very kind of you," said Kate sedately as he got in beside her.

"Oh, I was in Haystoun, anyway. It's market-day and I always have tea with the old lady when I'm in—she won't come up to my place, hates my housekeeper. So meeting you wasn't much bother," he told her. "You quite comfortable?"

"Perfectly, thank you. . . ." ('If Grey were here, he'd love to see me being a lady,' thought Kate. 'I wonder what the next remark ought to be? It's his turn now—')

The next remark when it came was so entirely unexpected that it left her gasping. "So you've come to help to pick up the bits and put 'em together again?"

"The *bits*?"

"The Lockharts' affairs, of course. I suppose you'll be on Lucy's side, all for Law and Order?"

Kate remembered that this man was a friend of her cousin Andrew. His tone said quite plainly that he was not on Lucy's side; but then, men always stuck to each other.

"I'm not on any side," she said with truth. ' It is none of my business."

"Very prudent of you," said Robin Anstruther. "Hullo, here we are, and I can see Aunt Jean peering through the fernery."

Kate quickly got out of the car, and without waiting for him, walked up the path to the door. She was furious with him. For some reason it is always maddening to be accused of prudence, and she began to think that she probably was on 'Lucy's side,' after all, if he was on the other.

At tea a brisk conversation was carried on between Kate and her hostess, who liked her. Robin Anstruther hardly opened his mouth—except to put bites of scone and mouthfuls of tea into it, thought Kate spitefully. But her sense of humour, which seldom failed her, returned before the meal was ended. It was really rather funny, when you came to think of it, that she, whom her family considered far too rash and inclined to leap without looking, should have been called prudent. And his opinion mattered so little. She was long past the agonizingly sensitive age of girlhood, when to be misunderstood was pure misery. Let him think what he liked of her, and be damned to him!

Mrs. Anstruther had fallen into a reminiscent mood and was reminding her nephew of old days at Soonhope, "when this girl here was only a baby. You and Andrew and Gavin Barlas used to play with them all on the lawn at children's parties, Robin."

Now it was Kate's turn to sit and smile, amused and, she hoped, aloof, while he roused himself to talk. "So we did, Aunt Jean. Which was the child who always asked to see my dragon? The one who called me 'Sailor'?"

Suddenly across Kate's mind flashed an early memory, disjointed but vivid, of someone who used to roll up his right sleeve obligingly to show her 'the *dear* wee dragon.' She could see the brown sinewy arm, startlingly white above the elbow, and the blue-and-red dragon boldly tattooed on it. Before she could stop herself, she had exclaimed incredulously: "But you—you *can't* be 'Sailor'?"

"Are you Kitty?" he countered as incredulously. "I don't believe it."

Kitty . . . she had not been called Kitty since she grew up, when, recognizing how utterly unsuitable it was, she had insisted that the whole family should adopt Kate, her father's favourite name for her, instead.

"I was Kitty, certainly," she said. "But I am always called Kate now."

Then, as he still looked doubtful, she remembered something else, and, "Look," she said, holding out her right hand, with the thumb bent, towards him. "I cut myself with your knife once. You can still see the mark."

He stooped to study the white crescent-shaped scar round the thumb knuckle. "Yes, of course. You bled like a pig and gave me a rare fright—and never shed a tear. I remember. And you were half-left-handed, too. I called you—what was it? 'Kar-handit Kitty.'"

Kate laughed. "I always thought it was unfair of you, when you're *kar-handit* yourself."

"So he is," said Mrs. Anstruther. "And always has been." She smiled kindly at him and at Kate. "It was clever of you to remember that."

"Not so very clever," said Kate. "After all, I could see him at tea, with his cup on the wrong side of his plate."

A smile broke over Robin Anstruther's harsh face. "And still you didn't remember me. Not so clever of you, that, I don't suppose I can have changed as much as you have in more than twenty years."

"Twenty-seven," said Kate soberly. "Doesn't it sound an awfully long time? More than a quarter of a century—"

He rose to go. "Well, we'll have to do what we can to bridge the gap," he said, shaking hands.

Kate, watching from the window the big car's almost silent departure, thought that quite a promising start had been made in gap-bridging in spite of his horrid remark about her being prudent.

'Prudent!' she thought again, resentfully. 'Such a *mean* virtue, if it is a virtue. Prudent! Ugh!'

2

"I can smell thunder," said Mrs. Anstruther, when Kate came into her room next morning to see her before starting for Soonhope. "There is going to be a storm."

"Darling, you sound exactly like a witch-doctor," protested Kate, who was not in the least afraid of her. "I wish you wouldn't be so bogy."

"Well, rake an umbrella in case it rains, but don't open it if there's any lightning, and don't shelter under trees or near a fence or wall—"

"And don't go near anything wet, or look in a mirror or approach an open window," chanted Kate, ticking off the items on her fingers. "And don't touch anything steel. I think I'll have to hide in a dark corner with my eyes shut."

"You are an impudent hussy," said Mrs. Anstruther. "My great-Aunt Isabella was killed by lightning, and my mother always used to sit in the wine-cellar with her fingers in her ears and a thick grey woollen shawl over her head all through a thunderstorm."

Kate was delighted by this picture of Mrs. Anstruther's mother, whom she knew only as a faded daguerreotype which failed to disguise the Roman severity of the features under a stately cap. Still laughing, and with a last promise to hide in the cupboard below the stairs at Soonhope if there was any lightning of the forked variety, she set out.

There was no doubt that thunder was in the air. The sky was darkening to a sullen lead colour with lurid copper lights between heavy banks of cloud, the hills loomed menacingly near. As Kate went up the winding avenue a sudden wind stirred eerily in the high tops of the beeches. It was almost dark in the avenue, a strange deep green twilight, with the smooth grey trunks of the great trees rising into the thick root of leaves which met overhead. Here and there a stray shaft of light struck fitfully against one of these pillar-like boles so that it gleamed as if under water. Kate felt oppressed yet strung-up as she always did before a storm, every nerve on edge, every hair of her head tingling to the electricity in the air. She walked quickly, eager to be indoors with some occupation to distract her mind.

The avenue ran out from the sheltering trees, curled round a lawn badly in need of mowing, and widened before the doorway into a sweep of gravel which had been laid when more than one carriage and pair had to be turned there. Kate, leaving the blankly staring uncurtained windows and shut door of the from, went to the right and across a flagged yard to the back door. This stood open, and from within she could hear a comforting sound of homely labour: the loud scrape of a scrubbing-brush followed by the slap-slap of a wet cloth on a stone floor.

Mrs. Pow from the lodge must be somewhere about, and presently, in answer to Kate's call, she appeared, a drugget apron tied round her waist over her print dress, her hand wet, bringing with her a smell of warm dirty water and strong yellow soap.

"Ay, the penter's here," she said, after suitable greetings had been exchanged. "A slow, potterin' body. He's dab-dabbin' awa' up in the big spare-room the noo. It's a maircy there's no' that muckle needin' dune, or dear kens when Mistress Lockhart wad get intil the hoose. An' hoo's yersel', Miss Kate? Ye're lookin' brawly."

"I'm feeling splendid, thank you, Mrs. Pow."

"Ye're no' thinkin' o' gettin' mairret yet?" asked Mrs. Pow with the privileged curiosity of the old retainer. She had known Kate since the days when a 'jammy piece' eaten at the lodge tasted better than cake in the drawing-room.

Kate shook her head, smiling. "No, Mrs. Pow. I'm an old maid. There has to be one in every family, you know. So useful."

"Hoot awa', Miss Kate, I'm sure there's naething o' the auld maid aboot ye. I'll wager there's plenty lads juist waitin' till ye gie them the nod, eh?"

"Lads are scarce nowadays, especially where we live," said Kate without bitterness, but it was obvious that Mrs. Pow did not believe her.

"So ye say," she answered, and added after a brief hesitation: "No, that I'm no' sayin' ye're mebbe better aft as ye are, the way things are nooadays. A' that die-voarce!" Mrs. Pow's tone was that of one who finds a slug in the salad. "Little did I think tae see that kin' o' trouble sae near hame—"

"Come, now, Mrs. Pow, there's no divorce in the family that I know of," said Kate lightly.

Mrs. Pow was not to be diverted. "Aw, mebbe it's no' ma place tae be speakin' o't, Miss Kate, but ye ken fine whit I'm efter. There's the maister, decent fally, beguilit awa' frae wife an' bairns by yon besom wi' her big een an' saft talk. Aye walkin' aboot the gairden, Pow tellt me, till it was a fair disgrace tae see the pair o' them, an' a' Haystoun wi' their lang lugs prickit. A bonny-like business tae come aboot at Soonhope! An' I'll never believe it was the maister tae blame, na, nor Mistress Lockhart neither. Whit way could yon Mistress Fardell no' bide at hame wi' her ain man?"

"I'm sure I don't know, Mrs. Pow, but there's nothing to be gained by talking about it, especially now that Mr. and Mrs. Lockhart are coming back."

There was a slight pause, during which Kate looked about the huge old kitchen with the high dresser running the whole length of one wall, the heavy table, white as sand with much scrubbing, the big range gaping black and cold. In the old days it had been a cheerful place, warm on the coldest winter mornings, filled with the pleasant smell of baking, the firelight throwing a rosy gleam on the shining bowls ranged along the dresser. It was melancholy work, coming back to a remembered house and finding it bare and chill. Kate was glad to think that it would soon be restored to its former condition; but she had a passing doubt as to whether the master and mistress of Soonhope could be as easily settled down again.

Leaving Mrs. Pow to her scrubbing, she wandered through the house. Except for one or two bedrooms there was no papering to be done, for though some of the walls had faded, Lucy had said that they were more in keeping with the old rooms than bright new papers. Privately, Kate thought that she did not wish to change the familiar aspect of the house more than could be helped. Everything, as far as appearance went, was to be as it had been. The solitary painter, a middle-aged man with straggling hair and watery, rather wild blue eyes, was pursuing his task in 'the big spare-room' at a snail's pace, whistling between his two remaining front teeth as he dreamily applied a brush to a cupboard door. He stopped as soon as he saw Kate, and seemed disposed for a refreshing chat on the political situation in Europe, which she brutally nipped in the bud.

"There's thunder aboot," he then said in a tone of foreboding. "I heard it reelin' awa' up in the Lammermuirs as I cam' through the toun. Ay, we'll ha'e a storrum, an' a storrum aye gangs tae ma heid. I canna be held responsible for ma wurrds an' acks gin there's a storrum. Mind, I'm warnin' ye for yer ain guid. It maitters nocht tae me, but it's yersel' I'm thinkin' o'."

Kate felt it would be wiser not to linger, but went to the drawing-room, after cordially assuring him that she would keep out of his way during the storm.

Though she had known that this room must be empty like the others, she must subconsciously have expected to find it as she had always pictured it, for it was a shock to cross the threshold and find it uncarpeted and blank. Only the cupids of the Adam mantelpiece still danced among the garlands that held them entwined, about the carved head of Pan in the centre. The light from a row of windows opposite glanced on his sly grin and budding horns. As a child, Kate had disliked this head because she was secretly afraid of it, but now he seemed friendly and familiar in the deserted room. There was nothing for her to look at except the fresh paint, so she made her way downstairs. Crossing the hall, she stood for a moment to admire the gracious outward curve of the wall, which formed a small bay on either side of the front door. Each bay held a window, curving also, with a wide semi-circular seat below. They gave the hall a character all its own, and were a notable feature of the fine old house, indoors and out.

Mrs. Pow, wearing a coat with a fur collar, and an amazing hat like a green straw coal-scuttle, suddenly appeared. "I'll awa' doon tae the lodge, Miss Kate. It's time for the bairns' denner, but I'll be back in a wee whiley."

Kate nodded absently, and looking from the window, watched her go stumping down the drive. A distant rumble of thunder reminded her of the painter, and for a moment she wished that she had asked Mrs. Pow it he was mentally sound. Then she told herself sharply that she was being simply silly. No one employed an insane painter, even in Haystoun.

She continued her prowling, coming to a stop in what was called the billiard-room, presumably because it had once contained a billiard-table, though not since Kate could remember—to stare at the large photograph of Andrew Lockhart which had been left hanging on the wall where everything else had been taken away to be stored. Nothing, it seemed to her, could so plainly have told the tale of the disaster which had overtaken the Lockharts. A foolish old nursery rhyme flitted through her head, and she found herself repeating it aloud to the photograph of Soonhope's owner:

> Humpty Dumpty sat on a wall;
> Humpty Dumpty had a great fall.
> All the King's horses and all the King's men
> Couldn't put Humpty Dumpty together again.

"Marriage, my poor dear Drew, is uncommonly like Humpty Dumpty. I only hope it won't be as impossible to put together again!"

A long roll of thunder rattled across the skies, ending in a heavy crash which sounded directly overhead, and shook the windows in their frames. As Kate stared wide-eyed, she saw lightning play wildly over the dark clouds above the trees, and then came a nearer peal, and the whole house seemed to rock.

Feeling that even the painter's society was preferable to none, Kate ran upstairs, wincing at every jagged flash, and threw open the door of the spare bedroom to the accompaniment of a particularly loud roll of thunder. The painter, his eyes whirling madly in his head until they looked as if they would meet over his nose and merge into one, stood at the window daring the elements with fine free gestures of his hands, one of which still clutched the paint-brush.

"It's the Day o' Judgment!" he bawled at Kate, standing transfixed in the doorway. "Did ye no' hear Gabriel's trump soondin'? Wumman, are ye prepared tae meet yer Maker?"

"I—I hope so," stammered Kate. "Are you?"

She put the question innocently enough, and simply because politeness seemed to demand an answer, and she could think of nothing else to say. But its effect on the painter was quite frightening.

"Am *I*? I wad hae ye ken that Saunders Fergus is ane o' the Elect!" he roared, advancing on Kate with a menacing wave of his paint-brush.

She thought afterwards that in a normal state she would have stayed where she was and braved it out; but when to religious frenzy was added thunder and lightning, she lost her nerve completely. For an instant she stood petrified, then, with one wild bound, she was outside in the passage, had slammed the door and locked it, and fled down the stairs. Once in the hall, she stood panting and listening to the furious hammerings and bawlings which filled in the gaps between the peals of thunder. "He'll make such a mess of the door!" she thought. "This is a grand start to looking after things for Lucy. I wish he'd stop!"

But when the noise suddenly did stop, to be replaced by absolute silence inside the house, though the storm outside continued unabated, she found something sinister about the hush, and longed for the painter to bang on the door again. At least while he was doing that she knew where he was. And: "Oh! *fool* that I am!" said Kate to herself. "I forgot the dressing-room, and he can get out that way!"

Still there was no sound from upstairs, and her heart was beginning to beat more steadily, when she heard a heavy step somewhere near the kitchen, in the passage. The painter, full of religious fury! He must have come down the back stairs, and by this time was probably thirsting for blood. Sheer panic overcame Kate. If she could only lock, him up in some place from which he could not escape. . . . She remembered the deep cupboard just beside her, which he must pass if he came through the swing-door dividing the dark kitchen passage into two parts. As always when badly frightened, she grew angry, and the welcome warmth of rage steadied her nerves. Her coat still hung over the end of the banisters, where she had untidily thrown it, and with some vague idea of muffling his head in its folds and shoving him into the cupboard while he struggled to free himself, she picked it up and crept towards the swing-door, with the cupboard gaping black at her left shoulder. The thunder was roaring too loudly for her to hear him now, but a flash of lightning lit up the dim passage for a moment and showed her that the door was being pushed open. Kate drew a long breath and clutched her coat tightly. Now for it . . . !

3

"What the *hell*—!" muttered Andrew Lockhart, struggling blindly in smothering folds of Harris tweed. He was pushed into a small space, a door was banged, hitting him a smart crack on the side of the head, and as he heard a key turn, a feminine voice said in tones of breathless satisfaction: "There, you brute! You can wait there until I can fetch the police to take you to the nearest asylum!"

"What the *hell*!" said Andrew again. He had succeeded in freeing himself from the tweed garment, but he was still, in every sense, in the dark. Once more he decided that he had been a damned fool to make this sentimental detour on his way north to shoot; but he could not pass Soonhope within a few miles without coming for a private view of the old place, and it had all been too easy, driving the car along the Loaning, unseen by any of Haystoun's gossiping inhabitants, and sneaking in by the garden and back door. And now he was in a pretty fix, locked into one of his own cupboards by an excitable female, who must be quite loopy, to wait until the local police discovered his identity. This would make a magnificent story for Haystoun, and so jolly for Lucy. He wriggled with discomfort in the narrow confines of his prison. Lucy would, quite justly, consider it all his fault. It would be another black mark against him, even if she did not find this last straw too much to forgive, it was so ridiculous, so undignified. If only he could escape before someone found out who he was! But push as he might against the heavy door, the stout lock and bolts refused to give. Raging, he stood still and longed passionately for a cigarette, but he could not move enough to get at his case.

Meanwhile Kate, in high feather at her own cleverness and courage, went springing upstairs to see what sort of mess the painter had made of the spare bedroom in his frenzy. Even the thunder did not frighten her now, and she unlocked the door and threw it gaily open to the sound of a peal which she hardly noticed. Neither noise disturbed the 'awfu' slow warker.' Recumbent on the floor, his grizzled head pillowed against the newly coated door, the painter lay wrapt in profound slumber, a beatific smile on his face, the brush fallen from his hand. Kate, blinking, stared at him in a wild surmise, then rubbed her eyes hard. If the painter was here, then whom had she locked into the press in the hall? However, that problem might wait for the moment while she dealt with what appeared to be some sort of apoplectic seizure. A powerful smell of whisky, which filled the air with every stertorous breath he exhaled, disclosed the cause of his stupor, and Kate's alarm promptly became rage.

"Wake up, you pig!" she cried, stamping her foot on the bare boards.

The painter, looking remarkably unregenerate for one of the Chosen of God, merely sighed in his sleep and continued to snore. Kate, deciding that violent measures were necessary, advanced, took him by his paint-smeared shoulders, and shook him hard.

He opened bleary eyes and groaned. "Eh, thae weemen!" he mumbled. "Never let a puir fally—hic—lie. Hic. Aye nig-naggin', nag-niggin'. . . . Lassie, can ye no—hic—me bide?"

"Pig!" cried Kate, losing her hold so that his head fell back against the fresh paint again.

"Ay. Ay. Bonnie wee—hic—pigs," said the painter blissfully. "Bonnie wee hics."

It was quite useless. Kate left him to his dreams and went downstairs, wondering how she was to deal with the prisoner in the cupboard. Listening with her head close to the panel of the door, she could hear nothing, and fear that he might be smothering assailed her. With a trembling hand she knocked on the cupboard door.

"Let me out, whoever you are!" said a voice from within, muffled but apparently not suffering from lack of air. "Who *are* you, by the way?"

"Who are *you*? is more to the point," retorted Kate.

"My good woman, what does it matter?" said the voice impatiently. "Let me out and you'll see who I am soon enough."

"I dare say, but I don't propose to open this door until I know who you are and what you're doing in the house at all."

"Oh, my God!" groaned the voice. "So we're no forrader than we were."

"There's nothing else for it. I shall have to go for a police-man," said Kate in despair. "Oh, dear, *what* a nuisance you are! Now there'll be all sorts of fuss, and Lucy will be annoyed—"

"Lucy?" roared the voice, so loudly that Kate jumped like a chamois. "Are you talking about my wife?"

This was too much. The man must be a lunatic. "Certainly not," Kate said in what she hoped were soothing tones. "Not your wife at all. Mrs. Lockhart, to whom the house belongs."

"It belongs to *me*, damn it!" bawled Andrew from within, almost bursting a blood-vessel in his efforts to make himself understood. "Do you hear? This is MY HOUSE!"

Instantly Kate forgot her newly-made resolution to deal with the madman in a politic fashion. "How can you talk such utter balderdash?" she screamed at him. "I suppose you'll tell me next that you are Andrew Lockhart?"

"That's just who I am!" shouted Andrew furiously. "And Lord knows who you are, but you must be mental!"

Before Kate could think up a reply, a new voice broke in. "What under the sun is going on here?" said Robin Anstruther. "I could hear you screaming like a peahen in full cry from the back door. You're making far more noise than the thunder, and you look like a fury."

"There's—there's a man in that cupboard!" gasped Kate, clinging to his solid arm in her ecstasy of relief. "I think he's *mad!*"

"In that cupboard? How did he get in there?"

"I locked him in," said Kate, not without pride. "He was prowling about the house, and—"

"Who's there?" called the voice from the cupboard. "Is it Robin Anstruther, by any blessed chance? If so, for God's sake, Robin, muzzle that female and let me out!"

Robin Anstruther gave one look at Kate, one at the cupboard door, and began to laugh. His shoulders quaking, he advanced and turned the key.

"What are you doing?" cried Kate.

The door opened, and a dusty, dishevelled figure burst out, cobwebs clinging to his hair, Kate's tweed coat still about his neck.

Often though Kate had pictured her next meeting with her cousin Andrew, and wondered how embarrassing it would be, her wildest imaginings had never drawn anything approaching the present situation. Dumb with amazement, she watched the two men grin and clasp hands, vaguely she heard the owner of Soonhope murmur as he brushed the cobwebs and dust-fluff from his head: "Who *is* she, Robin? And is she really loopy?"

Robin was thoroughly enjoying himself. "Not more so than most people," he said in a loud, clear voice. "This is Kate Heron, Drew. Second cousin of yours, isn't she?"

"Kate Heron! Kitty. . . . Good Lord, so it is. I recognize her now, of course," said Andrew dazedly. Then, as his eyes met Kate's, his mouth began to twitch, and he broke into half-unwilling laughter. "Upon my word, Kate, I never thought you'd turn out such a termagant!"

"I dare say not," Kate retorted, laughing too, thankful that the ice was broken and that at least she no longer had to dread meeting him. "But there's a drunk painter sleeping in the big spare bedroom—the carnation room, I mean, and with the thunder and being alone in the house with him, I rather lost my head. I do hope you weren't horribly squashed in that cupboard?"

"Squashed? I know just what pressed beef feels like," he assured her. "And I've swallowed pounds of dust. I'd give all I have for a pint of beer."

"I'm afraid that what the painter was drinking must have been whisky, and from his condition it's probably finished," Kate said sadly. "And I haven't any beer—"

"I have. I brought a couple of bottles and a lot of sandwiches along," said Robin Anstruther. "I thought a picnic lunch might be a sound idea, and Aunt Jean rose to the occasion. There's only two bottles of beer, but they're screw-tops, and anyhow you deserve to hand over part of your share to Andrew for locking him in one of his own cupboards."

"He can have it all," said Kate generously, "as far as I am concerned. What I want is a cup of tea. Several cups."

"Tea!" both men exclaimed with a look of horrified pity.

"Tea," said Kate. "I'm going to brew it now, in the kitchen, on the oil-stove. We'd better picnic in there. It's the most cheerful place, and a nice distance away from the painter."

"We must have a look at this painter of yours," said Robin Anstruther. "Sure he isn't all your imagination, like the burglar?"

"How mean of you. I hope he wakes up and comes down to threaten you with the Last Trump," said Kate, flushing under his amused stare.

"Well, never mind him just now. He'll keep till after lunch. I want to taste that beer," and Andrew led the way to the kitchen.

Kate, meditatively eating ham sandwiches in a corner beside the rather smelly oil-stove on which her kettle was slowly and unwillingly coming to the boil, could see the two men sitting on the table over by the window, quite silent, but apparently pleased to be with each other. She remembered how Robin Anstruther and Andrew had always been friends, and wondered a little if the break in Andrew's home life had made any difference. Probably not; there was no real reason why it should, and, in any case, men were much better about minding their own business than women. The kettle began to sing in a feeble protesting whine, and Kate's thoughts drifted. Why had Andrew Lockhart come to Soonhope in this odd, sudden way, without letting anyone know? It could hardly be pleasant to him to see the house which he had lived in all his life, dismantled and chill. . . . Of course, the place was unchanged, perhaps he was homesick and felt that he must have a glance at it. She had gathered from his few remarks to Robin that he was on his way north to shoot. 'I'd have done exactly the same thing myself,' Kate decided. She felt a fresh interest in this first cousin of her mother's, whom she had not seen very often since she grew up, and not at all for the past five years. But if he were so devoted to Soonhope, then to run away and leave it as he had done must have taken some influence so powerful that it was almost frightening to think about, like the sudden breathless shock of jumping into very cold water, or trying seriously to realize that each star in the sky was a world on its own. . . . Then the kettle boiled over, putting out the oil-stove, which revenged itself by smelling even more hideously than before, and Kate hurriedly made tea.

The men, gulping the remains of beer even more hurriedly, told her that the kitchen was no longer inhabitable by persons not equipped with gas-masks, and left. She could hear them talking, with an occasional burst of laughter, in the hall, before their voices died away. Evidently they had gone upstairs to view the painter.

"I wish them joy of him!" said Kate, flinging the window wide open, and sitting on the sill with a cup of tea in her hand.

4

The fumes from the oil-stove gradually became less obnoxious and finally vanished altogether, blown by the fresh air. Kate had finished her tea in great content, and was halfway through a cigarette before she began to wonder what the others were doing. The thunder had rolled far to the south, and the sun was making a million rainbows of the heavy drops that hung trembling from every leaf and blade of grass.

Loud bumping noises on the backstairs, which wound down from a turret to the kitchen, brought Kate to her feet, and as she reached the door at the foot of the stair and opened it, a pair of large hobnailed boots appeared in mid-air round the corner a little above the level of her eyes.

"Good heavens!" she said, recoiling.

"Steady with the feet, below there!" came Robin Anstruther's deep voice, a little breathless. "I don't want to scrape the Sleeping Beauty's head all down the wall. Bad for the plaster—"

"All dashed fine for you, but I'm going backwards, and the damn' things are sticking out over my shoulders," complained Andrew. "I hope we're nearly at the bottom."

Kate, with fascinated interest, watched the descent of a group which somewhat resembled the Laocoön in its involved embrace. The painter's inert form was carried with scant regard for his comfort, but he remained heavily asleep, disturbed only by the subterranean rumblings which broke forth regularly as a clock's tick in loud hiccups, and shook both his own person and those of his bearers from head to foot.

"Like carrying a bloomin' earthquake!" Andrew grumbled, as they staggered past the entranced Kate and out across the flagged courtyard. The procession was disappearing through the half-open doorway of the yard when she called after them: "Don't *hurt* him!"

Their reassuring shout came faintly to her ears, and she hesitated, for a moment half in mind to follow and see what they were going to do. Then she shook her head: better leave them to their own devices. Interfering never did any good, least of all to the interferer. 'Prudent again!' she thought, and was a little surprised at her new discretion. Perhaps it was force of suggestion? Certainly she had never been in the habit of thinking before she acted, until Robin Anstruther had commended her in a sneering fashion for her prudence.

The various excitements of the morning had unsettled her, and she wandered restlessly through the bare house until she found herself in the billiard-room, staring up at Andrew Lockhart's photograph again. He had changed a good deal since it was taken. He was thinner, graver with a kind of bitter gravity which had drawn lines from nostril to mouth, the ruddy hair had grey patches at the temples.

"Well? Having a look at the Prodigal Husband?" said Andrew's voice behind her, and she turned round with guilty haste. "Oh, I don't mind. I'm hardened to it," he added, as Kate was thinking of something to say.

Annoyed both with herself and him, she answered tartly: "You needn't be so proud of it," and then could have bitten out her tongue for saying it. "I'm sorry, Drew. That was horrible of me!" she cried.

"My fault. It was a rotten thing to say, anyway. Why shouldn't you look at the photograph, or anything else, for that matter, if you want to?"

"I was just—sort of *glaiking* at it," stammered Kate, and I thought you were outside with Robin Anstruther. What have you done with the painter?"

"Robin's dealing with him. There's a lot of the old lawless spirit still in Rob, that kind of freakish Border humour that likes a rather rough joke. I found I wasn't playing up properly, so I left," said Andrew. "Lord, how wretched the house looks like this, doesn't it? Pretty dismal for you, Kate. I understood that Aunt Robina was seeing to things here?"

"I'm only understudying her until it's time for the furniture and stuff to arrive," explained Kate. "I do so wish this hadn't happened—the painter, I mean. It makes me look so—so incompetent."

"My dear girl, why? You could hardly be expected to know that he was going to drink a bottle of whisky—we found the bottle, by the way, empty, in the cupboard he was painting."

"All the same, I'd hate Lucy to know. You won't tell her, Andrew, will you?"

"I?" Andrew Lockhart stared at her as if she had lost her senses. "Not likely. Lucy and I don't tell each other much nowadays. No, she won't hear anything about it from me—not even about your locking me in the cupboard."

"If you think the cupboard will amuse her, you can tell her that. I'll sound like a complete fool, but I don't mind much," said Kate generously.

"It wouldn't amuse her in the least," Andrew said, so coldly that Kate felt snubbed, and determined not to speak again.

"I'll have to push off," he said after an uncomfortable silence. "Damn' silly of me to come, really. I wish now that I hadn't. Good-bye, Kate. I suppose we'll see you sometime, when things are settled here?"

He was gone, leaving Kate to wonder if Lucy had omitted to tell him that she was filling the house with his relatives as soon as it was habitable, and what he would say when he found out. She was still wondering, still staring at the smiling photograph when Robin Anstruther shouted to her from the hall.

"Hi, Kate! Come out and see your painter!"

Kate found his loud voice so cheerful and heartening that she forgave him for alluding to the painter as hers, and gladly left the empty room to join him.

"Old Drew's looking a bit hag-ridden, isn't her" he said suddenly, as they walked over the flags of the courtyard, which the sun had almost dried by this time.

But Kate did not feel that she wanted to discuss her cousin, and she suspected that she was merely being driven into airing her views, so she said lightly: "Remorse, I expect."

He shot her a quick, curious look, and replied: "I expect that's it."

"What have you done with the painter?" Kate asked firmly.

"Don't be so impatient. You'll see in a minute."

"Impatience and prudence don't seem to go well together," observed Kate. "Oh! Here comes Mrs. Pow at last."

"Who said you were prudent?" he asked.

"You accused me of it," Kate said.

"And it's been rankling, has it?"

"Not in the least," said Kate loftily and untruthfully.

He answered with a provoking laugh, but before Kate had time to be annoyed she caught sight of the painter, and forgot everything else.

"Rather tasteful, don't you think?" asked Robin Anstruther, surveying his handiwork with fond pride.

The painter lay on an ancient mouldering hearthrug, under a drooping rowan beside the drive. His legs were crossed midway between ankle and knee, his feet rested against an empty whisky-bottle, his arms were folded on his breast with the paint-brush like a sword at his side. On his stomach, gently rising and falling with each deep breath, was pinned a large piece of cardboard, inscribed simply, 'R.I.P.'

"Don't you like it?" demanded the creator of the tableau. "I call it 'Hic jacet'—emphasis on the hic, of course."

"It's a masterpiece," said Kate, and broke into a peal of laughter that hastened Mrs. Pow's steps towards them.

On reaching the group she stopped, folded her arms, and nodded down at the sleeping knight with grim amusement. "Ay. Juist as I thocht," she said. "I might hae kenned he'd be at the whusky, but I keekit in his bag, and there was nae bottle in't this morning, that I'll swear."

"He was too clever for you, Mrs. Pow," said Robin. "The bottle was hidden in the spare bedroom cupboard. He must have smuggled it in yesterday."

"By! He's an awfu' ane!" said Mrs. Pow.

"Don't be too angry with him," pleaded Kate. "He's given us a laugh, anyway."

"Ou, I'll no' fyle ma tongue wi' him," retorted Mrs. Pow. "He can bide there till he wakens, an' if he isna roused by the time I leave the big hoose, I'll send ane o' the bairns doon tae the Sidegate an' tell his guid sister. He bides wi' her, ye ken, an' she's a warrior, I'm tellin' ye. *She'll* sort him. Ay," finished Mrs. Pow with grisly triumph. "He'll get his kale through the reek this nicht!"

"I'm glad you didn't say anything to Mrs. Pow about Drew having been here," said Robin Anstruther, as he walked back with Kate to his aunt's house. "Better not mention it even to Aunt Jean, I think."

"I'm not quite a fool," Kate said coldly. "Nor do I babble about other people's business, whatever you may think of me."

She put her hand on the little green gate of The Anchorage to push it open, but he held it against her while he said coolly: "I think, my dear, that you're a regular spitfire. But I hand it to you for pluck. After all, you didn't know it was Andrew you'd shoved into that press. It might have been a drunken tramp or anyone—"

"Thank you so much," said Kate with extreme bitterness. "I appreciate both your compliments very much. Good afternoon."

CHAPTER THREE

1

"HANNAH has some sandwiches for you in the kitchen," said Mrs. Anstruther, adding with splendid calm: "If you are going I should advise you to leave immediately, and by the back-door. I can see Flora Milligan hovering at the gate."

"Good Heavens! Has she seen me?" Kate made a bound for the door, then stopped. "No, she can't. Blessings on your fernery, darling. Is that why you cherish it?"

"I find it useful," admitted Mrs. Anstruther.

"I bet you do. Isn't it rather despicable of me to creep away and leave you at Miss Milligan's mercy?"

"I don't think," said Mrs. Anstruther dryly, "that I am as much at her mercy as she is at mine, poor Flora! But she has now screwed up her courage to open the gate, so really you had better go—unless you are anxious to see her?"

"Perish the thought! I'm gone. Expect me when you see me." And Kate made a hasty exit kitchenwards.

The grenadier, with a spasm of her grim countenance which passed for a smile, handed over a neatly tied packet. "Here yer lunch," she said. "Samwidges an' twa-three rock-cakes." Taking a huge orange from a drawer in the dresser, she remarked: "It's drouthy wark climbin'. Here an oranger. Mebbe ye'll no' fancy it as weel's beer, but it's a lang sicht better for ye. Fu' o' thae vitty-mings, as they ca' them, but that'll no' hairm ye."

Kate thanked her suitably, left her to answer Miss Milligan's timid ring, and went out into the fine morning.

She had put in five days of faithful overseeing, and now a particularly lovely day tempted her to play truant from Soonhope, the more so as Mrs. Pow now insisted on supervising the painter herself. "I'll learn him tae drink whusky an' pent his dirty heid instead o' the doors," she had said darkly. And so grimly did she carry out this intention that the painter had begun to wear the hunted look of a mouse which knows that the cat is lurking for it round the next corner. Though she could not help pitying him, Kate felt that Mrs. Pow's vigilance certainly had its uses. She was able with a clear conscience to take a holiday, secure in the knowledge that Mrs. Pow also would enjoy her day, monarch of all she surveyed, alternately harrying the painter and her husband, who was engaged in 'sorting' the lawn and 'redding up' the garden. So away went Kate through the town, along Riverside Street, where the old houses of great Lowland families, now converted into slum-dwellings for labourers, wore an air of wistful longing for the days when lords and their ladies came to Haystoun in winter, when the cobbled streets knew the echo of their horses' hoofs and the rumble of their heavy coaches. Her way led her over the narrow hump-backed bridge, with Alewater, reduced to a summer trickle, creeping beneath the arches, and then she was free of the town at last, and open country lay before her.

There was gossamer flying, sure sign of dry weather. The fairy strands, almost invisible, brushed her face or floated aside as she walked. At the first cross-roads she left the broad macadamized surface for a real country road, red as the soil of the fields it divided, velvet-soft with dust lying thickly to be stirred up by the slow-moving carts which had left long wisps of hay trailing from the hedges. Kate, seeing the glossy brown of her shoes gradually acquiring a greyish bloom, was carried back to her childhood. She could hear the singsong voice of Highland Nannie raised in mild and ineffectual reproof: "Kit-tay! Grey! Look-you-boots!" She knew again the lovely soft slippery scrunch under those stout boots, the satisfactory little dust-storms agitated by each guiltily scuffled step.

Of course the disappearance of those gritty clouds which teased eyes, nose and throat was a boon to motorist and pedestrian alike. Kate's common-sense and love of comfort forced her to admit this, but she felt that an arterial road, bare and ugly as its name, was something to be hurried over at top speed in a car, and avoided at all costs when walking. It was hard and unsympathetic to the feet, bordered by wires strung between concrete posts, adorned by hideous hoardings which even at night shouted the advantages of some hotel or patent food or cheaper petrol to the passers-by, and she held firmly to her private conviction that dust, a great deal of dust, would improve it by obscuring its immediate surroundings. Perhaps if trees were to be planted alongside it might be better, but the road-makers' ambition seemed to be to cut down every tree within reach and replace it by telegraph poles which, however useful, were hardly objects of beauty. 'The Utilitarian or Tin-Can-and-Cellophane Age,' thought Kate, and childishly pleased with this description, which struck her as excellent, went on in great content.

Round a corner came three carts, the drivers lying deep in the fragrant loads of hay, the horses' huge fringed hoofs clop-clopping gently in the dust, the harness jingling. Kate, forced almost into the hedge, stood on the grey-green leaves of the silverweed to let them pass on a wave of farmyard odour. The warm air was filled for a moment with the strong smell of horses and stables, of leather, of sun-dried hay, so essentially of a piece with the summer day that she sniffed it joyfully. As she did so she seemed to hear Lucy Lockhart's mild complaint, uttered years ago and never forgotten: "Kate is so dreadfully bucolic! She absolutely revels in all those horrible country things that smell of manure!"

A smile tugged at her mouth, and the man on the last cart, a rustic Lothario burnt almost black by constant exposure to weather, with a glint in his eye which spoke eloquently of many conquests, grinned at her and bawled a broad rural compliment above the dull rumble of the iron-bound wheels. Kate, rather wishing that Lucy had been there to look disgusted, waved gaily in reply. Presently the sound of their movement faded away behind her. She crossed a farmyard heavy with the silence of midday, and quite suddenly the road dwindled to a deeply-rutted track running straight into the Lammermuirs. A fresh breeze blew from their heights, a colder, stronger air very welcome after the heat of the valley. Larks were rising in a madness of shrill song to lose themselves in the almost colourless sky, thyme and lady's bedstraw and bluebells took the place of vetch and crane's-bill, heather began to show among the coarse grass.

She had eaten her sandwiches and was deep in the silent hills when she saw the sheep. It was lying with its short black legs sticking pathetically in the air, and as she caught sight of it, there was a convulsive struggle, a wild flurry of grey fleece and straining head. 'Silly creature, it can't get up,' thought Kate, and stood for a moment watching, hoping that it could right itself. But a fat ewe, once on its back in a hollow, soon becomes panic-stricken and exhausted if its first attempts to get up do not succeed. She realized that she must go to the rescue, and leaving the path, made her way towards it, wading knee-deep in heather.

The frightened animal, terror in its blank agate eyes, redoubled its efforts when it saw her. "I might be a wolf at least," she said to herself. A rank smell of hot damp wool rose to her nostrils as, avoiding the madly kicking hind-legs, she seized the sheep by its horns. It was a very large heavy sheep, but Kate was strong. Though she felt that she would probably sprain her wrists or break the beast's neck, she managed after several desperate heaves to set it upright on its inadequate legs.

"There!" she panted, scarlet with exertion and triumph.

The sheep rewarded her by promptly collapsing on to its back again in the same hollow.

"Ten thousand million devils!" cried Kate, justly annoyed by this display of ingratitude. "It would serve you right," she said severely to the struggling ewe, "if I left you here to die. However—"

Followed another brief period of violent activity, at the end of which the ewe had once more been hoisted to its feet and stood leaning against Kate, whose hands now clutched the dirty greasy fleece of its back.

"Well, I'm tired of grappling you," she said. "Can you walk now?"

The sheep, as if galvanized, leapt away from her, ran round in a tottering semi-circle, and fell over in its original helpless position.

"Of course, you know," Kate said sadly. "I don't believe you're really trying."

Plainly the creature was too feeble by this time to stay upright, and too stupid with fright to lie quietly and rest.

"Yet I can't just abandon you, silly old nanny," said Kate. "Oh, damn! I shall have to go and tell your shepherd all about you—if I can find him, which I doubt."

All round her was spread the lonely moor, mile upon mile of dim purple distance, and not another human being in sight. A dip in the hills about a mile to the west, where a few trees showed, seemed the only possible place for a small farm or a shepherd's cottage. Kate tied her handkerchief to a heather bush as a landmark, nodded encouragingly to the sheep, now lying hopelessly still, and set out on her mission.

When, flushed and dirty, with a large hole torn in one stocking by a vicious spike of burnt heather, she came to a halt and looked down into the dimple of ground which she had hoped might hide a house, she broke into helpless laughter. There was a shrunken burn running through the hollow, there were trees, there was even a little road which crossed the water by a tiny stone bridge; but the only house was a ruined shell, roofless, the garden a wilderness of nettles. . . . It seemed most unlikely that anyone would ever come along the little road, but Kate, having scrambled down the hillside, sat on the bridge and decided that she had earned a rest and a cigarette before she went any farther. The burn was very low and clear, the water ran like dark amber over its bed of smooth stones. Kate, looking down, could see the small trout so plainly that every red spot on their shining sides was visible. It must be pleasant to be a trout on a day as hot as this, to lie at ease under cool water with head upstream and tail gently moving to keep one's balance. She lingered alter the cigarette had been smoked to a stub, idly picking tiny pieces of moss from between the coping-stones of the bridge, the afternoon sun warm on her back. Lulled by the soft murmur of the water, she did not hear the car until it drew up.

When a man's voice said: "Lost something?" she was so startled that she jumped.

Indignantly she said: "What a fright you gave me, creeping up like that! I nearly fell into the burn."

And then she saw that the ancient tourer was driven by Robin Anstruther. Beside him sat a lean brown man wreathed in collies, most obviously a hill shepherd.

"Creeping?" Anstruther raised his eyebrows. "In this old tin-can, over a road like this? We came up making a noise like a fire-engine. But what on earth are you doing here?"

Kate had recovered. "I'm looking for help for a—a friend," she said.

"What? Another girl, d'you mean?"

"Well, I wouldn't exactly call her a *girl*," said Kate, considering the matter. "She's too matronly for that. A very womanly woman, I met her quite by chance."

His puzzled frown was too much for her gravity and she began to laugh. "It's a sheep. An elderly ewe. I found it lying on its back, and now *you* can rescue it."

Both men craned their necks as if they expected to see the sheep recumbent below the bridge.

"Not there. More than a mile away," Kate explained. "I was on my way to look for someone who could make it stand up."

This remark, perfectly sensible to her, seemed to amuse Robin Anstruther. He uttered his short laugh, which echoed loudly in the quiet place, and even the silent man beside him smothered a smile.

"The sheep and I," she pointed out coldly, "didn't find it very funny."

"Hah!" he said. "Where is this beast? Couldn't you have had a shot at setting it up yourself?"

"I did have a shot. Several shots," said Kate, still more coldly. "I should have thought that one look at me could have told you that I haven't been strolling idly about doing nothing. I don't get into this state of dirt for pleasure. And the sheep refuses to stay on its feet. It just falls down again, and as I got tired of supporting about half a ton of solid sheep, I thought I might get someone else to try."

"You can't have expected to find anyone in the burn," he said unabashed, and added with a chuckle, "unless you were looking for the kelpie?"

"I was tired and hot, so I stopped for a rest," began Kate on her dignity. Then, forgetting it immediately: "Is there *really* a kelpie?"

"Supposed to be. Well, come on and we'll go along the road with the car as far as we can. Duncan, you and the dogs will have to get in behind."

The shepherd got out in a wave of collies. "Doun, Tweed, doun, Glen, doun, Mirk!" he commanded as the dogs leapt about Kate. He proceeded to urge them into the back of the car, where he followed them.

"What's brought you so far afield? I thought you'd be at Soonhope looking after your painter," said Robin Anstruther, when they were bumping over the rough road.

"I gave myself a whole holiday. Mrs. Pow can deal with the painter far more efficiently than I can. He's really *her* painter now, not mine."

"Poor devil. With Mrs. Pow at his heels I pity him," he said. "Well, I was coming down this evening to Haystoun to see if you'd like to go to Baro Fair with me tonight, but you'll be too tired now."

"No, I won't, really I won't. I'd love to go—after we've rescued the sheep." Kate assured him hastily.

The car toiled on amid clouds of steam from the radiator. Grouse flew over them with a whir of swift wings, to alight at a safe distance in the heather and cry: "Go-back! Go-back!"

"I really think we'd better, you know," said Kate.

"Better what?"

"Go back, as the grouse advise. They are quite right. The car's boiling like a kettle."

"Pity we didn't bring any tea," he said placidly. "We might have had a cup, and you're so fond of tea, too. It's all right. Here we are at the top. Now where's your sheep?"

It was the shepherd whose keen eyes picked out the white speck which was Kate's handkerchief, and they set off towards it.

"Can you see the sheep?" she asked anxiously.

"I believe you're getting quite fond of this sheep of yours," observed Robin Anstruther.

Duncan said to him: "She'll be there a'right. Thae auld yowes are aye rowin' aboot. They're no' wise at a'."

The handkerchief was quite clearly to be seen when Kate stopped short with an angry cry. "Just look at that, will you?"

A solitary sheep had moved from behind a peat-hag and now began nonchalantly to crop the grass.

"Well!" said Kate, as Robin burst into a shout of laughter.

"Your sheep seems to have made a good recovery," he suggested, and the shepherd's polite decorum deserted him and his face became one broad delighted grin.

"Well!" said Kate again. "Isn't that exactly like a sheep? Not content with being a perfect fool itself, the ungrateful beast must needs make a fool of me into the bargain!"

2

Baro village lies high above Haystoun on the lower slopes of the hills, so cunningly enfolded by deep woods that from a little distance no stranger would suspect its presence. It can be approached from all sides by a network of small roads, but no main highway comes any nearer than the valley, where the buses roll heavily past on their way to England along the Post Road. Round Baro the farms have not yet been broken up into small-holdings whose over-driven tenants struggle to scrape a livelihood from an inadequate two acres of soil. Times are not very good, but the old order still prevails there, a survival of days when master and men were one large family working together with the same aim, that the land to which they were thirled might yield to its greatest advantage. It is true that Lord Soutra's great house, from which the village takes its name, stands empty for many months in every year, and his moors and coverts are shot by a syndicate of wealthy Englishmen who can afford to pay well for their sport. But a Heriot at least still owns the 'Big Hoose' and that counts for a great deal when so many estates have changed hands. The huge closed gates preside over the village, staring from the end of a grass avenue of lime-trees, now an extension of the Green, at the broken cross mounted on a seven-stepped pedestal which marks the centre of Baro.

"There are two pubs in this place," said Robin Anstruther as the car—the smart car, not the elderly tourer—came round a sharp corner by the old church. "One is rather pretentious, calls itself the Baro House Hotel, you know. Sun lounge, cocktails, food mostly out of tins. The other's just a pub where people stay who come for the fishing and shooting. Which d'you think you'd fancy?"

"Just the pub, please," said Kate promptly. It was obvious where his own preference lay, and in any case anglers and shooters usually chose a place which did them well in a plain fashion.

"Good, the Soutra Arms it is, then," he said in a voice of relief and turned the car away from the larger building behind the cross into a narrow road running alongside the lime avenue. "Here we are."

They had stopped before an old whitewashed house with a faded coat-of-arms hanging on a sign above the door. Across the road, on the Green and under the trees, the Fair was in full swing, noisy, colourful in the last of the sunlight failing between the leaves.

Baro Fair had once been famous throughout the south-east of Scotland, when the Haystoun High School boys 'got the play' to attend it. Farmers flocked there to buy and sell beasts, their wives, who did their shopping annually, came with them to inspect the wares of the weavers and shoemakers from Seton. Bickers and tubs had to be bought of the coopers, baskets of the wild swarthy gipsies. Nor was the Fair wholly given over to serious business. There were fortune-tellers, frowned on by the minister, but patronized behind his back by his parishioners, there were sellers of gingerbread, ribbons and trinkets and quack medicines, there were merry-go-rounds and wrestling matches and dancing.

Though stripped of its old use as an essential part of country life, and degraded to a cheap form of summer amusement, the Fair was still held every year. Games and dancing competitions took the place of the cattle sale, a circus had halted its wagons and pitched its dirty tents in a convenient field along the Haystoun road. The Green was set about with booths and stalls, where young ploughmen and hinds tried their strength or displayed their skill and accuracy of eye with darts, air-guns or quoits, hoping to win a gaudy prize for the giggling girls who accompanied them. In a dark corner a fortune-teller with an exotic eastern name, a gipsy costume of more than oriental splendour and a pronounced Glasgow accent lurked outside her dingy pavilion to lure passers-by within. The din was tremendous, and above the noise of showmen trumpeting their attractions, the laughter and loud talk of the crowd, blared the band of the British Legion from Haystoun rendering *Braw, Braw Lads* with every brass instrument it owned.

"Is the noise too much for you?" asked Robin Anstruther close to Kate's ear.

"No, no! I love it. Please may we go on the Green and see the fun?" Her eyes were shining, her cheeks pink with excitement. Robin, who had brought her partly because she amused him, a little out of half-lazy kindness, and more out of half-idle curiosity to see how she would take it, was, for some reason which he did not try to explain to himself, pleased with her.

"We'll have dinner first. I hope there's something to eat, and someone in to cook it," he said, and taking her by the elbow, gently urged her into the narrow hall of the Soutra Arms.

It was dark, quiet, and empty save for a pleasant smell of cooking, but while Kate was wondering where everyone was, a door flew open and a large woman in pink print, whose moon-face bore witness to her activities, advanced upon them, a basting-spoon in her hand.

"Eh, ye idle, guid-for-naethin' wee hempie!" she shouted. "If ye dinna set aboot yer wark this meenit ye'll can pack yer bag an' awa'!" Then, evidently realizing that the object of her wrath was not among those present: "Maircy on us! It's gentry!" she exclaimed on a lower note. "I'm *that* pit aboot, sirr, ye'll need tae excuse me. Here's the denner a' ready, an' no' a soul tae serve it, an' the three gentlemen in the settin'-room roarin' on their meat!"

"Well, Isa, we're roaring for ours," said Robin Anstruther. "Where's everyone? On the Green, I'll be bound."

"Oh, it's yersel', Maister Anst'er!" said the cook, adding bitterly, "ay, they're on the Green screichin' an' cairryin' on, an' me fair dementit."

A bell, pressed by an impatient finger in some room upstairs, trilled angrily through the house, and as if in answer to its summons a girl in a black dress and tiny apron, her coquettish cap over one ear, was blown into the hall from outside on a gale of high-pitched mirth.

The cook, swelling with fury, and looking like Boadicea urging her chariots against the legions of Rome, confronted her, while Kate and Robin fell back respectfully into an open doorway.

"Jessie!" thundered the cook with an awful wave of her basting-spoon. Kate trembled for the culprit, but she did not appear either abashed or intimidated.

"Eh, Isa!" she gasped, struggling with her laughter. "Noo dinna be vexed wi' me. I won twa prizes in the shootin'-gallery, an' baith for you—see, a poke o' sweeties an' a bonny wee peen-cushion wi' a dolly's heid on't!"

She held out the bribes and the cook in mollified accents said: "Weel, that was rale guid o' ye, Jessie. My, it's an *awfu'* bonny wee cushion. . . . But come awa' noo, hen, an' set the table for the denners. Here's Maister Anst'er brocht a leddy, an' the shooters up the stair are gettin' wild wantin' their meat. C'wa'."

In sweet accord they moved off towards the back of the hotel. Robin looked at Kate and smiled. "Mastery of matter over mind, don't you think?"

"Bribery and corruption," Kate said firmly.

"It seems to work all right. Look here, let's go into the dining-room and take a table by the window. Then you'll be able to watch the goings-on outside while I get you some sherry. Are you at the stage of 'roarin' on your meat yet?"

"Not quite. In any case, being a perfect lady, I shouldn't roar. But," said Kate rather wistfully, "I only had sandwiches for lunch, and we got back to Mrs. Anstruther's too late for tea. I could bear to be fed within the next hour."

"I'll try some more bribery on Isa, and see if we can't be dealt with before those wild shooters upstairs," he promised, and went off in search of sherry.

Watching the Green from where Kate sat at a table for two in the window was like looking at a stage from the front or a box. The noise was dulled, the moving figures and glaring lights that mocked the sunset slightly blurred by the glass between, and this gave a further effect of unreality to the changing scene. The hand was still play-ing its stock piece, and even the over-loud brass could not entirely spoil the lovely air. A small girl, wearing a travesty of Highland costume, her bonnet flaunting three feathers, her kilt disclosing a glimpse of frilled white drawers, her velvet doublet half-hidden by dangling medals, passed with a hard-faced woman who held her by the hand. 'One of the prize-winning dancers at the Games,' thought Kate, and smiled, remembering how angry it always made Greystiel Heron to see these over-dressed brats performing men's dances. 'Poor little wretch, she doesn't seem to be enjoying her triumph much.' The woman jerked her along, the child's tired sallow face was smeared with crying. . . . For the moment Kate was glad not to be out among the crowd. She was content to look on, a spectator of rough pleasure in which she had no part. And suddenly it struck her like a blow that she had spent far too much time looking on at life instead of living it. To sit here with the glass between her and the crowd outside was typical of her whole existence.

"It's all wrong!" she exclaimed aloud.

"What's all wrong?" Robin Anstruther, unheard by her, had come in from the bar carrying two glasses of sherry.

Kate looked at him seriously. "Nothing, really," she said. Instinctively she knew that she would never be able to make him understand, for he was the sort of person who would live as he chose, and yet expect women to want always to be sheltered.

He sat down opposite her, and smiled his slow ironic smile. "So you won't tell me?"

Kate laughed. "No, I won't. You'd never understand."

"Perhaps not. Women are unaccountable creatures," he said philosophically. "Aren't you going to drink your sherry?"

She picked up her glass and looked at him over it. The wine was almost the same colour as her eyes. "Unaccountable, quotha! Not so, sir. Men are the mysterious sex. We poor women are probably the simplest creatures in this complex world."

"Hah! Well, I'll take your word for it. Cheer-oh." He lifted his own glass and drank.

Kate nodded in reply, absentmindedly. She had to admit, as the meal appeared, carried in by Jessie at the gallop, that it was very pleasant to be taken out and looked after efficiently as Robin Anstruther did it. Perhaps there was something to be said for a sheltered life after all.

"Oh, raspberries, as late as this! And cream, lots of it. How lovely!" she said. "This is a very good dinner, isn't it?"

Robin nodded, smiling a little as he thought of other women who had dined with him. Some had fancied themselves to be in love with him, some he had imagined he loved, some he had merely found amusing companions, temporary sleeping partners, forgotten after a few days; but all had been alike in demanding the best restaurants, the most expensive and out of season dishes. No doubt they were quite right in setting as high a value as possible on their charms. They would have laughed at Kate Heron, enjoying this plain fare in a small country pub.

"Are you laughing at me because I'm greedy?" demanded Kate, undisturbed. She poured thick cream over a pyramid of dark red fruit and added sugar lavishly. "I am, and about such babyish things. Strawberry jam, and ices, and roast chicken. It's just one of the things about me that people have to get used to."

"As a matter of fact, I was thinking what good company you are," he said.

It was true. She was not so unsophisticated that she bored him; he shrewdly suspected that she could play the part of coquette if the mood took her, but there was no trace of it in her manner now, none of that rather wearisome consciousness of sex which so many attractive women wore like perfume. She had an unspoiled freshness of outlook, a keen 'delight in simple things' which made her seem at once younger and more interesting. There was only one other woman, he thought, of the many he had known, who shared that lovely faculty for making ordinary things exciting and romantic.

"I only know one other woman who can make an adventure out of nothing at all," he said, and realized with a shock that he had spoken aloud when he heard Kate say: "I didn't know *I* could do that. Who is the other one?"

He stared at her. "Did I say it? I didn't mean to speak," he said.

Kate had the grace to blush. "I know you didn't, and don't tell me if you don't want to. I shouldn't have asked. And it isn't fair, because I could see that you were thinking about something very hard, and just for fun I willed you to say it out loud. You know how easy it is to do it."

"I don't. I believe you're a witch," he said. "And I'm not in the habit of taking witches out to dinner, even in pubs. But there's no mystery really. The other woman I was thinking of was Elizabeth Fardell, as a matter of fact."

"Elizabeth Fardell?" For an instant Kate could not think why the name was so familiar, then suddenly she remembered. It had been mentioned in many tones of disapproval, anger and dismay through-out the family circle a few years ago. "Mrs. Fardell? You mean the woman who—the one Andrew ran away with? Am I like *her*?"

"Only in that one thing, I should think," he answered in a slow unwilling way. "There doesn't seem to me to be any resemblance apart from that. Are you offended because I compared you with her?"

Kate was puzzled by something in his manner, too vague to catch hold of, some tone in his voice, some passing look, in his eyes. Something which it was no business of hers to notice, and which she would do well to forget. "Of course I don't mind," she said hazily. "Why should I? I've never met her. I don't suppose I ever shall."

"I don't suppose so," he agreed, and added abruptly, "I didn't order coffee. They can't brew it here, it's always filthy. Do you mind?"

Before Kate, bewildered by this sudden change of subject, could answer, Jessie made a beaming entry behind a tray on which were two large cups of a greyish liquid.

"Isa minded that ye aye liked a cup o' coffee efter yer denner," she announced, setting her load proudly on the table. "So here ye are."

"Oh, Lord!" groaned Robin Anstruther after she had gone. "What are we to do?"

"Drink it, of course. We simply can't hurt their feelings," said Kate, bravely lifting her steaming cup to her lips.

"I doubt if you'll say that after the first taste," he warned her.

Kate put her cup back on its saucer with care. "No. I honestly don't see how we can swallow that. Please give me a cigarette to take the taste away."

They sat looking sadly at the cooling coffee through a thin veil of blue smoke, until Kate said in a thoughtful voice: "Do you suppose coffee would be bad for aspidistras?"

"This coffee would be bad for anything."

"But worse for aspidistras than for us? They're very hardy, I believe."

"Why?"

For answer she rose, took a cup in each hand and went towards the darkest corner of the room, where a large aspidistra blushed almost unseen in its pot on a high stand.

"I expect," she said, coming back and setting down the empty cups, "that it will do the thing a lot of good. Nourish it. Perhaps it will even *flower* after this."

He looked at her grave face and innocent eyes. "Entirely unscrupulous," he said.

Kate was indignant. "Resourceful, you mean, don't you?" she rebuked him. "The next time you come, that aspidistra will be hung with dear little coffee berries!"

"Well," said Robin. "We'd better go. If you're going to be resourceful you may as well practise on the coconut shies and lucky dips."

For an hour they wandered about the Green, trying their luck at various targets with little success, but much amusement on Kate's part. Robin, who had a straight eye, was not unnaturally less popular with the owners of the shooting galleries than his wildly erratic companion. At last, laden with prizes of repellent aspect, no value, and surprising bulk, they began to make their way back to the Soutra Arms and the car.

The crowd had become even more hilarious, the smell of whisky and strong tobacco and trodden turf and sweat was stifling. Kate, hesitating for a moment to glance at a set of girls and young men who were dancing an eightsome reel to the music supplied by two accordions and a mouth-organ, was separated from Robin Anstruther. A stalwart scarlet-faced youth, his yellow hair rampant above a streaming forehead, seized her arm.

"Hey, lassie! C'wa' an' dance wi' me. I'll gi'e ye a turn. Ye're a fine tall lass—"

He had probably had a drink or two, but Kate was pretty sure that gaiety and excitement rather than whisky had gone to his head.

"I'm so sorry, I can't. I have to go home now," she said, but she said it regretfully. Mad as the impulse was, she longed to dance.

"Ach, come on! Ye needna gang. It's early yet!" her would-be partner cried, and put an arm round her waist. "Can ye dae the Oxton Reel?"

Yes, I can, but—" said Kate, looking about her for Robin. She could not see him, and 'well, he oughtn't to have left me in the crowd,' she said to herself quite unreasonably. "It would serve him right if I *did* dance!'

Already the impromptu orchestra was playing a bumping strathspey tune, already couples were gathering on a cleared space of poached and paper-strewn grass. Kate flung discretion to the winds and allowed herself to be led into the arena in triumph. The next moment saw her deep in the intricacies of the Oxton Reel.

Robin Anstruther, turning to tell Kate to keep close to him, found himself addressing a large elderly female whom he had never seen before, and who froze him with a glare of such ferocity as she hissed: "Young man, I'll thank ye tae let me pass!" that he fell back several paces in sheer astonishment. The voice of his steward said in his ear with respectful enjoyment: "If it's the young leddy ye're seekin', sirr, I think ye'll fin' her dancin'."

"Dancing?" Robin stared at him, then, still laden with the ridiculous fruits of his prowess at the sideshows, strode back towards the dancing-floor, pushing his way through the throng with little ceremony.

He saw her almost immediately, her slim black frock showed up among the lighter colours worn by the country girls. Her hat was gone, her hair was ruffled, and she was dancing with a beautiful smooth grace as if she moved over polished wood instead of rough turf. The little upstanding white ruffle round the high neck of her dress made the carnation flush on her cheeks even more brilliant, but he was so angry with her that her evident delight in the dance only made him angrier. And he could do nothing until the Oxton Reel had bumped to a close. Then, thrusting all his tawdry burden into the surprised but ready clasp of an onlooker, be stepped forward and claimed her.

"Upon my word, young woman," he said grimly, when, her partner having relinquished her on the advice of a friend ("Let her gang, Johnny, she's got a lad o' her ain")—he was leading her through the press once more, this time with a firm hand on her arm. "Upon my word, you're not safe to take out. I suppose if I hadn't carried you off just now you'd have been dancing with that fellow again?"

"Very likely," agreed Kate cheerfully. "I love dancing. Most of my brains are in my feet."

"I can believe it," he said.

Looking at him, she could see that the deep furrow across his brow was even deeper than usual. "Are you peevish?" she asked with interest.

He gave her arm a slight shake. "It's no use trying that on with me," he said. "If I'm peevish, as you call it, I have reason to be. What would your people say if they knew you were out with a man who couldn't look after you properly?"

"Well," said Kate, "Daddy would be certain to blame you, but then he's prejudiced in my favour. Mother is much fairer. She'd probably say that no one bar a policeman with handcuffs could be expected to look after me. But I think you have taken care of me very nicely indeed. I've enjoyed every minute of it, and thank you most awfully."

He laughed, but unwillingly, and his voice was still grim as he said: "Here's the car. It's quite a relief to have got you safely to it without losing you again."

They drove off down the dim road under heavy trees, with the sweet air blowing cool in their faces. At the gate of The Anchorage he stopped the car.

"I won't come in. The old lady will be in bed, and I don't want to wake her. I'll see you the next time I'm in Haystoun."

"If it's during the next week-end, you'll find me camping out at Soonhope with Grey. He's coming from Friday night to Sunday."

"Well, you'll have someone to keep an eye on you," he said.

Kate looked at him. "Are you still cross with me?"

"No."

"I suppose Mrs. Fardell wouldn't have danced?"

"Elizabeth?" he said, his voice changing as he said the name. "Elizabeth would do almost any mad thing, but I've never actually heard of her dancing at Baro Fair. Good night."

"Good night—Sailor," said Kate. Feeling oddly subdued, she went into the dark silent house which seemed so stuffy after the night air and crept upstairs to bed.

3

"Abracabroccoloni says—" came the voice of Grey from the back kitchen, where he was laboriously scraping potatoes at the sink.

"*Damn* Abracabroccoloni!" cried Kate heartily. "If he is as slow as you, I marvel he ever cooks at all."

"My good girl," said Grey in shocked tones. "You don't suppose *he* performs such menial tasks as peeling vegetables? An army of scullions waits on his nod. The most he does is to add the pinch of seasoning that gives that *je ne sais quoi* to a dish, or very occasionally to make a special *sauce piquante* for some favourite client on a gala night." Grey, waving a knife, emerged from his lair and seated himself on a corner of the kitchen, table, prepared to enlarge on his theme in comfort.

"You needn't sit down," said his sister brutally. "Until you've finished those potatoes—that is, if you want to eat them this evening?"

"But this is oppression. This is sheer slavery. All the same, I'll make a bargain with you. You run and fetch me a bottle of beer, and I'll drink it slowly, and you can watch me, and then—"

"So the youngest son married the beautiful princess, and they lived happily ever after. You'll get your beer when the potatoes are ready, my love," said Kate. "Look upon me as Abracabroccoloni, darling, and yourself as one of his army of scullions."

Grey sighed. "And suppose—I only say *suppose*, I down tools and strike?"

"No beer."

"I could even go and get it for myself," murmured Grey, rising.

"You could. Only it happens that I locked the store-room door and hid the key."

"My sweet! You think of everything, don't you?" said Grey fondly.

"I know your pretty little ways so well, you see—Oh, heavens, Grey, listen! There's a car coming up to the house. Be an angel and see who it is, and don't bring them in here—give me a chance to tidy my hair—"

Grey, with a shrewd glance at his sister's suddenly flushed cheeks, grinned and strolled out of the kitchen. In a few minutes Kate, swiftly shelling peas into a yellow bowl with a feeling of complete security, was stunned to hear the perfidious Grey returning along the passage, and not alone.

"Sure you don't mind coming straight into the kitchen, sir?" he was saying. "It's the only room that's furnished so far. Kate's in there. She said just to bring you along."

They were at the door. There was no time even to dash across the kitchen and hide in the scullery. Kate, with one hunted look about her, took refuge in a cupboard among the crockery, holding the door so that only a crack of light filtered in.

"Hullo! She's not here." Grey's voice, sounding abominably pleased with himself. "I expect she's hunting out some glasses for beer. If she's in one of those cupboards, though," he raised his voice meaningly. "I hope she doesn't see a mouse and drop 'em."

"Is she afraid of mice?" Robin Anstruther's voice this time.

"Brutes and devils!" thought Kate in her cupboard. "I wonder if there *are* any mice really?"

A faint scrabbling noise made her jump, and her elbow knocked against a cup. To stay where she was after making a sound which seemed to her like an earthquake was merely silly. Flushed with anger, she pushed open the door and came out, blinking, into the kitchen.

"What were you doing in there?" asked Robin Anstruther with real male tactlessness. "I never met anyone so fond of cupboards as you! Are you playing Hide-and-Seek?"

"Not a bit of it," said Grey before she could speak. "She was looking for the glasses. Couldn't you find them, Kate? Well, have another look—oh, and by the way, you might as well give me the key and I can be fetching the beer in the meantime."

Kate, with a glance that spoke volumes, fished the key out of her overall pocket and handed it to him.

"Strategy and resource always win, don't they, sir?" said Grey cheerfully to the puzzled guest.

"Low cunning, you mean," retorted Kate. And to Robin: "You'll stay and picnic with us, won't you? I'm sorry to be so untidy."

"You look all right to me," he said. "I rather like that rig you've got on."

Kate, a blue overall hiding most of her pale summer dress, a blue ribbon tied round her hair to keep it out of her eyes, was really rather attractive, he thought. Not his style, and not exactly pretty, but somehow nice to look at.

"Now," said Grey, when he had brought the beer and poured out two brimming glasses. "Now I'll do those potatoes for you, my sweet."

"Oh, thank you, thank you, Grey," said Kate in a tone of deceptive meekness and gratitude. "How kind you are!"

"Anything to help you, Sis dear." And Grey, who knew her loathing of this particular form of endearment, and used it only to annoy, took himself off to his task in high good humour.

"I suppose I'd better do something to help?" suggested Robin.

Kate accepted his dubious offer with a composed briskness which secretly amused him. "Thank you, it would be very kind of you. Now let me see, what can I give you to do?"

"It looks as if the first thing you need is a fire in that range," he said.

"Oh, we aren't using that. It makes the kitchen so hot. Can't you smell your old friend the oil-stove? I'm going to call it Bouquet after the one in the 'Good Comrade.' We've moved it to the servants' hall, and it cooks all right, however odorous it may be. Grey found an oven belonging to it, too. Really rather intelligent of him. *I* thought it was a kind of tin hen-coop."

"Well, let me shell the peas. I can do that," he said, pulling a heavy wooden chair up to the table.

"Yes, that's a good idea, only don't eat too many of them raw, or there won't be enough to go round when they're cooked," said Kate, setting the basket of plump green pods, the half-filled yellow bowl, in front of him.

"What makes you think I'll eat 'em? Do I look peculiarly untrustworthy?"

"Grey always devours about half of what he shells. He's only safe with potatoes. And for all I know you may share his craving," Kate explained. "So don't let him near them. I'm going to look after the cooking."

She disappeared along the short stone passage leading to the servants' hall. Robin Anstruther soberly set to work at the kitchen-table, wondering what had possessed him to leave his own comfortable house and excellent dinner for this odd meal to be eaten in the kitchen of Soonhope.

However, to his relieved surprise he was given casserole of chicken, peas and potatoes in which he took more interest than usual, since he and Grey had prepared them, cheese-straws and very good coffee.

"I didn't know you were a cook," he said to Kate, when they were all washing up to the accompaniment of much talk and snatches of song, mainly contributed by the young Herons.

"It's one of my few accomplishments," she said gaily, and plunged into hot argument with Grey over some sea-battle of the eighteenth century, followed by swift altercation about the merits of Lee as a general.

"We're for the South, of course," Kate told Robin, when the point had been thrashed out at last. "It's a family falling to support lost causes, though we only do it second-hand, so to speak."

"Oh, I don't know so much about that," he said, going back with her to the kitchen, where they all sat down to smoke and drink more coffee. "After all, you're standing by here, aren't you?"

Kate stared at him, and Grey broke in: "You mean the Lockharts?"

"But—but—are they a lost cause?" stammered Kate in dismay. "I mean, they're coming back to live here all together—"

"It's a pretty badly patched affair," said Robin, "and patches are apt to show. I'm only saying this because I think you two could make things a bit easier if you realized that this business is going to mean heavy weather for everyone. You can't desert your wife and family for years and then come back and expect to take up your life again just as it was before the smash, can you?"

"I always thought," said Grey, gravely scraping the sugar from the bottom of his coffee-cup and eating it from the spoon with slow relish. "That Lucy must be a bit difficult to live with, especially for an easy-going chap like Drew."

"Oh!" cried Kate. "It isn't fair to blame Lucy! Think what she must have been through. It must be a dreadful position for her, and she'll never be quite sure that it wasn't partly her fault!"

"I doubt if Lucy will blame herself," said Robin dryly. "She's not that sort."

"How can you be so horrid, Robin? How do you know what she feels about it?"

"I've seen a good deal of her, Kate, you must remember," Robin answered, his cool voice in marked contrast to her angry cry. "And then Drew is my friend. I've never made any secret of the fact that I'm on his side."

"So am I," agreed Grey. "Every time. She must have driven him to it. He'd never have done it otherwise."

"And I suppose you're both on Mrs. Fardell's 'side,' as you call it too?" asked Kate bitterly, and without waiting for an answer she rushed on: "Well, I'm on Lucy's. It's disgusting the way men stick together however badly they've behaved! I think Lucy has been abominably treated, and it's most forgiving of her to come back here and live with Andrew again after what's happened."

"That seems to be that," said Grey. He had seen his sister in a fine partisan rage so many times that her latest display did not distress him.

But Robin Anstruther, to whom it was quite new, felt guilty and uncomfortable. He had not meant to upset her like this. When it was time for him to leave, and Grey had gone out of the kitchen ahead of him to see him off, he came over to Kate and took her hand.

"I'm sorry, Kate. I had no idea you were so fond of Lucy, or I'd never have said what I did."

"Fond of Lucy!" cried Kate in exasperation. "I'm not specially fond of Lucy, though I like her well enough. Can't you understand it's the unfairness of it that makes me so angry? It's got nothing to do with my feelings. I'm far fonder of Andrew than Lucy, if it comes to that, but I'm not going to back him up when I think he was in the wrong!"

"Be careful that in your anxiety to be fair to Lucy you aren't being unfair to Andrew," he said, still holding her limp and unresponsive hand. "You see, I could plead great provocation for him—"

"It's no use. We're on different sides," said Kate stiffly. "That needn't stop us from being friends, need it?"

"I hope not," Kate said slowly. "But it won't depend on us so much as on the other two, will it?"

"I think if we can make up our minds to be friends, no one else is likely to stop us," he said. "Good night, Kate. I'll be down to see you again before very long."

"Granny's coming next Friday, and Lucy the Monday after," said Kate.

"Your Granny and I are old friends. And I'll come and see you before Lucy arrives."

"There you are again, you see. You can't be fair to Lucy—and now you're laughing at me and thinking me obstinate."

"No, not exactly obstinate," he said gravely. "Loyal is the word I would use. Good night."

CHAPTER FOUR

1

INSIDE and out, Soonhope was ready to receive its mistress, who was due to arrive that afternoon. The windows sparkled in the September sunshine, the gravel, freshly raked, was as neat as a well-combed head.

Kate, feeling magnificently competent and business-like, and thoroughly enjoying the sensation because she knew it was really undeserved, sat at the big inlaid writing-table comparing the lists of china, glass and silver in Lucy's neat hand, with her own pencil-scrawled inventory, made as she and her grandmother had unpacked their cases. She faced a window set in the western end of the house, and behind her the drawing-room ran back to a great mirror which filled the farther wall, dimly reflected the furniture, and gave a distant glimpse of her own bent head and shoulders. Two rooms had been knocked together to make this drawing-room a cool and spacious place, one half brightened by the row of windows opposite the fireplace, the other sombre, lighted only by the reflections shown in the mirror.

Coming in by the door, which was set in the darkest corner, created an illusion of entering a gallery midway, for the mirror on the left doubled the length of the room while making it appear narrower than it was. Many times on winter evenings long ago, when she was a child and Andrew still unmarried, had Kate looked up from some uproarious game of cards with her cousins and Grey to see, always with the same start of surprise, almost of fear, that other table surrounded by laughing faces and wildly grabbing hands, far away down the room.

Almost she could imagine that those other players were not mere reflections, but independent persons engrossed in some game of their own; she always waited for the evening when she would see them do something which bore no resemblance to the activities at her own table. It was a never-failing relief to see actions, dresses, characteristic mannerisms, and movements faithfully reproduced, to be recognised after that first moment. 'Not a canny room,' she and Grey had decided while they were still very young, nor had they seen any reason for changing their opinions since. There was nothing unpleasant, it simply was 'not canny.'

That was only at night. In daylight the Soonhope drawing-room was too light, too airy, too filled with flowers, soft-toned chintzes, and gay cushions to disturb the most sensitive. Kate sat with her back to it quite composedly, nor did she look round when she heard the door open.

"How are you getting on, dearie?" Grannie's kind voice.

"Finished. Cast your beady little eye over the list and see if it's all right," said Kate, as Mrs. Barlas came up the room, her soft yet heavy step making the silver and china ornaments on the small tables tinkle.

"Read it out, Kate." Mrs. Barlas came to rest, a little out of breath, in an arm-chair close to the writing-table. "I haven't got my spectacles."

"You have, darling. They're nesting in your hair. But I'll read over my beautiful list to you, and there will be hell to pay if it's not correct," said Kate.

She took up her sheets of paper, shuffled them, and read slowly to the end. "How's that?"

"There seem to be some things broken," said Mrs. Barlas in a pained tone. "Such a pity, and Lucy is so particular."

"Well, we didn't do it. We unpacked them in bits, so it must have been the removal people or the storage. Lucy ought to be jolly glad it isn't much worse."

"Apart from that, then, dearie, it seems as it should be. The silver is all there," said Mrs. Barlas. "And the glass has escaped, which is a mercy. That beautiful crystal! Thank you for taking so much care and trouble."

"Don't thank me, Granny. I love this important organizing feeling, and my nose will be quite out of joint when Lucy comes this afternoon. I do think you've been clever about maids, though Miss Milligan has been prophesying woe, like the ancestral voices. Or was it *war* they prophesied? No matter, the principle's the same. She was very much afraid you would find it next to impossible to get any satisfactory girls here. Times are *so* changed, dear Mrs. Barlas, and girls *not* what they were. I gather that only about one in twenty 'keeps herself respectable.' An immoral town, Haystoun!"

"Flora always made a poor mouth over everything if she could," said Mrs. Barlas placidly. "It was a stroke of luck getting Florence back—you couldn't ask for a better cook. And though Nina Marshall is young, she waits very well and cleans silver beautifully. Then Mrs. Pow's May is coming as kitchenmaid, and she won't have to sleep in, which is a great relief with the house so full."

"Housemaids?" asked Kate in a practical voice.

"I've engaged a girl from Fenton—Phemie Paterson. She is a little rough, but Jean Anstruther knows the family and says they are all good workers. She and Nina ought to be able to manage, with Mrs. Pow coming in to help when we need her, and Lucy can get another housemaid later on if she finds it necessary."

"Phemie Paterson? Is that the red-handed young heifer I saw plunging down the avenue yesterday? Well, if she doesn't smash everything she touches, I expect she'll be all right. She has a nice honest country face, and certainly looks strong," said Kate. "Granny, I think you're a marvel. Now all we have to do is to wait for the balloon to go up. I do like to be behind the scenes. It gives me such an advantage over the others, poor things. I wouldn't be a mere guest arriving next week for a king's ransom."

"You have been more than useful, Kate, and I know Lucy will agree with me. Now would you like to come out to the garden for a walk round?"

"Of course. Do you want baskets and scissors and things?"

"I want my garden hat, Kate. It's hanging up in the cloakroom. Oh, and Kate!" Mrs. Barlas's voice rose to a shrill scream, terrifying to strangers, but treated by her family with the composure of long use, as her grand-daughter disappeared. "Ka—ate!"

"Yes?" Kate's head came round the edge of the drawing-room door.

"If you're hungry, dear, you'll find a new tin of ginger-snaps in the storeroom. There are apples, too."

"Thank you, Granny. I'd like an apple—"

It would never do to spoil Granny's touching belief that they were constantly in need of some small snack to stave off the pangs of hunger. The storeroom in Granny's day had always contained supplies of biscuits and fruit to appease the insatiable appetites of growing children. The two Lockhart boys, Adam and Henry, were the only ones who would really appreciate it nowadays—that is, if

Lucy allowed them to eat between meals, which did not seem prob-
able. Kate, for the sake of old times, when the storeroom had been
a treasure-house, rummaged about in its dark recesses, smelling
of scented soap, coffee, spice, China tea and the wooden silver-
paper-lined boxes which contained it, until she felt the hard yellow
apples, each wrapped in a wisp of blue tissue paper, which from a
high shelf added their winey scent to the rest.

Next door to the storeroom was another dark deep cupboard,
glorified by the name of cloakroom, with a smell all its own, of
rubber, leather, and damp. A row of pegs, empty now, waited to
receive waterproofs. Mrs. Barlas's garden hat of black straw, wide-
brimmed, with a ruche of white muslin underneath the edge, and
long white muslin streamers to tie under her chin, hung there alone,
her small goloshes stood neatly on the floor below. Kate took the
hat, which gave her grandmother an oddly Tudor look as of a gentle
lady beefeater, and went out to join Mrs. Barlas at the front door.

"Geordie Pow has done wonders with the lawn," said Mrs. Barlas,
pausing to cast an approving look over the close-mown turf, the
neatly trimmed edges. "If his boy can help him, he will soon have
the garden tidy again."

"The garden looks remarkably well, I think, considering."

"Oh, my dear!" Mrs. Barlas shook her head sadly. "Geordie is no
good; unless you keep an eye on him, he does such stupid things.
All the good plants seem to have disappeared—no doubt they are
flourishing in the gardens of Geordie's friends by this time. And,
of course, there are no annuals to speak of this year, and I do miss
them, the larkspur especially."

They reached the garden and went in, Kate to walk about enjoying the tangled mass of colour under the blue sky, Mrs. Barlas to
go purposefully from one border to another, giving directions to
Geordie Pow, or pulling out some weed that particularly offended
her eye with a small but capable hand.

"Rack and ruin!" she murmured occasionally, uttering one of
the heavy sighs which did not denote any deep distress, but were
merely habit. "Rack and ruin!"

Mrs. Barlas, in fact, was completely absorbed and happy, free for
the moment of disturbing thoughts about Lucy and dear Andrew.
The earthy presence of Geordie Pow, the dump of his spade as

he dug just out of sight behind the gooseberry bushes, a fleeting glimpse of Kate in her pink linen frock, were soothing, until the garden began to be peopled with ghosts of the happy past. Their memory was not distressing, but Mrs. Barlas knew that a woman of over eighty was apt to live in other days, and too much of that sort of thing was not good for anyone. So when she found herself thinking that it was time to call the boys in to wash their hands for luncheon, she raised her voice instead in a scream to summon Kate.

"Darling, you made poor Geordie leap miles into the air," protested her granddaughter, joining her on the teak seat under the big pear tree. 'I never heard anything like it. You really surpassed yourself that time. The welkin, whatever it may be, must still be ringing! Do you want anything?"

"Just a little light conversation," said Mrs. Barlas, unperturbed.

"You shall have it. It's probably your last opportunity for a little conversation with *me*. Once Lucy is here, your mind will be ta'en up wi' the things o' the state, won't it?"

"I suppose it will," said Mrs. Barlas, and this time her sigh was a genuine one.

"Don't worry, my pet," said Kate, patting the plump hand that fidgeted uneasily with the folds of her black skirt. "It'll be all right on the night."

Then she stopped to wonder if this had perhaps been a rather indelicate remark for a grandmother's ears, and quickly said the first thing she thought of. "It's queer, considering that Lucy has lived here for so many years—she and Andrew have been married for twenty, almost, haven't they?—that she never really seemed to *belong*, somehow. I always think of you as being mistress of Soonhope, Granny. And I'm pretty sure the others think the same."

"Lucy always ran the place very well. She is an exceedingly good housekeeper," said Mrs. Barlas.

'And that's about all,' Kate said to herself, but instantly felt guilty. Was this how she backed Lucy up? Robin Anstruther would have very little reason to think her loyal if he knew. . . . And she hadn't seen Robin since that evening when he had come to supper with her and Grey in the kitchen, and they had taken sides, she so hotly, he with cool amusement. 'Oh, dear!' thought Kate dolefully. ". . . I'm so sorry, Granny, I didn't hear what you said?"

"I said that after lunch I am going to lie down, to be fresh for Lucy when she arrives. And I think you should rest, too, Kate. I'm sure you must be tired."

But after luncheon, when she had seen her grandmother comfortably tucked up under the eiderdown on her bed, and had left her with the promise that she should be roused half an hour before Lucy was due, a very demon of restlessness seized on Kate, and she prowled the house like a caged lioness. Everything was as spotless and orderly as the combined efforts of Mrs. Pow, Nina, and the red-handed Phemie could make it. The bedrooms, big and airy, were exquisitely clean, smelling of flowers and fresh linen and lavender. Each drawer was lined with smooth white paper, carefully cut or folded to fit exactly, the old mahogany furniture was polished to a soft gloss. Surely Lucy would be pleased to find Soonhope restored to its former state of comfort and home. Kate, feeling a little soothed by the perfection of the rooms, leant out of the window above the front door, sniffing in the scents of cut grass and late roses, and idly watching Nina, neat in her conventional afternoon black and white, tripping down the drive with a jug in her hand.

'Florence must have forgotten the cream, and sent Nina for it— just like her,' she thought indulgently, as Nina vanished from sight. 'Thank goodness Lucy isn't due for an hour yet!'

A roll of wheels, the clop-clop of a slowly trotting horse roused her, and she looked up to see the ancient cab from the station trundling round the curve of the avenue. It appeared to be laden with luggage, and suddenly a black umbrella of the old-fashioned type, armed with a long sharp ferrule, was thrust out of one window and poked by no uncertain hand in the aged driver's ribs. Kate saw a face, sharp-featured and witch-like, framed in a rusty black hat, before she drew back from the window to subside weakly into the nearest chair.

"Who on earth can it be?" she muttered. She heard the cab stop, the bell ring, sounds as of someone being shown into the parlour—Granny still clung to the old name for the downstairs sitting-room—then the hurried footsteps of Florence thundering on the stairs.

'Of course, Nina *would* have been sent out on a message so that Florence has to answer the door,' thought Kate, going out into the wide corridor which ran all along the front of the first floor. She knew and had often been amused by the cook's ill-concealed passion for admitting visitors, but this time it seemed a little unfortunate.

"Who is it, Florence?" she asked in a low voice, with a warning glance at the door of Mrs. Barlas's room.

"Oh, Mary, Joseph, an' Jasus, Miss Kate!' hissed the crimson-faced Florence excitedly, relishing to its fullest extent the drama of her announcement. "'Tis an old lady says she's come to stay, bein' a mimber o' the fam'ly, no less, and the name of her's Miss Charlotte Napier, an' her never expected, the creature!"

2

"Cousin Charlotte!" Kate had heard her visits to Soonhope spoken of with horror by her mother as one of the nightmares of her childhood, but to the younger generation 'Granny's Cousin Charlotte' was a legendary figure known only by name. Grey, who had once seen her, used her as a model for all the witches in the interminable fairy-tales with which he had wiled away long wet afternoons. In Kate's mind, Cousin Charlotte was inextricably tangled in a maze of spells, deep forests, and wood-cutters' fair daughters, through which, dark yet clearly defined, moved an old woman with a hooked nose, a grizzled moustache, and a large black handbag containing among other mysteries a quantity of peculiarly strong peppermint drops.

So: "Granny's Cousin Charlotte!" she said now, with more excitement than dismay in her voice.

"What'll we do with her, then, Miss Kate? Mrs. Lockhart could niver bear the sight of her."

The unholy joy in Florence's eye, her appreciation of this last-minute situation and the difficulties it involved roused Kate.

"Whatever happens, I won't have Mrs. Barlas disturbed and worried. Mrs. Lockhart can deal with Miss Napier herself when she comes. Oh, and, Florence," she added with a horrified glance at the wild figure facing her with arms akimbo, tousled grey hair, wrinkled stockings, and an apron held together by a lavish display of large black safety pins. "Did you have to send Nina out at this inconvenient time? And couldn't you have sent Phemie to answer the bell?"

"Is it that young gerril? And isn't she scared out of her wits this moment with the terror that was on her lest she'd have to go to the door? And for Nina, there's a kindly soul for ye, now, Miss Kate! She'd be after knowing that I had the soles fair worn off me feet with the goin' and comin', and says she, 'I'll away out and seek the cream for ye.' And the mistress not bein' expected till later," Florence explained with a glibness that left Kate quite dazed, "I saw no harrum in goin' my own self, though not engaged to answer the front door. But I was never one to be disobligin', Miss Kate."

"I see," said Kate. It was quite hopeless to remonstrate. Granny had been trying without success for twenty-five years to break Florence of her habit of answering the front door bell, and had given it up as a bad job long ago. The alternative of parting with her cook had never even occurred to Mis. Barlas. Florence was faithful and willing, and though she was heavy-footed, her hand with pastry was light as a fairy's. Now she stood awaiting orders, pleased and thrilled, like a dog who has just brought back a thrown ball and is ready to rush after it again. Kate wondered whether Lucy would be so tolerant of her faults, and rather feared not. It was so entirely incorrect for the cook to open the door to visitors, especially when the cook happened to look like Florence.

"That's all, Florence," she said. "Tell Phemie that the yellow room will probably be required to-night. It's all ready except for putting a hot bottle in the bed. And, of course, there will be one extra for dinner. . . . What's that queer noise?"

A dull thumping sound which she had heard for some moments without really noticing it had suddenly become loud enough to impress itself on her consciousness. It seemed to come from downstairs.

"That? It'll be the old one in the parlour, it's likely," said Florence equably. "Didn't I lock her in nice and safe the way she wouldn't be troubling Mrs. Barlas? Thinks I, it'll take a key to keep that one within in it, and I'll just be making sure she'll stop where she's put."

"Good heavens, Florence! Do you mean to say you locked Miss Napier in? You ought to be ashamed of yourself!" cried Kate, making for the wide stair. "Granny will be furious, and so will she. And as for what Mrs. Lockhart will say, I don't like to think—" To herself she added: 'There's a sort of curse on this house. Everyone is seized with a mania for locking other people into rooms—or cupboards!'

Florence's reassuring answer, hissed in a loud conspiratorial whisper over the banisters: "Ah, sure now, Miss Kate, the old one in there'll be thinking the door's stuck someway, and as for the mistress, praise be she'll never hear of it till she's had her rest," fell on deaf ears.

From behind the parlour door came the determined thumps and bangs which sooner or later could not fail to waken Mrs. Barlas, if they had not already done so. Kate, flying across the stone-floored, sunny hall, called: "I'm so sorry! I'll open the door for you at once!"

This promise, however, proved impossible to fulfil, for the simple reason that the key was not in the lock. "That *idiot* Florence!" muttered Kate savagely. "Fire from heaven ought to fall on her for this!"

"Who's there? Will you open this door immediately?" said a harsh voice, old and cracked, but full of vitality. "Is the house full of lunatics besides the one who showed me in here? Either let me out or come in yourself."

"I'm afraid the door has stuck, Cousin Charlotte," said Kate, feeling that it would be far from politic to confess that it was locked. "Would you mind waiting just a minute? It's the—the damp, you know," she added, improvising wildly.

There was a snort from within. "Damp? Huh! Driest summer we've had for thirty-six years."

Kate turned upon Florence, who had followed her downstairs and now stood breathing heavily behind her. "Give me that key, quickly!"

"The key, is it, Miss Kate? Glory be to God, is it not in the door, then?" Florence fumbled uselessly in the sagging pockets of her apron. "Now where would I have been after mislaying it?"

"Heaven knows," said Kate bitterly. "But you'd better find it before Granny comes down."

"What's all that mumbling and clucking out there?" came Cousin Charlotte's voice from the parlour. "Are you or are you not going to open this door?"

"I'll come round to the window and explain," said Kate in despair. "Find that key!" she threw over her shoulder at the now thoroughly dismayed Florence, and ran out to stand among the antirrhinums under the parlour window.

It was more than a pity, she thought now, that her great-grand-father, who had admired the picturesque, should have had this window divided into three small casements, none of which, even when opened to its largest extent, could let any person larger than a child climb through. The furious old lady who thrust her nutcracker face out so close to Kate's anxious countenance that she staggered back a pace was very small indeed, though her voluminous garments swelled her to at least double her normal size; but somehow Kate did not see herself inviting Miss Charlotte Napier to struggle out by the window.

"Now what does all this mean? And who are you? You can't be one of Andrew Lockhart's children. Not young enough. What *is* this piece of tomfoolery? A practical joke? If so, you have played it on the wrong person, let me tell you," said Miss Napier with appalling ferocity.

"Indeed it isn't a joke, and please would you not make quite such a noise?" said Kate. "Granny's resting and I don't want her to be disturbed."

"Granny? Hah, you mean Robina, I suppose. Then you must be one of Eleanor's children. She married that man Heron—nothing that *his* family would do could surprise me. And don't try to dictate to *me*, young woman. I shall make as much noise as I choose." And she thumped on the door with the umbrella which she still clutched like a rapier in one bony hand.

Kate, with a courage which afterwards, when she had time to think of it, amazed her, glared angrily back at Granny's Cousin Charlotte. "You will do nothing of the kind," she said firmly. "I will not have Granny wakened. She's tired. I'm exceedingly sorry that you can't get out just now, but it won't do you or anyone else any good to be noisy about it. Can't you be bad-tempered quietly?"

"I could, no doubt, but it gives me very little satisfaction. Nobody knows when you are in a rage unless you let 'em hear it," was the surprising answer. More surprisingly still, Miss Napier's grim visage creased into an unwilling smile. "Now I am certain that you are a Heron," she said. "No one else would have dared to stand up to me. Perhaps, though, you will be good enough to answer a few inquiries. What is your name?"

"Kate," said Kate, repressing a desire to answer, 'N or M.' "It's Katharine, really, but I'm always called Kate."

"Good sensible name. I dislike those fancy ones. Now tell me where Lucy Lockhart is, and why Robina and you are here?"

"Lucy is coming some time this afternoon. I do hope," added Kate, forgetting to whom she was speaking, "that she won't arrive until after we've got you out! And Granny and I came to get the house ready for her—take the cold air off, you know."

"She should have done it herself. No sense in shirking unpleasantness," said Cousin Charlotte. "Yes, I can quite believe that you are anxious to have me out before she comes. Not only out of the parlour, but out of the house. Eh?" with a glance of piercing directness.

"Not—not exactly," stammered Kate. "But, you see, she isn't expecting you—or anyone. Even Andrew won't be here till next week."

"I prefer you when you are speaking the truth. You know very well by hearsay that Lucy and I are like cat and dog. But I made up my mind to come and see how things were going, and here I am. She's having a family party, isn't she, to celebrate the joyful reunion?" Cousin Charlotte spoke with a sneer horrible to witness.

"Yes," said Kate. "At least, my people are coming, and Granny will be here, of course."

"Very poor taste, but Lucy never did know how to carry things off, I remember," pronounced Cousin Charlotte. "Well, I have no intention of leaving before I have seen this family gathering. But I will at least spare your anxiety so far. I will refrain from asking why the parlour door will not open, and if you will fetch me a chair, I shall try to get out by the window. Quietly, of course. We must not disturb Robina."

"Do you think it's safe?" began Kate. "The window is so small—"

"My good girl, I may be old, but I am not decrepit," said Cousin Charlotte tartly. "Do what you are told, and don't argue. It is a most deplorable habit, in any person under forty-five."

Kate went into the house and fetched a chair from the hall, without further protest. She was not looking forward with any enthusiasm to helping Cousin Charlotte to escape by the window, but there seemed nothing else to do.

"If you would give me your umbrella and handbag, Cousin Charlotte, and take off your cape," she suggested, "it would be so much easier for you."

"I shall get out as I am, or not at all," was the reply, and one narrow foot in a black elastic-sided boot was placed firmly on the window-ledge.

'It will be not at all, I should think,' Kate said to herself, as, dodging the umbrella, which was waving perilously near her eye, she seized Cousin Charlotte's heavily caped form and pulled.

Lucy Lockhart, driving her own small car up the avenue, found her feelings of faint melancholy changing to acute irritation as she saw Kate trampling on the flowering antirrhinums, and trying to drag what looked like a large black bundle out of the sitting-room window. Not for the first time she reflected with disfavour on the oddness of her husband's relations. The Hallidays—she had been a Halliday—had never done the queer things which seemed to come naturally to these others. She drew the car up capably beside the front door and got out, only to be further offended by the sight of Florence surging through the hall towards her, and looking as if she had robbed a scarecrow. In the background hovered a young housemaid with goggling eyes and one large red hand clapped over her mouth as she rocked with soundless merriment.

"Holy-Mary-Mother-of-God, 'tis herself!" ejaculated Florence in horror, recognizing the disapproving figure on the gravel. "And the old mistress not out of her bed yet. Run, Phemie, an' let a cry on her that the mistress is here!"

Lucy, ignoring Florence altogether, said to Kate: "I suppose you know that you've ruined the antirrhinums? And what are you doing with that bundle of old clothes?"

In justice to Lucy, it must be admitted that Miss Napier, whose cape had fallen over her head, temporarily extinguishing her, did look like a bundle of old clothes.

"Oh, it's you, Lucy," panted Kate. "You're early, aren't you? This is Cousin Charlotte. She's stuck, and I wish you'd help me to get her out."

"Cousin Charlotte! Miss Napier!" Lucy fell back, almost colliding with Florence, who had stolen up behind her to see the fun. "What is *she* doing here?"

"If you would have the goodness to help me out, I will then talk to you, Lucy," snapped Cousin Charlotte, freeing herself from the cape with a violent struggle, and darting a fiery glance at her hostess. "But it is just like you to bother about inessential details at the wrong moment. You've done it all your life, and I suppose you will be doing it on your death-bed. Pull me *out*, I say!"

Before the petrified Lucy or the exhausted Kate could obey, the stout figure of Phemie mysteriously appeared in the parlour. Kate saw her without astonishment. So much had happened that it seemed perfectly possible that Phemie had got into the room by the keyhole. With one vigorous shove from behind, the housemaid propelled Cousin Charlotte forward into the arms of Kate and Florence, who, to the final destruction of the flower-bed, had plunged to the rescue in the nick of time.

"There, now. Sure ye're grand now!" she said proudly as she righted the old lady with a deft twist which reminded Kate of pancake tossing, and set her on her feet on the gravel.

"And now perhaps someone will explain what all this is about?" Lucy asked patiently. Florence, muttering something about tea and the kettle, discreetly withdrew, and Phemie had already vanished from the parlour window.

Kate shook her head in a feeble manner. "Don't ask me to begin. It's all so muddled—"

"Not at all. Perfectly simple"—this was Cousin Charlotte, of course. "Some fool locked me into the parlour and presumably lost the key, and as I was tired of being in there, I decided to get out by the window."

Kate really felt sorry for Lucy, but wished ardently that she would laugh, which was what she longed to do herself, but dared not alone.

"I see." Lucy's tone and expression said clearly that she considered this a joke in exceedingly bad taste. "Don't you think it a little odd that the sitting-room door should be wide open now?"

"I am talking about the parlour," said Cousin Charlotte.

"And *I* call it the sitting-room, Cousin Charlotte. It was very good of you to call, though a little unexpected. Are you staying in the neighbourhood?"

Kate stole away, feeling too dazed to enjoy this meeting of Greeks. She heard Cousin Charlotte's incisive reply: "I am proposing to stay here, Lucy, if you have no objection. I understand there is to be a house-party of his relations to welcome Andrew home, and as he has always been a favourite of mine, I decided to join you."

There was a sting in the tail of that, thought Kate, as she went thankfully into the cool hall, a gentle reminder that Andrew or his children *might* be Cousin Charlotte's heirs. "Lucy will ask her to stay, loathing the necessity, and probably thinking that if I'd been really clever I could have got rid of her."

Phemie was coming heavily downstairs, and on seeing Kate instantly burst into wild giggles, and then stuffed what looked like half of her apron into her mouth to stifle them.

"What's the matter, Phemie?" asked Kate.

Phemie removed the apron just in time, from her appearance, to prevent suffocation, and gasped: "Eh, it wis the auld leddy, an' the key! I've lauched till I wis fit tae burrst wi' it!"

"Well?" said Kate, whose patience had been worn threadbare, and whose tone of disapproval sounded quite like Lucy's.

"Well, Florence gied me a key tae unlock the dairy, an' it wadna fit, an' syne I cam' an' pit it tae the parlour door, an' megsty! if it wasna the parlour key a' the time! An' the auld leddy sclimmin' oot by the windy!"

"Really, Phemie, I never heard anything so stupid," exclaimed Kate angrily. "I think you must all be out of your senses this afternoon."

"Eh, but ye havena heard the best o't yet!" cried Phemie, swelling with triumph. "D'ye ken whit it wis I was tae fetch frae the dairy? The *cream*, nae less. An' there's Nina awa' tae the ferm seekin' it. She'll be black angered, I doot, gin she wins back wi'oot it. A' that walk for naethin'!"

"I hope," said Kate sincerely, "that she will do something dreadful to you and Florence."

But Phemie only giggled again, and retired to the kitchen to report to Florence that "the leddies wis a' ragin' thegither fit tae be tied, except Mistress Barlas. She juist said never tae heed, an' it didna maitter ava'."

To Lucy's obvious regret, Kate's astonishment, and Cousin Charlotte's grim amusement, this was Granny's view. Fortified by tea,

Kate told the whole story, sparing Florence as much as she could, though Lucy's impatient "Tchah!" did not sound too promising.

Mrs. Barlas sipped her tea and smiled placidly. "*What* a pity Andrew wasn't here," she said, beaming at them. "Dear Andrew, he would have enjoyed it so *much*!"

3

When Lucy said after dinner, "Then I shall expect you here after breakfast, Kate, and we can go through those lists together," even the most limited intelligence would have understood that Kate was intended to return to The Anchorage to sleep; and though Granny was inclined to be indignant, Kate left with a sense of escape, was received by Mrs. Anstruther with pleasure, given elderberry wine and sponge-cake, and described in detail the harrowing circumstances of Lucy's homecoming. "And I hope," she concluded, "that there won't be any more adventures for a long, long time. I've had my fill of them lately."

"Now that Lucy is here, things will be very cut and dried," said Mrs. Anstruther.

"I really hope so," Kate answered, fervently. "Nothing would please me better."

She awoke in the same frame of mind, and walking down the road towards Soonhope, saw a familiar figure approaching, whose every angle spoke of a horror of adventure in any form. Perversely enough, Kate groaned aloud.

"Oh, dear, here comes Miss Milligan, and there's no means of escape!"

Miss Milligan, fluttered bird-like up to her and stood twittering. "Good morning, Kate, my dear. I am so lucky to have caught you. Now I needn't go on to The Anchorage, or up to Soonhope, and that will be a saving of precious time, as I must go to the grocer's for Mamma's Allenbury's diet, which I most stupidly forgot to order yesterday, and she will want it at lunch."

"Can I take a message for you to Mrs. Anstruther? Or Granny?" asked Kate.

"No, no, thank you. It was you I wanted to see. Would you come to tea this afternoon, Kate? It would give Mamma and me so much pleasure. I think she has been feeling a *leetle* dull lately, and you would cheer her up."

It was on the tip of Kate's tongue to refuse, when she thought that having tea with Mrs. and Miss Milligan would surely keep her safe from any adventure. Also she remembered Mrs. Anstruther's caustic description of 'Mamma,' whose greatest interest in life was bullying her daughter. She thought she could read a dim appeal for help in Miss Milligan's small bright eyes, and heard herself answering: "Thank you. I'm sure I can be spared at Soonhope, and I should like to come very much indeed."

'What have I let myself in for?' she wondered, as, leaving Miss Milligan to turn back towards the grocer's in Crossgate Street, she went in at the gates of Soonhope.

There seemed to be a good deal of noise going on at the lodge, she could hear voices raised in what sounded like loud, shrill lamentation, mingled with curses uttered in Geordie Pow's deeper tones. But why was Geordie not up at the garden? Kate stopped, wondering if she ought to inquire into the matter, when the eldest daughter of the house, the fashionable young woman known throughout Haystoun as 'Mrs Pow's May,' and destined to be kitchenmaid at Soonhope, burst from the open doorway wringing her hands, with large tears rolling down her round pink cheeks and splashing unheeded on her newest jumper.

"May! Is anything wrong?" asked Kate in dismay.

"Oh, Miss Kate! Oh, dear! A nawfu' thing's happened!" wept May.

"Is it Mrs. Pow? Or has Jimsy fallen into the fire?" asked Kate, all sorts of horrors flashing vividly through her mind.

"Oh, no! It's my Dadda's leeks! They've been stole in the night!"

Kate, after the first moment of relief and consequent annoyance at having been frightened for nothing, began to appreciate the full extent of the calamity which had befallen the Pows.

"Not his leeks for the Show, May?" she said anxiously.

"Ay! The finest leeks ever ye seen, nane better in the county!" sobbed May, her genteel accent leaving her in this hour of stress. "An' the Show on Setturday firrst, an' him sairtain o' the Firrst Prize!"

Round the corner of the lodge came Mrs. Pow, breathing threats of vengeance, and terrible as a volcano in full eruption. "Thae dirrty thievin' tinklers o' Barries! I could burrn the hoose aboot their lugs, the blagyirds!" she proclaimed in trumpet tones.

"Then you know who took the leeks?" said Kate.

"Fine I ken. Whae else wad it be? Barrie's aye been second tae Pow, an' black jealous, an' this year he's gaun tae be firrst or ken the reason why," said Mrs. Pow grimly. "C'wa' you roond tae the back, Miss Kate, an' see for yersel'."

Kate threw all thoughts of Lucy and her neat little lists to the winds. With the weeping May at her heels, she followed Mrs. Pow's stormy progress to the patch of garden behind the house. Here Geordie was discovered, a statue of woe, his whole figure drooping, even the leather straps which secured his earthy trousers below the knee eloquent of loss, staring gloomily into a large hole in the ground.

"Ay," he muttered in answer to Kate's murmur of condolence, spoken in a hushed tone, for she felt as if she stood beside an empty grave. "Ay. Three o' the bonniest leeks ever I grew. Little did I think they were tae gie John Barrie a firrst at Haystoun Show."

"Can't you get them back, Geordie?"

He uttered a short sardonic laugh. "Is it get them back? Ae leek's geyan like anither when it's in the grun', an' I've nae trade-mark on mines. Forbye John Barrie's guid sister's mairret on the polis-ser-geant, an' if I gaed tae the station he wadna heed me. I was juist mak' a fule o' mysel' for the hale burgh tae lauch at. Na, na, Miss Kate, they're a lossie. I doot I'll juist hae tae thole."

On hearing these words May's sobs were redoubled, and even Mrs. Pow applied a corner of her apron to eyes which were notice-ably dry with fury.

"I'm terribly sorry, Geordie," said Kate. "I wish there was some-thing we could do."

"Aweel, there's naethin' we'll can dae but struggle on," said Geordie in tones of manly resignation. "We'll no' say a wurrd o' this, mind ye"—with a threatening look at his wife and daughter, who had made rebellious noises, for they had looked forward to telling their wrongs. "I'm no' gaun tae hae the hale toun ken that Geordie Pow canna keep his ain gairden frae robbery.

"Mind ye," he added, "it's no' juist for mysel' I'm heedin', but I'm rale vexed aboot it wi' the maister an' mistress new hame an' a'. The fowks used wi' readin' i' the *Advertiser* that George Pow,

Soonhope Lodge, has got a firrst for his leeks, an' I doot they'll be wonderin' whit's gane wrang. As like as no' they'll think I wis keepit that throng in the big hoose gairden that I hadna the time tae grow my ain leeks, an' that's no' richt. An' this the very year we'd be wishin' tae hae a'thing at its best. There'll be mair clash nor ever. Na, it's no richt ava'.".

"Certainly not," Kate agreed. "But all the same, Geordie, I don't see what you can do except keep quiet."

With this cold comfort she left him, went on up to the house, and spent a long and rather tiresome morning with Lucy's little lists. It was a very great pity that Lucy made it so difficult for anyone to sympathize with her, when she was undoubtedly in the right. Perhaps it was because she never let it be imagined for a moment that she could have been wrong? Kate was not sure, but she was feeling ruffled and tired when she went back to Mrs. Anstruther's to put on a hat and collect a pair of gloves before going out to tea with old Mrs. Milligan. She decided to walk along the Loaning behind the houses, and reach The Anchorage by its back door. She could not tell what had prompted her to take this road which passed the small cottage tenanted by the nefarious Barries, but she found herself peering over their garden wall as guiltily as if she were the thief. Certainly it was maddening to see, in a sunny patch of rich black soil, screened from the house by a bank of enormous shaggy dahlias, a large glass bell-jar carefully set over some treasure—in all probability the stolen leeks. Feeling ran high as the date of Haystoun Show approached, and ladies who were rivals in butter-making or 'jeely' were frequently not on speaking terms for days before and after the great event of early autumn, and at least one family feud had raged for eleven years over a baking of dropped scones. Choice vegetables had been known to be spirited away overnight to appear as some other competitor's entry in the cottage gardens' produce section. But never before had it happened so near home. A clannish feeling of rage, which made her own sister to Mrs. Pow, began to stir in Kate's heart. Why should these vile Barries get away with it, and laugh in their sleeves at Soonhope?

"They shan't," she vowed through clenched teeth. "If I have to steal them back myself!"

There was a moment when she remembered her hope of no more adventures, but it passed almost immediately, for the idea, once formulated, instantly became a plan, which is rather a habit with ideas. Still not quite knowing what had put it into her head, Kate walked on. It was very strange. Only two minutes had passed since she had paused merely to look sadly over the Barries' wall, and now she was going straight towards the telephone kiosk near Mrs. Anstruther's back gate, and her intention was to ring up Mrs. Anstruther's pet nephew and invite him to assist at a burglary. It was an outdoor burglary, but that wasn't likely to make it look any better in the eyes of the police-sergeant so inconveniently married to John Barrie's sister-in-law.

All this was at the back of her mind, for her present urgent anxiety was to see whether she had enough pennies in her pocket for the call. If fourpence was not sufficient, she would take it as a sign; if it were, well, then, it was still a sign. Even as she asked for Robin Anstruther's number clearly and firmly, and, obedient to the disembodied uninterested voice of the exchange, put her four pennies into the slot, Kate knew that sheer obstinacy would have made her go home and fetch more money if necessary, sign or no sign. It would have been a waste of time for her to have taken the omens in old days; nor did it occur to her that he might be out, a more unfortunate augury still.

Her confidence was rewarded. "Hullo?" he said, sounding very gruff.

"This is Kate Heron," began Kate, who suddenly realized that it was not going to be too easy to explain her beautiful idea to him. There was a long pause, then they said "Hullo?" together, and Kate swallowed a longing to giggle.

It sounded in her voice as she said again: "Hullo. Are you still there?"

"Still here. What's the matter? You sound as if you were trying to confess a crime. Have you murdered my aunt?"

"I haven't murdered anyone," said Kate. "If I had, it would have been much more likely to be Lucy than your aunt. But I'm going to burgle a garden tonight, and I want you to help me. Sailors are supposed to be so good at odd jobs."

"Haven't you forgotten that I'm a farmer now, not a sailor. And this is really a very odd job. Damned odd. Fishy, in fact."

"It's an act of justice," Kate said solemnly. "And I can't manage alone. You simply must help me."

"Suppose I say I won't?" he asked coolly.

"Oh!" Kate's gasp of dismay was audible even over the telephone. She was so taken aback that she could think of no argument or appeal likely to move him. "Oh, well, if you won't, there's nothing more to be said," she ended in a flat voice, and hung up the receiver.

As she left the stuffy little kiosk, a smile broke over her face. "Hanging up like that was an unconscious stroke of genius. If he's as curious as most men, he won't leave it there."

4

It seemed so indecorous to be planning a burglary while seated at Mrs. Milligan's prim tea-table that Kate was hard put to it to restrain her smiles; as a result of which Miss Milligan and Mamma had quite a little argument after their guest was gone, Miss Milligan bravely maintaining that Kate wore a very pleasant expression, while her parent trenchantly observed: "Nonsense, Flora, the girl sat there grinning like a hyena. I wouldn't be surprised if she had a *want*, mark my words."

Kate, however, was quite unaware that she had aroused such grave suspicions of her sanity in her hostess's mind, and continued to listen with only half an ear to current Haystoun gossip, and to smile irresistibly whenever she thought of the leeks. With an effort she brought herself back to Mrs. Milligan's bedroom, where tea was always served to those persons whom the redoubtable old lady wished to see. It was dark as a cave, heavily furnished with large Victorian wardrobe, chest-of-drawers, dressing-table and wash-stand, all looming from their corners, and dominated by the huge four-poster, hung with maroon curtains, from which Mrs. Mulligan ruled her little world.

"Yes," Kate heard her say complacently. "Your grand-mother and I were the beauties of Haystoun in our day, when we didn't depend on paint and powder to help us, either."

Startled, Kate looked at her, trying to find traces of bygone beauty in that enormous puffy white face, so reminiscent of unbaked dough, the owlish eyes magnified by round glasses, the cruel hooked nose. Her tiny pursed mouth, perhaps, had been a rosebud?

"You wouldn't think it to look at me now," added Mrs. Milligan grimly. "Oh, you needn't bother to say anything. I have the use of my eyes and can see myself in the mirror, thank you. Jean Anstruther was a handsome young woman, too. I remember her coming here as a bride, nearer sixty than fifty years ago. But she was very sharp-tongued even then, and it's grown on her. How do you like staying with her?"

Kate murmured truthfully that she liked it very much indeed.

"Do you see much of that nephew of hers?" was the next question in the catechism.

"Not a great deal. Of course he comes regularly to see Mrs. Anstruther on market-days."

"H'm. I heard he had been in the town pretty often lately," said Mrs. Anstruther with a meaning look, which Kate returned with an innocent stare.

'Dreadful old woman,' she thought, but she was struggling with yawns now, not secret smiles, and felt too sleepy to be indignant. The room was very hot, for a large fire burned in the grate in spite of the sunshine outside, and though Mrs. Milligan and her daughter appeared to bask pleasantly in the heat, Kate suddenly was overcome by an agony of drowsiness. A row of horrible little greenish-yellow bobbles hanging down from the strip of velvet which covered the mantelpiece, wavered before her eyes, now swelling to a monstrous size, now dwindling away almost to nothing. Extraordinary things seemed to be happening to Mrs. Milligan's voice, for it had sounded no louder than a mouse's squeak a moment before, and suddenly it was roaring in her ears.

"I suppose he and Andrew Lockhart won't be so friendly now as they used to be?" it was saying.

"He? Robin Anstruther? Why not?" Kate heard herself ask stupidly, and was instantly wide awake, for Mrs. Milligan replied.

"Well, it must have been a blow to him when Mrs. Fardell ran off with Andrew. Everybody knew that Robin Anstruther would have given his eyes out of his head to be in Andrew's shoes. He was silly about the woman."

Kate pulled herself together. This was gossip with a vengeance, and somehow it seemed to threaten Robin, tearing a veil from a dark secret place in his life for curious eyes to peer at. She mustn't listen to another word. "I didn't know that. But I can assure you that he and my cousin Andrew are very good friends," she answered casually, and rose, pulling on her gloves. "I ought to be going now, Mrs. Milligan. It is much later than I thought, and I'm sure you must be tired."

"Tired? Not at all," Mrs. Milligan was annoyed both by the implication and the cutting short of interesting chat. "I leave that to you young people, and to old maids like Flora. Flora is always tired."

Restraining an almost ungovernable desire to slap the soft shapeless cheek nearest her, Kate said good-bye, and thankfully left the room, full of pity for Miss Milligan.

She seemed to be rather proud of her terrible parent than otherwise. "Mamma is so full of life," she said to Kate in the hall. "It is a great trial to her to be bedridden, far more so for a person of her active nature than it would be for me, my dear Kate. I always remind myself of that."

Kate felt that she would have to spend all the time reminding herself. 'I begin to understand why some people are murdered," she thought, as she set out on her walk home through the town. "I'd put a good pinch of arsenic in Mrs. Milligan's arrowroot without a qualm."

She went the longest way round, by the oldest streets, past tall houses with queer roofs bulging out into unexpected windows, or caving in with age and neglect, with odd little outside stairs, half-ruinous, lived in by the poorest of Haystoun's population, teeming with overcrowded life, slum-dwellings fit only to be pulled down, yet so beautiful in decay that Kate hated to think of their destruction. Beside the river, screened from the street by a high wall, the remains of an old castellated building which had once belonged to Bothwell was slowly falling to pieces. Not for the first time Kate pondered the curious lack of perception shown by Mary of Scotland in her choice of husbands: that inane two yards of foppish arrogance Darnley and the swaggering bravo Bothwell to whom she had mistakenly turned for strength. Between them and her own temperament she had brought disaster upon herself, a not uncommon fate of impulsive women even in these modern days. As witness Mrs. Fardell. . . . Kate's thoughts swung to Robin, whose unlucky love had been shot at her like a cannon-ball by Mrs. Milligan. Now she knew why his voice changed when he spoke of Elizabeth Fardell; and she had worked up a fine pity for him, bound to the enchantress who had not cared about him, by the time she reached The Anchorage, where she found him leaning over the gate, an ancient pipe between his teeth, puffing clouds of more or less fragrant smoke on the still air.

"Well," he began teasingly, his manner anything but love-lorn. "You've kept me waiting here long enough, young woman. Miss Milligan must be a damn' sight more amusing than she used to be."

"Oh," said Kate innocently. "Were you waiting to see *me*? How sweet of you."

"About this burglary—"

"I thought you weren't going to have anything to do with it?"

"I want to hear what you're up to. Then I'll tell whether I'm going to have anything to do with it or not."

"Suppose I don't need your help any more?" suggested Kate provokingly, but he was not to be drawn.

"Don't tell me Miss Milligan's offered herself as your accomplice," he said.

The picture of Miss Milligan digging up leeks in someone else's garden at midnight made Kate laugh.

"That's better. You don't look well with your nose in the air," he said. "Now come on and let's have this plot of yours."

"Won't Mrs. Anstruther wonder where we are?" asked Kate, as she started walking with him down the road.

"Not she. Don't start developing a criminal's conscience before you've committed the crime. I told her I was going to post letters."

"And I'm coming with you to lick the stamps?"

"That's it. Am I going to hear about this burglary or am I not?"

"Well," began Kate, "it's really more like poaching than burglary." Breathlessly she told him the story, breathlessly waited for him to speak. They were standing outside the Post Office now, and he dropped a bundle of letters through the yawning brass-bound slit before he answered.

"This is a fine play," he said at last, turning to walk slowly back. "You realize, don't you, that Barrie will suspect Pow of having pinched the leeks back again?"

"Does it matter much? He can't say anything, any more than Geordie can, once they're in the lodge garden."

"'Wha fin's, keeps', in fact?"

"Yes. And 'wha losses, greets.'" Kate said gaily. "It's all *too* simple."

"So simple that I expect we'll find Pow there himself on the same errand," said Robin Anstruther.

Kate shook her head. "I don't think so. Quiet dignity is his line—but you said 'we'! You're going to help me?"

"Someone's got to keep an eye on you," he said. "Yes, I'll help, but we mustn't be caught. I'm a J.P. and it would be a pretty thing if the police found me raiding a garden at dead of night."

"You are a pet," said Kate.

"I look like a pet, don't I?" he growled. And his air was so singularly unpet-like, his frown so savage, that Kate began to shake with laughter.

"Now look here," he said. "I'll leave the car at Aunt Jean's gate. I have to dine with some men at the 'bell' anyhow—and I'll come back about midnight or a little after. You'll have to get out of the house quietly and meet me in the road—"

"This is lovely. I feel like a conspirator," said Kate.

"What an exciting place Haystoun is. I've never had so many adventures before."

"I hadn't noticed any excitement until you came," he told her dryly. "And I expect you and adventures, as you call them, rush madly at each other like two bits of quicksilver. Don't stir us up too much, or you may get a shock some day."

"I'll risk that," Kate said, and went indoors to spend an evening which seemed interminable to her strung-up senses. Never had a meal been so dull—minced collops with little strips of toast arranged in a star pattern on top, cornflour shape and stewed plums—or so long-drawn out. Yet, when they rose from table, and Kate helped Mrs. Anstruther in her stiff painful progress across the hall to the sitting-room, only half an hour had been spent over it. Eight o'clock. For two hours Kate must sit and pretend to read, or watch Mrs. Anstruther play a complicated game of patience called 'The Fascinator,' which involved the use of two packs and never seemed to come out. As the grandfather clock on the upper landing wheezed ten, the grenadier brought a glass of hot water to her mistress, who sipped it slowly; at half-past ten Mrs. Anstruther went upstairs to bed, leaving Kate and the grenadier to go round the house, bolting windows and locking doors. On this particular evening Hannah, who usually entrusted the fastening of the front-door to Kate, chose to do it herself, and in consequence Kate, stealing downstairs just at midnight, found that not only had she to turn a key which squeaked protestingly unless very tenderly handled, but to shoot two bolts and undo a clanking chain. This was so eating that she quite forgot the slight tremors which had troubled her earlier in the evening, and passed out of the house on a warm wave of annoyance, only to find that her fellow conspirator was nowhere in sight.

It was a soft dark night, moonless, with clouds sweeping slowly across the sky, hiding the stars to reveal them again. A light breeze carried in its wake all the scents from the gardens bordering the road. The clock on the Town Hall chimed in a cracked voice: "Ting-tong! Ting-*tong*!" which meant half-past twelve, and Kate, all the pleasant angry heat oozing out at her toes, shivered. Deeds of the sort she contemplated ought to be done quickly, as Macbeth knew, and not deferred until conscience and a belated sense of law and order had time to raise their small chill murmurs of disapproval.

"I wish Robin would come," she thought nervously, and heard a quick light step on the road. He was with her, he had taken her cold hand in his warm one, he was saying in his half-teasing voice: "You'll never make a conspirator, standing there shaking in your shoes and jumping at a shadow."

"I wasn't," protested Kate. The whole venture took on a new colour, a new glow of enterprise, the stars winked encouragingly before a fresh band of cloud could veil them.

Time, which had crept so slowly, now took wings. Almost before Kate had realized that they had started on her poaching expedition, they were climbing the Barries' garden wall. A smothered yelp and a scrambling noise brought her heart to her mouth.

"What on earth—" she whispered.

A stout Aberdeen terrier landed beside them with a heavy thud and shook himself.

"My God, it's Wat!" muttered Robin. "The old devil must have followed me all the way from Pennymuir and hidden in the car. It's a favourite trick of his. Never mind, he'll keep us warned if anyone passes along the Loaning."

Kate felt privately that the gang now numbered one too many, but she kept this opinion to herself, and in the difficulty of locating the bell-jar without leaving incriminating footprints all over the soft earth she soon forgot Wat.

"Here it is," she whispered at last, as she almost fell over it.

"All right. I'll hoick out the leeks if you'll keep watch."

The bell-jar was carefully removed, and in the faint glimmer of the September night the thick white stalks of the prize leeks shone palely. They were strangely hard to move.

"Did you bring a trowel or anything?" asked Robin Anstruther, straightening himself.

"No. How could I? They can't be very firmly in, after all. It isn't as if they'd *grown* there."

He grunted. "Isn't it? Well, all I can say is that they feel as well-rooted as trees. I can't shift them."

"I'll help." Kate went down on her knees beside him, and together they tried again. "Do be careful! If you hurt them they won't be any good to Geordie!" she hissed in his ear.

"Damn Geordie and his leeks, too. And don't make noises like a snake at me. I'm nervous."

"We'll have to shovel away the earth with our hands," said Kate decidedly, though still in an undertone. Her partner in crime groaned.

"Come on!" She was quite ruthless by now, and started digging like a terrier about the roots of the leeks.

"I don't believe you really need to throw all that mud in my eye. I got a mouthful just now," complained Robin.

"A mouthful in your eye? Keep it shut, then," panted Kate, scraping furiously.

"I've found a potato," he announced after a few seconds' silence.

"I wish I could find a leek's roots! Pouf! What a smell of onions—"

"Did you expect 'em to smell like lilies-of-the-valley? Careful, now, they're coming!"

Two pairs of dirty hands met round the smooth coldness of the yielding leeks, and just as by a combined effort, they pulled them, undamaged, triumphantly out of the ground, bedlam broke loose.

A cat, mincing along the roof of a small shed against the garden wall, intent on courtship, raised its face to the skies, and uttered a long musical cry, tremulous with passionate love. At the same moment the dog Wat, hearing the voice of an hereditary foe, opened a mouth like a crocodile's and roared a savage bass reply to what he took to be a challenge. Someone threw open a window in the cottage and flashed a light over the garden. To Kate and Robin Anstruther, cowering behind the dahlias, it appeared as powerful as any searchlight. Voices were heard, angry voices which sounded as though their owners had been roused from well-earned sleep.

"Is there a' body i' the gairden, Jone?"

"Wife, I'm no' a hoolet. I canna see in the dairk."

"Wha belangs tae yon dog? It's frichtenin' the pussy."

"Never heed the cat. It can mind itsel'. Awa' back tae yer bed, there's naebody ootbye."

"Jone Barrie, are ye no' gaun doun tae see? Think shame o' yersel', man!"

"I tell ye, wumman, there's naebody there."

While the argument was in progress, Robin touched Kate's arm. "Come on," he whispered. "We can get through between the peas, but we'll have to crawl."

Obediently Kate followed him on hands and knees, wincing as her hair caught on the spruce branches on which the peas, now withered, had been trained. It was extraordinarily damp, and she wondered what sort of a trail they were leaving behind them.

Robin Anstruther apparently shared her thoughts, for he stopped in his painful travelling, and putting his face close to hers, muttered with a smothered laugh: "It must look as it a tank had been let loose in here!"

"Have you got the leeks?" asked Kate in an undertone hoarse with anxiety.

"Yes. Can't you smell 'em? But you'll have to take them now. I want to get hold of that infernal dog of mine."

A moist oniony bundle was thrust into her unready arms, and he had slipped away so quietly that she did not know he had gone until, putting out her hand to touch the rough tweed of his sleeve, she felt nothing. Clasping the leeks to her bosom, Kate made her way as fast as she dared towards the wall, no longer on her knees, but crouching low and moving like a lapwing leading someone away from its nest. She guessed that the garden was no place for her now that she was in possession of stolen goods; if Robin by ill luck was caught, she supposed that he could put up some sort of a story of having climbed over the Barries's wall to find his dog.

Nothing so desperate happened, and before Kate bad dropped carefully into the Loaning, the voices had ceased, the cottage window had been shut with a rattling bang, and peace reigned again. A sudden sharp shower of rain made her shiver, and she wished that Robin, whatever he might be doing, would hurry. It seemed a very long time until he and Wat landed on the road beside her.

"Sorry, but I had to clear up a bit," he said. "I don't think we'll be so easy to trace now. Give me the leeks. I suppose the next thing is to plant them in Pow's patch?"

"I suppose so," Kate said blankly, for this necessary part of the plan had completely escaped her mind.

He laughed. "I knew you'd forgotten. Never mind, our luck ought to hold now."

In fact, the rest of the proceeding passed off so uneventfully that there seemed no adventure left about it, and Kate was frankly yawning when she and Robin arrived back at the gate of The Anchorage.

"You've been wonderful," she said to him. "I can't thank you enough."

"It was good fun while it lasted," he said. "but I am glad it's over, and no one has seen us."

This last statement was too optimistic, for though no one had seen them to connect them with a robbery, they had been noted and recognized with bulging-eyed delight by Mrs. Milligan's peroxide-blonde Mima, who, herself absent without leave, was sneaking home from a dance at one of the farms outside Haystoun. It was a pity, Mima considered, that, in the circumstances, she could not pass on this titbit to Miss Milligan without betraying her own unlawful outing, or her means of entry, which involved the pantry window.

Still, she was not debarred from telling her intimates, and to them she could freely retail the story of having seen "yon Miss Heron" with Mrs. Anstruther's nephew, walking up the road as cool as you please, in the middle of the night.

CHAPTER FIVE

1

"It is too naughty of Andrew not to have arrived. I fully expected him in time for tea,' said Lucy, who looked distractingly pretty standing behind a small table laden with the old Worcester cups and saucers, the heavy Georgian silver of teapot and hot-water jug.

She spoke to the party at large, in a light, almost careless manner, but Kate thought she noticed an edge to her voice, a trace of nervous irritation in the fluttering movements of her small white hands. Granny's soothing murmur was drowned by Cousin Charlotte.

"What did you expect?" said the old lady sharply. "If a man *can* avoid a tea-party he'll do it. I don't blame him." And she swept the men in the room with an eagle glance that made them feel mere worms.

"But Andrew didn't know—" began Lucy, and bit her lip.

"I thought not. You never told him, eh? What a pleasant surprise he'll get," said Cousin Charlotte, with a cackle of malicious laughter. Everyone looked miserably uncomfortable until Greystiel Heron, in the courtly eighteenth century manner which he could assume so well when he liked, engaged her attention, and conversation broke out again.

There were twelve people gathered for tea in the old billiard-room at Soonhope, where their absentee host's photograph smiled gaily down on them as if he shared a secret joke with each. Kate sitting in a corner by herself, looked about interestedly, from Lucy, capably pouring out smoky China tea, to the youngest of her three children, Henry, who was carrying a plate of feather-light hot scones round the room in an absent-minded fashion, quite forgetting to hand them to anyone, but devouring an astonishing number himself. The other two young Lockharts were standing together, Anne's lovely head of dark auburn curls very close to Adam's red head. They were amazingly like their father, and had all his former gaiety and charm, while Anne, fortunately for her, had also inherited her mother's dainty hands and slender narrow feet. Henry was the plainest, a lanky boy with a big nose, but Kate rather fancied that he was the most interesting of the three. Apart from appearances, she had had no opportunity to judge, for they had only arrived that morning, a few hours before the rest of the family gathering. Grey and Robin Anstruther, who, except for his aunt, was the only person present not related to Andrew Lockhart, were deep in shooting and fishing. Kate could hear her brother's "lost a beauty a twelve-pounder at least by the look of him, and clean-run," as she turned her head to see her father still bending over Cousin Charlotte all courteous interest, while every line of his elegant figure in its disgraceful old tweeds said to those who knew him best, 'damned old harridan.' Mrs. Anstruther and Granny were unravelling genealogical tables, while Mrs. Heron strove to make conversation with Lucy, whose distrait look and mechanical smiles showed that her thoughts were probably with her delaying husband. Finally Kate saw her mother glance at her despairingly, and left her corner to go to the rescue.

Robin Anstruther smiled at her as she passed him, a friendly smile which made her feel warm and happy inside, and then she was standing at the table saying to Lucy: "Such a lovely tea, Lucy. And a very good idea to have it in here. This room's so big that people have space to move about without bumping into each other all the time."

"I thought it would be easier for Mrs. Anstruther if she didn't have to climb the stairs," said Lucy, and while Kate was rejoicing at the real consideration shown in these words, spoilt the whole effect by adding: "Besides, I hate crumbs all over the drawing-room carpet. It marks so."

Mrs. Heron, with well-concealed relief, had removed herself to join her husband, now wearying of Cousin Charlotte, and Kate was left looking ruefully at Lucy's grateful down bent head as she filled the cups which her sons had just brought to her.

"I say, Kate," said Henry, whisking round so that a billow of tea slopped over the brim of the cup he held. "Kate, did you—"

"Be careful, Henry, you're spilling the tea," said his mother. "And don't you think 'Cousin Kate' would be more polite?"

"Oh, please—" began Kate, feeling at least Cousin Charlotte's age. But Henry had already gone calmly on.

"That's quite out of date, Mother. Even if she were an aunt of mine I'd probably still call her Kate. I say, Kate, did you really lock someone into that cupboard in the hall because you thought it was a burglar? Robin said you did."

"Really, Henry, what nonsense you talk. Why should Kate do such a stupid thing? And I will not have you calling people so much older than yourself by their Christian names," said Lucy with asperity.

Henry gave her a patient look. "It wouldn't have been silly if it *had* been a burglar, Mother. And he likes it," he explained. "He told me so. Besides, life's too short for all these titles. Look at all the people in this room that I'd have to call Cousin if I began." He gesticulated again with the cup, and this time the tea descended in a scalding flood on to his grey flannel legs, causing him to dance in agony. "Gosh, my only decent bags! And I'm burnt!"

"Go and change them at once. They'll have to go to the cleaners now," said Lucy.

"Don't you care about me being burnt? If an area equal to one-third of the human body is burnt," said Henry with gusto, "the patient usually succumbs. It's true. I read it in Anne's First-Aid book. I shall probably die."

Kate laughed heartlessly, took the now empty cup from him and said: "Yours can't be worse than a burn of the first degree, Henry. Off you go and change, and then see for yourself just how bad it is. I'll take that cup for you when it's refilled."

What a boy," sighed Lucy, filling the cup once more; but Kate could tell that Henry was the adored of her rather cold heart.

"He's great fun," she said, and went to deliver the tea its rightful owner.

"Kate," said Robin Anstruther close beside her, "will you come out into the hall with me? I can't get a word with you in this crowd."

"All right. In a minute," Kate promised, annoyed to that her heart was thumping absurdly.

As they left the billiard-room, they could hear Lucy saying to Anne: "I *can't* think why your father isn't here yet. It is too bad of him."

Robin gave Kate a quick ironical look. "Poor Drew!" he murmured. "Not a good start, is it? I wonder where he is."

Andrew, who could easily have been at Soonhope early in the afternoon, had dawdled deliberately on the way, holding his car back over stretches of good road, stopping frequently to look at the countryside. As a boy his favourite hour for arriving had been just before dinner, and he wanted to recapture, if he could, the joy of coming back to Soonhope in the clear evening light, when the sun, nearing the west, left the sky a cold pure green behind black banks of trees.

Reaching the top of Soutra he drew in to the side of the road and shut off his engine while he gazed, dazzled, at the brilliant stretch of richly coloured land running away northward to meet the Forth, which was a strip of molten gold. Once again he marvelled at the pigheadedness of people who seemed to shut their eyes and label Scotland a grey country. In weather like this it had all the changeful glories of a fire-opal, variations of colour which he had never seen in England. . . . 'And never will,' he thought, feasting his eyes on the bright blue of the sky, flecked with gold-tipped clouds, on the rolling miles of heather, on fields of ruddy wheat, ripe for the cutting, on emerald pasture, richer green of roots, heavy dark woods, and a line of white where waves were breaking on a distant sandy beach. Edinburgh lay half-hidden in a veil of blue smoke from her chimneys, with Arthur's Seat brooding over the old town. He had a glimpse of a tenuous spider's web which was the Forth Bridge, he picked out the islands in the Firth, black dots in that golden stream. Then he turned to look towards Haystoun, and found he could wait no longer to get there. It was queer, but this delight of homecoming was a pure happiness which nothing could spoil, not his long estrangement from Lucy, not even his parting with Elizabeth. Starting up the car again, he drove slowly down into the broad valley, taking all the by-roads he remembered so well, noting the burns where he had fished for trout, the narrow bridge over Alewater where he had seen a kingfisher for the first time in his life. He almost felt again the sudden stab of painful delight which he had known at sight of that blue-green flash, vivid as a flame against a background of dim grey willows. . . . And then quick as the kingfisher's flight, there came a verse of Housman's which robbed him of his quiet happiness. Try as he might to forget them, the words sang through his head in time to the throbbing engine.

Into my heart an air that kills
From yon far country blows:
What are those blue remembered hills,
What spires, what farms are those?

That is the land of lost content,
I see it shining plain,
The happy highways where I went,
And cannot come again.

'And cannot come again!' he thought sadly. Truly this was a land of lost content for him, and always must be now.

Haystoun seemed unchanged, dreaming under a calm sky as he came into the town from the West Port, passed the railway station, and turned in at the old gates of Soonhope. Nothing was changed except himself, and he must pretend that he had not changed either. Unless he could delude himself into believing that, life would not be worth living, he thought, and at the same time, so strong is habit, waved a hand and smiled cheerfully to Mrs. Pow at the lodge door.

All in a minute he was coming round the bend in the drive, and the house was before him, waiting for him in its beauty of curving front and gracious lines, all the indefinable charm which made it lovely. Its air of happy peace was laid like a spell on Andrew, restoring to him some of his former content. He left his car standing at the door, took the two shallow steps up to it at a bound, and walked into the hall, which smelt, as it always had, of fresh air, fresh flowers, and a faint suggestion of pot-pourri. Two figures moved towards him from the shadowy arched entrance of the passage leading to the billiard-room: Kate Heron and Robin.

"Hullo!" said Andrew. "This is a pleasant surprise."

"You—you didn't expect to see me—us?" faltered Kate for want of something better to say, though she knew perfectly well that he expected to see no one but his wife and children.

"No. I didn't, but I'm very glad, all the same."

"Drew, old fellow," said Robin, taking pity on Kate, who was wondering how best to break the presence of the party. "I hope it really is a *pleasant* surprise, because we're only a small part of it. Lucy's got a regular house-warming gathered here to welcome you back."

"The devil she has!" muttered Andrew, at a loss. Then, sharply: "Who's here, Robin?"

"Your aunt Mrs. Barlas, all the Herons, and that redoubtable old warrior, Cousin Charlotte," said Robin. "Aunt Jean and I are only here for tea. Your offspring are also among those present, of course."

Andrew sighed. "Oh, well. It might have been worse, I suppose," he said. "I say, Kate, I'm sorry. It sounds damned rude, I know, but it's—well, a bit unexpected, you see."

"I should be furious if I were you," Kate said. "To come home and find your house full to the root of guests whom you hadn't invited."

"Oh, what does it matter, after all?" said Andrew carelessly. He had recovered himself, and was feeling faintly amused. It was so like Lucy to barricade herself against him behind a bunch of his own relatives. "All in the family. But I can't quite understand Cousin Charlotte. Lucy never could bear her."

"She came off her own bat," said Robin with a chuckle. "And she's been causing terror and dismay to all around her ever since."

"She would," Andrew agreed. "I'd have liked to be present at the merry meeting of Cousin Charlotte and Lucy. It must have been worth seeing—and hearing."

"Kate saw it, didn't you, Kate?" said Robin. "Go on, girl, tell Andrew about it, and don't look so scared. He won't bite."

Kate shuddered. "I beg that you won't remind me about *anything* that happened on that awful afternoon," she said faintly.

"Fun and games?" Andrew looked hopeful.

"Well, if you like to call it fun and games. Cousin Charlotte got locked into the parlour, and Lucy arrived just as I was trying to prise her out by the window, where she stuck midway."

"More locking doors. I won't forget that cupboard in a hurry," said Andrew feelingly. "Have you been up to anything else in that line?"

He was looking at her with smiling eyes, and Robin said: "Wait till you've heard. Come on into the parlour for a minute, Drew, and I'll tell you all about her ongoings."

Andrew hesitated. "What about the party?" he asked, jerking his head in the direction of the billiard-room. "I ought to go and see 'em all, I suppose."

"They don't know you're here yet, and you won't another chance like this for a devil of a long time," Robin pointed out. "But if you want tea, of course—"

"Too late for tea. I could do with a drink, though."

"I'll get the whisky and soda," said Kate. "Unless you'd rather have sherry?" Then she paused uncertainly. "I'm sorry. This is awful of me, playing the hostess to you in your house—"

"Don't be an ass, my dear," said Andrew kindly. "Fetch the whisky and a siphon and a couple of glasses. Three, if you'll join us?"

Kate shook her head, and presently slipped into the parlour with a laden tray, to find the two men sitting on the window-seat filling their pipes. "There was a plate of sandwiches. I brought them too," she said to Andrew, as she set her tray down on a table beside him.

"Gawd bless your kind 'eart," he said. And to Robin: "The girl's got brains, hasn't she? Knew I was starving."

In spite of the fact that she was the subject of Robin Anstruther's libellous stories, Kate enjoyed what Andrew called their 'cads' party' in the parlour. The tale of the leeks was told with embellishments, and caused Andrew to roar with laughter.

"We'll have to go to the Show," he gasped at length. "When is it? To-morrow, I suppose? First Saturday in September."

"To-morrow it is," said Robin. "But I've arranged a small shoot up at Pennymuir, the first of the partridges. Greystiel Heron and young Grey, and you and myself—and Adam. He's keen to go. What about it?"

"Good enough. But we must drop in for a few minutes and see those leeks," Andrew said. "Your father won't be pleased, Kate, if I sneak away, even for an hour, but I dare say his opinion of me is so bad by this time that it can't be much worse."

He spoke lightly, but Kate was distressed by the bitterness which must have prompted the words. She hesitated, not knowing quite what to say, and in the silence that had fallen on all three of them, they heard the billiard-room door open, and Lucy's clear voice proclaim: "Andrew must have come. I'm sure I heard his laugh."

"I knew that laugh of yours was far too loud," growled Robin. "Now we're for it. Caught in the act."

Lucy's quick step crossed the hall and came, almost without faltering, towards the parlour.

"Andrew?" she said, opening the door and coming in. "What on earth are you doing in here?" Then, seeing the glasses, the decanter and siphon and the empty plate, her face hardened. "Couldn't you have come into the billiard-room?" she asked. "Or didn't you know we were there?" This with a suspicious glance at Kate and Robin, who stood by in guilty silence.

"Yes, I knew. I wanted a word with Robin, and a drink in peace before I faced the mob," said her husband. "I'm sorry, Lucy. Let's go in now and see them all."

"It's a little late," Lucy said coldly, but she led the way back to the billiard-room.

Kate thought that there could hardly have been a stranger meeting between a husband and wife who had been separated for years. Then, remembering the reason of that separation, she felt that it might have been much worse. The clarion tones of Henry, now attired in a pair of incredibly dirty trousers, smote on her ears as she entered, and seemed to sum up the situation very aptly. "Gosh!" he was saying. "Gosh! We're thirteen now that Father's here. Isn't that unlucky?"

2

There was a tap at Kate's bedroom door, followed by the voice of Nina, discreetly lowered. "If ye please, Miss Kate, could I speak tae ye a meenit?"

"Come in," called Kate, who was twisting and writhing in violent efforts to do up her black dinner dress, which fastened at the back and caused her to curse heartily every time she wore it. "What is it, Nina? Hadn't you better go to Mrs. Lockhart if anything is wrong?"

"There's nothing wrang, Miss Kate," said Nina. "Will I do yer dress for ye? It's just Mrs. Pow's May says can she see ye afore she goes hame."

"May? Very well, tell her I'll be down soon," said Kate, adding inwardly: 'I suppose she's broken something, and wants *me* to break the news to Lucy. I only hope it's nothing valuable.'

But when she went downstairs and met May hovering by the backdoor, there were no signs of dismay on that damsel's cherubic face, only a suppressed excitement which threatened to bubble over into giggling.

"Please, Miss Kate," she began breathlessly "The queerest thing ever ye heard tell o's happened. My Dadda says could ye come down to the lodge an' see his leeks?'

"His leeks, May?" Kate simulated what she hoped looked like genuine astonishment.

"Ay. His leeks," said May, nodding her bobbed and waved head and pursing up her lips as if afraid to say too much.

As Kate also was afraid that she herself might say too much and rouse suspicion, she replied briefly: "I'll try to come down after dinner."

"That's fine. Ye'll get an awfu' big surprise," May promised her, and pattered off across the courtyard on her absurdly high heels.

Kate wished that she could invite Robin Anstruther, her partner in crime, to go with her, but Geordie would probably wonder, and they could not afford the risk of making anyone wonder. Then, with a guilty start, she realized that the gong had boomed through the house, and she must be keeping everyone waiting. Tripping over her long skirt, she ran upstairs, and slunk into the drawing-room, where Lucy was beginning to look impatient, her hostessly mind obviously concerned with the fear that dinner might be spoilt. As soon as Kate entered the room she rose briskly, and saying, "Shall we go down now? I think we are all here," set the party in motion.

Henry, proceeding downstairs by the simple method of draping himself over the banisters and propelling himself with a casual thrust of the toe on every fourth or fifth step, suddenly found that he had overtaken Kate. So he raised his person to an upright position and sang in her ear:

> *"Cousin Kate, you are awfully late,*
> *And Mother has been in no end of a bait!"*

"I know I was late, Cousin Henry, you nasty little boy," said Kate crossly. "Don't boo in my ear."

"Are you in a bait, too? Kate's in a bait because she was late. Which do you like best?" said Henry.

"Neither," said Kate.

Henry, unabashed, continued his progress beside her. "Are you very hungry? I am. There's an ice-pudding and mushrooms on toast," he told her. "If you don't care for ice-pudding, you can give me your share, and I'll let you have my mushrooms. I hate them."

"Thank you, Henry," said Kate, her slight ill-humour ending in a laugh. "But I happen to like ice-pudding myself—*and* mushrooms. Never mind, I dare say you'll manage to get two helpings of pudding."

Seated at table between Adam and Cousin Charlotte, she found that very little was required of her in the way of conversation, Adam not being as talkative as his brother, and Cousin Charlotte entirely engrossed with her share of an excellent meal, through every course of which she doggedly munched her way, displaying an appetite only equalled by Henry's.

They were no longer thirteen, for Mrs. Anstruther had home, but Robin was there, sitting at Lucy's left, on the same side of the long table as Kate. She had caught a glimpse of him in the drawing-room, and thought that his swarthy face looked even darker against the shining starched shirt. He was much more squarely built than the other men, but they were all nice to look at, from Henry, proudly conscious of his first dinner-jacket, and blissfully unaware that he had crumpled his shirt abominably during his passage downstairs, to Greystiel who wore kilt and silver-buttoned doublet with a grace and distinction which no man could surpass.

Outside, the sky in the west was pale primrose, but the dining-room was always rather dark, owing to its panelled walls and ceiling, and Lucy had dull blue candles burning in two-branched Sheffield plate candlesticks on the polished table. A glass posy-bowl in the centre held a Victorian bouquet of small bright flowers with one dark red rose at its heart. Little silver dishes were filled with salted almonds, candied violets, and bright green peppermints. It was a charmingly arranged table, Kate thought, and Lucy matched it in her dull blue taffeta with the puffed sleeves and tight bodice, her fair hair shining in the soft candle-light.

'What a pretty creature she is!' thought Kate without envy, 'Oh, if only she had a few human failings! . . .' "I'm so sorry, Adam," she apologized, suddenly aware that he had muttered something. "I didn't hear you."

"I only said that Cousin Charlotte's laugh sounds like a hen that has just laid an egg," he said.

Certainly the cackle which some remark of Andrew's had caused Miss Napier to utter was astonishingly like a fowl, Kate had to agree, but she said in a warning undertone: "Don't let her hear you saying anything like that, or I tremble to think what would happen to you."

Cousin Charlotte's voice, indeed, broke in on these very words. "What are you and That Boy mumbling about?" she demanded, levelling a suspicious lorgnette framed in tortoise-shell at the boy in question, who turned a guilty scarlet. "I thought so. Mischief," she added with tremendous satisfaction. "No boy is ever out of mischief, even at the dinner-table."

Adam turned even redder at this insult addressed to him as if he were a child at a prep. school; he, a house prefect, a member of the Fives Ties, and well in the running for his First XV colours next term—and in front of that kid Henry, too!

Henry, of course, was not slow to take advantage of his elder brother's discomfiture. "Gosh!" he exclaimed in his piercing tones. "Adam's as red as a tomato!" As Adam, speechless with rage, glared at him across the table, Henry burst into such hearty laughter that a portion of ice-pudding, too large for anyone's mouth but his, flew from his spoon to land with a plop in Cousin Charlotte's glass of Vichy water.

"Henry!" said his mother disapprovingly, and it was Henry's turn to blush, for Cousin Charlotte could be heard remarking acidly: "This is what comes of allowing boys to dine. That one ought to be having bread-and-milk in. the schoolroom at his age."

"What was Andrew saying to make you laugh, Cousin Charlotte?" asked Kate, carrying the war into the enemy's country with a bravery that delighted the two boys.

"None of your business," said Cousin Charlotte promptly. "Don't be so curious."

"I'm sorry," said Kate with great meekness. "I thought you wouldn't mind my asking, as you asked *me* what Adam and I were talking about."

"At my age, one is allowed a little licence. You are an impudent hussy," said Cousin Charlotte, but it was felt to be a very poor comeback, and Adam hissed joyfully in Kate's ear: "You win, Kate!"

Not long after that, Lucy collected the women with one swift look and marshalled them upstairs, and Kate, seeing that her hostess was occupied by Cousin Charlotte to the exclusion of everything else, seized the first wrap which she could find from the cloakroom, gathered her trailing skirts high above her silver shoes, and ran down the avenue to the lodge. All the way she practised amazed remarks. "Your leeks, Geordie! You've got them back! How *wonderful*!" she said aloud, in a high, artificial voice ending in a squeak.

"The leeks, Geordie," she murmured again. "No, that won't do at all. I'll just have to leave it to chance and the moment."

Geordie, in his shirt-sleeves and carrying a lantern in hand, answered her knock so quickly that she was convinced he had been standing just inside the door waiting for her. He shut the door behind him, and said in a loud whisper: "I've sent the wife tae the pictur's, an' May's ben the hoose patchin' ma breeks, for ye see, Miss Kate, I've a wee surprise for ye."

"The leeks, Geordie?" (Better this time.)

"Ay, the leeks. But—" with a dark look at her, "there's mair aboot yon leeks than ye ken. Ye'll mind the wife was cairryin' on aboot Barrie stealin' them?"

"Y—yes," said Kate, a very faint doubt beginning to creep into her mind.

"Weel, weemen—if ye'll excuse me, Miss Kate—are awfu' anes tae blether. Sae I juist let her gang on, an' kin' o' gied her the notion I thocht Barrie wis the man masel'. But I had a suspeecion a' the time that I'd need tae luik some ither place for ma leeks. An' last nicht I took a daunder doun tae Paterson's the shoe-maker's, for I'd heard tell o' some unco guid leeks he had in his gairden, an' thinks I, that's kin' o' queer, his leeks no' bein' byordinar' guid as a general rule—"

All through this speech Kate had been silent, but as Geordie appeared to be a long way from reaching the point of his story, she could bear the suspense no longer. "Go on, go on!" she cried, her voice hoarse with dread, which Geordie, taking it for interest, was gratified to hear.

"Sae," he continued deliberately, "I went doon, as I was sayin', an' took a guid luik at the leeks. Thae leeks, thinks I, were never grown by Jems Paterson. There was naebody about, an' I gied a wee bit pu' ye ken, an' they cam' up in ma haund as canny as ye like."

"Oh!" gasped Kate, remembering with what difficulty she and Robin had unearthed their leeks. "Well?"

"Syne I cam' back hame an' plantit them whaur they cam' frae, Miss Kate. But this morrnin', when I gaed oot tae see them afore gangin' up tae the hoose—'By'! says I. 'Geordie, ma man, ye're seein' double, an' it no' Ne'erday neither!' Miss Kate," he spoke even more slowly and impressively, "if ye'll believe me, there was *twa* lots o' leeks, bonny, bonny leeks, in the grun'. Noo, wull ye come awa' roon' an' see them?"

Kate, who was past speech, tottered rather than walked round to the garden, to see, as Geordie had said, two lots of handsome leeks growing in beauty side by side. May had promised her a big surprise, and she had certainly got it.

"Wh—what will you do, Geordie?" she said at last, after Geordie, swinging the lantern to and fro in a gloating manner, stood upright again.

"Dae, is it? I'll show them baith! If I dinna lift Firrst an' Second as weel, ma name's no' George Pow! But, mind ye, Miss Kate, I'm trusting tae ye no' tae mention this. The wife an' May are fair mystified, an' I'm juist for lettin' them bide that way. Nae need for them tae ken that I'm dumbfoondered as weel."

"They won't hear a word about it from me," Kate assured him with such fervour that Geordie was more than ever sure that she was a 'rale nice young leddy, aye takin' an interest.' She started to walk back to the house in the twilight, her mind whirling.

Under the beeches of the drive it was already dark, and she only knew that two persons were coming towards her by the two small glowing points that were lighted cigarettes.

"Hullo, who's this?" Andrew's voice.

"Oh, Andrew!" cried Kate, peering at his companion. "Who is that with you?"

"Only your fellow conspirator," said Andrew, laughing. "But where have you been? Down viewing the leeks you rescued?"

"Rescued?" echoed Kate with an hysterical laugh. "Rescued? *Stole*, you mean!"

"If this is remorse," said Robin Anstruther, "it's come on very suddenly, and too late to be any good."

"What's wrong, Kate?" This was Andrew again, kind and steadying.

"Everything," babbled Kate. "Geordie's got his leeks—"

"Don't I know it?" Robin interrupted with feeling. "Considering that I sweated blood to get 'em last night, it's no news to me."

"Yes, but he got them himself! The ones we took out of Barrie's garden were his—"

"There's a confusion of personal pronouns here that I can't disentangle," said Robin. "I know they were his."

"No, no, not his! Barrie's!" cried Kate, becoming more and more confused in her agitation.

"Wait just a minute," said Andrew. "Kate, my dear, are you trying to break it to us that Geordie rescued his own leeks, and you went and lifted Barrie's?"

"That's what I've been saying all the time, only you kept on interrupting. We've stolen Barrie's leeks, and now the poor man won't have any to show to-morrow!"

There was a second's silence, broken by the loud laughter of Andrew and Robin. Kate did not join in.

"Can't we do something about it even now?" she asked, and the laughter ceased abruptly.

"Listen to me, Kate," said Robin, taking her by the arm and shaking her gently. "If you're suggesting that we should go all through last night's performance again, starting at the other end this time, Let me break it to you that there is nothing doing. You understand? *Nothing*."

"Absolutely dam' all," agreed Andrew. "No, Kate, you can't do it a second time. You'd be caught, for one thing—"

"But Barrie—"

"Barrie must suffer. He'll be able to tell everyone that if it hadn't been for foul play, he'd have got first prize. Now come on, we'll have to show up in the drawing-room, or Lucy will wonder what has become of us. There was some chat about bridge."

They walked back in silence until they were at the door, when Andrew remarked with an irrepressible chuckle: "After this, nothing is going to keep me away from Haystoun Show!"

3

"Cousin Kate! Are you going to the Show?"

"Yes, Cousin Henry, I am," said Kate. "Aren't you?"

"Well, I'm not sure," said Henry mysteriously. "It rather depends, you see. Who else is going?"

"Dear me, are you so particular? I'm going, Anne's going unless she changes her mind in the meantime, and your mother, and my mother. We shall be four lorn females if you don't take pity and escort us."

"Oh, it's not that I mind being seen about with you," Henry told her generously. "Only—look here, Kate, do you like dogs?"

"Most dogs, yes. I have met one or two whom I cordially disliked," said Kate, "Why?"

"Come with me," said Henry, "and I'll show you something."

He conducted her out of the house in a stealthy manner, and after a hunted glance to right and left, darted round to the courtyard, and went in again by the back door, Kate, bewildered but obliging, following him as closely as she could, for it was difficult to keep up with him at one moment, while the next, owing to one of his unexpected stops, she was liable to bump into him from behind.

"What are we doing? Playing Follow My Leader?" she asked a little breathlessly as Henry, giving a quick peep into the kitchen, hurried past the door and up the turret stair. For answer he put a dirty finger to his lips and rolled his eyes alarmingly.

"If you do that again I shall be sick," said Kate, and he withdrew the finger to indulge in a burst of silent laughter. Almost immediately he resumed his expression of frowning intensity. "Never know when there are spies about," he said.

Half-way up the spiral stair a door led to the passage off which the maids' bedrooms opened; but the end room, Kate remembered, had once been the nursery, and was no longer used. Perhaps Henry had adopted it as his own special lair but she still could not understand the secrecy and caution with which he stole towards the door. Drawing a large key from his pocket ('More locked doors,' thought Kate), he fitted it into the lock, and at once a strange scratching and snuffling began inside.

"You go in," said Henry. "I want to have a last look round. We may have been followed." His manner was so like that of one of Mr. William le Queux's better heroes that Kate allowed herself to be pushed into the room through the very small crack which he opened.

Almost before she was inside she realized why Henry had asked her if she liked dogs, for a very odd and woolly specimen was leaping frenziedly upon her with growls of delight.

"Down, Virginia!" said Henry, who had sidled in behind Kate and locked the door. Not content with this precaution, he was also shooting the bolts, and only when they were thus barred in did he turn to Kate.

"This is my dog," he said in an off-hand manner which could not conceal the pride of ownership. "How d'you like her?"

"She won't keep still long enough for me to see her properly," said Kate, looking at the small creature dancing on its hind legs round Henry like an animated dark grey woollen ball. "But I like her high spirits. "Why is she called Virginia?"

"Oh, because of the American Civil War," said Henry. "I'm for the South. If she hadn't been a—a—" he broke off, apparently embarrassed.

"A bitch?" supplied Kate, and received a look of relief.

"Yes, a bitch. If she hadn't been one I'd have called her Lee or Jackson or Forrest or Jeb Stuart, but there didn't seem to be any female names, so I decided on States, and Virginia's the most important and the one I like best."

"I see," said Kate, sitting down on the floor and allowing Virginia to leap exuberantly on to her knee.

"When she has puppies, I'll call the bitches after the other Southern States, and the dogs after Confederate generals." Henry joined her on the floor and dragged Virginia into his arms.

"Is that likely to happen soon?" asked Kate, for the little dog seemed barely to have ceased being a puppy herself.

"Well, no," said Henry reluctantly. "She's not easy to match. She's a—a Very Rare Dog," he added, with a stern glance, as if defying criticism of this statement.

Kate looked respectfully at the Very Rare Dog. Whatever its pedigree, Henry obviously adored it, and Virginia, now licking her owner's face with a moist pink tongue of astonishing length, as obviously adored Henry.

"Where did you get her, and why must the poor little creature be kept shut up here?" she said.

"Oh, er—I picked her up," Henry said vaguely. Kate discovered later that this was, quite literally, the case. The puppy had come and seized him by a shoe-lace when he was walking back to his House from afternoon school, and he had instantly taken her for his own. By what means he had succeeded in keeping her for the rest of the term, Kate never heard in detail, but it had involved much worry, and the boot-boy bad played a prominent part in the intrigue.

"You'd have thought," Henry went on bitterly. "That it would've been easy enough once I'd got her here, but it's not. Mother doesn't like dogs. They make a mess in the house, she says."

"Isn't Virginia house-trained, then?"

"Of course she is!" Henry was indignant at this slur on his beloved's manners. "It's not that kind of mess. It's pawmarks and bones and things."

"Oh," said Kate, and after a pause: "Does anyone know about her except me?"

"Florence does. She's pretty decent about giving me things for Virginia to eat. But it's company Virginia misses," said Henry, his face drawn with care. "She hates to be left alone, it's so dull. She never squeaks or whines, but she looks so unhappy, Kate."

"Why don't you tell your father? I'm sure he wouldn't mind the little dog."

Henry shook his head and mumbled something about "not fair to Mother to tell *him* when she doesn't know," for which Kate gave him full marks.

"Well, I suppose you want to take Virginia to the Show. Is that it?"

"Yes," said Henry, and added gloomily that he saw very little chance of doing so.

"Will you *swear* to me that she'll behave?"

"You don't understand Virginia," said Henry with a glance of quiet disdain. "She's used to going about. She behaves *beautifully*."

"Very well," said Kate. "Then I think we can do it quite easily. The others don't want to go till after lunch. You and I can take sandwiches with us and walk down to the Show at about twelve. Virginia will be able to see all the life of the town, such as it is, and we'll lose ourselves in the crowd if we see any of the others coming near us."

Henry solemnly rose, shook hands with her and made Virginia do the same. Then he fell upon his dog, and the two indulged in a growling match on the floor that made the window rattle.

'I wonder if I should have done this,' thought Kate as she watched them. 'Lucy would probably think I ought to have gone straight to her and told her that Henry has a dog in the house.' But Henry's—and Virginia's—wistful eyes had been too much for her; and she couldn't help feeling that it was hard on Henry not to be allowed to enjoy his dog openly. Something would have to be done about it.

They had no difficulty in leaving earlier than the rest of the party. As Anne said indifferently, if they liked to make themselves uncomfortable and miss a perfectly good lunch for the sake of seeing endless sheep-dog trials and giant cabbages, it was their funeral. Kate bore away with her the conscience-stricken remembrance of Lucy's gratitude for amusing Henry, but in the excitement of getting Virginia safely down the drive unnoticed, soon forgot it.

Virginia, with a ludicrously large feathery tail curled over her back, caracoled and pranced round them until she looked like seven small dogs, and Henry was in a state of delirious happiness far beyond mere words.

Haystoun Show had always been held in a low-lying meadow beside Alewater, just outside the old East Port of the town, on the first Saturday of September. It was almost the only day in the year which brought back to the ancient royal burgh some degree of its former bustle and importance. The whole county, high and low, men, women and children, flocked to the Show, and the sheep-dog trials which were a feature of it, could boast of entries from as far afield as Carlisle and Newcastle-on-Tyne.

As Kate and Henry, attended by the greatly exhilarated Virginia, walked down the High Street, the big blue buses, each full to the door, went roaring past them, bringing the country people, whose great annual outing this was, from their lonely villages and farms at hair-raising speed.

"Not much of a crush, is there?" said Henry, finding his tongue at last, the delighted sparkle in his eyes belying the careful boredom of his tone.

"Just wait. There will be more than enough of a crush in a minute," prophesied Kate who remembered the Show of old.

They turned into the Nungate, a narrow old street which wound towards the East Port from a long-vanished nunnery. "This is more like a crowd. If they'd only hurry a bit it might be the people leaving Atlanta," said Henry with satisfaction and called Virginia sternly to heel. The street was a steady stream of humanity, which had overflowed the pavements on either side and now walked stubbornly on the cobbles of the roadway, moving aside a mere grudging foot or so to allow the cars which hooted impatiently at their backs, to pass. Old women padded along, bent on seeing what the 'Rurals' had produced in the shape of needlework and knitting; their even older husbands, bowed and gnarled by years of field-work, hobbled beside them in thick, respectable tweed suits and stiff collars. Shepherds walked with their easy swinging step, lone crook-handled sticks in their hands, tremendous boots with turned-up toes, the inch-thick soles decorated with artistic arrangements of 'tackets' on their feet. There was a fine free holiday feeling in the air, encouraged by the smell of whisky wafted about them by those whose merry-making had begun early.

Presently the houses dwindled to a straggle of small cottages, roofed with mellow red pantiles, separated from the road by strips of garden where hollyhocks stood almost as high as the walls, and dahlias and asters made a gay showing. Now they could catch a glimpse, between the bobbing heads in front, of the wide green field, where two large marquees were pitched, they could hear the noisy braying of a brass band above the hum of voices. On the left of the road an open gateway, the ground churned into a sea of mud, was labelled hopefully: 'Car Park, 2s. 6d.,' and through the mud to the field beyond it cars bumbled and bumped, directed by a red-faced young policeman whose white cotton gloves appeared to embarrass him greatly. Kate, turning to ask Henry if he thought it would be safer for Virginia to put her on the lead, found that he was no longer beside her. She saw him in a moment, at the farther side of the road, pressing something into the free hand of a ragged man whose other hand was engaged in holding a mouth-organ to his lips. If he was playing, he could not hope to make himself heard in the medley of sound about him, but even while he nodded acknowledgment to Henry he continued to blow and suck with ardour.

"I'm sorry, Kate," said Henry breathlessly, darting back, with the puzzled but obedient Virginia at his heels. "I had to give him something, you know. It must be pretty rotten to see all the rest of us going to have a good time and not be able to have one yourself."

"I know," said Kate, who never could pass a beggar herself without giving him what she had, or apologizing if she had no money, which was frequently the case. "What did you give him, Henry? I'll go halves."

"Well, I'm glad you said that," he answered in a relieved voice. "Because, as a matter of fact, I gave him our sandwiches and a shilling. He looked hungry," he added.

"Wouldn't the shilling have been enough?" Kate asked mildly.

"Well, you see, I thought he could keep the shilling for the next meal. Never mind, Kate, I'll stand you lunch. Father tipped me this morning. Ten bob."

It was on the tip of Kate's tongue to offer to pay for lunch herself, but she managed to stop in time. Henry would probably feel insulted. She said instead: "Thank you, Henry, that will be very nice. Lunch in the tent will be fun, and I'm sure Virginia will enjoy it. But if you're going to give me lunch, you must let me pay at the gate. That's only fair."

"Very well," Henry agreed, a little reluctantly, but his reluctance disappeared when Kate handed him a florin, saying in a casual manner: "It looks so much better if the man pays, I think."

They were at the gate, they had been given two strips torn from a roll of tickets, and. then they were walking on the trodden grass among a crowd which even Henry should have found sufficiently large and congested.

"What'll we see first?" he bellowed in her ear. Kate hastily consulted the catalogue which she had just bought from a small schoolboy with a shining pink face and water-sleeked hair.

"I don't believe anything really exciting begins before one-thirty," she said. "Don't you think it might be a good thing if we had lunch first?"

"Come on, then," said Henry, leading the way briskly towards one of the marquees, outside which a gang of shrill-voiced women with rolled-up sleeves was washing plates in frenzied haste and tubs of very dubiously clean water. They worked to such an accompaniment of crashing crockery that Kate was amazed to see anything emerge whole from the tubs into which it was flung with cheerful abandon. Every now and then a waitress dashed from the marquee and shot a fresh consignment into the water, while the washers-up juggled the clean plates into piles like stage professionals.

Virginia, always friendly and interested, pattered over to speak to them, and was received with a deafening increase of yells. "Eh, *whit* a fricht I've got!" screeched one enormous woman, whose apron would have made a mainsail. "I near drappit a' thae dishes!" "Dinna dae that, Elsie!" bawled her next-door neighbour. "They're clean anes."

Henry called to Virginia, but in vain. She was entranced by the company in which she now found herself the centre of attraction, growled and made playful snaps at their heels, and finally proceeded to pounce upon and worry a dishcloth so well-used that Kate felt faintly sick at sight of it.

"Virginia!" roared Henry in the voice which all dog-owners resort to sooner or later, and which their dogs can invariably gauge at exactly its true value. "Virginia! *Come here!*"

Virginia gave a start of affected surprise. "Dear me, did I hear someone mention my name?" she said, her soft ears pricked, her teeth still clenched on the dirtiest portion of the dish-cloth. "Well, I must go and see what he wants, girls, I suppose. It's the owner." She gave her treasure a last regretful shake before dropping it, and toddled back with a careworn expression to her master.

"Naughty girl," said Henry in loving tones. "Isn't she sweet, Kate?"

But Kate's horrified gaze was riveted on the fat woman, who, without an instant's hesitation, had seized the dish-cloth from the grass where Virginia had left it, and begun to dry glasses with it at top speed.

"Henry," said Kate faintly, "do let's have lunch quickly, before they start using the washed-up plates and things. With luck we may get ones that haven't seen those tubs and towels."

"I expect," said Henry, hastening his steps obligingly.

"That they're every bit as dirty in hotels and restaurants."

"Very likely," retorted Kate. "But at least I don't see them doing it there!"

"Lunch-tickets half a crown, please," intoned a young man with a weary air, seated behind a small table at the entrance to the big tent. While Henry in a lordly manner pulled a ten-shilling note from his pocket and waited for change, Kate peered inside. The dim and odorous place was a seething mob of people, some sitting chewing as placidly as cows in a field, some trying to push their way out, others struggling to find seats at the long trestle tables. Among them flitted the waitresses, carrying laden plates and brimming glasses as though they were in an empty room.

"Come on," said Henry, and dived in between two large tweed figures who were standing, deep in argument, their broad backs to the doorway. Kate meekly followed, but as she made her plunge, the two leaned towards each other, and she was jammed in the middle, "like a piece of ham in a sandwich," as Henry described it.

There was a torrent of apology and explanation, all delivered without movement on the part of the tweed persons, so that Kate was held prisoner while they boomed above her head. "No idea there was anyone there. Very sorry indeed, miss, if we squeezed ye a bit." "A fine-looking lass, too!"

Kate, feeling that these personalities were liable to become embarrassing, especially as they were uttered in voices that resounded throughout the tent, gave a frantic wriggle and succeeded in breaking away from between them.

"Oh, do come on!" shouted Henry, dancing with impatience. "I've got two places for us if you hurry."

They were the last two seats at the end of a bench plated on a slope. The table sloped down towards them, and it was far from easy to keep from falling backwards off the bench onto the grass, but Henry was triumphant, and had already ordered two portions of veal and ham pie, with plum tart to follow.

After this meal, which seemed to consist mainly of very solid pastry, and was washed down with ginger beer, luke-warm and soapy, Kate staggered rather than walked out into the fresh air again. Henry and the effervescent Virginia, apparently revived by their lunch, bounded after her. There was a blast of music from a gramophone mounted in a van, with a loudspeaker attached, and a hoarse voice proclaimed: "The Competeetion in Scottish Country Dencing for school-children will now commence!"

Kate and Henry, pressing towards the announcement, found themselves at a railed-off circular piece of ground, with a small dancing-floor of boards in the middle. Teams of small children, shepherded by school-teachers who ran round their charges like anxious hens, stood solemnly by awaiting their turn. A snuffy elderly man in a Trilby hat at least two sizes too small for him took his seat impressively on an inadequate camp-stool.

"That must be the judge," murmured Kate.

"What, him? He doesn't look as if he'd been much good at dancing even in his prime, and he must have forgotten all about it by now, at his age," was Henry's disparaging rejoinder, delivered in clarion tones, which evidently came all too clearly to the judge's ears, for he frowned reprovingly in their direction, and shifted uncomfortably on his rickety stool.

Fortunately before Henry could say anything more, the first team of children appeared on the platform, acutely conscious of the lonely splendour of their position, and at the same instant such a roar of country-dance music issued from the loud-speaker that nothing else could be heard. During the interval between the second and third dances, a fluttering voice addressed Kate. "Such dear little things," it said. "Such sweetly pretty dancers."

Looking round and down, Kate saw Miss Milligan, whose eager eyes were fixed in avid curiosity, not on the dear little dancers, but on herself. In her innocence Kate supposed this was due to the fact that she had come from Soonhope. She could not guess that Mima, discovered by her mistress trying to stuff the shattered remains of a Spode teacup which had come away in her hand, into a convenient mouse-hole below the kitchen sink, had diverted the wrath to come by telling Miss Milligan how she had seen Kate with Robin Anstruther walking up the road after midnight, and adding the interesting detail that she had 'heard tell' that Miss Heron had danced with a ploughman at Baro Fair. Even the kindest of women, if her interest in living is only kept alive by gossip, could not be expected to hear such momentous news unmoved, and Miss Milligan fed on gossip. So she now stared at Kate as if she must bear some traces of her midnight ramble, with such intense interest that the object of her attention became restive.

"I hope your mother is well, Miss Milligan?" she asked politely.

"Oh, yes, indeed, thank you. Mamma is very well, very well indeed," answered Miss Milligan. In fact Mamma, who had interviewed Mima herself and had sent her daughter to the Show to see if anything else of moment could be seen or heard, was in a state of such extreme vitality, not to say irritability, that Flora would have been exhausted had this temporary means of escape not been opened to her.

"Very well, very, very well," she went on in an excited bleat, so reminiscent of the Sheep in *Through the Looking Glass* that Kate had to bite her lips to stop a smile.

"And are the gentlemen not with you? Are you all alone?" pursued Miss Milligan archly.

"The gentlemen," said Kate with praiseworthy gravity, "are out killing partridges, but I am not all alone."

"Ah, yes, the poor sweet little birds, but so good to eat," murmured Miss Milligan vaguely, and added much more sharply: "Then who is with you?"

"Henry Lockhart. The youngest," said Kate. She turned to her cavalier, who was vainly trying to broaden Virginia's mind by showing her the dancing. "Henry, I'm sure you must remember Miss Milligan?"

"D'you do?" muttered Henry gruffly.

"How do you do, Henry? And how are your dear Mamma and—er, your Papa?"

A gleam of devilish amusement flickered in Henry's eyes and was gone. "As well as can be expected, thank you," he answered with mournful solemnity.

This unexpected rejoinder silenced Miss Milligan for the moment, but as Kate, seizing him by the arm and hurrying him away before he could commit further indiscretions, said to him:

"Henry, how could you do it? That remark of yours will be all over Haystoun by to-night."

"I know, " he said cheerfully. "That's why I said it. And they're quite well, and that's to be expected, isn't it? Oh, never mind the old girl, Kate. Let's go and see the ponies."

They went and saw the ponies: musical ride, bending race, potato race, and all; they saw the serious collies being judged by even more serious shepherds, who examined their every point with infinite care; and they had some difficulty in getting Virginia away from them, for she suddenly became coquettish and flaunted her charms so brazenly that they left to an outburst of canine lamentation; then, Kate rather weary, Henry still fresh as a daisy, they sought the sheep dog trials. Once there, it was plain that Henry would not be willing to move for a long time. He was enthralled by the uncanny prescience of the shaggy black-and-white collies, not much to look at, for these were working dogs pure and simple, which each brought their three sheep up to the pen between two posts with no further assistance from their masters than a wave or an occasional shrill whistle. Kate, feeling thankful that there was a prospect of rest, unfolded the shooting-stick which so far had proved more of a burden than a help, and perched herself on it.

The crowd began to thicken. Where, half an hour earlier, it had been largely composed of shepherds and farmers with their friends, it was now increased by the arrival of men in plus fours or riding-breeches, smartly tweeded women, girls with tiny skull caps on their curled hair and strings of small but obviously authentic pearls on the necks of their hand-knitted jumpers. It amused Kate to look at their feet. Where all were dressed more or less alike as far down as their skirts, the only variation to this uniform of suits and high-necked woollies was to be seen in shoes. There were high-heeled brown-and-white pumps, there were Newmarket boots, there were stout brogues laced round slender ankles. Cigarettes were lighted, the reddened tips thrown on the grass to be trampled out were stared at with disapproving interest by the older shepherds. There was a buzz of well-bred voices, laughter and conversation.

"Whose dog is this now? Number thirty-three. Look in the catalogue, Jim dear, will you? . . . Of course, it's James Brown from

Redheugh. I *thought* I recognized him. Dear old man, I hope he wins.
. . . Oh, look, isn't that Uncle Tim's shepherd in the brown cap?"

It was all very friendly and pleasant, and Kate began to wish
that someone she knew would appear. For the first time it struck
her that, coming from Soonhope, she might be looked at with more
curiosity than friendliness, and she hoped, as much for Henry's sake
as her own, that no awkward meeting would take place. While she
was thinking, she absently noticed that a pair of exceedingly elegant
shoes, punched white buckskin with dark brown trimmings, long
and narrow, and evidently of American design, was coming very
close. They halted just beside her own plain brown brogues, and a
voice said: "Isn't it Kate Heron?"

Kate looked up into a charming face under a rather wide brimmed
felt hat. The soft white hair, the beautiful long blue eyes fringed
with black, the wild-rose complexion and tall willowy figure, could
only belong to one person.

"Lady Charteris?" she said, rising from the shooting-stick, and
taking the hand held out to her. "How nice of you remember me."

"I thought I wasn't mistaken. Tell me, are you staying with the
Lockharts? I heard that they had come back to Soonhope, and I am
so glad," said Lady Charteris in her slow, rather deep voice. "Aren't
any of them here this afternoon? I want to see them again."

Nothing awkward about *this* meeting, anyhow, thought Kate
gratefully as she pointed out Henry and explained that his mother
and sister had probably reached the Show by this time.

"Dear me, is that tall creature Henry? I should never have recognized *him*. He was a little boy in shorts when I last went to Soonhope.
And the girl. Isn't she grown-up by this time? I seem to remember
that she and my Sybil are much of an age."

"Anne is nineteen," said Kate. She leaned forward and poked
Henry with her shooting-stick. Henry, deep in conversation with
an elderly farmer, merely wriggled, and paid no attention until the
third prod, which was a shrewd one, impatiently delivered. Then
he turned and came slowly and reluctantly towards her. "Kate, do
you know what he was telling me?" he began eagerly.

"Lady Charteris, this is Henry Lockhart," said Kate, ruthlessly
interrupting the sheep-dog enthusiast.

"How d'you do?" said Henry, and looked with some dismay at the beautiful cream-coloured glove which Lady Charteris extended to him. "Really I'd better *not*,' he said hastily. "My hands are a bit doggy. Do you know what that man was telling me?"

"I hope you are going to tell *us*," said Lady Charteris with a smile which had always created havoc, and made a deep impression on Henry.

"Well, if you're interested," he said gratified. "*He* says that the dogs that go in for the big sheep-dog trials, the international ones, you know, are trained on *chickens*!"

"Never!" cried both his hearers in genuine astonishment. Kate at least picturing these pampered collies dining off roast chicken every day.

"He says so, and he seems to know all about it. You see, they don't need to run so far as if they were herding sheep, and chickens are much easier to drive," said Henry, his face aglow. "And Kate, don't you think I could teach Virginia with hens? She's a sort of—sort of sheep-dog, you know."

It seemed to Kate that there would be a considerable lowering of the fowl population if the volatile Virginia were deliberately incited to chase them; but she hesitated, unwilling to hurt Henry's feelings, and was spared the necessity of having to answer by the appearance of her mother, Lucy and Anne.

"Here you are!" said Lucy briskly. "'We've been looking for you everywhere."

"I told you that Henry would be sure to be at the farthest possible point," said Anne languidly. "And I was right, wasn't I, Henry?"

Henry favoured her with a long slow look. "No wonder it was ages before you got here," he said amiably. "You've been giving your mug an extra coat, haven't you?"

"Pig," said his sister without rancour.

Privately Kate thought it rather a pity that Anne should have decorated quite so freely with lipstick, rouge, and mascara. It was a charming face, even when plain and unadorned. But after all, one had to be in the fashion, and Anne certainly looked very well in green tweeds with a rakish little green *suède* cap cocked on her mahogany curls.

Lucy, in blue, was more like a Dresden china figure than ever. Her first faint defensive air had melted to genuine pleasure under the warmth and charm of Lady Charteris's friendly greeting.

"Lucy dear! How very nice to see you again, though it is quite absurd to think of you as the mother of those two."

Lucy smiled. "Do you know my husband's cousin, Mrs. Heron? Of course you do, how silly of me! But, my dear Vera, you have worn so much better than I have, really. You don't look a day older than when I first met you."

"Couldn't we go? We must be missing no end of things, and besides, there's Virginia," muttered Henry in a hoarse aside to Kate, whom he considered his special companion for the day at least. "It wouldn't be rude. They're jabbering so hard that they'll never notice."

This seemed true, though impolitely put. Leaving Lucy and Lady Charteris deep in arrangements for 'their young people' to meet, while Mrs. Heron looked at the sheep-dog trials and Anne seemed content enough to stand by, Kate allowed herself to be hauled away by the anxious Henry. Having seen the sheep-dogs, he now proposed to see the sheep themselves, and made across the field towards the pens like an arrow from the bow. It was unfortunate that the shortest way led straight over the track where flat-racing was just about to begin. As Henry said afterwards with righteous indignation: "How was I to know what those silly little flags were for? It's the stupidest thing I ever heard of to have the quarter-mile round and round in the middle of everything else."

Stupid or nor, this was the time-honoured method employed at Haystoun Show. Just as Henry reached the sacred circle marked by the silly little flags, a pistol was fired, and a bellow of enthusiasm from hundreds of spectators announced the start of the quarter-mile. Kate, realizing that she was in the danger-zone, fell back, but Henry went on, and Virginia, not quite so close to his heels as she might have been, was appalled to see a rush of wild figures, bare hairy legs working like pistons, spiked shoes spurning the ground, bear down upon her. In this crisis she lost her head completely, and deaf to Henry's shouts, turned and fled blindly among the legs of the justly incensed runners. Two jumped over her, the third she nearly upset, causing him to lose his place In the race, and then she was gone like a streak of dark grey lightning among the crowds on the other side of the track.

"Dod! That ane's a rinner, richt eneuch!" said a beery voice close to Kate. "It's a peety they hadna a quarter-mile for the dowgs!"

Kate did not wait to answer him, but ran as fast as she could in the direction that Virginia had taken, Henry galloping ahead of her, the sheep, the Show, his dignity, everything forgotten except his darling Virginia.

Several cars, belonging to stewards, judges, or other important persons, had been parked on the Show ground, and Henry, who had stopped running, was peering into each as he passed it. Kate came up to him and said breathlessly: "Oh, Henry, I'm so sorry! Poor Virginia—"

"Oh," he said in an off-hand manner which did not hide deep anxiety, "she's probably gone to ground in one of these cars, I expect. We'll just have a look in case."

After the excitement and distress which she had caused, It was a little tactless of Virginia, Kate thought, to he discovered lolling at ease on the beautiful pale grey upholstery of a large Daimler whose owner had left one door slightly open. But in face of Henry's relief she did not say anything.

"Pretty clever of her, you know, Kate!"

"Oh, very," said Kate dryly. "You'll notice that she has picked the best-looking car of the lot, too. It isn't the only one with an open door. She could quite well have got into that Ford shooting-brake, but she is evidently Daimler-minded."

Henry chuckled. "She'd have got into a Rolls if there'd been one," he said with pride. "But she's really frightened, Kate. Look at her, she's shivering like anything."

Violent tremors were agitating all Virginia's hairs, and she flatly refused to leave her haven. 'Drag me out if you like,' her flattened ears and lustrous eyes said, 'but short of brute force I will not come.'

As another shot and its attendant yells told that a second heat had begun, Virginia cowered down among the rugs and trembled more than ever.

"We'd better leave her here for a bit," said Henry. "I'll come and get her before the car goes away." He shut the door as he spoke.

Between the two evils of having Virginia found there by an indignant car-owner, and the certainty that she would be greeted with rage on the running track, Kate hesitated, but only for a moment. Then she decided that it would be easier to pacify one person than a multitude, and allowed Henry to shut his treasure into the Daimler.

"And *now*," he said, quite satisfied with this arrangement, "we'll go and look at the sheep."

From the catalogue there appeared to be a bewildering number of entries, and Kate soon gave up trying to distinguish between a 'Fed Cheviot Gimmer' and a 'Hill Cheviot Gimmer'; or a 'Half-bred Young Ewe' and a 'Half-bred Ewe Lamb.' It was a relief to see the black-faced sheep, with their horns and jetty plush faces. She and Henry wandered from pen to pen, looking at the Cheviots, dipped pale buff or primrose, their broad flat backs each adorned by a ticket with a number, or the coloured placards which proclaimed that their bearers had won a prize. She was trying to think what 'Family of half-bred Ewe, Gimmer and Ewe Lamb, unfed, clipped bare and buisted' might mean, when Henry said: "Robin's shepherd has won a First for a pair of hirsel half bred sheep. Look, number a hundred and fourteen, with a red label." And in the same breath: "Here's Father! I thought he'd still be up at Pennymuir."

"Hullo," said Andrew cheerfully. "Admiring the Pennymuir exhibits? Kate, have you been to look at the vegetables yet?"

Kate gave a guilty start. "No! I'd forgotten all about them. Where are they?"

"In the dirtier of the two marquees. I think the *leeks* might interest you," said Andrew with a look of devilish amusement, which showed plainly the source of Henry's wicked glances.

Henry was charmed at the prospect of further sightseeing with his father as an addition to the party, and lost no time in herding them to the marquee.

"Oughtn't you to go and find Lucy?" asked Kate, as they were swept into the stuffy heat of the interior.

"In a minute. I want to see your face when you see the leeks."

"I say, Father! Kate!" Henry's voice, as usual, dominating all other sounds. "Look here! Geordie's done awfully well—George Pow,

Soonhope Lodge, first *and* second for six leeks grown by exhibitor in his own garden!"

But Kate, who had just caught a glimpse of a lowering whiskered face which she rightly concluded to belong to the bereaved Barrie, had turned tail and fled from the tent without seeing anything but an array of knitted socks, intricate and beautiful in design, fearsome in colour, which had been contributed by members of the W.R.I.

"You craven!" Andrew, laughing openly, had forced his way out after her. "You might have commiserated with Barrie, at least, if you didn't want to congratulate Geordie!"

Kate put her hand up to her flushed face as if she could stem the flood of guilty colour rising there. "One would be as bad as the other," she protested. "Oh, don't ever mention leeks to me again!"

4

"Well, Andrew, as you're here, I hope you will drive us home." Lucy spoke in her most gracious tones, and smiled at him. "Eleanor and I are quite worn out with all this—aren't you longing for a cup of tea, Eleanor?"

"I should like several," said Mrs. Heron, who looked remarkably cool and unwearied. "Dear me, Kate, how hot and untidy you are."

"I know," said Kate, who had been taken by the indefatigable Henry to watch a wrestling contest, and had only left because she feared that the wrestlers, whose trousers appeared to be supported on their stout forms by faith alone, might become even more undressed at any moment. "But I have really done the Show thoroughly, Mother. If you had been squired by Henry, you'd look every bit as hot as I do!"

"Father! One of them is wearing red flannel underfugs," said Henry's stentorian voice. "Long ones, right down to his ankles. You really ought to see 'em. They're worth a look."

"No, Henry, we're going home now, in the car, said Lucy hastily.

Henry's face became anguished, and Kate realized that he had suddenly remembered Virginia, still, presumably, immured in the Daimler.

"Oh, Mother! Can't I walk? I'd much rather—"

"Nonsense, Henry. We are all going in the car, or we'll be late for tea. Come along at once," said his mother. Then, seeing the look on her youngest son's face: "What's the matter, dear? Don't you feel well?"

It was an exceedingly awkward moment, and Kate felt full of sympathy for the wretched Henry, who, seeing that there was nothing for it but the truth, gulped miserably and stammered: "Well, you see, I've—I've got a little dog—"

"A *dog*?" cried Lucy in horror, as if he had claimed ownership of a black mamba. "Where did you find it? Leave it here and its owner will get it."

"But you don't understand, Mother. She's mine."

"*She?* Good Heavens, Henry, a bitch? You know perfectly well I won't have the brute in the house!"

Henry bit his lip, but said nothing, and Kate was wondering if to champion what looked like a lost cause would only make matters worse, when Andrew unexpectedly intervened.

"Well, we can't stand here arguing about the dog," he said, his cool tones falling like rain on the general excitement and dismay. "Henry will have to bring it home with him, Lucy. We can decide there what's to be done with it."

"Where is the creature, then? You understand, Henry, that I am very angry with you, and that on no account will you be allowed to keep it," said Lucy.

Henry, as near tears as any boy of fourteen may be, muttered unsteadily: "She's in a car. That big Daimler over there."

"Go and fetch it, then," commanded his mother.

"No, Henry. Wait a bit," said Andrew, rather pale. "I think if Kate doesn't mind, she'd better go."

"Why?" Lucy whirled round. "Why should Kate have to go tramping about on Henry's errands? Let him go himself." Then she looked over towards the car, beside which a tall grey-tweed clad figure was now standing, and where Andrew had paled, she flushed an unbecoming bright red. "Of course you *would* have to choose that car, of all cars!" she exclaimed in a stifled voice, so obviously upset that Kate was suddenly sorry for her. "Didn't you know whose it was? It's—it's Colonel Fardell's, and there he is—"

She turned away and walked quickly to the entrance, followed by Andrew, who looked miserably ashamed. Mrs. Heron gave Kate a quick meaning glance.

"Fetch the dog, Kate," she said. "Henry, Anne has gone to the car already. You and I will walk quietly on and Kate will catch us up."

Henry, subdued by more than the fate which threatened his dog, nodded and went with her, and to Kate was left the unwelcome task of retrieving Virginia.

As she went slowly towards the Daimler, her mind revolved a dozen forms of apology and explanation which need not introduce her name; but when she reached the car, whose owner was still standing by the door gazing in astonishment at the strange dog asleep on his rug, she could think of nothing to say.

He turned, showing her a handsome stupid face which reminded her of a good-looking carp. There was little kindliness or humour about him, she thought; his most salient characteristic, unless his appearance belied it, was a dull obstinacy. But though his eyes held no warmth, he spoke civilly enough. "Your dog? Couldn't think how he'd got into my car."

"I must apologize," said Kate in her best manner, which, seldom used, was usually effective. "She was so terrified by the men running and the shots that started them that she came here of her own accord and we, very impertinently, I'm afraid, left her here. I do hope you don't mind very much. Her feet weren't muddy, and she is perfectly clean otherwise. "

"Quite all right. Quite all right," he answered, a faint light beginning to gleam in his fishy eyes. Kate might have been, as her mother said, hot and untidy to a woman's glance, but most men would have found her attractive at that moment with her flushed cheeks and parted lips, and the short ends of wavy hair clinging to the edge of her small cap. "I've got a dog that's gun-shy myself. A springer spaniel. Brute goes to ground as soon as he hears a shot fired. Found him in the box-bed in a shepherd's kitchen one day. Don't apologize. She's doing no harm. Let her stay here."

"Oh, thank you," said Kate, trying not to dislike him, but suspecting that if Henry or any other mere boy had come on this errand, he would not have been either polite or good-natured. "But we're going home now, and I've come to fetch her. It is really very kind of you not to be annoyed. We took an unwarrantable liberty."

"Can I give you a lift? I'm goin' home myself," he said with heavy gallantry. "Perhaps I go your way?"

"No, you don't," answered Kate without thinking. "I go—er—west, you see."

"So you know that my road's to the east, do you? You have the advantage of me, my dear young lady, for I don't know who *you* are."

"No? Oh, well, it doesn't matter," Kate said wildly, knowing only too well that she had blundered. "We aren't likely to meet again, you know."

"I should consider that a very great pity if it were true. But this is a small place, you know, and neighbours are always meetin'. Won't you tell me who you are?"

Kate had opened the car door and scooped the somnolent Virginia into her arms. "Yes. I'll tell you, but you won't like it a bit," she said bluntly, forgetting to finesse. "I'm Kate Heron, a cousin of Andrew Lockhart's. And I'm staying at Soonhope. I need hardly say that of course I didn't realize that this car belonged to you. Good-bye." She sped away, leaving behind her a most disgruntled and astonished Colonel.

The car-load which was borne hack through the town to Soonhope was equally disgruntled, the pleasure of the day spoiled for all of them. Packed closely together, Mrs. Heron and Lucy in front with Andrew, Henry seated between Kate and Anne in speechless misery which threatened to turn to shameful weeping every time Virginia licked his hot cheek, they drove and were driven in absolute silence. On reaching home, Andrew took complete command of the situation with a firmness that impressed Kate.

"Henry, you are to stay in the car with your dog just now," he said. "Until we have decided what is to be done. Your mother and I will talk it over in the parlour."

Lucy's face was still patched with the ugly red that betokened anger and distress. "There is nothing to talk over, Andrew. I won't have the dog in the house, and Henry knows it quite well."

"Mother, how *can* you be such a beast?" This violent cry came, most unexpectedly, from Anne, who, Kate had always imagined, was strongly pro-Lucy. "Let him his dog, and be thankful he doesn't want a motor-bike to break his neck on!"

"Don't interfere, Anne. This is nothing to do with you," said her father abruptly. "Henry, stay where you are. Now, Lucy, if you're ready?"

And Lucy, without another word of protest, though her rigidly held head gave little hope of yielding, walked into the hall in front of him. The group standing by the car heard the parlour door shut, and still they said nothing. It did not seem fair to offer hope to Henry, sitting in a heap with his thin arms clutching Virginia to the point of suffocation; and the sharp tones of Cousin Charlotte, who appeared at that moment, struck on their ears almost as a relief.

"Well, what are you all doing, standing here like mutes at a funeral? And what has That Boy got? A dog? It will give him fleas. All dogs have fleas."

Anne, with a sound of suppressed fury, turned and rushed past her aged relative and upstairs like a whirlwind. "Dear me. Has Anne caught a flea already?" was Cousin Charlotte's acid comment. "Well, something must have happened, I can see that, and you may as well tell me what it is. Eleanor?"

"It's rather unfortunate, Cousin Charlotte," said Mrs. Heron. "But the dog belongs to Henry, and Lucy doesn't wish him to keep it."

"What a fool the woman is," said Cousin Charlotte dispassionately. "Why shouldn't the boy have his dog? They are both dirty animals by nature, and therefore admirable companions."

"Virginia isn't dirty," said Henry with a snuffle, and bending his head, he wiped his nose surreptitiously on Virginia's back. "And she hasn't got any fleas."

"Can't be healthy, then," said Cousin Charlotte at once. "But if the creature hasn't got fleas—which I don't believe for one moment—what objection can Lucy possibly have to it?"

"Oh, I don't know—" said Mrs. Heron with a distraught look at the parlour window close beside them. "And I really think we might talk of something else. Lucy and Andrew are in the parlour, discussing what is to become of the dog, and—"

"It you're afraid that Lucy heard me call her a fool, Eleanor, you need not worry. Lucy must know my opinion of her by this time."

Kate had an inspiration. "Cousin Charlotte, we're simply parched with thirst," she said. "And I saw Nina carrying the tea-tray into the billiard-room. Come and pour out for mother and me. Our need is urgent."

"Anything to get away from the parlour window, eh? Well, come along. You can tell me about the Show," said Cousin Charlotte. Kate and her mother drew deep breaths of relief, but they had not yet succeeded in inveigling Miss Napier from where she stood, her elastic-sided boots firmly planted on the gravel. "What about That Boy? Is he to have no tea?" she demanded, pointing a bony finger at the wretched figure in the car.

"Oh, he'll have his presently. We needn't wait for him," Kate said hastily.

"Humph! Waiting to hear the verdict, I suppose? He needn't suppose that his father will be able to get permission for him to keep his flea-ridden dog. Lucy never did listen to Andrew, and if I know her, the mere fact that he asks her to do a thing will make her do the opposite, especially now. Oh, you needn't look so suffering, Eleanor. If you were in the habit of speaking the truth as I am, you would say the same."

"Thank Heaven she doesn't," said Kate, losing her patience suddenly. "Truth, when it is carelessly used, as you do, Cousin Charlotte, is quite the most unpleasant thing in the world. Mother, you and I will go and have tea. Cousin Charlotte won't be able to flaunt her opinions or speak the truth if we aren't there to be horrified."

"Kate! Dear!" said poor Mrs. Heron faintly, appalled by this outspokenness. "How very rude!"

"Impertinent minx," said Cousin Charlotte. "Give your arm to the billiard-room."

In the parlour Andrew Lockhart looked at his wife with a faint smile. "Cousin Charlotte evidently hasn't much opinion of my powers of persuasion."

"You mean, she hasn't any opinion whatever of me, and never has had," retorted Lucy quickly. She was fidgeting with a glass ash-tray on a small table, and that her hand was trembling could be heard plainly. "But I really don't mind what she thinks. And I will not have that dog in the house. Henry must get rid of it immediately."

"Suppose he kept the poor little brute in the stable?"

"That's begging the question, Andrew. I told Henry, when he asked me about a year ago if he might have a dog, that I wouldn't allow it, and I have not changed my mind," said Lucy. "He has disobeyed me deliberately, and you are encouraging him."

There was a pause before Andrew answered her. He seemed to be considering how best to put what he had to say. "Does it never occur to you, Lucy," he said at last, and though he spoke slowly, there was no hesitation in his voice, "that you are running a serious risk of losing the children's affection by being so arbitrary? Henry isn't a baby any longer. He is quite old enough to have a dog and to look after it himself to use the example nearest to hand—and it seems a very reasonable wish, in a place where the dog has plenty of room to run about. Every boy wants a pet, and a dog is by far the most satisfactory all round. If it had been white rats, now," he added with a conciliatory smile, "I'd have been more inclined to back you up."

"To back me up?" Lucy echoed bitterly. "'When have you ever 'backed me up'? Have you forgotten that for the last four years you've left me to look alter the children alone? And now the first thing you do is to undermine my authority with Henry, and then threaten me with losing their affection!"

"That is not true, Lucy, and you know it," said Andrew sternly. "I have never interfered in your dealings with the children, but in this case you are exercising tyranny, not authority. Let Henry have his dog. You'll be very glad in the long run."

"If you are so interested in the children *now*," said Lucy obstinately, "I wonder that you didn't think a little more about them four years ago."

"You are quite justified in saying that, though it's ungenerous. But—what do you think made me come back?"

"What? Why, Soonhope, of course. You care more about this place than about any person living!" cried Lucy, frightened of the storm she had raised, but refusing to draw back. The swords were out now, and husband and wife stared at one another unflinchingly.

"Yes. I love Soonhope. I'm not happy away from the place for long," Andrew admitted. "But I came back really because of the children, though you may not believe it."

"Oh, I believe it. As long as you don't try to make me believe that you came back for *my* sake!" said Lucy with a bitter laugh. "I suppose you'll tell me next that I've lost your affection—"

"You don't try very hard to keep it, do you? You never have," said Andrew, bitter himself now.

"I? When did I ever fail you, Andrew? Haven't I always tried to be a good wife to you?"

Andrew sighed. That was the difficulty with Lucy. She never could admit to having failed in any respect, and, indeed, according to her own lights, she never had. But it was a very great pity that virtue had to wear such a forbidding face. "Well," he said wearily, "I dare say you're right, Lucy. You generally are. And I know I have failed you, often."

This admission, which should have cheered her with a knowledge of victory won, left Lucy instead with a desolate feeling of doubt. She had lost Andrew, the real Andrew, she knew that now, and was left with this courteous and patient shell of a husband. What if he were right, and the children, in whose loyal love she had always gone armed, should cease to care for her, too? The thought alarmed and distressed her so much that she sank on to the neatest chair, covered her quivering face with her hands, and burst into tears.

Andrew, half-afraid that she would repulse him, yet unable to see her suffering without trying to comfort her, crossed the room to her side and stood patting her shoulder awkwardly and calling himself a brute.

"Oh, Andrew, I can't bear it if the children stop loving me!" she sobbed.

"I was a brute to frighten you with the idea," he said remorsefully. "Don't cry, Lucy. The children have always been more yours than mine, and they won't turn against you unless you try them very high."

"You—you think I ought to let Henry keep that horrible dog?" said Lucy, still sobbing, but beginning to fumble with her handkerchief. Unlike so many women, she could always find it even in moments of stress such as this. "It—it seems to me so *weak*, Andrew, and Henry will despise me for giving in to him."

"Not at all. Give the boy credit for some decent feelings," said Andrew. "He'll think all the more of you if you do."

"Will you tell him, then?"

"No," said Andrew, though he would have liked to be the one to brighten Henry's unhappy face. "You must tell him. That's only fair."

Henry, when his mother went out to the car and said, "I've decided that you may keep the dog, Henry," took Virginia's reprieve so quietly that Lucy was disappointed.

He said: "Thank you, Mother. It's awfully decent of you," but his eyes sought Andrew, standing a little apart with his shoulder against the sun-warmed stone of the doorway.

And it was to Andrew that he said, as if rewarding a service rendered: "Would you like to see Virginia having her tea, Father? She has a bowl of tea with one lump of sugar in it every day, because it's good for her coat. You'd enjoy watching her. She's an awfully neat lapper."

CHAPTER SIX

1

"It isn't fair," Anne said, all the more hotly because secretly she sympathized, "to take Andrew's part just because he's more easy-going and pleasant than mother. After all she's had the worst of it all round."

"Well, she doesn't let us forget it, does she?" drawled Adam, who happened to be in a bad temper.

"Oh, Adam! How can you be so mean?" cried Anne. "That's a horrible thing to say."

Adam looked a little ashamed of himself. "It's true," he growled. "All the same, I admit it was pretty foul of me to say it. And she did let Henry keep Virginia."

"It was Andrew who did that," said Henry from the floor, where he was engrossed in combing Virginia to her pretended anguish. "You know it was, Anne."

All three young Lockharts were crammed into the summerhouse on the lawn, beside a collection of rotting deck-chairs, disused croquet-mallets and large wooden balls, their paint almost gone. As children they had found it a spacious, almost a palatial, playroom, but now they filled it to capacity. Henry and Virginia occupied the entire floor, and the other two were perched, Anne on the croquet-box, and Adam half-in, half-out of the open window, his long legs occasionally hitting Henry on the head, his fingers slowly disentangling a mass of ancient fishing-casts. In spite of the fact that Anne was grown up and Adam loftily conscious of the three-year gap between himself and 'the kid Henry,' they were in the habit of all conferring together as equals. They had assumed complete responsibility for their own actions, and were inclined to resent parental interference. Though they seldom put it into words, they felt that both parents had failed them and had no longer the right to try to order their lives. For a long time they had clung staunchly to Lucy, for they had been bewildered and distressed by her grief when Andrew had left them, but even before the return to Soon-hope they had begun to realize that there might be something to be said for their father. Lucy, they discovered, as they grew out of childhood, was not easy to live with. She made too many rules, laid too much insistence on small, unimportant points, kept them in on every side, and if they rebelled, was a little too apt, as Adam had said, to remind them that she had had to be both father and mother to them during those years of change. So they had come to rely on their own judgment, and found, when they pooled their opinions, that these were sounder than Lucy could be made to believe; also that when they presented a united front, their mother could be made to yield, though grudgingly and with many laments over their ingratitude.

Now they were discovering that the father on whom they were prepared to look with suspicion, ready to pounce on the first offi-cious assumption of paternal rights, had apparently no desire to exercise authority over them. He was interested in them, but treated them as rational beings entitled to their own views. It remained to be seen what be would do or say it they tried to get their own way in some outrageous demand. The meeting summoned in the summer-house had debated for a long time over the expediency of trying this on; but the difficulty appeared to be to find a suitable test case, and as Adam said: "It would only make them think that we really are senseless fools. I vote we just go on, and if anything crops up we'll soon see where we stand."

This having been approved, they passed on to a frank discussion of the merits and demerits of each parent, a proceeding which would have annoyed and distressed Lucy, and interested Andrew. On the whole, they were just, though not very merciful. The young are not given to a great display of mercy, considering it 'soppy.' At the same time, it is not easy to be absolutely impartial where one's own mother and father are concerned, and it was a certain tendency to be lenient to Andrew which had made Anne break out in defence of Lucy.

After Henry had made his remark about Virginia, a silence fell, for they were all thinking it over. What Henry said was perfectly true. If it had not been for Andrew, Virginia would not have been lying on the floor of the summer-house with tightly shut eyes and forepaws prayerfully crossed while her master combed her bushy tail. Andrew had stepped in, and somehow had persuaded their mother to let Henry keep his dog. That was only fair: there never had been any real reason why they should not have a dog; but what interested them now that the crisis was over, was that Andrew had quietly asserted himself, behaving as the master of the house and head of the family without any fuss. His children began to think that if it came to a trial of strength, easy-going Andrew might win over all comers. . . .

"Of course, mother never did let Andrew have much to do with us, even when we were kids, you remember," said Adam, suddenly breaking the silence. "She always sort of disapproved and stopped him from playing with us, or anything. Didn't she?"

"The real truth is," said Anne, ignoring this unfortunate fact, which she remembered very well indeed, "that Andrew and mother should never have married each other. They just don't fit."

"Who would mother fit with?" asked Henry, sitting back on his heels, a very dirty comb, its teeth full of Virginia's hair, in his equally dirty hand. "Or is that a rotten thing to say?" he added conscientiously, as his elders frowned.

"It may be rotten, but it's dashed difficult to answer," said Adam. "*I* don't know. The misfit's plain enough to see, but the other—! What do *you* think, Anne?"

"I think we'd better stop, because they *are* married, misfit or not," said Anne, wishing she had not spoken her thought aloud.

"I know who Andrew would have fitted in with," said Henry dreamily. "Someone like Kate."

"That's easy," said Adam with a laugh. 'Haven't you noticed that Kate's a bit like Mrs. Vardell in some ways?"

"Kate wouldn't run away with another person's husband!" cried Henry, resenting this as a slur on Kate.

"Oh, do let's stop!" said Anne uneasily. "Honestly, boys, we oughtn't to discuss the parents like this—now. It was different when Andrew wasn't here, and we felt he hadn't anything to do with us."

"The trouble is," mumbled Adam through a mouthful of casts, "that we've been thinking for ourselves for so long we've got out of the habit of bothering about the parents."

"It looks as if we'd have to start bothering about Andrew. He means to run the show," said Anne. "And I believe it will be quite a pleasant change."

"If he does run the show, I hope he'll let me learn to drive the car," said Adam thoughtfully.

"I think he will if you ask him," Anne said thoughtfully. "He seems very reasonable."

"Do you suppose we ought to stop these meetings of ours, Anne?" asked Adam.

Anne, relieved that she had not had to make the suggestion herself, agreed eagerly. "Yes, I do, unless anything frightfully crucible needs discussing," she said, meaning, of course, *crucial*, but she and her two brothers were quite pleased with crucible. ". . . Oh, Henry, is Virginia finished? The darling! Doesn't she look divine?"

The conclave broke up in a general hugging of the complaisant Virginia, during which the door, bumped into by Adam, flew open and a cascade of boy and dog fell out on to the lawn. Anne, following more carefully, sprang over the heap of struggling bodies, to find Kate gazing at them all in some surprise.

"A battle? A bear-fight?" she suggested.

"A dog-cuddle, that's all," said Anne. "At least, it started as one, inside the summer-house. I don't know how it will finish. Were you looking for any of us, Kate?"

"Not exactly. I came out to escape Cousin Charlotte, who is making herself peculiarly obnoxious to your mother in the drawing-room."

"Poor mother," said Anne, her face clouding. "She does suffer from that old she-devil. I wish we could get rid of her."

"It would take a bomb or an earthquake," said Kate. "Boys! Wouldn't you like to go up to Pennymuir this afternoon? Robin has asked us to tea."

"A tea-party?" demanded Adam suspiciously, rising from the heap, but keeping one large foot planted on his writhing younger brother.

"Not a polite one," Kate assured him. "Neither your mother nor mine seems keen to go. What about you, Anne?"

"I'm playing tennis at Charteris, I think," said Anne. "They asked you, too, Kate."

"I know, but my tennis is so frightful. Unless the party turns out to be a series of low-comic turns, I won't be much asset to it," said Kate. "Really, tea at Pennymuir with the boys is more in my line."

"I'd better go and see if I have a respectable pair of shorts," said Anne, and moved off across the lawn towards the house.

When she came out again, after giving her best white piqué shorts to Nina to have the pleats pressed, there was no sign of the boys or Kate. Only Andrew could be seen, talking to Geordie Pow near the garden door. Anne hesitated. She felt awkward with her father, partly because she had been discussing him so recently, partly because she was afraid of growing too fond of him, which would have seemed like a breach of loyalty to her mother. But Andrew waved a hand to her, and she walked slowly down the drive until she was close to him.

Dismissing Geordie with a nod, he turned to Anne. "You look if you were at a loose end," he said. "Would you like to come in to Edinburgh with me? I have to sign some papers at Dickson's office—the lawyer, you know—but it won't take long. We'll be back in plenty of time for luncheon."

"Oh, Father, I'd love it!" cried Anne, suddenly realizing that she was a little bored. "Let me get a coat and a pair of gloves—"

"What about your mother?"

"Mother's in the drawing-room writing letters. Cousin Eleanor is in her room writing letters. Aunt Robina is in her room writing letters, unless Cousin Charlotte has gone to interrupt her. Father, wouldn't it be easy if you could just say those little spots that people write under a line when they're repeating a thing?"

"You could always say 'ditto, ditto,'" said Andrew gravely.

"So I could. I wish I'd thought of it sooner. I won't be a minute, Father."

Altogether, it was a pleasant morning. Edinburgh was looking clean and sunny, and the tourists had thinned to an occasional two or three untidily dressed persons armed with cameras, who ate chocolate in the streets and loudly discussed the idiosyncrasies of the Scottish as though the people near them could not understand what they were saying.

"It's a pity that a nation is so often judged by its tourists," said Andrew mildly as he and his daughter walked along Princes Street. "Tourists are really a race apart, and a very odd one."

Anne laughed gaily, the clear, carefree sound causing several heads to turn and smile in sympathy at this good-looking father and daughter. She was thoroughly enjoying herself. Andrew had bought her some beautifully fine silk stockings, a blue *suède* bag and a pair of gloves to match', and, which Anne liked almost better, a spray of 'Royalty' carnations, looking like shot blue-and-pink silk, to wear in her coat.

"We've time for a drink," he said, crowning the whole morning by this careless suggestion, and led the way into the American bar of a famous hotel. "What would you like, Anne?"

"Well, truly, I'd rather have tomato-juice than anything," said Anne. "But if it would look better, you choose me something not too strong."

"Tomato-juice looks as well as any other drink, and tastes a great deal nicer than most. I suppose I'm old-fashioned, Anne, but I am really rather glad you don't like cocktails."

"They make me sneeze," explained Anne, sipping her tomato-juice. "Father, this is simply too divine."

"What? The tomato-juice?"

"No, though it *is* marvellous. No, I mean the whole thing, coming in to Edinburgh, and everything."

"Surely, now that you're grown up, you must have been taken out by other people a lot more amusing than a mere father?" said

Andrew, wondering just how tight a rein Lucy had kept on this young creature.

"Oh, yes, I have been taken about by boys, but not awfully often. Mother was never very keen on it, unless she knew them and their fathers and mothers and things. But you know so *much* better how to do it than any of them," said Anne, and then blushed at her own tactlessness, for of course her father must have had a lot of practice taking Mrs. Fardell to places like this divine little bar with the high, red stools and the clinking cocktail-shakers and the amusing frescoes on the walls.

Andrew, however, appeared to notice nothing, and answered with complete composure: "At my age, my dear, one ought to know a little about the business. Have a potato chip? Or a cheese straw? It would go very well with tomato-juice."

Shortly after this they left. "It would be a pity to spoil it by being late for lunch," Andrew said, and Anne heartily agreed. She did not want any unpleasantness to dim this delightful outing.

They were driving very slowly eastwards along George Street when an old man, rather shaky on his feet, but attired with the utmost elegance and neatness, tottered out in front of the car, heard the warning horn, stepped back and shook his fist as they passed. "Damned road-hogs!" they could hear him cry in a shrill voice of fury, and Andrew chuckled.

"Know who that was?"

"No. Ought I to?"

"Well, he's your mother's Great-Uncle Henry, a Victorian survival of the naughty nineties, and a kind of male Cousin Charlotte."

"How dreadful!" said Anne, twisting her head to catch a last glimpse of the doddering but jaunty figure. "One Cousin Charlotte in the family is more than enough. And oh, Father! Couldn't you possibly think of some way to get Cousin Charlotte out of the house? She is driving mother mad, and I really don't wonder."

"It might be done. I've got an idea. Great-Uncle Henry and Cousin Charlotte hate each other like poison. Suppose I suggested that old Henry—by the way, he's Henry's godfather, so it is all the more appropriate—ought to be asked to Soonhope. There's no hope or fear of his refusing an invitation to live free for a week or two, and unless I'm very much mistaken, Cousin Charlotte will be packing her boxes within the next hour."

"Father, how marvellous of you!"

"It all depends on your mother, of course," said Andrew dryly. "She may refuse to have anything to do with it."

"I don't think so, not if it means good-bye Cousin Charlotte."

"I'll try it, then, at the first favourable moment," Andrew promised, and changed the subject by saying: "I suppose you can drive, Anne?"

"Only—only unofficially, Father. I mean, no one at home knows I can."

"I hope you haven't been fool enough to drive about without a licence? That's a mug's game," said Andrew, but not at all in the fatherly manner which Anne would have resented at once.

"Oh, no. I went round plastered with 'L's' for about a fortnight, with a providential licence in my pocket, and then I passed a test and got a proper licence."

"And where did all this take place?" asked Andrew, hiding a smile at the 'providential' licence.

"When I was staying with a girl I was at school with," Anne said ungrammatically. "Her father was giving her driving-lessons, and he very decently said I'd better learn, too, at the same time. So I did."

"Without telling your mother?"

"Well, Father, Mother always drives her own car herself. She'd never let us, because I've heard her say often that a car is far better when only one person drives it."

"I think you're old enough to have a small car of your own," said Andrew. "I'll see you drive first, though—and I suppose," he added, but to himself, "that Lucy would say I was bribing Anne! It can't be helped. . . . "What's that, Anne? I didn't hear you. Sorry."

"I only said, thank you, Father," said Anne in a small voice. "And *please* could Adam share it with me? All his friends drive, and he's been crazy about it for more than a year—"

'We'll see. Adam will have to be taught to drive without danger to himself or anyone else before I promise anything more.'

But Anne was content. "Father, you are a darling!" she said gratefully, and fell to blissful dreams of having a car of her very own.

Andrew, after a half-rueful glance at her rapt face, was silent also. She had called him a darling, she had enjoyed being with him, but how much was it all worth? It seemed very unlikely that Anne or the other two should feel particularly fond of him: and Lucy would be right, as she usually was, if she accused him of bribery, for it was the sudden longing to see Anne's face brighten, to attach her to him by gifts if by nothing else, which had made him promise her a car so recklessly.

2

"What are you going to do this afternoon, Granny?" asked Kate, feeling, rather remorsefully, that she had seen very little of her grandmother since the house had been filled with people.

"I am taking Charlotte out to tea with Jean Anstruther," said Mrs. Barlas. "If that doesn't humble her a little, nothing will."

"You're a brave woman. I don't know that I'd care to be present at a party where Mrs. Anstruther was hostess and Cousin Charlotte guest."

"It will be very good for both of them," said Mrs. Barlas placidly.

Kate was in her room, powdering her nose before going to Pennymuir with the boys, and her grandmother, seeing her door open, had come in for a talk. She now sat down in a small chintz-covered arm-chair beside the open window and said: "Wouldn't you rather have gone to the tennis-party with Lucy and Anne?"

"Not I. The boys' society is about on the same intellectual level as my own, and besides, I want to see what Pennymuir is like."

"It used to be a lovely house when I was a girl," said Mrs. Barlas. "There was a large family of young people, Hume was their name, and we had such picnics and dances and walking excursions. Of course, driving all that way in the wagonette was an amusement in itself, though I dare say the horses didn't care for it much. Old James, my father's coachman, used to make us walk up all the hills, I remember, out of revenge for having to go at all. We used to take our ball-dresses with us and stay the night. . . . But I don't know what Pennymuir will be like now. A bachelor so often seems to live uncomfortably to our ideas, though I believe Robin Anstruther has an excellent cook-housekeeper. You must tell me all about it when you come home."

"Of course I will, darling, but I dare say Mrs. Anstruther could tell you far more than I'll be able to after one short visit."

"Oh, Kate! Kate!" suddenly shrieked Mrs. Barlas as her grand-daughter moved towards the door.

"Granny darling, what a *skelloch*," said Kate. "I'm not going away, you know. I'm still here."

"I very nearly forgot what I came in on purpose to say," explained the unrepentant Mrs. Barlas. "It's this, Kate. I think Lucy is almost certain to ask you to stay on for a bit and I want you to say that you will."

"But dear me, Granny, why this thusness? I mean, the party's breaking up already, with Daddy and Grey gone back to business, and mother leaving to-morrow, to keep a watchful eye on them. I thought that by the end of this week I ought to be going—"

"Lucy will ask you to stay, and I wish you would, Kate. It is an uneasy household, and having someone like you would be a help."

"A buffer state? What a delightful prospect," said Kate. "And when it's between husband and wife, a little invidious, don't you think?"

"Well," said her grandmother defiantly. "I'm sorry for Andrew. I know he behaved badly, very badly, but he's trying to make up for it now, and really poor Lucy is enough to try anyone's temper. So insufferably *good*," ended Mrs. Barlas angrily. "And about as much sense of humour as would lie on a threepenny bit!"

"So you would sacrifice your grandchild for your nephew?"

"Andrew has always been like a younger son to me," Mrs. Barlas went on, unheeding. "He and your Uncle Gavin were brought up together, for his mother died not long after your grandfather, Kate, and I came back here with the children—your mother and Aunt Jane and Gavin—to keep house for my brother Adam, Andrew's father. Ever since Gavin was killed in 1914, Andrew has tried to take his place, and I don't like him to be so unhappy."

"But, Granny, haven't you ever thought—Lucy must be unhappy too!"

"Lucy has never understood Andrew or made allowances. She should have married an elderly minister or a desiccated professor, not a young man with hot blood and a high spirit. I don't think I am a vindictive woman, Kate, indeed, I pray to God every night to make me less *judging* of Lucy, but I find it very hard to forgive her for what she drove Andrew to doing."

Kate realized that it was quite useless to try to make her grandmother see things from Lucy's point of view, so she only said: "Very well, Granny, if Lucy asks me, and if you really think I'll be a help to any of them, I'll stay."

"You'll be a help to me if to no one else," said Mrs. Barlas, rising as a bellow came up from under the window.

"Hi, Kate! Kate, aren't you nearly ready?" bawled Adam. "You must look like the Queen of Sheba by this time!"

"Have you been ''tiring your head?'" shouted the shriller voice of Henry. "And painting your face?"

"Silly ass, that was Jezebel," Adam could be heard answering.

"Never mind," said Henry with fine indifference. "She's taking ages anyhow."

Kate dropped a kiss on her grandmother's soft cheek and hurried downstairs.

Lucy was talking to Andrew in the hall. "But I thought you were coming with us to Charteris, Andrew."

"Sorry, my dear. I want to see some beasts of Robin's that he thinks might suit me," he said.

"Lady Charteris will think it so *odd*," complained Lucy. "And I accepted for you."

"No one will think it in the least odd if you explain. After all, a farmer's time isn't altogether his own, especially at this season of the year."

"I wish you wouldn't call yourself a farmer," Lucy said fretfully. "It sounds so disgustingly rural."

"Well, I am disgustingly rural," said Andrew with unabated good-humour. "Hullo, Kate. You ready?"

Kate, conscious all up her spine that Lucy was looking frowningly after them, walked out to the old stable, now a garage, with Andrew by her side and the boys and Virginia rushing on ahead.

"Couldn't you have gone to Pennymuir another day?" she asked. "I'm afraid Lucy is disappointed."

"Lucy's always disappointed with me. She'd miss it if she weren't," he said cheerfully. "And she only wants to drag me to Charteris to prove to everyone what a reunited couple we are."

"Oh, Andrew! You shouldn't talk like that," said Kate, painfully aware that she sounded both priggish and feeble.

"Now, Kate, don't you begin worrying about me. Just make up your mind that I'm a hopeless case and you'll feel much better about it," he said.

Kate, angrily wishing that she could remember always to count ten before she spoke, said with an impatient sigh: "The tongue is an unruly member!"

"Cheer up. Yours isn't half as unruly as some. Think of Cousin Charlotte."

She had to laugh. "I'm glad, at least, that I'm not as bad as that!"

Then they were at the garage, where the boys had already occupied the back of the car, with Virginia leaping from one pair of bony knees to the other in a vain search for a comfortable seat.

"Longstreet's forces being rushed to Chattanooga in the cars," announced Henry as they started. "Drive as fast as you can, Father, or we'll be too late to help old Bragg."

"'What on earth is the boy talking about?" Andrew asked Kate.

"American Civil War, I should think. He lives in it the whole time," said Kate. "I've learnt quite a lot about it since Henry took me in hand, though I can't master tactics."

"You've learnt quite a lot about Henry," he said. "You know him a great deal better, in this short time even, than I do."

"Oh, parents often don't hear very much about their children's private affairs. You probably have a better chance than most fathers if you start now," Kate said.

"Why so, my clever cousin?"

"Because you can see them in a more detached way, as if they were just other people," explained Kate, her words vague, but the idea behind them, as Andrew realized, not only clear-cut but extremely sound. "Parents and children hardly ever think of each other as persons. I suppose that's the fault of so close a relationship. But you, after not seeing them for a bit, ought to be able to judge them pretty fairly."

"That is very acute of you, Kate. I didn't know you studied human nature so deeply."

"I don't. It's more instinct than anything. A woman's instinct!" said Kate in a deep, mysterious voice, and laughed. "Dear me, I'm talking clichés now. Do you ever do that? It's rather amusing, played as a game."

"You mean 'I always say there's nothing like a good cup of tea,' that sort of thing?"

"Yes, that's it exactly. And 'how small the world is' and 'a fire brightens up a room so.'"

"But hang it all, it *does*!"

"Of course. Clichés are nearly always true," said Kate. "That's partly why they're so irritating, I expect. Oh, Andrew, isn't this lovely?"

While they talked, the car had been climbing steadily up out of the valley, and now they were almost on top of the long ridge of the Lammermuirs. All about them rolled the hills, purpled with fading heather, which deepened in the hollow places to an exquisite soft dark brown. Far ahead the narrow unfenced road ran winding down into Berwickshire, the Cheviots filled the southern horizon, and away to their left could be seen a dim line of sand, white fringed, which was the shore at Berwick-upon-Tweed.

"There are the Eildons," said Kate, gazing at the three-headed hill standing up so abruptly in the plain near Melrose.

"Where? That's Look-out Mountain," Henry said dreamily. "The dam' Yanks are massed behind it."

"Shut up about that war of yours," ordered Adam, cuffing his younger brother's head. "We're all sick of it. Father, are there trout in those burns we crossed?"

"Any number, or used to be," said Andrew, who had stopped the car and was looking through half-closed eyes at the wide scene. "We'll go and see one of these days, Adam."

"Are we far from Pennymuir?" asked Kate.

"No, but you can't see it, from here. There's a green valley running to the south, just below that dip in the road," said Andrew, pointing. "It's quite near the hills, but so sheltered that the crops are earlier than on any of the neighbouring farms. The ground drops sharply here, and it doesn't lie nearly so high as you'd think."

He started the car again, and they ran slowly down the winding road. Quite suddenly it turned to the left, and instead of heather on either side there was a great stretch of purple-tawny grass in seed, the burnished stems shining bronze in the sun. Below her, Kate saw the green valley, threaded by links of a burn, and half-way down its length a cluster of tall trees stood about a house, which was built on a level piece of ground above the water. A drift of blue smoke from the high chimneys rose straight up into the windless air, there was a hoarse cooing of wood-pigeons. Beyond it, where the valley opened out, were fields of darkening wheat, fields of vivid green turnips, meadows where black cattle lay dreaming.

They crossed the burn by a solid wooden bridge, which Henry looked at hopefully, murmuring to Virginia, his sympathetic listener: "They'd have to burn that bridge behind them if they retreated."

Unfortunately, Adam overheard. "At it again?" he said sternly. "And anyhow, what would be the good of burning the bridge? They could walk over the burn easily."

The burn certainly was disappointingly shallow and narrow.

"Never mind, Henry, I expect it runs red in winter, when the snow melts in the hills, and almost up to the bridge," said Kate, turning to smile at the Confederate behind her.

"It wouldn't be easy to get guns and wagons over," muttered Henry, this time so low that only Virginia heard. He tickled her ear when he whispered, but she only twitched it once or twice, and lavishly licked his hand. 'Dear Virginia!' thought her besotted owner. '*She's* interested, if no one else has the sense to be!'

Several dogs rushed from the house and galloped, barking furiously, round and round the car. Virginia promptly sat up and barked back, and the clamour was becoming deafening when Robin Anstruther, in breeches and gaiters, appeared on his door-step and roared, "That will do!" whereupon the dogs, all except old Wat, the Aberdeen, whom Kate recognized immediately, hurriedly departed, with an occasional last bark, to some point of vantage among the trees.

'Pretty bachelor-ish,' thought Kate, as they went into a hall furnished with an oak settle along one wall and a narrow oak table along the other. Both were strewn with an engaging variety of odds and ends: dog-collars, muzzles, a shoe-horn, several ancient tweed caps, a pipe or two, and a tin of tobacco. Among these, on the table, a small lustre mug crammed too tightly with antirrhinums looked pathetically lost.

'Not as uncomfortable as Granny seemed to fear,' she added to herself, for the sitting-room which they entered was sunny, the worn leather chairs large and inviting. 'But, oh heavens, *what* a smell of dog!'

It was obvious that dogs were accustomed to sit where they pleased, for one by one the pack stole quietly in, and with growls and sidelong looks at each other, proceeded to their favourite chairs. Virginia, her nose in the air, sat bolt upright on Henry's knee, loftily ignoring the blandishments of Wat and a peculiarly dirty wire-haired fox-terrier.

'A woman's touch is what's needed here,' thought Kate, wishing that she could repeat her cliché aloud to Andrew. As he and Robin were already deep in talk, and the boys seemed inclined to be silent, she had time to look about her. A large writing-desk, open, was littered with papers, which had overflowed on to the mantelpiece, where they stacked on either side of a clock and behind one or two bits of old china. The clock, Kate noticed, was not going. There were two bookcases full of books, with yet more papers on top of them; there was a large wireless in a corner, and, rather surprisingly, several good etchings and dry-points on the walls, and a small landscape in oils, of a red East Lothian field caught by the sun on some day of early spring. But the cushions, and the cretonne loose covers of the sofa and some smaller chairs, had a draggled look, and the leather of the arm-chairs was scratched, and even in places torn, by dogs' paws or teeth.

'I suppose he prefers it to look like this, or he wouldn't let it get in such a mess,' thought Kate, but she had received a severe shock, for her idea of sailors was that they were always neat, and liked to have things 'shipshape.' Though not naturally very tidy herself, her fingers itched to set this room to rights, to straighten one of the dry-points that hung crooked, remove the collection of spent matches from the coal-scuttle, and sweep the dusty papers out of sight.

The boys showed signs of becoming restive, and Robin rose. "You'll find some of the plums ripe on the garden wall," he said to Adam. "Would you and Henry like to have a look at them before tea?"

"Yes, please," answered both, and instantly disappeared, followed by Virginia and a trail of other dogs.

"I don't know how to entertain you, Kate," went on the host with a worried frown. "Drew and I are going to walk down to the low meadow to see some bullocks—"

"I'd like to come, too, it you don't mind. But if you want to be all boys together, I can explore by myself," said Kate.

"Nonsense. You'll come with us, of course," said Andrew.

When they reached the meadow, Robin turned to her. "What do you think of them?" he asked, waving a stick at the placid bullocks, who gazed at them from large, soft, stupid eyes and blew out their moist black nostrils questioningly. Their long ears flapped at flies, their tails switched peacefully, their black coats shone like satin over their sleek flanks. Kate wanted to cry: 'I hate to look at them, poor beasts, when I know that they'll all end in the slaughter-house!' But she realized that this was hardly likely to meet with approval, so she narrowed her eyes judicially, pursed her lips, and finally said in a carelessly knowledgeable tone: "They seem a nice level lot."

The surprise and suspicion that struggled with respect in the men's faces was too much for her gravity, however, and she began to laugh.

"It's no good," she said at last. ""You see, I've learnt the proper thing to say about bullocks, and pigs, of course, are straightforward. You just prod them with a stick and look profound. But if you had shown me sheep, I should have been undone."

"You shameless creature," exclaimed Andrew admiringly. "Did you ever hear of such duplicity, Robin?"

Kate was indignant. "I think I've been very honest. Far too honest. And you know you only asked me what I thought in the hope that I'd make an ignorant remark for you to snigger at."

"There speaks the true woman," said Robin. "As usual, turning the tables to shift the blame on to the Mere Man. But I'll give you this satisfaction, for you deserve it. You're perfectly correct in saying these beasts are a nice level lot. They are."

"I hope," Kate said rather anxiously, "that you won't give me away? I find it such a useful thing to say in farming circles."

"Your guilty secret is safe with us," Andrew assured in his best mock-heroic manner. "We are dumb. Aren't we, Robin?"

"Silent as the grave," Robin agreed. "Now, Drew, good look at 'em. They're nice, you know. Not too long in the leg—"

The conversation became highly technical, and soared beyond Kate's very slight grasp of the subject. She found herself, for the second time within an hour, a silent onlooker. The two men forgot her presence altogether, and she passed the time in contrasting them. Certainly Andrew was the better-looking of the two: beside his slim height Robin Anstruther appeared almost too broad of shoulder. Andrew's fine, clean-cut features and long, rather melancholy grey eyes were set off by his red hair, and he had a manner to wile a bird off the tree. Robin was blunt, rather harsh, with the furrow scored across his forehead which gave him the look of a perpetual frown; Kate did not even know what colour his eyes were, for he crinkled them up when he did smile so that they were half-shut, and at other times his brows were drawn down close above them. She supposed they were dark, to match the thick, greying hair. And yet, comparing the two men, so utterly different, but such staunch friends, she could not think why Mrs. Fardell had chosen Andrew, not Robin. If what old Mrs. Milligan had said was true—and Kate was sure that it was—then Robin loved Elizabeth Fardell, too, and had lost her to Andrew. A curious mingling of feelings disturbed Kate: relief because that woman had preferred Andrew, rage at her blindness in not seeing that Robin was by far the better man. . . . And they were still friends. Truly men were odd creatures, and in many ways so much nicer than women. . . .

"Kate! You must be bored to death. I'm truly sorry!" It was Robin speaking, and she turned to him with a dazed smile. In an instant, like a clap of thunder, she understood both her relief and her anger. She had fallen in love with Robin Anstruther herself.

With an enormous effort she forced herself to say in an ordinary voice: "No, I'm not bored, really, thank you. It's lovely just to be out on an afternoon like this."

She would have said exactly the same thing if they had been standing in heavy rain in Haystoun's worst slums. To be with him was enough for Kate just now, and she felt a spring of such pure happiness welling in her heart that she was afraid its effects must surely be noticeable. But Robin only said:

"That's good. We'd better be going back for tea now," and they turned and walked back up the sloping meadow.

For Kate the afternoon had suddenly become quite different from even the finest of September afternoons. Colours were all intensified, the grass was as green as the flames from a burning log of sea timber, everything about her swam in crystalline air that dazzled her eyes. The barberry bushes in the hedge, her favourite of all hedgerow trees, were hung with waxen tassels of fruit, rose-pink and orange-tawny on their black thorny stems, lovely beyond belief, and even the hawthorns were weighted down with haws which were brilliantly red, and not the usual rather dingy crimson. Robin picked a spray of barberry in passing and gave it to Kate, and she held it so tightly that the thorns ran into her hand, but she never felt them.

It was like falling over a cliff to come into the prosaic atmosphere of a chilly and formal dining-room, where a solid tea had been set out on the round table. Plates of massive girdle-scones, plates of rock-cakes which looked extraordinarily like their name, a heavy, dark gingerbread, a lump of shortbread, and on the sideboard a brown and a white loaf on a board. Evidently Robin's cook-house-keeper was accustomed to catering for gargantuan appetites. There must at least half a pound of butter on each of the two glass dishes, there was an enormous jam-dish. Even the cups looked to Kate like soup bowls, as she sat down behind them, hidden from the others by the massive silver teapot and hot-water jug, which she could only lift with difficulty.

"Strawberry jam, Henry?" asked his host, pushing jam-dish towards him. "I hope it *is* strawberry, by the way. I told Mrs. MacOstrich not to give us anything else."

Henry, courtesy struggling with truthfulness and a love of strawberry jam, finally murmured: "I think this is plum jam, sir, but it doesn't matter. I'm sure it'll be awfully good."

Robin seemed to Kate, who now found his every slightest gesture or change of expression important, to brace himself as he rose and rang the bell. "We'll have strawberry jam," he said.

A measured tread could presently be heard approaching, each heavy step by its slowness asserting its owner's dignity and dislike of being summoned. The dining-room door opened and a figure, beside whom Mrs. Anstruther's grenadier would have seemed like a simpering girl, stood gazing sternly at them. Mrs. MacOstrich, if this were she, was not tall; in fact, she was not larger than a twelve-year-old child, but every inch of her small, tautly held person, every line of the oblong, wooden face from which two china-blue eyes looked disapproval on the world in general, was awe-inspiring. Her sparse grey hair was combed off her face into a tiny knob on top of her head, her hands were folded on the small square of lace-edged apron which covered the front of her black dress.

"You rang, sir?" was all she said, but a sort of shudder passed over the petrified party seated round the table. Kate thought that it was actually Mrs. MacOstrich's tininess which made her so terrifying; Henry said that he felt like a person with a cobra swaying to and fro in front of him; Adam said that he felt like a worm being put on a hook; and Andrew said with feeling: "Poor old Robin! He can't get rid of her, you know. I believe she mesmerizes him."

But all that was later, driving home. While Mrs. MacOstrich was present in person, no one spoke a word except Robin, and he only with an obvious effort.

"I asked for strawberry jam, Mrs. MacOstrich. This is plum. There must have been some mistake."

"There was no mistake, sir. The plum was opened, so I put it out. There's not a jar of strawberry open."

"I see," said Robin, and Kate's heart was full of pity for him, bullied by this dwarfish creature, who ought to have been housekeeper to a troll. "But I think you'll have to open a pot of strawberry jam, all the same."

Silence. Then: "It's the *new* strawberry, sir," said Mrs. MacOstrich. "Maybe you didna know that last season's was finished?"

"Never mind, never mind. Bring the new stuff," said Robin hastily.

With a look which said eloquently that she washed her hands of all responsibility for such wanton extravagance, Mrs. MacOstrich left the room. When she returned, it was to place on the table a plate containing a section of honey, and in a silence that forbade remonstrance, she slowly ebbed away once more. The door closed soundlessly behind her malevolence, and the blight which had stricken Robin's appalled guests began by degrees to vanish.

He looked miserably upset. "The old she-devil," he muttered. "Wait a minute, boys, and I'll fetch that jam myself."

But a chorus of voices negatived this suggestion, which all felt to be a forlorn if valiant attempt, and the boys ate honey freely, making themselves and, Kate was rejoiced to see, the polished table exceedingly sticky in the process.

"Why doesn't he dismiss her, Andrew?" she asked when they had started on their homeward way. "Did she save his life in infancy or something tiresome like that?"

"No. I can't see the MacOstrich troubling to save anyone's life, can you?" said Andrew thoughtfully. "She's new since I was last there. It's difficult to explain. She runs his house efficiently, and like a good many men he simply hasn't the moral courage to say to her, 'Mrs. MacOstrich, I find that I can dispense with your services. Here is a month's wages in lieu of notice, and I should like you to leave to-night.' No, she's like the Old Man of the Sea who burdened poor Sinbad, and he can't get rid of her."

"Is she so very efficient?" murmured Kate. "I didn't see many traces of it. The sitting-room was awfully doggy and untidy, and the dining-room about as gay and homelike as a dentist's antechamber. I wouldn't stand her—or the dogs!"

"No, but you're a woman, and have the dauntless courage of your sex where female servants are concerned. Robin would turn off a ploughman or a gardener as fast as some people, but he is wax in the hands of his housekeeper. As for the dogs—don't tell him I told you, or he'd be livid, but everyone who wants to get rid of some dog they don't want goes to him with a sad tale and a pack of excuses and reasons for having to 'part' with them, and poor Robin takes 'em all in. I don't believe there's one of his own there bar old Wat."

"Poor fellow!" said Kate in accents of profoundest pity.

And then the mere fact that she had been speaking of Robin sent her soaring away again in a silent ecstasy, helped by the swoop of the car as it topped the hill and flew down into the valley of the Alewater. It was amazing, this feeling. Kate had been in love before, but she had never known this boundless happiness, this sense of increased beauty and richness in all about her which made it a joyous adventure even to breathe. In the first exaltation following on her discovery that she loved Robin Anstruther, Kate was not troubled with his feeling towards her. Disappointment and disillusion would come later, perhaps, but for the present she only hugged her delicious secret joy closer. She was still in this dreamy mood, at peace with the whole world, wanting everyone to be as happy as herself, when they arrived at Soonhope to find that the tennis-playing contingent was back from Charteris.

Lucy, indeed, was crossing the hall when they entered, the boys once more clamouring for food in spite of their large tea. "Did you have a nice time?" she asked, in a tone which lacked its usual undercurrent of faint disapproval.

"Lovely," said Kate; and then, seeing from Lucy's surprised face that possibly 'lovely' was an overstatement except to her own ear, added rather confusedly: "It was so beautiful up on the Lammermuirs. Such a—a grand view."

"Well, I'm very glad," said Lucy. "And if you are enjoying it at all, Kate, I do hope you will stay here for a bit, and not cut your visit short? Eleanor said she could spare you, and we should all be glad. Wouldn't we, Andrew?"

"Of course. Delighted," he said with his ready smile, pleased at Lucy's hospitable impulse. "Do stay, Kate."

Stay here, within reach of Robin? Stay here, where even if she did not see him, she was in the place where he lived? How could she do anything else? "Yes, I'd love to. Thank you so much, Lucy—Andrew." And Kate, with a faint, dazzled smile at both, went upstairs to dress for dinner.

Andrew looked after her with a puzzled frown. "Funny thing," he said confidentially to Lucy, "I never noticed it before, but Kate's uncommonly good to look at, isn't she?"

Nor did he notice his wife's quick, suspicious glance at him, and she only said: "Yes, Kate is really very handsome this evening. I think the air here must suit her." 'Which was as well for his peace of mind.

3

"Really, there are times when I think that Florence is half-witted," said Lucy, coming into the parlour, as everyone but herself still persisted in calling it, a few mornings later. "To-day, for example, I couldn't get a word out of her. She just stood staring at me with her hand over her mouth, all the time I was in the kitchen. And yet on other mornings I haven't had a chance to speak because of her flow of conversation. Aunt Robina, are you quite sure she is all there?"

"Oh, I *think* so," said Mrs. Barlas placidly, looking up from the fine crochet which never seemed to tire her amazingly youthful blue eyes. "I know she is a little odd in some of her ways, Lucy, but she is *such* a good cook."

"Oh, yes, she is an excellent cook," Lucy conceded, "I've never had a better one, and I think it was wonderful of you to get her back for me. But really, Aunt Robina, it is a little nerve-shaking to be *goggled* at when you are giving orders for the meals—and no suggestions about puddings or a savoury for to-night! Not a word. Just blank silence, clutching her face. I found it most upsetting. Was she in the habit of behaving like that when she was your cook?"

"N—no. I don't think she was," said Mrs. Barlas slowly, "Never mind, Lucy dear. She'll send in a triumphant pudding and a quite new, exotic savoury, and all will be well," added Kate, who thought her grandmother suddenly looked a trifle upset, and supposed it was because Florence did not altogether meet with Lucy's approval.

"I dare say she will," said Lucy more cheerfully. "She has never failed me so far. Only this evening I do particularly want things to be quite perfect, with the Charterises coming to dinner."

"Florence loves a dinner-party and will do her very best," said Mrs. Barlas over her shoulder. She had risen and was moving to the door.

"Do you think I've offended Aunt Robina by saying that about the paragon, Kate?" asked Lucy as the door closed. "I didn't mean to."

"Don't worry," said Kate consolingly. "It'll be all right. You know Granny doesn't really mind in the least."

"Well, I only hope that Florence's manner will be a little more normal to-morrow morning," said Lucy. "Or I shall be really frightened to speak to her at all, and you will have to do it."

She had never seemed so human before, and Kate thought: 'If she were only like this always, what a nice person she would be!'

A sharp voice could be heard raised indignantly in the hall. "Boy, call off This Animal. It's biting my boots."

"Cousin Charlotte!" breathed Lucy with a hunted look in her eyes. "Heaven send she doesn't come in here!"

There was a delighted growling, a scampering of toenails on the tiled floor, a scuffling, and Henry's voice, admonishing Virginia. "Naughty girl. Wicked girl. Mustn't bite ladies' boots!"

"As if that cooing sort of talk is likely to stop the little monster," said Lucy, who had grown almost reconciled to Virginia's presence about the house. She and Kate looked at each other and had to smile, so tender was Henry's scolding.

"There, Cousin Charlotte. She won't do it again," he said confidently.

"I don't trust the Creature within a yard of me. I shall go to the garden, where I understand dogs are not allowed." And Miss Napier's footsteps died away. Presently Kate, peeping cautiously round one of the long curtains which hung at the parlour window, saw her black hat bobbing determinedly down the drive.

"Gone to heckle Geordie Pow. We're safe," she announced to Lucy.

"For the moment," retorted Cousin Charlotte's unwilling hostess gloomily. "But I shall not feel *really* safe until she leaves. And then I'll go to the station and see her off, just to make certain that the train doesn't go without her."

Kate laughed, but she was sorry for Lucy, knowing that Cousin Charlotte reserved her most unpleasant home-truths for her. "Does she bother you so much, Lucy? It's a shame."

"*Bother* me? I can't tell you, Kate, how grateful I'd be to the person who could send her away—without being outrageously rude to her, of course."

"Mother!" shrieked Anne, suddenly springing up from the sofa where she had been curled unnoticed with a book. "Mother! Do you mean that?"

"Anne, what a fright you gave me! Of course I meant it," said Lucy. "Why?"

"Then wait here a minute. Don't go. Stay here till I come back." And Anne tore from the room.

"Do you suppose that half-wittedness is catching and that Anne has taken leave of her senses, too?" asked Lucy plaintively.

"I hope not. A half-witted cook could be got rid of at pinch, but a daughter in that state would be a much more serious problem," laughed Kate. "Lucy, I must rush to Granny and tell her that I see the postman coming. She has some foreign stamps for him, and you know what a passionate philatelist he is. Wouldn't that make a nice title for a book or a play? *The Passionate Philatelist?*"

"With Laidlaw as the hero," suggested Lucy, raising her eyebrows as she glanced out of the window at the rather unromantic tubby figure coming up the drive pushing a bicycle.

"Well, no. Perhaps not. But I must tell Granny—" And Kate in her turn went tempestuously out, leaving Lucy, obedient and curious, but puzzled, to wait for her daughter.

Because she never liked to be idle, she went to the handsome bow-fronted bureau of inlaid wood, its surfaces polished to a mellow sheen, and began, with a frown—it was one of Lucy's more human traits that she had to count on her fingers—to add up the monthly books. But half-way up the second horrid column of pennies, ". . . and one makes fourteen, that's one-and-fourpence. No, it isn't, it's one-and-two, oh, dear!"—there was a scud of hurrying feet, the door burst open, and Anne, dragging her bewildered father by the coat-sleeve, dashed in.

"Now. Father, *tell* mother!" she cried, breathless but triumphant. "Mother, father has a plan!"

"Tell your mother *what*?" and:

"A plan to do *what*?" said her parents in a duet.

"Dear me, how stupid you both are!" said Anne, stamping with impatience. "Mother, didn't you say you'd be internally grateful if someone could tell you how to get rid of Cousin Charlotte? Father, you *know* you said you had a wizard idea about it. Well, then!"

Andrew looked at his wife and nodded. "It's true. I did have an idea, Lucy, but whether you like it or not is a different matter."

"It would have to be pretty frightful to be worse than Cousin Charlotte, don't you think?" said Lucy dryly, "Yes, Andrew, tell it me. I'm sure I've racked my brains without result. The only thing *I* could think of was to burn the house down, and then she'd have to leave."

"This isn't quite as bad as that," he promised her. "It was just this: you know how dearly Cousin Charlotte and your Great-Uncle Henry Halliday love each other? All you have to do is to invite the old man here for a few days, and I'm willing to bet you ten to one that she'll go by the first available train."

"Andrew! How wonderfully clever of you," said Lucy, the first honest approval of him that he had seen for at least ten years in her eyes. Then her face clouded. "It wouldn't be fair, Andrew. *You* would have to bear the brunt of Great-Uncle Henry, and he's my relation. Perhaps we'd better stick to Cousin Charlotte."

"No, no, my dear." He was touched by her thought for him. "If it comes to that, Cousin Charlotte belongs to me, and you've borne with her gallantly. It's my turn now. I'll take on old Henry. If you'll be content to leave it to me, I'll say carelessly at luncheon that I've written and asked him to come, and you must back me up."

"Oh, I will," Lucy said fervently. "With all my heart."

"That's grand," said Anne with immense satisfaction. "And no one will be exactly prostituted with grief over Cousin Charlotte's departure!" She skipped away, leaving her parents to smile over her quite unconscious malapropisms.

In the meantime Kate had gone to her grandmother room, got the promised stamps, and given them to the gratified postman, and was returning to deliver his messages of thanks, when Nina came scurrying along the corridor from the direction of the back-stairs, an expression of horror blended with delight on her demure face.

"Could I get speaking to Mrs. Barlas, Miss Kate?" she asked breathlessly.

"I should think so. Granny, Nina wants to see you about something," said Kate at her grandmother's door.

"Come in!" screamed Mrs. Barlas. "Yes, Nina, what is it? Was Laidlaw pleased with his stamps, Kate?" she added at once in the same breath, before Nina could speak.

"Charmed. But go ahead, Nina. My news can wait," said Kate.

"Oh, if ye please, mem," gasped Nina, with a giggle hurriedly curtailed for propriety's sake. "Florence has lost her teeth!"

"Lost her *teeth*?" This was Kate.

Mrs. Barlas showed no surprise. "I knew it," she said heavily. "Very well, Nina. You can go and tell Florence to have a good look for them, and I'll see her presently." And when Nina had reluctantly left them, she went on: "As soon as Lucy told me about Florence saying nothing and standing with her hand to her mouth, I remembered. Kate, I didn't dare to tell Lucy! You know how disgusted she would be. I had to leave the room in case I gave it away."

"But, Granny, after all, what does it matter to Lucy? Of course, it is very awkward if Florence can't or won't speak, and I hope she'll find them soon, but what is so disgusting about it?"

"Kate," said Mrs. Barlas, with mournful solemnity, "you would be disgusted if I told you some of the places where Florence's teeth have been found. The last time they were only in a plant-pot, among the leaves of a fern—and I never felt the same about that fern again, even after leaving it out in the rain for two nights. But the time before *that* she had baked them in a cake. A seed-cake, I believe— or was it one of those soda cakes she makes so well? Fortunately, it was a cake for the kitchen, and the teeth were in the middle of a slice, so they weren't damaged. But both the other maids gave notice and left at once. It was no laughing matter," she ended reproachfully. "The house was full of guests, and I had to get new maids at a moment's notice, and the boot-boy was making beds and the gardener washing up."

"Oh, Granny, I'm so sorry!" cried Kate, unrestrained tears of mirth streaming down her cheeks. "It was a picture of the kitchen tea, with Florence's dentures grinning at them all from a slice of cake that did it! You shouldn't be so funny."

"It will be far from funny," observed Mrs. Barlas with a bitterness almost up to Cousin Charlotte's standard, "if she serves them as a savoury this evening. I know Florence. Until she finds those— those *damned* teeth of hers, she will only be fit for a mental home. I shall have to go and see her."

"I'm coming, too. I can't miss this," said Kate. "I promise I won't laugh, Granny darling. You couldn't be such a pig as not to let me come with you?"

But at sight of the scene of havoc in the kitchen, where drawers and cupboards had been torn open, and Florence, one hand still glued to her mouth, was scrabbling frantically among the contents of bins and boxes which stood empty on the table, Kate's composure threatened to desert her. Only her grandmother's ferocious look, her hissed, "Behave yourself!" made her gulp down her laughter and try to show a fitting severity.

"Now, Florence, what is this? Yes, I know you have lost them," said Mrs. Barlas, as Florence, from behind her hand, made mumbling and unintelligible noises. "If you keep the things in their proper place, which is your mouth, you wouldn't lose them. Have you looked in the coal scuttle?"

"Glug!" said Florence, nodding so madly that her cap fell over one eye and made her look wilder than ever.

"If ye please, mem," broke in Nina glibly from the door leading to the scullery, where she, the open-mouthed Phemie, and Mrs. Pow's May were all clustered, charmed spectators of this novel scene. "Me 'n' Phemie's looked under her pillow, an' in amang the pitatoes, an' a' places, an' we canna see them."

Phemie and Mrs. Pow's May gave vent to a burst of giggling, and Mrs. Barlas turned on all three of them.

"Why aren't you girls doing your work?" she asked. "You ought to be ashamed of yourselves, standing giggling there. Off you go!"

"If ye please, mem, it's eleeven o'clock," ventured Nina.

"It may be midnight for all I care. You can't have your cups of tea in this mess," said Mrs. Barlas, such a martinet that Kate hardly recognized her gentle grandmother.

Without a word the three gathered dusters and brushes and faded away, and Mrs. Barlas resumed her one-sided examination of Florence.

"Not in the dust-bin? Thank goodness. You haven't dropped them into the soup, I *hope*?"

"Glug!" said Florence, this time shaking her head as violently as she had previously nodded it. Her cap flew to the back of her head and hung there on a single hair-pin.

"Well, it seems quite hopeless," Mrs. Barlas said at last, with a sigh of despair and exasperation. "You'll have to do without them just now, Florence, and if you go to the dentist this afternoon— mercifully this is the day he is in Haystoun—he may be able to fit you with a temporary set. I'll pay for them—" As Florence glugged and waggled her head in dissent: "If Mrs. Lockhart hears of this, I expect she will dismiss you, and I shall not blame her."

Florence, with her free hand, flung her dirty apron over her head and sobbed behind it, and Kate, feeling that her grandmother was being really very severe indeed, was about to plead for the culprit, when, like a young horse galloping over a field, Phemie charged into the kitchen.

"Here they're! See, I fund them for ye, Florence! Dinna greet, wumman! Here's yer art teeth!" With a noble gesture she opened one red hand and flung a complete set of the most obviously artificial teeth Kate's fascinated eyes had ever beheld on the floor at the cook's feet.

Florence uttered a shrill cry, swooped on her recovered treasures, and all in one movement slapped them into her mouth, switched the apron from her face, and broke out volubly:

"The good God will reward ye for this, Phemie, that He will! And where were they at all, that I niver clapped me own two eyes on thim?"

"In the dust-pan!" cried Phemie triumphantly. "I heard a kin' o' a rattlin' noise, and I luikit, an' there they were. Eh, I'm that pleased, Florence. Ye were awfu' hard up wantin' them!"

"Well," said Mrs. Barlas, "I hope this will be a lesson to you, Florence. See that this mess is cleared up before you and the girls have your eleven o'clock tea." Her tone was once more mild. "How could they have got into Phemie's dust-pan, I wonder?"

"Sure, it's no wonder at all, ma'am," said Florence happily, hurling tins back into cupboards at top speed and with deafening clatter. "Seeing I put thim there meself. Thinks I, it's there they'll be safe while I give me mouth a rest, for Phemie's that thoughtful, if she sees thim she'll niver cast thim out!"

4

"Well, you've been long enough in coming to see me," said Mrs. Anstruther, as the grenadier showed Kate into the drawing-room at The Anchorage. "I began to think you had forgotten me altogether."

"I know. It has been rather a long time, but it isn't always easy to get away when one is a mere visitor," Kate said, coming forward and kissing Mrs. Anstruther's withered cheek. "Now I have been asked to stay for several weeks, at least until the boys go back to school, so Lucy feels that I can be left to amuse myself, I suppose. . . . Oh, how do you do, Miss Milligan? I'm sorry I didn't see you before, but it's so sunny outside that my eyes are dazzled."

She shook hands with Miss Milligan, who had crept mouse-like out of a very large chair.

"Sit down," said Mrs. Anstruther, "and tell me what you've been doing at Soonhope. Flora is dying to hear, too," she added with a malicious side-glance at her other guest.

"One thing we did was to go to Pennymuir for tea the other day," said Kate.

"Yes, Robin told me you had been up, with Andrew and the boys. How is the place looking? Like a pigsty and full of other people's unwanted dogs, I suppose. You know I refuse to go there at all, while he persists in keeping that woman."

Miss Milligan's nose grew pink at the tip and quivered with excitement, scenting scandal.

"Oh, I don't mean what *you* think, Flora," said Mrs. Anstruther, and gave her sudden hoot of laughter. "The woman is his cook-house-keeper and it is all quite as respectable as you could wish."

Then, as Miss Milligan, overcome with confused indignation, subsided, Mrs. Anstruther continued blandly, as if she and Kate were alone in the room. "A truly dreadful woman, my dear. The last time I went to Pennymuir she was intolerably impertinent to me, and I vowed that I would never go to the house again until Robin paid her off. But the creature is a termagant, and Robin appears afraid to tell her to leave. *I'd* do it with pleasure, but she wouldn't take it from me."

"Men hate changes, don't they?" Kate suggested. "They always seem to prefer the evils that they know, even to possible unknown blessings."

"Well, there's one change I should like to recommend to my nephew," said Mrs. Anstruther. "And that is marriage. It's about time he took a wife. In another year or so he will be so encrusted in bachelordom that he will be a hopeless case. Even as it is, I pity any woman who marries him. What with getting rid of that MacOstrich and most of his dogs, she would have her work cut out for her."

Kate said nothing, for this mention of marriage had brought to her mind the remembrance of Robin's unhappy love-affair. Of course, it Mrs. Fardell's husband were to grant het the divorce he had refused up to the present, she could be free to marry Robin. But how awkward a situation would arise if he brought her as his wife to Pennymuir! And Kate's heart cried "'No!" more loudly than any thought of the difficulties attending this possibility. Her silence was not noticed, and she blessed Miss Milligan for having piped up as soon as Mrs. Anstruther had ceased to air her views.

"Oh, surely, dear Mrs. Anstruther, you are being a *little* hard on your nephew. Such a charming man, I am sure anyone would be pleased to marry him." And she darted a look at the unconscious Kate.

"Now, Flora, don't talk nonsense. What do you know about Robin? Or about any man, if it comes to that?" said Mrs. Anstruther. She knew that she was being unkind, but she had endured a long session with Miss Milligan, and was thoroughly weary of her. Besides, her arthritic pains had been more troublesome than usual lately, and her patience and temper were equally short.

"Perhaps I had better be going," said Miss Milligan with maddening meekness and long-suffering. "Mamma will miss me if I am not home soon."

"Don't forget to tell her that Kate will be at Soonhope for longer than she expected," said Mrs. Anstruther.

"I won't. And I hope, Kate, that you will be able to spare the time to come and see Mamma and me?" said Miss Milligan, eyeing Kate so intently that she made the object of her scrutiny feel acutely uncomfortable.

"Why has Miss Milligan taken to staring at me like that?" she asked impatiently as soon as the door had shut on the small, spare figure with the inevitable basket in one hand. "It is most embarrassing."

"Oh, poor Flora, she has to have something to stare at," said Mrs. Anstruther, a great deal more charitably than 'poor Flora' would have believed. "And it might as well be a pleasant-looking creature like yourself. But I did think that it was a peculiarly piercing look. Have you a guilty secret on your conscience? If you have, Flora will ferret it out for a certainty."

Kate, on whom the effect of the leek-stealing and its consequences had worn off long since, denied possession of a guilty secret, and their talk presently turned to other topics. But when, after having had tea with Mrs. Anstruther, she started to walk down the road to Soonhope, she still could not shake off the unpleasant sensation which Miss Milligan's gimlet-like, boring look had caused.

'Even if she knew that I'd fallen in love with Robin—and she couldn't possibly unless she was a clairvoyante,' thought the puzzled and irritated Kate, 'she'd have no business to glare at me as if I'd done something disgraceful.' Then she told herself that she was bothering herself to a morbid degree about the opinion of a local busybody, and began to think of the approaching dinner-party. The principal guests, Sir Hugh and Lady Charteris, with their elder daughter Sybil and their son John, she dismissed with a careless 'nice people!' For her the guest of the evening was Robin Anstruther, and she wondered anxiously if he would like her in the leaf brown velvet dinner-gown, the new one which Granny had given her, which she thought so becoming. Then she remembered that he probably would never notice what she wore, for with his mind's eye he must always see his love, Elizabeth. Kate's first careless rapture was over now, and the pangs which follow that exaltation were upon her. She was very sober when she met Andrew in the hall, and he could not imagine what had made him think his cousin Kate good-looking. This evening she was really very plain indeed.

Kate, had she known what he was thinking about her, would have seconded it, unflattering though it was. She looked at her reflection in the mirror on her dressing-table, and made a disgusted face at it. Indeed, to be truthful, she so far forgot her age and sense as to put out her tongue, and then drew her brows right down to her eyes, shooting out her lower lip at the same time. The result was appallingly ugly, and she was startled and annoyed to hear a yell of laughter which told her that she had an audience. Whirling round, she saw Henry rolling on her bed in agonies of mirth.

"What a really horrible little boy you are, Cousin Henry," she said. "And who gave you permission to creep into my room without knocking?"

"Now, Cousin Katy, be decent," he implored her. "Do be decent. I did knock, but you were so busy making faces that you never heard me. So I thought I'd have a squint, and if you'd been in your under-fugs or your corset-cover, or whatever women wear under their dresses, I was going to steal modestly away, though I've seen Anne tons of times in next to nothing. I say! Could you make that marvellous face again? It was like a sick bulldog."

"I could, but I'm not going to, Henny Penny, And could you stop carousing on my bed?"

"Och, Kate, you might do it again, just once, to cheer me up. I need cheering up," he added darkly.

"I'm sorry, but even for your sweet sake I won't repeat the performance. Even in its hey-day that face was never made more than once a week."

"When was its hey-day?"

"Oh, a long time ago, before you existed, if imagine such dim ages, when I was Leader of the Fifth at Saint Cymbeline's," said Kate, who was feeling better, improvising rapidly as she made up her face. "I used to be bribed to do it at mistresses who had incurred our displeasure. Ah, Cousin Henry, those were the days! I remember at the height of the great Boot-hole Riot, when the whole of the Lower Fifth was singing the Red Flag among the hockey-sticks in that subterranean retreat, and Miss Chipping Norton, the geography mistress, was sent to quell the disorder and fine each rioter ten Order Marks, I made The Face, and she swooned into a boot-hole. And when she did come round, she was a raving maniac. What do you think of that?" said Kate impressively, and waved her lipstick.

"There ought to be a girl who sneaked on the rioters to Miss Weston-super-Mare," said Henry thoughtfully. "There always was in all the girls' stories that Anne used to read."

"Oh, you mean Matilda Ramsbottom? Yes, to be sure, she sneaked—(and the name was Chipping Norton, Henry. Miss Weston-super-Mare was the games mistress, and everyone adored her and used to hang about the passages for the exquisite pleasure of seeing her emerge with her hockey stride from the Staff Room after eleven o'clock milk and biscuits) but Matilda's subsequent fate was so awful that I wasn't going to sully your innocent ears with it. She was forced to eat the whole form's share of Spotted Dog on the following Thursday, just before she played in the great match against Saint Perkin's, and she burst in mid-field and the bits had to be sent back to her sorrowing parents in a hamper. They were immensely rich, and she was, of course, an only child."

"That's prime. You ought to broadcast," said Henry, chuckling. "Oh, I say, Kate, isn't it a shame! Mother won't let me dine to-night because it'll make thirteen at table. I told her I wasn't superstitious, but she wouldn't listen to me."

"Henry, I'm awfully sorry, but I don't see that I can do anything," said Kate. "It won't be so very thrilling," she consoled him, "and Florence is sure to see that you get your share of everything—especially the puddings."

Henry brightened. "Yes, Florence is a good sort. If you could *just* save me one or two of those crystallised fruits, Kate, it wouldn't be too bad."

"Very well, I will," Kate promised rashly. "And now I must fly. Telling you that bedtime story has taken up a good deal of time."

She patted his shoulder, and went along the corridor to the drawing-room, praying that she wasn't late, for she had heard a car arrive while she was talking to Henry.

But the drawing-room was empty save for one broad-shouldered figure leaning against the mantelpiece. Kate stopped short. "Robin!" she said.

"Robin it is," he answered, straightening himself and coming to meet her down the long room. "You're looking very nice this evening, Kar-handit Kitty."

The unexpectedness of seeing him had brought a sparkle to Kate's eyes, an added touch of colour to her smooth cheeks. In her velvet gown with its wide skirts, she seemed taller than usual, the puffed sleeves tightening to fit closely to her wrists and the square-cut neck all gave her a passing resemblance to some old picture, for choice by Van Dyck.

"That rig suits you," he said. "You look so stately that I feel there is only one thing to do." He took up her left hand as it hung at her side, and lightly kissed it.

Kate had been watching them both in the long mirror, with her old childish feeling that she was looking at someone quite different, and not herself and Robin. At the touch of his lips she started as if wakened from a dream. "Oh, Robin!" she said, catching her breath, seeing her brilliant eyes shining back at her from the glass. Then she recovered herself quickly, afraid of giving her secret away.

"Are you in the habit of making these pretty compliments? Did you often do—that—to Mrs. Fardell?"

"No," he said slowly. "I don't believe I ever kissed Elizabeth's hand. Why do you ask, Kate? Why her especially?"

"Tell me what she's like," said Kate hastily. "I've so often wondered. You said once that I—I reminded you of her."

"Only in some of your ways. Not at all in looks" he said, and Kate's silly heart sank like a stone. Still staring at the mirror, she listened to him. It almost seemed as if that other woman was slowly appearing from his description, and must be visible, standing beside Robin's reflection in a moment, so vividly could Kate picture her.

"She is a little creature, to begin with . . . black hair that curls at the ends and is quite smooth on top of her head, and a mouth that curls at the corners, and eyebrows like wings, every hair in its place, and big shining eyes greeny-grey; and that fine pearly skin, not dead white, you know, and not thick enough for 'magnolia pallor,' but a sort of warm white like milk . . . and she has rather ugly ankles," he added suddenly, but he didn't sound as if the ankles mattered very much, Kate thought sadly. They obviously hadn't to Andrew.

"Very, very attractive," she murmured, feeling that she must say something or she might cry, which would be disastrous as well as stupid, and so awkward just before a dinner-party.

"Very," he said briefly. Having to give a description of Elizabeth had shaken him, as thinking or speaking of her always did; and yet, he found with astonishment, though he immediately longed to see her, it was not quite the old desperate longing, but a gentler melancholy, not altogether unpleasant. He looked at Kate, whose eyes were dark with the tears she had managed to keep out of them, and thought: 'Kate has more interesting eyes than Elizabeth.' But he said carelessly: "How is it you're so early this evening? I thought you rather specialised in being late."

"I thought I *was* late," Kate answered, as lightly. "I was trying to cheer poor Henry, who isn't dining to-night, because with him we should be thirteen at table."

"Hard lines," said Robin. Then, suspiciously: "What is it, Kate? I seem to know that look in your eye—"

"Only if you're sitting next to me, Robin," pleaded Kate. "I want to smuggle some crystallized fruits and things for him, poor exile. He does love the flesh-pots. And I've nowhere to hide them. I thought you wouldn't mind perhaps putting them in your pocket?"

"I do mind," he said hastily. "No, really, Kate, it's a bit too much to ask any man to fill the pockets of his dress-suit with sticky sweets. I'd do a good deal for you, but I draw the line at that."

"I'll wrap a clean handkerchief round them first," said Kate with a wistful look, and he laughed.

"Oh, Kate, Kate! You are an awfu' ane, as my old nurse used to say to me. I suppose I'll have to do it, if you promise not to forget the handkerchief."

5

"Of course, my dear Lucy," said Cousin Charlotte in a tone which could have bitten through a sheet of copper, so acid was it, "if you have already invited that elderly male gossip Henry Halliday to stay, I must leave immediately. Be good enough to look up a suitable train for me at once."

"Great-Uncle Henry isn't coming for three days yet, Cousin Charlotte," murmured Lucy placatingly. "You really needn't hurry."

"The mere thought that he is coming is quite sufficient to poison the place for me," retorted Miss Napier, "However, I shall stay until the day of his arrival, as I have to pack. Why you saw fit to have him here, I cannot imagine, a creature so doddering that it takes him half the day to cross a room. He might die on your hands at any moment."

"He's Henry's godfather, after all, Cousin Charlotte," said Andrew in response to a glance of appeal from his wife. "And pretty hale still. I don't think he is liable to die for quite a bit yet."

"The more's the pity," said Cousin Charlotte, and Henry, who had been playing with Virginia unobserved in a corner of the room, could contain himself no longer, but burst into a strange snorting sound which was a laugh smothered in Virginia's hair.

"Put That Boy Out," ordered Cousin Charlotte, with a venomous glance at Great-Uncle Henry's godson. "I must say, Andrew, that you showed some sense in making Halliday his godfather. That Boy is exactly like him, and will be more so as he grows older."

"Outside, Henry, and take Virginia with you," said Andrew quietly, seeing that Henry was about to engage in argument. Henry, who was beginning to know his father well, rose without a word and made for the door. "And by the way," added Andrew, "if you go up to the big garret and look in that old black trunk, you'll find a whole pile of the *Illustrated London News* of the 1860's, with pages of American Civil War pictures in them."

Henry uttered a whoop of delight that caused Virginia to hark and Cousin Charlotte to groan angrily, and rushed from the room, banging the door after him.

"Quite mannerless. A real Halliday," said Cousin Charlotte with tremendous satisfaction. "Not a trace of Lockhart about *him*."

"He's the living image of my grandfather, old Adam Lockhart," said Andrew mildly, but to no avail.

"His looks bely him," was Cousin Charlotte's reply. "Well, Lucy, I wish you joy of your Great-Uncle Henry, and his visit. I shall go and pack." And having had the last word, she went grimly away.

"I hope it won't be out of the frying-pan into the fire," said Lucy apprehensively. "It does seem hard that we can only get rid of one frightful relative by asking another to stay. Why can't we be at peace in our own house?"

Andrew's restraint had become almost perfect since his return, and he forbore to point out that the necessity would never have arisen if Lucy had not chosen to hedge herself about with a family party; but he wondered how Lucy's memory could possibly be so short where things that went wrong were her own fault. And Lucy, to whom the same thought had reluctantly occurred, could not humble herself enough to admit that it *was* her doing. With an effort she said: "I really am more grateful to you than I can say, Andrew, for your idea. Cousin Charlotte was preying on my nerves."

"There's no need to talk of gratitude between you and me, Lucy," said Andrew. "And by the way, I think Cousin Charlotte might be driven right in to Edinburgh, and the car can bring old Henry back."

"Who is to drive her? You?"

"I thought Anne might do it. You know I'm shooting the next four days."

"Anne! But can she drive? Has she got a licence?"

"Oh, yes. She can, and she has. As a matter of fact, Lucy, Anne is a very good driver. She has your clear head and cool judgment, she knows the rules of the road and sticks to them, and she's easy on the car—"

"Andrew, I will not have Anne driving my car, understand! I think it is very underhand of Anne to have done all this behind my back, and never said a word about it," said Lucy indignantly.

"Oh, parents don't know half of what their children ate up to nowadays," was Andrew's most unfortunate reply.

"*You* seem to know a good deal about all three of them, far more than I do. It's most unfair that I should always be kept in the dark."

"No one is keeping you in the dark, Lucy except your own constant disapproval of whatever they do," said Andrew, a little impatient by this time. "And it's partly that, as Kate said to me, I've come to see the children from an outside point of view, and that's how I happen to know one or two things about them that the average parent never has a chance of learning."

"*Kate* said to you? Do you mean to say that you have been discussing our affairs with *Kate*?"

"If you think that, you'd think anything," said Andrew in weary disgust. "Of course I haven't. Kate wouldn't anyhow. You ought never to have asked a thing that."

Lucy, in the wrong, had a habit of instantly seizing on some other point which might in some twisted way help her to prove herself right. She did so now. "So you're rewarded for having left your children and neglected them for four years, by knowing more about them than I do, who had to be both parents to them during your absence!"

"Lucy, it's quite impossible to talk to you when you persist in being so utterly unreasonable," he said. "Of course I don't know more about the children than you do. It's more than I deserve to find that I know anything about them at all."

"It certainly is," said Lucy in a low tone full of bitter anger.

"Well, anyhow, Anne is to drive Cousin Charlotte in to Edinburgh, and bring Great-Uncle Henry back with her. She can have my car. Until the small one which I have ordered for her is delivered, she can keep her hand in on the Humber." And before Lucy could find words to disapprove, he swung round and left her.

But his face was drawn with temper and weariness, and he said to himself: "Can I possibly carry on with this? God knows I'm to blame, but unless Lucy can manage to stop reminding me of it every time I speak to her, it won't be bearable. It's unbearable now."

He found some slight consolation in Anne's pride and delight when, two mornings later, she brought his car round to the door, prepared to drive to Edinburgh. And Lucy, once she had seen the black hat and cape, the old-fashioned boxes and wraps which belonged to Cousin Charlotte, finally disappear round the bend of the drive, offered him as much of an apology as she could ever make.

"Anne does drive very well, Andrew. I'm glad you are going to give her a car of her own. And you must blame Cousin Charlotte if I lost my temper the other day. She really has worn my nerves to shreds."

Andrew, being Andrew, accepted the explanation with ready courtesy and a rather tired smile. He supposed that Great-Uncle Henry's effect on Lucy's nerves would supply her with a reason and an apology for any wounding thing she might say during the next week or so; but after that, what excuse would she have? Then, he decided, she would have to fall back on the original theme of his unworthiness. Anyhow, for the moment the sky was clear again, and he made the best of it.

As Great-Uncle Henry preferred to arrive just in time to dress for dinner, and Cousin Charlotte refused to put off her departure to convenience him, Anne had to spend the day in Edinburgh, and Andrew had returned from shooting Robin Anstruther's partridges by the time the car was heard coming back.

"Come on, Lucy. I'll meet him on the doorstep with you," said Andrew. "It always looks well."

They went out, and the others, Adam, Henry, Kate, and Mrs. Barlas, took up strategic positions in the hall where they could see the arrival.

The car came slowly round the curve and drew up at the door. Lucy uttered nails into Andrew's arm.

"It can't be—" she said.

"It damned well *is*," answered Andrew, as he went forward to the car, opened the door, and helped out the too familiar figure of Cousin Charlotte. Beyond her could be seen the Wellingtonian nose and white hair of Great-Uncle Henry, who, refusing Anne's assistance, climbed shakily out and tottered up the shallow steps. Over their heads Lucy signalled a frantic glance at Anne. She responded with a shrug and a look of helplessness.

"Well, Lucy, no doubt you are surprised to see me back, and not too well-pleased," said Cousin Charlotte. "I happened to meet Henry in Princes Street, and he had the effrontery to tell me that he was sorry I should not be here during his visit, as he wished to renew his victories over me at chess. His victories, indeed! As if he ever—"

"How do you do, Lucy, me dear," said Great-Uncle Henry, cutting Miss Napier short as few dared to do with a ruthlessness due partly to deafness and partly to enmity. "It is a long time since I had the pleasure of staying under your hospitable roof. Very kind of you and Andrew to invite an old man to join your happy party on this auspicious occasion. I well remember when I first visited you here. You were a bride, me dear, and a very charming one. You recalled to me a little dear Lady Margaret Gold-Finch, or was it Lady Rosamond? Tut-tut, I forget. I fancy it must have been Lady Rosamond, as I did not have the pleasure of meeting her sister Lady Margaret until later. She married Sir Warren Waveney, and—"

"Stop talking snob, Henry. You're a walking Debrett," said Cousin Charlotte, whose indignation, smouldering throughout this speech, now burst into flame. "Let me remind you once again that you have never checkmated me."

"Only at chess, Charlotte. Only at chess," said Great-Uncle Henry with a courtly bow and a wheezing chuckle at his own wit. "Which reminds me of the splendid struggles Lord Westwater and I used to have. Many a time they continued for days."

"I have always been able to beat yon within two hours," said Cousin Charlotte, flinging down the gauntlet.

"Never!" cried Great-Uncle Henry, picking it up with a flourish. "Never, Charlotte."

"Well, I have come back for no other reason but to prove that. I am right and you are wrong. After dinner we will start," said Miss Napier. "Lucy, perhaps you will be good enough to see that the chessboard and men are set out on that solid card-table—nothing rickety or too small, remember—in the billiard-room—"

"Not the billiard-room, Charlotte. The light is not good enough. The parlour," said Great-Uncle Henry.

"The billiard-room, Henry!"

"The parlour, Charlotte!"

They glared at one another, while the entire family, too stricken for speech, stood dumbly by like an audience at a play.

Finally Great-Uncle Henry, with a bow, waived his claim. "The billiard-room let it be, Charlotte," he said.

"We can play in the parlour to-morrow, Henry," said Cousin Charlotte in a voice which was almost a coo.

Together they passed through the hall in happy harmony, and Lucy looked at Andrew. "Two of them!" she whispered.

"My fault. I was too clever," he answered with a groan.

"My poor Andrew, how could you foresee this? It is an Act of God."

CHAPTER SEVEN

1

"It's a dashed dirty trick to make us work in the hols., I think," said Henry gloomily, kicking the stout teak of the garden bench on which he and Kate sat side by side eating half-ripe plums. "Did they set you a piece to learn in the summer holidays when you were at Saint Thimbleine's, Kate?"

"Far worse than mere learning, Henry. Sickening things like making collections of pressed wild flowers or doing a bit of embroidery. Not that I ever did them. Which doesn't mean," Kate added hastily, "that you are to neglect your holiday task, Henry. What is it?"

Henry spat out a plum-stone with vigour, watched it soar over a clump of lavender, and said: "Actually, ours isn't as rotten as that. But to have to learn the whole of *Julius Caesar*'s pretty steep, Kate, don't you think?"

"Oh, I don't know. It's a play that you're bound to know bits of already. How far have you got?"

"As far as that good fat scene between Brutus and Cascara, you know, the 'let me tell you, Cassius, you yourself Are much condemn'd to have an itching palm' one. I like it, but it's dull being both of 'em turn about."

"If I could have the book, to look up the pieces I forget," said Kate cautiously, "I might be one of them."

Henry dragged a mangled copy of *Julius Caesar* from his pocket and handed it to her. "There's a bit in the middle where Virginia put her feet after she'd been in the pigsty that's rather difficult to read," he said. "But I dare say you can manage."

'I dare say, if I don't have to hold my nose. Is it very piggy?" Kate sniffed suspiciously at the page which bore the imprints of paws, and decided that it was not too bad. "Who do you want me to be?"

"Cascara, it you don't mind, because I know him best. I'd better have a shot at the noble Brutus."

They began, and as Henry lost his first self-consciousness and desire to giggle, the drama of the scene took hold of him, and he and Kate thundered at each other to their mutual satisfaction.

"It's great stuff, really. Old William's not as sickly as those poets they make us read," said Henry condescendingly when they stopped for a rest. "I say, Kate, let's do it again—"

Once more they were 'within the tent of Brutus,' two Roman generals quarrelling fierily. Kate had reached Cassius' most dramatic speech, and declaimed with much feeling.

> *"Come, Antony, and young Octavius, come,*
> *Revenge yourselves alone on Cassius,*
> *For Cassius is aweary of the world:*
> *Hated by one he loves; brav'd by his brother:*
> *Checked like a bondman; all his faults observed.*
> *Set in a note-book, learn'd, and conn'd by rote,*
> *To cast into my teeth. O, I could weep*
> *My spirit from—"*

"'Enter Caesar, in his nightgown,'" observed Henry incorrectly.

"You little monster! You've spoilt my best bit!" cried Kate in a rage. "I hadn't even time to offer you my dagger! Oh—" she broke off, seeing for the first time that they had an audience of one. Andrew, approaching silently on the turfed path, stood near them, with one hand on the old pear tree.

"Excellent, Kate," he said. "Henry, your mother is looking for you. Something about red stockings for school. She wants to know if the old ones are to be thrown away. You'd better go and see about it for yourself."

"Gosh, I'd *better*. Those stockings are to be refooted. I'm not going back with new ones," said Henry. "'Thou shalt see me at Philippi,'" he muttered to Kate, and fled towards the garden door, Virginia dancing round him.

Andrew smiled, but Kate thought he looked tired and hipped and altogether forlorn. "Sit down and talk to me," she said. "It's nice here in the sun."

"I'm not very good company to-day," said Andrew, but he sat down beside her on the bench. "What was that speech were in the middle of when I interrupted?"

"Cassius and Brutus. You must know it."

"I'd like to hear you say it again. You've got a good voice for Shakespeare, Kate."

A little against her will, Kate repeated it. He said nothing for a moment, then:

"'All his faults observ'd, set in a note-book, learn'd and conn'd by rote, to cast into my teeth,'" he murmured. "Oh, well, I suppose I deserve it."

"Andrew!" cried Kate. "Surely no one does that?"

"You don't certainly. You've never cast my misdoings in my teeth," he said. "Though I can't imagine that you approve of them."

"No, I don't," Kate answered honestly. "But I think that you probably don't care for them much yourself."

"My God, if you knew what an utter cad I feel!" he muttered, so miserably that Kate was distressed.

"Oh, Andrew, don't take it so to heart," she said. "After *all*, you've done what you can to put it right. You've come back. Surely Lucy—"

"Lucy? I'm not thinking about Lucy!"

"Not?"

"No. It's Elizabeth. Think what a cad I've been to her."

This was quite a new point of view for Kate. Up till now, if she thought of Mrs. Fardell at all, it had been as the temptress, the woman who had made Robin unhappy, who had lured Andrew from his home, his wife and family. That *she* might also have been wronged simply had not occurred to her, until Andrew spoke. Then her imagination began to picture what it might be like for Mrs. Fardell. She had thrown away the security which every normal woman prizes for Andrew, and now had lost him too. It was her own fault, of course. How easy it had been to leave it at that, thought Kate, until one's eyes were opened to the consequences. Quite possibly Mrs. Fardell had not been happy with her husband, who looked so like a handsome carp, and, as far as could be told from one casual meeting, was as cold-blooded and dull as the fish he resembled. But at least she had had a home in a most lovely countryside, a settled position, friends and acquaintances. To Kate the worst thing was that not being able to return to the familiar shadow of Lammermuir, the rolling miles of hill and valley, the jagged sea-coast, Alewater winding between old willows, Haystoun dreaming in the sun. . . .

> Happy the craw
> That biggs i' the Trotten Shaw
> And drinks o' the Water of Dye,
> For nae mair may I.

She knew what had brought Andrew back, that love of the land which was stronger than any other tie. It had all been made comparatively easy for him because he was a man. . . .

"Oh, it's so unfair!" she burst out.

"What, particularly?"

"That you could come back, and she can't. Did she—was she fond of this country?"

"Yes, very. But leaving it could never have meant to her what it meant to me, you know, Kate. It's in my blood, while she was an in-comer. An old aunt of her husband's left Darnhall to him, or they'd never have come here. Sometimes I wish they hadn't."

"You left it for her, but you couldn't stay away. I know," said Kate. "I've always known that it must have taken something very big to make you desert Soonhope."

"It was something pretty big, all right," muttered Andrew. "Of course, neither of us was happy at home, and that drew us together to start with. We knew, without a word said. But we weren't so happy once we'd gone," he added, talking, Kate saw, more to himself than to her. "I suppose we've all got consciences, and ours were continually bothering us, spoiling what little happiness we had. All for love and the world well lost didn't apply to us. Perhaps we weren't young enough for that. Not that we minded about the world, but we had responsibilities, and I kept dreaming about Soonhope. she who made me write to Lucy. I'd have stuck it out, but she said she'd rather send me away than watch me hankering after home, and gradually blaming her for everything. I don't believe I would have done that, though, but I couldn't help my homesickness. . . . Oh, well, it's all over now. We might have been happy if things had been different, but happiness isn't life by any means."

"Everyone has the right to be happy," said Kate rebelliously.

"No doubt. But snatching at happiness that's out of reach doesn't do any good, Kate. Believe me, I know what I'm talking about."

"But suppose Lucy had divorced you, and Colonel Fardell had divorced his wife, you could have come back together and lived here—"

"And what about Adam? This place will be his some day, you know. It is his right to live here, and it couldn't have been done any other way but this. Lucy was right when she refused me a divorce," said Andrew with grim fairness.

"I'm very, very sorry for all of you," was the only thing Kate could find to say. "For you, and her—yes, and Lucy, too. "

"Why not add Fardell to your list of pitied? Isn't he in the same boat?" asked Andrew, laughing harshly.

"I don't believe he is. I don't feel sorry for him, somehow. If he was hurt at all it was only in his vanity," said Kate.

"As it happens, you are perfectly correct. Did you hear, by the way, that he is divorcing Elizabeth? Yes, now. After waiting for four years."

"Now? I wonder why—"

"Oh, he has probably seen someone he'd like to marry, and as, legally, he is merely an injured husband, a righteous man wronged, I haven't a doubt he will find a wife who will sympathize with him and tell all her friends that his first wife didn't understand him," said Andrew bitterly. "Now can you begin to see how I feel? Here am I, restored to my home and family, forgiven—on the surface, anyhow—by my long-suffering wife. There's Fardell, quit of a woman he drove almost mad by his selfishness and lack of all human feelings, free to marry anyone he fancies. And Elizabeth—Elizabeth carries back the can!"

Kate, her heart sticking somewhere at the back of her throat, her knees turned to pulp, gulped and said in a thick voice: "What—what about Robin? If Colonel Fardell divorces her, she could marry Robin."

She spoke so huskily that she was afraid that he wouldn't hear, and then he would ask her what she had said, and she would have to repeat the words that clamoured in her ears: "She could marry Robin." But Andrew had heard, and turned an amazed face to her.

"Upon my word, Kate, you're the most astonishing young woman. I didn't know you knew about Robin, poor devil. Who told you?"

"Remember, Andrew, this is Haystoun," said Kate with a flippancy which sounded lamentably false to her. "Who told me? Old Mrs. Milligan, of course. She knows everything that goes on. Nothing is hid from her, from people's most private love-affairs to what they pay for their Sunday joint."

"Old bitch! Sorry, Kate, I meant *witch*, but the other is more suitable."

"Poor Virginia!" murmured Kate pensively, and was rewarded by hearing him laugh.

"Yes, you're right. We'll leave it at witch. But about Robin— Lord, how angry he'd be if he guessed that it was public property, and no wonder. This place is a cess-pit of gossip and scandal," said Andrew angrily. "What made you say that Elizabeth could marry him, Kate? She always liked him. I never could see why she didn't prefer him to me, but she didn't and she doesn't love him. She'll never marry again, I'm pretty sure. If she did, it wouldn't be Robin. Anyhow, I think he's getting over that affair now. It's four years ago now, remember."

"'Love's not Time's fool,'" said Kate.

"I fancy that wasn't written about love that was not returned," said Andrew shrewdly. "And though your solution sounds excellent, a fine easy way out, happy-ending sort of business for all concerned, there are so many holes to be picked in it that it would soon look like a fishing-net."

"You know far more about it than I do," said Kate meekly, though she was not convinced of this. "It was just an idea. I hoped it might make you feel better about it."

"It wouldn't if I believed it. We're selfish brutes, Kate, and I can't say I fancy the thought of Elizabeth and Robin married. Dog in the manger, of course, but there you are! Don't you worry, anyhow, bless your kind heart. I do feel better after making my moan to you," he said, putting his arm round her and giving her a hearty hug.

It was unfortunate that this innocent and brotherly act should have coincided with Lucy's appearance.

"Andrew!" she exclaimed, her voice sharp with annoyance, her eyes darting suspiciously from one to the other. "I've been looking for you everywhere. I sent Adam and Henry to find you, and finally had to come myself, though it was most inconvenient at the moment, when I am busy going through the boys' school clothes."

"Well, Lucy, I'm sorry. I should have thought I was easy enough to find. I haven't been hiding," said Andrew good-humouredly, though his brows had drawn together in a displeased pucker. He disliked this hectoring tone of Lucy's at any time, and before Kate he considered it in the worst of taste. "And now that you've discovered me, what am I wanted for?" he ended dryly.

"A man has come down from Pennymuir with some bullocks, and wants to know which held they are to go into," said Lucy, her annoyance changing to sulkiness as she realized that she had roused Andrew to temper. "I can hardly be expected to know about the farm as well as everything else."

"Certainly not," Andrew agreed with a smoothness which struck Kate as dangerous. "I'll come."

"By the way, Kate, there was a note for you, from Robin, brought by the cattleman," said Lucy, producing a letter from her jersey-pocket. "I thought I might find you with Andrew."

"Thank you," said Kate, and watched them walk away. 'I know Lucy was hoping I'd ask if I could do anything to help her, so that she'd have the pleasure of refusing,' she thought.

As she turned again on the garden-seat, she kicked something at her foot, and found that it was Henry's forgotten copy of *Julius Caesar*. "Now lies he there," she murmured, picking it up. A loose page fluttered out, and as she stooped again, she recognized it as the one used by Virginia as a mat, with the speech which she had repeated to Andrew on it. She put it back in its place, and her eyes fell on Brutus's reply, and she read it through.

"'Cassius, you are yoked with a lamb,' she said aloud. "For 'Cassius' read 'Lucy,' and it's true. I know he didn't treat her as he should have, but I wonder if it ever, ever enters her head that she is behaving absolutely abominably to him?"

When she heard the click of the garden door shutting, and knew that she was quite alone, Kate looked at her letter, the first she had ever had from Robin Anstruther. The envelope bore several excellent impressions of the cattleman's prints, but that did not matter. There was her name: 'Miss Kate Heron' in a decided black handwriting . . . At last, after she had turned it over and examined it thoroughly, she opened it and read:

> *My dear Kate* [wrote Robin],
> *It seems a long time since I saw you except at dinner parties and such, which don't count, do they? I have to go to London for a few days—deuced awkward with the harvest in full swing—but when I get back, will you dine with me in Edinburgh and go to a show if there's anything decent on? Say Tuesday or Wednesday of next week. Send me a note to Pennymuir. Yours, Robin.*

For a long time Kate sat, the letter in her hand, staring at the garden without really seeing it. Gladiolus, dahlias, first of the Michaelmas daisies, all danced before her eyes in a brightly coloured haze. Robin had written to her, Robin had said that it seemed a long time since he had seen her, Robin had asked her to go out with him, just the two of them.

If the unwelcome thought crept into her mind that this was all because she was like his lost love in some ways, she pushed it determinedly away again. Nothing was going to spoil this for her, nothing!

Something did, of course, as it so often does. Feeling happy, and wanting to please other people if she could—Kate was never so good as when she was happy, adversity had the most souring effect on her—she accompanied her grandmother to tea with Mrs. Milligan. She had not been asked, and thought both her hostesses looked at her very queerly indeed. And in that hot room, where human voices buzzed like flies caught in the web of Mrs. Milligan's gossip, she heard the old woman say, with many meaning nods of the head and wavings of the fat useless hands: "I hear that Robin

Anstruther has hurried off to London. Of course we all know *why*. With harvest going on and everything, it would take a good deal to drag a farmer away from home at this time of year. Yes. Mrs. Fardell is in London. I have it on the *best* authority. A friend of mine saw her in Harrods's and mentioned it to Flora in a letter. And you've heard . . ."

Buzz, buzz, buzz.

Kate, trying to talk to someone else, straining her ears against her will to catch the rest of this piece of news, only heard the end of it.

". . . Divorce all arranged, and much as I dislike and disapprove of it, one can hardly blame Colonel Fardell, poor man. Once she is free, of course. . . . Of *course* that is the reason of this hurried dash to London—really a trifle premature, but what can one expect? You know he always cared for her, though I must say I never saw anything very remarkable about her looks. And as for her morals . . ."

2

"There's nothing worth bolting dinner and giving ourselves indigestion to go and see," said Robin cheerfully as be drove Kate towards Edinburgh. "So I've brought you out under false pretences. Do you mind?"

"Not a bit," answered Kate with equal cheerfulness. Her first impulse, after bearing Mrs. Milligan discoursing to her friends on the reason for Robin's going to London, had been to write to him and contradict her acceptance of his invitation. But a very little thought had shown her that this must lead to questions, and she left it alone. Now that she was with him, friendliness and the gaiety proper to the occasion must be her line, and it was not proving as difficult as she had expected.

The Post Road stretched straight in front of them, the car ate up the miles as if trying to catch the sun, which was sinking, a globe of fiery orange, into the invisible Firth. Already in the east a large primrose-coloured full moon was floating in the hazy sky, there were drifts of mist in the hollows, the Lammermuirs were cut of pure amethyst.

"Well," said Robin, glancing at her for a moment, "what shall we do? Just sit and talk, or have sixpenn'orthhand of hot hand at the movies, or dance? I seem to remember your once saying that all your brains were in your feet."

"Whatever you like. I really don't mind a bit. You choose," said Kate, the cheerfulness stop pulled out to its fullest extent.

"I don't seem to recognize this meekness," he said. "It doesn't suit you, Kitty. I don't think I care for you meek."

"'Yoked with a lamb,'" murmured Kate, but he heard her and gave a short laugh which sounded extremely heartwhole and free from care.

"Which is the lamb?" he asked rudely. "No one could have been less lamblike than you on your leek-stealing expedition."

"That was a special occasion," said Kate with dignity.

"I refuse to be yoked with a lamb this evening," he said. "So you'd better hurry up and say what you want to do."

"Dance, then, if you're good at it. If not, sit and talk."

"That's more like you. 'If I'm good at it!' My dear child, I was dancing before you were born."

"Perhaps that's what I'm afraid of. Dancing has changed a lot since then. And anyhow, if you were dancing before I was born, it must have been at a dancing-class for little boys," retorted Kate. "And you were the worst-behaved of the lot."

"Quite wrong. As a really little boy I was surprisingly good," he told her. "All right, we'll dance. There's a do on at one of the hotels, a gala night of some description. We'll go there."

"Must we go to Edinburgh at all?" suddenly asked Kate.

"Now you're being contrary," he said reprovingly. "I think, if you remember, I asked you to dine with me in Edinburgh. It's not for you to pick holes in the place once you've accepted."

"You see, I'm so bucolic," pleaded Kate. "All my tastes are for the country, and it's much too lovely an evening to spend in any town, even Edinburgh. Besides, haven't you had enough of streets and lights after being in London?"

"I'll take you over into Berwickshire, then, and if you have to wait a long time for your dinner don't blame me."

"I won't," Kate said gaily, her carefully assumed cheerfulness quite forgotten, as he turned the big car into a side road leading south towards the Lammermuirs. They passed farm-steadings, the red roofs of the cottages rosy in the last level rays of the sun, the gardens brilliant with dahlias, they crossed Alewater where willows traded silver-grey branches in the dark water, and as they began to climb, the sun disappeared. Now, looking back, Kate could see all the valley filled with milky vapour behind them. The moon, growing every moment more luminous, hung like a yellow Chinese lantern in the south-eastern sky, the evening star shone, the first hunting owl swept across the road on broad silent wings, plover cried plaintively in the grass fields. It was almost dark in the low ground, but when they reached the ridge of the hills they could still see, and not until they were swooping down the southern slope did Robin switch on the lights, showing scared rabbits scampering before them along the roadside, white scuts bobbing, and the occasional green eyes of a wandering cat.

The ruins of a castle stood up sinister and jagged against the cold duck-egg green sky, and presently they whirled into a little town and drew up on a large open space of ground before an hotel. Above the modern A.A. and R.A.C. signs on the lichened walls were gilt capital letters, a little out of the straight now, but still easy to read: 'Post Horses.' The door stood open and light streamed broadly out to welcome them. Kate, as she went up the steps, said with a sigh of satisfaction: "This is *much* nicer than "Edinburgh."

A competent young woman in a well-cut tweed skirt and hand-knitted jersey assured them that they could have dinner as soon as they had drunk the sherry ordered by Robin, and they were shown into a lounge where a large fire was burning.

"I'm not at all sure you aren't right," said Robin, leaning comfortably against the high mantel. "But of course Edinburgh isn't much good until winter. Suppose I'd offered you dinner at a really good London restaurant instead of this, which would you have chosen?"

"This," said Kate promptly. "I'm not at all smart myself, and smart places usually terrify me. Very occasionally I long to sweep into one of them looking too dazzling for anything but a mannequin, but it never happens, of course. If I am asked, I haven't a dress worthy of the invitation, and have to slink to the table looking and feeling the complete country cousin that I really am."

"You have too much poise for a country cousin," said Robin gravely, looking at her as he drank his excellent dry sherry. "And then, you walk so beautifully. You know, Kate, the first time you walked into the Soonhope dining-room in front of me in that black dress you were wearing, the only words that fitted it were those hackneyed ones, 'she walked like a queen.'"

"Oh, thank you, Robin! Grey always teases me and says I go about like Little-Johnny-Head-in-Air."

"Certainly you don't slouch. Do you want to? I should think that round-backed, head-poked-forward position could be learnt quite easily but I hope you'll never adopt it," he said. "Now, what about dinner?"

It was a simple but well-served meal, and their fellow diners appeared to be a party who were staying in the hotel for shooting, the women not too smart to frighten Kate, the men, their weather-beaten faces very red and brown above their white shirt-fronts, eating hungrily, and when they talked at all, speaking only of bags and drives and beaters.

"They come here every year," said Robin, noticing that Kate had glanced across the room at them, "It's a syndicate, of course. They start with grouse, and about now or a little later they get any number of geese. You ought to see the geese flighting, Kate, it's a wonderful sight. I'll speak to Drew about it."

Later, as they went back to the lounge for coffee, he said, "I don't think we'll stay here for long. I know one or two of these fellows slightly, and if we get mixed up in a poker game or something with them, Lord knows when we'll ever get home. So we'll push off as soon as we've had coffee, if you don't mind."

Leaving Kate by the fire, he went to pay the bill, and having done so, met the two men he knew in the hall.

"Hullo! What are you doing here, Anstruther?"

"Dining," said Robin rather shortly. "No, I can't stay, Bruce. I've got a lady with me. What sort of bags have you been getting this season?"

"Never mind the bags—they'll keep. I've been hearin' stories about you, my boy. Hear you've taken to roamin' round Haystoun in the middle of the night with your girlfriends. A bit careless, eh?"

"I don't know where you get hold of your gossip," said Robin, his dark, face unpleasantly pale with anger, "but you've been misinformed in this instance."

"Oh! Well, it's all over the place," said his acquaintance, who had obviously dined very well indeed. "Some old trout dropped in here to tea one day when we happened to be in a bit earlier ourselves, and they were full of it. Couldn't help overhearin' them, they were at the next table. All rumour, no doubt, and, anyway, what's the harm in it?"

"None, if it happened to be true, which it isn't," said Robin. "I'd be obliged if you'll contradict it the next time anyone says it to you." Inwardly he was cursing, it was quite evident that some busybody had seen Kate and him on their leek-stealing excursion. First and last, those leeks had been an infernal nuisance.

"Cert'nly, cert'nly, old boy," said Bruce obligingly, trying to slap Robin on the back and almost losing his precarious balance as Robin moved aside and he smote empty air. "All between friends. And how's Lockhart these days? Hear his wife's taken him back; and he's up to his old tricks already, carryin' on with a cousin of his he's got stayin' at Soonhope. Damned useful, these cousins, what?"

"That," said Robin very gently, "is a damned lie."

"Eh? Call me a liar, would you?" Bruce was becoming belligerent. "No man can call me a liar and get away with it."

"I can, and I do," said Robin. "And if you weren't drunk it would give me great pleasure to knock you down."

"What? What? Knock me down? Try it and see—"

"Oh, take him away and put him to bed," said Robin wearily to the other man, who had stood all this time looking on with a sardonic smile. "It's all he's fit for."

As Bruce, still loudly proclaiming that he'd show anyone who called him a liar that he was a liar himself, was dragged off by his friend, Robin turned and went back to the lounge.

Kate, her coffee untasted, was standing in the middle of the room, her eyes sparkling with anger. "I heard it all," she said, as he looked anxiously at her. "The girl who brought the coffee left the door open. How dared that revolting man say such vile things? I'd like to kill him."

"So should I," said Robin. "Except that he isn't worth swinging for. He's a friend of Fardell's, which explains a lot. Don't let it worry you, Kate. What does it matter if the whole of Haystoun saw us that night?"

"Us? I'm not thinking of that. There's no reason why we shouldn't dance a rumba in front of the Town Hall at two in the morning if we choose. It's what he said about Andrew. Robin, has Andrew always got to have things like that said about him just because of what he did when he was so unhappy that he couldn't help himself?"

"It doesn't matter what damn' fools like Bruce say. No one pays any attention to him," said Robin, thankful that she had not noticed her own connection with the piece of slander. The next moment, however, he knew that he had been thankful too soon.

"Cousin, indeed!" she said scornfully, with a laugh. "Cousin! Was the creature talking about *Mother*, do you suppose? She's Andrew's cousin—" Something in his look stopped her.

"Think again," he said.

"But—but who? Robin, he can't possibly have been talking about me?"

He nodded. "I'm afraid he was. I wish now that I *had* knocked him down, drunk or not, the foul-tongued brute."

To his great relief she was astonished and angry, but still for Andrew's sake. "How absolutely absurd!" she said. "I never heard anything so silly in my life, did you? I'd laugh at it if it weren't that it's such a shame for poor Andrew. I wonder they don't accuse him of making love to Cousin Charlotte!"

"You've taken up the cudgels for Andrew now, I see," he said. "I thought you were on Lucy's side?"

"It's all so difficult," sighed Kate, her brow puckered in a puzzled frown. She sat down and drank some of the lukewarm coffee. "You see, I still know that Lucy is in the right, but she is so awfully nasty about it. Why is it that so many people who are right have the effect of making you prefer the people who are wrong? I know that Andrew behaved very badly, yet now, every time I see him with Lucy, it's *he* who behaves well, and Lucy who is horrible. If I were sure I was right I'd be so pleased with myself that I'd be nice to the other person."

"A bit involved, aren't you?" said Robin, "but I know what you mean. It isn't a question of right and wrong, really. It's just that Andrew has the knack of attaching people to him, partly by his own kindliness, partly by what's rather loosely called 'character' these days; and Lucy hasn't the knack, and so she feels it and takes it out of Drew. It's been like that all along, Kate. It will always be like that, because you can't change a person s nature."

"Well, I'm dreadfully afraid that unless Lucy is a great deal nicer to Andrew, he won't be able to stand it. And this time he'll have Anne and Adam and Henry on his side, right or wrong," Kate said soberly. "and what will Lucy do then?"

"God knows, but *we* can't do anything. To interfere would only make matters a hundred per cent worse," said Robin.

"Can't we? Couldn't you? Lucy likes you——"

"Not a hope," said Robin firmly. "You don't drag me into any more escapades, my dear. Do you realize that you've got to live down the 'orrid scandal of being seen with me at midnight in Haystoun?"

"Pooh!" said Kate. "Do you mind much?"

"I can bear it. Now come on, and we'll get away before any more of Bruce's tiddly friends come and annoy us. My temper's a bit frayed already, and you don't want to be mixed up in a vulgar brawl, do you?"

"I'd love it," Kate assured him. "You may as well know it, I'm a fishwife at heart, and no lidy. I'd take part in a brawl joyfully."

"I believe you would," he said with a groan. "But you're not going to have the chance. Come on." He took her by the arm and almost ran her out to the car.

"We aren't going *home*?" she asked disappointedly as they started.

"Haven't you had enough excitement for one evening?"

"No. I want something to take the nasty taste out of my mouth after dear Mr. Bruce. Could we drive rather slowly and go by all the little roads? It's not much after nine o'clock."

"It'll be after ten by the time we get back to Haystoun," he reminded her.

"Ten? What's ten to a person who is seen out at midnight?" said Kate magnificently. "Unless you're tired of me?" she added with a sudden drop in her voice.

"Now you're talking like a fool," he said. "I won't reassure you, you don't deserve it. but I'll go slowly, by the side roads, and we'll probably be lost and have to stay out all night."

"That will give Haystoun something fresh to talk about," said Kate, settling down under her rug and laughing.

The moon, riding high, was a silver honesty penny, shedding a wan clear light on the fields, which had all been led in this low, sheltered land, and now lay bare, the blonde stubble glimmering faintly under the moon. Hedges and trees and houses were black silhouettes, an occasional signpost at a cross-roads showed like a ghostly figure with arms outstretched. The lights of the car picked out details haphazard—a rat scurrying across the road, evil sharp nose and long tail, a clump of tall grasses, their heads heavy with seed, a hawthorn bush, the polished haws shining, a hedgehog, its spines laid along its round back, toddling doucely homeward. The unpleasant encounter at the hotel began to seem vastly unimportant to Kate, on whom the strange beauty of the country at night was having its effect.

"Where are we now?" she asked idly after a time.

"I haven't the least idea. We're going vaguely in the right direction, unless this road changes its mind, but beyond that, I don't know," he said, as if it did not matter much.

All that mattered to Kate was that she was sitting beside him sharing this magic. If she had been in the habit of quoting Browning, which she was not, for she had an absurd dislike of him, she would have found her feelings expressed for her with a poet's easy eloquence in *The Last Ride Together*.

"Look, there's a light!" she exclaimed as they turned a sharp corner. "Oh, Robin—music! Do stop, it's a dance or something!"

Resigned and amused, he stopped the car beside a small building which from its shape and size seemed to be one of those wooden, corrugated-iron-roofed huts so frequently erected as village halls in remote parts of the country. "I believe it's a kirn. They don't have many nowadays," he said, as the sounds of music, the stamping of many heavy feet, came more clearly to their ears.

"A kirn?"

"A harvest-home dance. We might go and have a look at it."

"What fun they're having!" said Kate, as the *Flowers of Edinburgh*, recognizable only from the short snatches of tune heard at intervals, pounded gaily on. A middle-aged bearing the fine hallmark of shepherd from his keen, clear eyes to his enormous boots, saw them, and tramped relentlessly through the dancing crowd to speak to them.

"Ay, it's a kirn. This is Wideopen an' Seefew ha'. Step ben, sir, an' the leddy. It's no' sae warrum ootbye as it is in here. By! if it's no' Maister Anstruther o' Pennymuir! Ma maister bocht in three score Cheviot yowes aff Pennymuir a fortnicht syne at Bo'sel's mart! Ye're welcome, sir," as Robin, thanking him for the invitation, went inside. Kate was already over the threshold, her foot tapping in time to the merry air ground out by a piano and two accordions.

"Ou, it's juist a sma' affair, oor ain, an' nae incomers," explained the shepherd, producing, as if by sleight of hand, a hard wooden chair, and setting it for Kate out of the draught from the open doorway. "There's singin' tae. They'll be giein' us anither sang in a meenit. It gies them time tae get their breath, an' pleases the auld fowk. Sit ye doon."

As it was one of the dancers who, wiping his face with a large red handkerchief, and panting visibly, jumped on to the tiny platform as soon as the dance ended, Kate felt that he, at least, was not being given much opportunity to 'get his breath;' but he seemed delighted with his importance, and burst without pause into a long chant about an 'Ah-rab steed.'

> *"Ma bee-autifu', ma beautifu'*
> *That stahndest meakully by,"* he bawled mournfully.

His audience sighed in an ecstasy of sentiment, and the shepherd, with pride, muttered in Robin's car; "Ay, he's the lad, is Dand. it's aye a sang aboot horse he gies them, him bein' horseman at Wideopen, ye ken."

It seemed an excellent reason, and satisfactory to everyone, for when the singer, having given up his Ahrab steed, announced the fact in a last bellow of manly resignation, and jumped off the platform, he was applauded with such vigour that the dust, which had subsided a little, swirled through the place like a sand-storm.

"Are you being choked?" said Robin, as Kate sneezed several times.

"Yes. But it is worth choking for. It's grand entertainment. Do please let us stay," she answered before another burst of sneezing checked her.

"They're wantin' anither sang, an' there's no' a soul can oblige," said the shepherd, who appeared to be master of ceremonies, anxiously. He turned his appealing eyes on Robin, who affected a fine air of unconsciousness. "Sirr?" he murmured hopefully.

"No, no. They don't want to hear me. Let them, sing themselves," said Robin hastily.

"Robin, do you sing?" asked Kate in surprise, for she had never suspected him of this accomplishment.

"I make a noise," he said most reluctantly. "I have never called it 'singing.'"

"Then make your noise!" Kate turned to the shepherd. "Mr. Anstruther will sing," she said, heedless of Robin's frown.

"You take a good deal upon yourself, don't you?" he growled, as the shepherd made a suitable announcement from the platform.

"I want to hear you, Robin. Don't be cross."

"Well, you'll have to vamp an accompaniment and help with the chorus," he said, taking her by the hand and helping her up the single high step to the stage, where he led her to the piano stool. He did not seem in the least nervous as he turned to face his hushed and expectant audience, and said in his careless, commanding voice: "I'm going to sing my one and only comic song to you. *Phil the Fluter's Ball*, and you can all join in the chorus, or I'll stop singing."

Kate, wildly picking out what she hoped were appropriate chords on a defective piano, had not much attention to spare for the singer, but she liked his voice in the cheerful piece of Irish nonsense, and it was plain that everyone else liked it too from the continuous stamping of feet in time to the music, and the thundering cheers which nearly lifted the tin roof at the end.

"No more. I told you I only knew one song," sad Robin. "Besides, I came here to dance. Where's the band?"

Amid laughter, the band arrived on the stage and struck up *The Dashing White Sergeant*, and Robin, seizing Kate with one hand and an elderly ploughman's wife with the other, whirled them into the dance, a riotous measure in the course of which each set of three progressed round the room, meeting all the others and exchanging backchat with them at the full pitch of powerful country lungs.

While they sat regaining their breath and an earnest young woman recited: "*The Highwayman*, by Alfred Noyes," the shepherd creaked over to their bench and whispered proudly, "I've askit the baun' tae gie ye ane o' thae modderrun dances, a fox-step, for the next."

"Oh, thank you!" murmured Kate, struggling with laughter and lack of breath combined. "How very good of you. And to Robin, when he had tiptoed noisily away again: "We'll have to do this most superbly, or they'll be so disappointed."

"A fox-step," said Robin thoughtfully. "Well, we can only try, but it sounds difficult. I wonder what the 'baun' will play for us?"

It was a little disconcerting to find that the fox-step was apparently in the nature of an exhibition number, and for a little they sat nervously on their bench, unable to bring themselves to take the floor. But the two accordions, loudly playing *Phil the Fluter's Ball* as an additional compliment, the grieved look on the shepherd's weather-beaten face, finally brought them to their feet.

"Come on, some of you, and dance," said Robin loudly. "You don't expect us to do it alone?"

"Gie's a lead, man, an' we'll folly ye!" roared some man, bolder than the rest, from the safe shelter of a grove of his companions.

"Right!" said Robin. He put his arm round Kate and swung her into the middle of the floor.

The first step told her not only that he was an exceedingly good dancer, but that their steps matched admirably. Kate forgot the onlookers, forgot the humpy floor, the wheezing, grunting accordions, and danced as she had never danced in her life. Her feet felt as if they had wings attached to them, she followed his intricate steps without trouble, and all the time she was conscious of his hard arm holding her, of her fingers lying in the palm of his other hand, of wishing that they need never stop.

It was a shock when the exhausted band suddenly ceased to play, and they found themselves left standing rather foolishly on the dancing floor. "We'll go now," said Robin suddenly. "You've had enough of this." He spoke harshly, and Kate, still caught away by the enchanted rhythm of the dance, to which her heart had not stopped beating or her feet tingling, felt as if she had fallen without warning into a snowdrift. Looking at him, she saw that the frown, deep and straight as a sword-cut, disfigured his forehead, and she sighed. 'Remembering that he used to dance with *her*, I suppose,' she thought resentfully.

"Are you ready to go home? It's late," he said more gently.

"Yes, I'm ready," Kate said in subdued way, and in a minute they had exchanged the heat and dust and clamour of the but for the cool night wind and the sailing moon, remote and small now in the middle of a dark blue arch of sky. The soft air, carrying with it the faint sweet scent of stubble fields, cut corn stalks and dying clover wet with dew, blew refreshingly in their hot faces, there was a stir in the heavy-leaved dark trees.

"Cross with me for dragging you away?" Robin asked in his old half-teasing, half-fond voice, after they had left the hall a mile or two behind.

"Cross? No, I'm not cross. I thought *you* were."

"Is that why you're so quiet? I've managed to frighten you?" he said, and added: "Very good for you, Kate."

"Pig," said Kate, but she said it drowsily, for her head was nodding already, and presently she slipped lower in her seat and fell asleep in earnest, her head against his arm. Robin, after one look at her, stared straight ahead at the strip of road and hedge-row which leaped into life as the car lights flashed over it. Now that she was sleeping, her thoughts ranging free, and probably far from him, he was more acutely conscious of her than ever before. Even when he had danced with her, feeling the springing vitality of her body against his arm, she had not impressed herself so strongly on him. At first faintly amused by her, finding her good company, it had given him a kind of painful pleasure to trace her fleeting resemblance to Elizabeth Fardell, shown in some impulsive act, some chance word or quick gesture. Now he wanted her company always, he wanted to go on finding her amusing and dear all the rest of his life. A little gloomily he remembered the sixteen years between them; but Kate had never behaved as if he were so much older than her brother, young Grey. She treated all men as if they were both older and younger than herself, from her father to Henry Lockhart . . . . He drove very quietly through Waystoun, and half-way up the Soonhope Drive, stopped the car.

"Kate," he said, putting an arm round her, "wake up. We're at Soonhope. Will you walk to the house from here? If I take the car all the way someone's sure to drag me in for a drink, and I want to get home."

"Home—to that awful dwarfish MacOstrich," said Kate drowsily. "I wonder you can bear to call it home. A woman like that would give an Institution feeling to the cosiest cottage."

With a pang he realised that she was right. There would be no welcome for him at Pennymuir except from the dogs, and perhaps the chill disapproving figure of his housekeeper hovering in the background silently condemning his lateness.

"I must get rid of that woman!" he exclaimed aloud.

"You never will, my poor dear. Someone will have to do it for you," said Kate, sitting up straight and rubbing her eyes. "Oh, dear, I am so sleepy! What cheerful company I must have been for you, Robin, all the way home. I'm really very sorry."

"I don't mind. I was thinking."

"I've been dreaming. I dreamt you were still in London," said Kate. "And I couldn't think who was driving me about the country. Even in my dreams I was worried that it might be Andrew, and Lucy would be cross with him. The result of that horrid man at the hotel, I suppose."

"Never mind him. Forget all that," he said. "Now I'm going to walk up the drive with you and see you safely into the house."

He drew her hand through his arm, and they started, stumbling a little at first in the thick darkness made by the beech-trees.

"So you dreamt I was in London, Kate? What do you think I went up for?" he asked. He was paving the way, leading up to what he wanted to say to her: that he was free of his love for Elizabeth, had done what he felt was the only decent thing he could do, and was finished with it. Would Kate understand that he wasn't really fickle? That his love for Elizabeth, though true enough, had been woven of dream-fabric, unable to stand the wear and tear of everyday life, grown out of a desire for what he could not possess . . . In his rather blundering fashion he imagined that Kate would realize what he was driving at, and he was taken by the little quiver of distress in her voice as she said: "If what old Mrs. Milligan was hinting is true, you went to see Mrs. Fardell."

"Damn that old woman!" he said uneasily. "She never utters a word that isn't poisonous." For of course he had not expected this, and it made his next remark take on a meaning which sounded more misleading than he guessed.

"Yes. I went to see Elizabeth." They were very near the door now, and Kate was pressing on as if in a hurry to be in. He held her back, gently enough, but firmly, while he continued. "She's getting her divorce—or rather, Fardell's getting his, and though the decree nisi is through, I only heard of it the other day—just before I went up to town. I—I asked her to marry me, Kate."

"Yes?" Kate sounded breathless, as though she had been running, and they were at the door. Her foot was on the lowest step.

"She refused me," he ended rather lamely, worried by her manner. And he was still more worried when she cried, softly but with a kind of rage in her voice: "She refused you? Oh, Robin, poor, poor Robin, I'm so sorry! And it was all the sweeter of you to take me out this evening, and I have loved it, but now I'm so—so awfully tired, I *must* go in!"

Indeed, she was perilously near to tears. It was bad enough to be reminded of how much he loved this woman who cared for no one but Andrew: so much that he had gone at once to London to ask her to marry him when he had heard she was divorced; but to be expected to sympathize with him was more than she could bear after the lovely evening which she had enjoyed so much in spite of the after-dinner contretemps. She must be alone to pull herself together. So: "What can I say, Robin?" she repeated piteously. 'Except that I am—was afraid this might happen, and I—I'm so *very* sorry!"

She ran up the steps, pushed the door, which fortunately for her, yielded at once, and next moment was inside the darkened house, pushing home the bolts, turning the key as if afraid that he might follow her in.

5

Kate woke next morning heavy-headed, with a dismal feeling of having failed Robin when he needed her help and comfort. This was not lessened by the sound of rain falling steadily out of low grey skies which looked as it they could go on weeping for days on end. Going down to breakfast, she found the others hardly more cheerful. Henry, moping over his porridge, was already in the depths of woe at thought of his approaching parting with Virginia and the fear that his beloved would be miserable in his absence. Anne and

Adam, who had been looking forward for days to playing in a tennis tournament at Charteris, which the rain had now obviously made impossible, ate in mournful silence. Those two ancient enemies, Cousin Charlotte and Great-Uncle Henry, indulged in gloomy prophecies as to the practical certainty of a World War which would instantly annihilate the entire civilian population, breaking out at any moment; while Lucy, in a state of tense annoyance aggravated by their croaking, frowned alternately at the silver teapot, on which were several smeary fingerprints, and the small fire which she had ordered to be lighted, and which was fulfilling Florence's fears by smoking gustily. The only person who seemed in her usual mood of quiet content was Mrs. Barlas, and Kate suddenly loved her more than ever as she smiled back at the peaceful blue-eyed face. Dear Granny! Always anxious that everyone should be happy, she was looking warningly from her grand-daughter to Lucy as if to say: "Look out for squalls."

Andrew, entering the dining-room in unsuspecting good spirits, brought the smouldering embers of several tempers to a blaze.

"Good morning, everyone. Sorry to be late, but I had to dash up to the farm and see the grieve," he said. "Lucy, my dear, your fire's smoking."

"So I see," said Lucy with a baleful glance which should have extinguished the fire at once.

"Any news?" he added cheerfully, clattering the lids of various dishes on the hot-plate. "I suppose some of you have seen the morning papers by now?"

"I am sure that either Cousin Charlotte or Great-Uncle Henry will be delighted to tell you all the gloomiest bits of news," said Lucy, filling his cup with cold tea and forgetting to add any sugar. "Personally, as I have several things to do and have already been treated to a résumé of all the horrors, I must ask you all to excuse me. Henry, stop being idiotic about that dog and come with me to look at your navy-blue shorts. They seem to me to be far too small for you." She rose and left the room, shutting the door with a furious gentleness infinitely more alarming than a mere bang.

"Dear me!" murmured Andrew mildly as he brought a plate of kidney and bacon to his place. "Something seems to have upset Lucy?"

"Apparently," said Great-Uncle Henry with tremulous dignity, rising and twisting his table-napkin as if he were wringing someone's neck. "Apparently the mere presence of Charlotte and myself, far more our innocently expressed opinions, seems to be sufficient to upset Lucy. That being so, I propose to return to Edinburgh this morning, Andrew. I believe there is a train at eleven-fourteen from Haystoun. I don't know what Charlotte intends to do, but for myself, I certainly cannot stay in a house where my hostess so obviously resents my presence."

"I quite agree with you, Henry. I shall travel to Edinburgh by the same train," exclaimed Cousin Charlotte, also getting up.

"This is very sudden," said Andrew, still unperturbed in appearance at least. "Adam, open the door for Cousin Charlotte. There's no necessity for you to forget your manners because your tennis-party has fallen through. Anne, go and tell your mother that Cousin Charlotte and Great-Uncle Henry are leaving almost at once." And as the four, a little disconcerted, went from the dining-room in a body: "Give me a cup of hot tea, will you, Kate?" Andrew continued. "And if there's none, ring the bell."

Kate, her own troubles momentarily forgotten in an increasing amusement, rang the bell, and sat down again beside her grandmother, who was still eating toast and marmalade.

The door flew open and Lucy came in. "Andrew! What's this I hear?" she cried.

"I don't know what you've heard, my dear," said Andrew. "Oh, Nina"—as the table-maid hovered in the background expectantly. "Make me some fresh tea, please, and not too weak."

Lucy waited, fuming, until the maid had gone, and Andrew placidly ate kidney and bacon.

"Anne came to me with an absurd tale about Cousin Charlotte and old Henry," she burst out, as he said nothing. "She said that they were leaving this morning. Is it true?"

"Perfectly, unless they change their minds," said Andrew. "But they not only announced that they were going, but mentioned a train. The eleven-fourteen, I think it was."

"But what *happened*?" almost screamed Lucy. "Don't sit there eating as if nothing had *happened*! Tell me at once why they're going. You must have offended them somehow."

"On the contrary, I haven't spoken to either of to say good-morning," answered Andrew. "And as you find them so much on your nerves, Lucy, why worry? Let 'em go. You've wanted to get rid of them since they came, and now it's being handed to you on a plate."

Kate trembled for Lucy's self-control, but she said quite quietly: "You know very well I didn't want them to go like this, in a rage. Are you *sure* you didn't annoy them? I want to know."

"Absolutely certain," said Andrew. "Ah, here's my tea. Thank you, Nina. Do you mind pouring out a cup for me, Kate? There's nothing I dislike more than half-cold tea. No, Lucy my dear, if you must know, it's you who have annoyed them, tiresome old reptiles. They resented your remark about the news, it seems, and to such a degree that they are, for once, in beautiful accord with each other. I fancy it's been boiling up for some time, and this was the climax."

Lucy subsided limply into a chair. "And you can sit there and *eat*," she said in deep reproach.

"Well, I see no reason for going without my breakfast. You've had yours, and I'm dashed hungry after being out."

Lucy sprang up again and began to walk about the room. "Andrew, you must go and apologize—for me, of course!" she added impatiently, as he shook his head. "They musn't leave like this."

"Not I," said Andrew. "They're better away. As it is, we never know from one hour to the next when there's going to be an explosion, and I'd like a little peace in the house for a change. I won't do anything so ridiculous as you suggest, and if you're wise, neither will you."

"But—" began Lucy.

"Andrew is right, Lucy," said Mrs. Barlas, speaking for the first time. "They must go if they wish. I don't suppose Henry will bear malice for long, and Charlotte will come round quite soon enough. Just say good-bye to them, and don't attempt any explanations or apologies. It's always a mistake."

"I can see that you're all against me, even Kate, though she's so careful to say nothing," said Lucy bitterly. "If you'd helped me a bit with them I might have been able to keep my temper better. But I suppose you are quite pleased, so they can go, and I hope they will *never* come back." She went away, followed after a moment by Mrs. Barlas who, Kate was sure, would be able to soothe her.

"My God, what a jolly start to the day!" said Andrew, heaving a sigh of mingled relief and exasperation. "Well, I don't care. I'm going to have some ham." His expression of defiance as he slashed thin pink and white slices from the home-cured ham made Kate laugh, and at the sound he laughed a little too.

"That's better," he said. "I hope the day won't go on as it's begun, but with this rain we'll all be boxed up together in the house, and anything might happen."

"Anything," agreed Kate sadly, and they were still staring at each other in a foreboding way when the door was kicked open to admit Henry, who sidled in clutching Virginia.

"Father," he began at once. "Would you mind very much if I didn't go back this term? I never learn anything anyway, old Stinky said so in my last report, and I can't possibly leave Virginia. I was reading about a dog the other day that pined away and died because its master left it behind."

Virginia lavishly licked his face, already grimy, though the day was comparatively young.

"I'm afraid I would mind a good deal," said Andrew. "As I've paid large sums in advance for your so-called education. And Virginia isn't such a fool as to pine to death. Here, Virginia, have some ham fat. I'll look after her myself, Henry, I promise you."

"It's not just feeding her and drying her ears when she's wet," said Henry in a voice that quavered. "She likes company and walks and being talked to a lot."

"Well, she'll get all that with me, I need someone to be friendly company, and you have plenty of that at school, so don't be self-ish, old chap. Lend her to me in term-time. I'd be no end grateful."

Henry brightened a little. "Oh, in that case," he said, much more briskly. "If you *really* need her, Father, of course I'll lend her to you. That's different. No more ham, Virginia," he added sternly. "Come and be brushed." Virginia, ears and tail hanging down, followed him meekly from the room.

"If all our problems could be solved so easily!" said Andrew as he pushed back his chair. "Well, I'm going to the farm, Kate. Take my advice and keep out of harm's way in your room until luncheon."

Kate, feeling that though he was probably right, the prospect of a whole morning spent moping in her room was not enlivening, wandered into the hall. Here, with considerable bustle, the luggage belonging to Cousin Charlotte and Great-Uncle Henry was being dumped by Phemie. Anne, like her namesake, leant against the rounded wall of one of the embrasured windows, gazing dismally out at the dripping trees and sodden grass and steady rain.

"What a foul day!" she observed dispassionately as Kate came to stand beside her, "Nothing to do, nowhere to go, and Mother liable to catch me any minute and find some useful job about the house for me!"

Kate was sorry for her. She had neither a dog nor fishing-tackle to absorb her, and as she said, Lucy might quite possibly tell her to do a dull household task which would last the whole morning.

"It's the sort of day for making toffee and playing charades," she said. "Or reading a nice sloppy old-fashioned novel while eating the toffee after it's made. Only it is really too early to start that kind of thing yet."

"I'd like to make toffee after lunch," Anne said dreamily. "Lots of toffee, the stick-jaw sort. But as you say, we can't do it at ten in the morning."

"I shall go out," said Kate, suddenly coming to a decision. "Rain outside is far better than sitting in the house watching it fall. You come too, Anne."

"Ugh, no, thank you," said Anne with a shudder. "I'm not ambidextrous like a frog or something. I'd rather stay in and keep dry."

"You'll be caught and have to do something," Kate warned her.

"I'm pretty wily. I'll pretend I'm helping with the Aged Relatives' goods and shackles," said Anne.

"Too late, I'm afraid," murmured Kate, as Lucy came quickly downstairs.

"Did I hear you say you were going out, Kate?"

"Yes. I thought I'd have a tramp in the rain—unless I can do anything for you?" said Kate, remembering that she owed a duty of politeness to her hostess.

"As a matter of fact, the only thing you can do for me is take a message to the farm, it you *really* mean to go out in this downpour," said Lucy, turning her disapproving glance at the weather.

"Of course I will, with pleasure. What is it?"

"I've written it down, so that there can be no mistake. All you have to do is give it to the grieve's wife," said Lucy, producing a neat little note. "Oh, Anne!"

"Yes, Mother." Anne, who had started to creep quietly away, turned round.

"I've got something I want you to do, dear. Those new pillow-slips that came yesterday from Robinson and Cleaver, the embroidered ones, linen, all need to have names sewn on them; that will fill up your morning nicely."

"Like hell it will!" muttered Anne rebelliously. Kate, thankful that her job did not involve a needle, in the use of which she was deplorably lazy, went to put on her thickest shoes and a waterproof. As she came down to the hall again, she had a glimpse of Anne, laden with snowy linen, going towards the billiard-room, her work-bag swinging from her arm, and laughed unfeelingly.

"You brute! There's two dozen of them!" hissed Anne, but Kate only laughed again as she opened the door and went out into a flurry of raindrops and soft air.

As the farm had not originally belonged to Soonhope, but had been bought by an enterprising Lockhart during the Napoleonic wars when corn prices had soared to an astonishing height, the steading lay unusually far from the house, a fact on which Lucy, who heartily disliked farms and everything about them, always congratulated herself. Naturally, this arrangement did not please Andrew so well, but Kate, whose object was to walk, did not mind having to go along the Loaning and then turn to her right up half a mile of very muddy farm road. As she had said to Anne, wet weather was never so bad once you were out in it, and she walked fast, the first falling leaves pattering to the ground with the rain pale yellow elm and lime, which were brought down by a wind and did not wait until the shrewish nip of frost detached them from their twigs. Ahead of her, nestled in under the side of a gently sloping hill, were the farm buildings, roofed in old red pantiles which the rain had washed to a deeper tint than usual. On either side of the road the cut corn stood in stooks, waiting to be carried to the stackyard as soon as the rain stopped and a west wind rose to dry it. To-day the extra hands taken on for the harvest would be sitting idle in the barn or bothy, sleeping, eating, and playing cards. Only the shepherd would have to be out and about as usual, and of course the cattleman, wearing an old sack over his shoulders to keep off the wet. Kate suddenly began to laugh at the thought of the cattleman, for she remembered the story, passed on to her quite recently by Grey, of Lucy's first visit to the farm-steading. Andrew had been talking to the cattleman when the town-bred Lucy, hearing a dismal lowing, and thinking of bereft mothers robbed of their calves, had exclaimed: "That poor cow! What can be wrong with it?" And before Andrew could offer some more refined explanation the old cattleman, brutally direct, had answered. "Och, she'll juist be wantin' the bull!" The incident had set the final seal of Lucy's disgust on all things pertaining to agriculture, and she never again went near the farm if she could possibly avoid it.

'I must be very coarse,' thought Kate, but not nearly regretfully enough, and her lips were still twitching when she turned the last corner and saw Andrew coming towards her.

"Hullo!" he said. "I see you aren't frightened of the rain. And you look as if the day was turning out better than we expected."

"Nothing's ever so bad out-of-doors," answered Kate, blinking the raindrops from her lashes. "I know my nose is the colour of a ripe cherry, and my feet are soaking, but what boots it?"

"What indeed? And your nose is merely an artistic shade of sunset pink. It's your cheeks that are cherry coloured, and that's the right way round. But—I didn't know that you had discovered that things are always more bearable when you're not under a roof," he said. "I didn't think you had many cares, Kate. I hope not."

"Oh, we all have our troubles," said Kate both lightly and tritely. She had no intention of burdening Andrew, or for that matter, anyone else, with hers. Better that concealment should prey on her damask cheek, though even that she hoped to avoid. For one's family is often apt to make solicitous inquiries about headache or indigestion, and however much kindness and anxiety prompts these questions, they are hard to parry without irritation. So she laughed and went on quickly: "It's lovely once you've made up your mind to be really damp, isn't it? And you can squelch freely through mud and wet grass. I'm going to the farm with a message from Lucy."

"As you're out anyhow, and wet already, would you like to take a turn across the fields after you've delivered your message?" said Andrew. "I'd be very glad of your company."

So, having put the note into the hand of the grieve's wife, wet and red with the scouring of what already seemed a spotless stone floor, Kate felt that she had done her errand properly and was free to go with Andrew. They waded through long wet grass up to their knees, and saw the bullocks brought from Pennymuir standing disconsolately in the shelter of a high hawthorn hedge, their tails to the wind and driving rain; they crossed fields of sodden stubble, where the lines of stooks were darkening with wet, and fallen sheaves had to be set up again here and there. Kate plunged recklessly into a burn too swollen to jump, and laughed at the chill of the water and the bubbles squeezed out of her shoes.

"You are a baby, Kate," said Andrew. "Fancy anyone so childish in her ways—except one," he added as an afterthought.

"You mean—Mrs. Fardell, of course."

"Yes."

"Am I so like her? Robin has told me so too," Kate.

"I suppose you are, now I come to think of it. That's perhaps why we both like being with you."

Kate rebelled at this. "Of all the tactless things to say!" she said angrily, frowning at him resentfully from under the hair which had been sprayed by the wind over her forehead. "I wish I didn't remind you of her. I'd rather be liked for myself. It isn't much of a compliment to know that people want to be with you just because you're like someone else."

"It's not just because of that," Andrew said, unravelling her involved and ungrammatical sentences without difficulty. "But you must see, my dear, that in my case at least it's an—an added attraction."

"Well, I don't like it at all. From now on I'm going to be quire different, sensible and competent and—well, just *sensible*," insisted Kate, walking at a great rate up the steep meadow into which they had come by way of a gap in the hedge. "I don't believe it's good for you to be reminded of her."

"Probably not. But don't change too quickly, Kate. I like you very much as you are."

"I dare say you do, but it's bad for you."

"It's about the only thing that helps me to carry on," he said.

"And what will happen when I go home?" she asked.

"God knows," said Andrew. "For I don't," and his tone was so recklessly miserable that she was frightened.

They had come to the top of the meadow, and now stood, looking down the southward slope to the red roofs of the farm, and farther off beyond the wet slates of Soonhope glimmering like water among the trees, the clustered houses, the noble tower of the Abbey Church, the gardens and streets which, all bound within the links of Alewater, made up the ancient royal burgh of Haystoun. For once Kate did not really see the scene at which she was staring blankly, she was even blind to the dark mass of the Lammermuirs, over which the heavy clouds were rolling like waves. It seemed to her very hard that she should have to be the one to deal with Andrew and his difficulties, she, who did not know, except as an onlooker, what made marriage a success or failure, whose sympathies were entirely with the man while her reason and sense of justice told her that the wife had right on her side. But there was no one else, and she knew that her conscience would never cease to plague her if she did nothing, and at last with a sigh she turned to the man standing gloomily beside her.

"Andrew," she said firmly. "You can't go on like this, and you showed me yourself why you had to come back. Now you're here you've got to go through with it. Just coming back wasn't enough, for you are still thinking of Miss Fardell, and that's hopeless. Would she like to know that you're thinking of giving up?"

"For God's sake, Kate—" muttered Andrew. "Don't make it any worse than it is. It's easy enough for you to talk, but you know that if Lucy would only lend a hand I'd manage all right, but she doesn't—"

"You can't alter Lucy," said Kate.

"I can't alter myself, either!"

"No, I know. But you married her, you know what she's like by this time, surely? There's so much more in your favour than in Lucy's that you ought to do more—you will have to make all the effort, don't you see?" argued Kate not very hopefully. "And it's not as if you stood alone, Andrew."

"Don't I?" he said with an ugly laugh.

"No. Everyone likes you. You make friends of nine of ten people you meet. And—the children are all with you now. You must have seen that, surely? The four of you are a pretty strong combine. No, it's Lucy who is alone! Poor Lucy, she's the one to be pitied, really, Andrew, and all the more because she'll never know why. Oh, dear, I oughtn't to be talking like this to you about your wife," said Kate in dismay. "But it's true."

He did not answer, and she could think of nothing more to say. Whether she had done more harm than good, Kate didn't know. She stared at the broad valley, and now she saw it suddenly glorified, for while they talked the rain had stopped, the sun had come out, and every blade of grass was hung with diamonds, changing to all the colours of the prism as the sun caught them: and arched above the dark sky was a brilliant rainbow.

"Forgive me, Andrew," she said. "I had no right to preach to you at all."

"Oh, that's all right," he said absently, as if in a dream, "We'd better be going home. It must be almost lunch time."

Silently they went down the hill, across one field after another, along the Loaning where ruts full of water were blue as the sky they reflected. Only when they reached the garden, Andrew stopped inside the door and took her hand.

"Thank you, Kate, my dear," he said. "You've been a great help. And you needn't try to be competent and sensible—for my sake, anyhow. I'm going to be sensible myself, whatever happens."

"Well, Andrew!" said Lucy's voice sharply, and Lucy herself came round the sweet-pea hedge post in time to see him drop Kate's hand. "I had no idea that you and Kate were out together. The telephone has rung for you several times. Of course I had to say that you were out and I didn't know in the least when you would be in."

"That was quite true, and if it was anything important they can ring up again," said Andrew serenely. "Have the aged relatives gone?"

"Yes. Kate, aren't you wet through? You ought to change, after being out so long," said Lucy, with a glance which brought to Kate's mind the hateful remark of the man in the Berwickshire hotel the night before. Her cheeks burned. Surely, surely, Lucy couldn't be so dreadfully silly and small-minded as to be suspicious of *her*? But Lucy's eyes were more than suspicious, and Kate's blush grew hotter than ever, though she held her head up and proudly returned the look, her own eyes full of the anger and shame of innocence accused.

"I am going to change," was all she said, and walked away, sore at heart.

Andrew, being a man, had noticed nothing. He only wished that Lucy had not such a forbidding manner, especially with Kate.

4

"Stop prowling about the room like a hen on a hot girdle, you make me feel nervous," said Mrs. Anstruther, her black eyes snapping. She looked anything but nervous, bolt upright in her big arm-chair, and Kate could not help laughing a little at the mere idea. "That's better," said Mrs. Anstruther. "It you look in that old tea-caddy, the tortoiseshell one on the chest-of-drawers, you'll find some peculiarly strong Turkish cigarettes. Smoke one, it will probably make you feel rather sick, and that will take your mind off whatever is bothering you."

"Counter-irritation?" suggested Kate, meekly taking one of the cigarettes and lighting it. Almost at once she began to cough.

"Something like that. Now sit down and tell me what the matter is," said Mrs. Anstruther.

Kate was neither frightened not disconcerted by her abruptness. In some queer way it seemed to steady her—or perhaps that was the effect of the powerful cigarette?

"It's all rather difficult, and you'll think I'm silly," she began hesitatingly.

"Very likely. The young are frequently intensely silly," said Mrs. Anstruther promptly. "I suppose Lucy has started being jealous, eh?"

Kate dropped the cigarette on the carpet in her astonishment.

"Pick that horrible thing up and put it in the fire. You've smoked quite enough of it," commanded Mrs. Anstruther. "So that's the trouble. I thought as much." She sounded rather pleased.

"How—how did you know?"

"For one thing, I know Lucy. She has spent most of her married life being jealous unnecessarily. For another," said Mrs. Anstruther dryly, "I've had it hinted to me by several people, among them Flora Milligan. It was bound to come."

"I never really believed before that Haystoun was such a vile place for gossip!" burst out Kate furiously.

"Living here has its drawbacks. Of course you didn't believe it until it touched yourself. Who does? To comfort you, I believe that there is also a good deal of gossip about you and Robin."

"Don't you care? Don't you see how horrible it is?" asked Kate incredulously.

"I would, if it weren't that during the many years I've lived here I have come to realize that the only people who have an unblemished reputation in Haystoun are those whose feelings are always subject to soulless conventionality," said Mrs. Anstruther. "Bless you, Kate, your grandmother and I suffered in our day too, and were made acutely miserable at the time, and as you see, we have weathered it and are none the worse."

"I *can't* stay at Soonhope with Lucy thinking that about me," Kate said wretchedly. "I came to ask it you'd take me in for a day or two. The house is full at home. Mother has a cousin from New Zealand and his wife staying until the end of the end of the week, or I'd have gone before."

"If you go home so suddenly, or come here, you'll give a handle to all the gossips—and Lucy will think the worst at once. No, Kate, you will have to face it out."

"I have, for ten days. It's ten days since I knew what Lucy was thinking about—about me."

"Then you can manage another week, till the boys go back to school," said Mrs. Anstruther briskly. "Then, in the bustle of their departure, yours won't be noticed. Besides, Andrew will miss you. He's doing his best, but he needs all the help he can get. The strong have to go to the wall, Kate, for the sake of the weak. The meek shall inherit the earth, and the strong win their inheritance for them and hand it over. You're strong, my dear, and you must pay the penalty of it. And what would Robin say," she added in a different tone, "if you fled away without warning like this?"

"Robin? It won't make any difference to him. I'm sure you must know, as you know so much, that he and Andrew like me because they think I'm like Mrs. Fardell!" cried Kate.

Mrs. Anstruther looked at her in silence, seeing everything which Kate imagined she had kept hidden. When she spoke it was only to say indulgently: "Men have such silly fancies. Well, leaving Robin out of it, Kate, will you be a good girl and stay at Soonhope? For your grandmother's sake if for nothing else."

"It's the thought of Granny that has been worrying me most," Kate admitted with a sigh. "Very well, Mrs. Anstruther. I suppose I was a coward to want to get out of it, but it's very unpleasant and difficult altogether."

"Life often is," retorted Mrs. Anstruther. "But it's always interesting even at its most disagreeable. Remember that, Kate, as a pearl of wisdom. And you've done nothing to be ashamed of, so you don't need to worry about what people say."

That was all very well in the shelter of The Anchorage drawing-room, thought Kate as she went down the road up which she had almost run in her impulsive haste an hour earlier. But it didn't seem to work when, for example, she met Miss Milligan, as she did at Soonhope gate, and had to endure the piercing curiosity of her look while exchanging polite remarks about the fine weather and old Mrs. Milligan's health. Escaping at last with a hot face and hotter anger, Kate walked up the drive and into the house. 'Everything,' she thought passionately, 'is perfectly disgusting. And why can't I be left in peace with my own worries?'

So far she had not had time to realize that this sea of extraneous troubles was a blessing, however well disguised. When she had time to sit and brood over her unhappiness about Robin, she might wish that she had something else, no matter how disagreeable, to divert her mind. 'If Lucy appears and gives me one of those looks of hers, I'm liable to forget all Mrs. Anstruther's good advice,' was her next thought.

Fortunately, it was not Lucy, but Anne, who came flying downstairs at top speed, her face eager. "Kate! Isn't it lovely?" she cried. "Grey has just rung up to say he's coming for the week-end!"

This was good news to Kate, who felt that with a member of her own family, particularly Grey, on the spot, she would not be so alone and unprotected; but Anne's delight seemed excessive, and she could not help saying: "Are you so fond of Grey, Anne?"

'Of course I am, he's a darling," said Anne quickly, and to Kate's ears, evasively. And she went on in a great hurry:

"Oh, and Robin Anstruther rang up too, something about going to see some geese, of all things! Father knows. He'll tell you."

She went on across the hall and out over the lawn like a bird in flight, and Kate saw that she could only express her pleasure at the thought of Grey's coming by swift movement; and she smiled and then sighed. Nothing like that could help her, not if she ran like Atalanta. "But this is a revolting state of mind, this mess of sickly self-pity that you're wallowing in!" she told herself severely. "For goodness' sake stop it."

"Talking to yourself is a sign that you're going mad, Cousin Kate," said Henry, popping out of the storeroom with suspicious speed and stealth.

"Very likely, Cousin Henry. And eating between meals is a sign that you'll be disgustingly fat when you reach your father's age," retorted Kate. "'With an enormous stomach and no neck.'"

"'Fair round belly with good capon lined,'" said Henry cheerfully. "I won't mind a bit. I wish it was lined with good capon now. I've only put a few biscuits and things into it."

"Is *that* all? And in ten minutes it will be teatime!" said Kate pityingly. "And only three hours ago you ate a luncheon that would have fed three normal boys. Poor little fellow."

"I say, Kate, do you know Grey's coming to-morrow?" asked Henry, quickly changing the subject. "I'm glad, aren't you? I like Grey."

"So do I," said Kate, laughing.

"So does Anne. She's been doing her nails and things ever since he rang up," said Henry. "What tosh, isn't it? As if Grey's going to notice Anne's nails!"

"He won't be able to avoid noticing yours," Kate answered unfairly. "If you don't have at them with a trowel or some suitable implement."

"Back chat isn't wit. Old Stinky says so," said Henry, and rushed away with a wild whoop of triumph before Kate could punish this final piece of impertinence.

"What a boy!" she said aloud, and Andrew, coming in, heard her.

"Who? Henry? What has he been up to now?"

"Nothing," said Kate. "Merely the usual impudence, which is a good sign, when you consider that his parting from Virginia is only a week away, poor dear."

"You're far too decent to the brat. . . . Will you come with Robin and me to-morrow evening to see the geese flighting to Crooked-shaws Loch?"

He evidently expected her to accept with pleasure but Kate had several reasons for hesitating. First of all, she was not sure that she wanted to see Robin—yet. Later, perhaps, but not yet. Then there was Lucy, who if she did not openly object, would manage to let her silent disapproval fill the house like a clinging sea-mist. And the boys and Grey might to go too, and if Grey went, Anne would go, and that would make so many of them that they would probably frighten the geese. This was what Kate said, after a pause, since her first two reasons, though the really important ones, could not be spoken.

As she had feared, Andrew brushed it aside. "They'll all be going to play tennis," he said. "The tournament has been fixed for to-morrow, and even Henry has been asked to play, with some girl who is staying at Charteris and hasn't a partner. Poor girl. If she only knew it, she'd be better playing with Virginia than Henry, but no matter. And Lucy will be going to look on, of course. No, you can go with a clear conscience. I'll let Robin know it's all right."

A clear conscience Kate could certainly achieve, but she could not rid herself of a foreboding of trouble, which remained with her throughout the evening and haunted her dreams all night.

Grey's cheerful arrival at midday seemed to blow through the house like a wind from the hills. Kate felt heartened as he thrust his hard cheek against hers in a careless brotherly kiss, the boys were noisily exuberant, Anne very quiet, though her eyes shone as if a candle had been lighted in each. Even Lucy, who was fond of Grey, lost the forbidding look, the tightly closed lips and suspicious carriage of the head which Kate had come to dread, and welcomed him in what was for her a positively gushing manner.

In spite of this change, there was still a faint uneasiness in Kate's mind as she went up to her room to put on the thick shoes and stockings and tweed suit which Andrew had told her she ought to wear for her own comfort and because it would not be seen by the geese against the heather as a lighter garment would. But she reassured herself by supposing that she was not looking forward to seeing Robin with unmixed pleasure. The thought that Lucy, as well as the others, would have started for Charteris, made her run downstairs much more cheerfully than she had gone up. For however clear her conscience was, she had no wish to rouse any further evidences of that absurd jealousy and suspicion which Lucy had already shown her.

It was a considerable shock, and a most unpleasant one, to find Lucy standing in the hall watching her descent of the last flight of steps. For one moment Kate wanted to turn, run madly up again, and lock herself into her bedroom. She felt as though minutes had ticked away while she clutched the banister rail on which her hand had rested lightly until the smooth cool wood hurt her palm, while the atmosphere thickened with the sense of approaching crisis. Actually she made no perceptible pause, but continued on her downward way steadily, if rather more slowly.

"I see you are going out," said Lucy at once, as if she had been waiting patiently for Kate's foot to reach the stone floor of the hall before she spoke. "With Andrew, of course."

"With Andrew—and Robin Anstruther," answered Kate so lightly that she surprised herself. It did not seem possible that with legs turned to melting jelly, a heart that thumped and banged in one's ears, a general feeling of some nausea, one could still manage to behave in quite an ordinary way.

"Robin Anstruther!" There was complete unbelief in Lucy's short high-pitched laugh, and Kate remained silent. She was not going to try to justify herself by explanations which would be received like this. "I can't stand this any longer," Lucy went on rapidly. "I suppose you imagine that I've noticed nothing? But I have, I assure you. There's very little that I miss when it concerns Andrew."

"In this case," said Kate, finding her voice, and thankful that it obeyed her, "you have been noticing what doesn't exist, Lucy, except in your own mind. Can't you ever forget what Andrew has done, and be fair to him?"

"Fair to him? Fair? What is he to me?" cried Lucy in the hysterical tones of repression suddenly let loose. "The other affair was bad enough, but *this*, in his own house, with you, is too much. I never thought that even Andrew could—"

"What have I been doing now?" Unnoticed by either of them, Andrew had come in from the front door, and stood looking at them steadily, his face quite white, his blue eyes blazing. "Now, Lucy, tell me at once what you are making a scene about."

"A scene? Am I to stand by and watch you being unfaithful to me again, with one of our own guests, and your cousin at that?"

"How dare you?" said Andrew, and though he did not raise his voice the anger and scorn it held made Lucy shrink. Kate, once more frozen into silence, shiver a little. It was so frightful as to be unbelievable that she, Kate Heron, should be standing here having to listen to this.

"I've tried my best since I came back, Lucy," he said. "God knows you haven't made it easy for me, but I have tried to go on with this. But no one could be expected to stand your pettiness, your bullying, and now this foul slanderous talk—about Kate, of all people!"

"That's enough, Andrew," Kate said sharply. "Please don't say any more. I don't deserve to have to listen to either of you. I shall go home at once, as soon as I have packed a suitcase. Perhaps you'll see that the rest of my things are sent after me?"

She turned and walked upstairs, so numb with rage and disgust that she felt nothing but the immediate necessity to leave Soonhope.

5

"So you see, Grey, there was nothing else for it. I took Kate to the station and saw her into the train, and sent a wire to your people telling them when to expect her. I can only apologize for myself as well as Lucy. It is unforgivable that anyone staying in my house should have been treated to such a scene, and I feel it is very largely my fault. I should have seen it coming."

Andrew and Grey faced one another in the billiard-room, both rather pale, and Grey puzzled as well as angry. "Of course I'll leave too," he said at last. "Nothing to do with you, Andrew, but I can hardly stay when Kate—when Kate—" he broke off. "Lucy must be completely loopy," he ended lamely.

"It's my fault," Andrew still stood rigidly by the fireplace. "If I hadn't given her cause to feel jealous and suspicious, this would never have happened."

"Rot, my dear fellow. Lucy'd have been just the same if you had never so much as looked at another woman. She could be suspicious of a clothes-horse if you hung a petticoat on it," said Grey robustly. "Look here, let's have a stiff whisky and soda. You obviously need it, and I wouldn't mind one myself."

Andrew suddenly sank into a chair, his face in his hands. "Yes. You might get it, will you, Grey?" he muttered.

Grey went out, and in the dark passage almost fell over the three young Lockharts, who were huddled there, a cluster of white tennis clothes and pale faces. "Adam, you and Henry get the whisky and siphon and glasses," said Grey.

The two boys detached themselves from Anne.

"Just tell us first, Grey, is it another row?" said Adam huskily. "Is it as bad as the one when Father left us?" Henry made a sound like a sob and tried to turn it into a cough.

"Good God, I hope not! But it's bad enough," Grey said, realizing that, young though they were, the state of affairs between their parents entitled them to be told. "Your mother's made a fool of herself, a damn' fool of herself—about Kate, and Andrew is livid, and Kate's gone home, and myself presently."

Anne gave a small cry and seized his arm. "Oh, Grey! Oh, Grey! I knew something like this would happen!" she wailed. "But why should it spoil everything for us?"

Grey said to the boys: "Go and fetch that whisky, will you?" and as they crept miserably away, took Anne in his arms. "It's not going to spoil anything for you, beautiful," he said.

"But you'll go, and how can you come back now that Mother's been awful to Kate?"

"It'll blow over in time, I hope. I mean to speak to Lucy myself. She may listen to me," said Grey more hopefully than he felt, for a woman as madly unreasonable and self-righteous as Lucy would be almost impossible to argue with. "Perhaps I can frighten her into common sense. She must see, when she comes round, that she's been a bloody fool—sorry, Anne, you know I don't say things like that to you as a rule, but there's no other word for it—about Kate. And in the meantime—well," he went on, stroking the tumbled head that lay on his shoulder. "You weren't so keen about me an hour or two ago, my sweet, and you're so awfully young. We'd have to wait till you grow up a bit anyhow, wouldn't we?"

"That was quite different, when I knew you were here, and I could see you any time I wanted to. I was just giving you a little wholesome negligence for your own good. But you know I love you truly, Grey. I couldn't love you any more if I was a centurion!"

Grey kissed her, moved by her earnestness, and never even noticed the malapropism which would have delighted her father. "Well, we'll tell Andrew, shall we? Would that help?"

"Oh, yes, it would! He always understands," said Anne, and then the boys came back, and they all went into the billiard-room.

"Andrew," said Grey, pushing a glass of practically neat whisky into his hand. "Take a pull at this and listen. Anne and I want to marry each other."

As he had hoped, this was as effectual in rousing Andrew as a sudden cold shower. "Are you trying to be funny?" he said. "Or is this with the kindly idea of counteracting one shock with another?" Then, looking from his sons' stricken faces to his daughter, holding tightly to Grey's hand: "No, I see that it isn't meant for a joke. But why choose this moment to spring it on me?"

"Well, you see—I ought to call you 'sir' if you're going to be my father-in-law—this—this crisis has sort of brought things to a head," explained Grey.

"I see. And who said I was going to be your father-in-law? Have I given my consent yet?"

Grey grinned broadly at him. "It's no good, Drew. You can't do it," he said.

"But look here, Grey. Is this a time to tell me that you're going to snatch my only daughter from me?"

"But he isn't, Father! Not for ages!" cried Anne, running to him and putting her arms round his neck so that whisky splashed all over both of them. "We only want to be engaged! We don't want to be *married*!" she ended in shocked tones.

"Oh, if that's all, you can he engaged with my blessing," said Andrew wearily. "Give me some more whisky, Grey, I need it. And as you are all concerned in this, you'd better give me your opinions. Kate, as you probably know already, has been driven out of this house, by what was as much my fault as anyone's. Don't contradict me,"—as a murmur rose from Grey and Anne. "You must take my word for it. Whether she will ever forgive us and come here again, I don't know, and it's too soon yet to hope for that. In any case, what I really want to put to you is this: Is it any good my staying here? Adam, you'll soon be old enough to manage this place with a grieve as capable as Purdie. Anne, you're settled in life, as engagements usually lead to marriages, and Henry will have several years of school yet to occupy his attention. I seem to have done more harm than good by coming back. Has it made any sort of difference to you having me here? The truth, mind you, and nothing but the truth. This is no time for sentimental lies."

"*All* the difference, Father," said Anne in a low voice. "You know it has. We couldn't go back to where we were without you, could we, boys?"

Andrew looked at his sons, who stared at him from over-bright eyes. "I've only this to say," said Adam huskily. "If you go, I won't take Soonhope. Not while you're alive. If you go, Father, we're going with you." He nudged Henry savagely.

"You needn't dig my ribs to pieces," said Henry. "Of course we are going with Father—and Virginia too. You wouldn't leave her, Father? When are we starting?"

Andrew gave a long sigh, and with it, finally relinquished all his hopes of getting away. "Well, I don't propose to cart you all over the place with me," he said. "So it looks as if I'd have to stay here."

Everyone showed vast relief except Henry, who looked woefully disappointed. "Then I'll just have to go back to school next week as usual? he said. "I might have known it. Gosh, what a sell!"

CHAPTER EIGHT

1

THE slow weeks carried the year on from autumn into winter. Kate, at home again, found that she could still laugh at Abracabroccoloni's culinary advice, delivered through Grey, still enjoy a crisp frosty morning and a clear saffron and rose sunset, still eat with appetite and sleep, as a rule, peacefully through the nights. If life for the present had lost all flavour for her, no one suspected it. She had come home sick and shaken, her distress over Robin thrust into the background of her mind by the scene with Lucy. Her parents asked no questions, for which she was thankful, but her mother noticed how she shrank from any mention of Soonhope, and was intensely angry at the cause, which Grey had hinted to her. Greystiel Heron said nothing, except once, and then it was to mutter to his pipe: "I never liked Lucy Lockhart. Too cat-faced."

Anne and Grey wrote to each other at great length, but he never went to Soonhope, nor would she go to what the family called 'the Heronry.'

In the meantime, she wrote in her large untidy hand, *we're better to meet at the houses of neutral friends*.

"So silly," commented Kate, when Grey read this out to her. "As if we were at war or something."

"She means 'mutual,' of course," said Grey tolerantly. "You'll never get Anne to use the right word. After I'd heard her talking about the *Four Horsemen of the Acropolis* I knew it was no good."

Kate laughed, as she was intended to do and knew it, but she said, "Grey, I don't see why you and Anne should suffer because of me. It seems very hard lines. Why don't you go to Soonhope sometime?"

"Because I don't choose to see Lucy," he said, all the Heron obstinacy in his out-thrust chin. "I told her a few home truths before I left, and I'm not going back in a hurry. She'll have to apologize to you first."

"Well, it seems that all I can do is wait for that to happen, and accept it with indecent haste when it does," said Kate. "But I think it most unlikely, Grey. Lucy was never very much good at apologizing."

"Lucy has never been quite so obviously in the wrong before," Grey said dryly. "And what with Granny going back to Edinburgh, and Andrew having his chance to be disapproving, Anne says her mother is very subdued these days."

"Poor Anne! What a lively time she must be having, and newly engaged, too," said Kate. "And poor Lucy, too. It must be awful, when you've always been so certain you were in the right, to be in her position now."

"'Poor Lucy!'" echoed Grey in disgust. "Really, Kate, I sometimes wonder if you aren't a bit *saft*! Why should you pity her?"

In spite of her brother's scorn, Kate's instinct was right: Lucy was most certainly to be pitied. With the boys at school, Anne moving about in a dream of her own from which she only emerged to smile at her father, with Mrs. Barlas gone in displeased silence, and Florence threatening to follow her, Lucy was in a desolate state. She felt disapproval in the polite but rather distant manner of her acquaintances, and she had too much sense to appreciate the barbed sympathy shown by people like Miss Milligan, for she realized its true worth to be less than nothing. Above all, Andrew, on whom she was used to look down as little as being slightly inferior to herself in every respect, was now in the position of judge. Not that he rubbed it in, as she would have done, and indeed, had done; he spoke to her seldom, and always with grave courtesy as to a stranger whom he had no wish to know better; but each time she met his glance she read condemnation in it. This, to Lucy, was unbearable. She grew thin and pale, and quite lost her look of Dresden china youthfulness during the weeks of that Christmas term. No longer was she upheld by the comfortable feeling of conscious virtue which, she remembered now with a tinge of shame, had given her a melancholy pleasure when Andrew left her. She was haunted by the fear that he might go away again, and this time she would know that he had been driven by her, that no one else could possibly be blamed for it.

It was the desperate need of confiding in someone, no matter how unsympathetic, that drove her one chill afternoon to call on Mrs. Anstruther.

That redoubtable lady, seated before an extravagant fire with her black silk skirt turned back over her knees, received her without enthusiasm.

"Pull a chair in and sit down," she said. "You don't often honour me with a visit."

"It seems a long time since I saw you," Lucy murmured, taking her seat on the small hard chair which she had chosen.

"Why that uncomfortable chair?" asked her hostess dryly. "Is it a stool of repentance?"

Lucy rose quickly. "I suppose you think I ought to be sitting on one," she said rather resentfully, giving the chair a spiteful push back to its place and drawing up a large cushioned one with an upholstered back and arms.

"That sounds more like you," said Mrs. Anstruther. "As for what I think, it is of no importance to anyone but myself. It's a pity, since you chose to call to-day, that you didn't come a little earlier. You would not have missed one of your most ardent admirers then."

"I didn't know I had any," said Lucy dismally, het resentment already gone. "'Who was it?"

"Flora Milligan. And if you wanted cockering up, I don't know why you didn't go to see *her*."

"Because, poor though your opinion of me is, I have enough sense to know that the admiration of Miss Milligan and company is a dangerous thing and not to be encouraged," said Lucy with spirit. "If you don't want me to stay, I can go home. I shall *not* go to the Milligans."

"No, I don't believe you would. You're so extraordinarily silly at times that one is apt to forget that you are really quite sensible," said Mrs. Anstruther thoughtfully. "Don't go. Stay here and have tea and hot buttered scones, and we can be disagreeable to each other."

"Must we be disagreeable?"

"It's warming on a cold day, and I need an antidote to poor Flora. She's as sweet as—no, not honey or sugar, they're both of them genuine fattening sweetnesses. I'll say saccharine, instead. It gives the illusion of sweetening without doing you any good."

"Very well. We shall be as acid as we can," said Lucy. "I certainly don't feel sweet."

"No, it's hardly your nature, is it?"

"I suppose not," said Lucy with a sigh, forgetting to be acid. "The truth is that I have a very nasty nature, and I only just discovered it."

"None of us can claim to be perfect if we look at ourselves truthfully. Your trouble is that you have always seen yourself in some pose or other, usually noble."

"You believe in plain speaking, don't you?" said Lucy, wincing.

"Yes, and that is my particular trouble. It has done me a great deal of harm, let me tell you. But you didn't come here to talk about me. What is the matter at the moment?"

"I seem to have made the most frightful mess of everything," said Lucy.

"It's a sign of grace that you realize it," was Mrs. Anstruther's comment. "Don't tell me any more, or you will be sorry one day. It is a very great mistake to confide in other people. Here is Hannah with the tea."

"But I thought you might be able to help me," said Lucy desperately, as the grenadier carried in the tea-tray and placed a covered dish which gave forth warm, tantalizing odours, on a trivet by the fire.

"Have some tea first. You won't need help so much after that. Tea is a wonderful restorer of morale to a woman," said Mrs. Anstruther, pouring out a cup and handing it to her guest. "Eat several of those hot scones, too. You are far too thin."

And when Lucy, with a strange, not unpleasant sensation of being back in the nursery, had obeyed, Mrs. Anstruther looked at her and said: "Now?"

"I *do* feel better. I'll try to get out of my difficulties myself. But," added Lucy dolefully, "I don't believe Andrew will ever forgive me."

"I'm glad that you've stopped harping on the string of forgiving Andrew. Of course he'll forgive you. It isn't in Andrew's nature to bear malice. You may have to wait for it, you know, and you may," said Mrs. Anstruther, with a shrewd glance at Lucy's pretty downcast face where lines showed now that had been invisible a month before, "you may have to do things that come hard to you, like climbing down and taking back words you have said. In my opinion it would be well worth it, but of course that is for you to decide. And in the meantime," she went on briskly, giving Lucy no time to speak, "the best way to stop brooding over your own troubles is to brood over someone else's."

"Whose?" asked Lucy.

"Robin's, for a start," said Mrs. Anstruther promptly. "He must get rid of that frightful housekeeper, and he hasn't the courage to do it. I believe you could. Why don't you try? Drive up to Pennymuir and have tea with him and see what you can manage. I can't see you letting yourself be defeated by Mrs. MacOstrich."

Lucy rose to go. "Well, I can try, If you like, and I will, because you have been far kinder to me than I expected or deserved," she said.

"And I just hope," said Mrs. Anstruther to the empty room when her visitor had left, "that my unexpected kind-heartedness hasn't made me do a very foolish thing."

The very next day Lucy, whose reforming zeal have been passed down to her undiluted from some Calvinistic ancestor, drove alone to Pennymuir through the brown hills. She thought that she would be prepared for the worst from what she had heard the boys and

Andrew say of Robin's cook-housekeeper, but the tiny figure which stood in the doorway, and by sheer force of character appeared to block it entirely, rather startled her.

"The Master's not in," said Mrs. MacOstrich.

"Then I shall come in and wait for him," said Lucy, after the first moment, was not in the least afraid of her. "When do you expect him?"

"He'll be in to his tea."

"Good, I'll have tea with him." And Lucy so evidently intended to enter that Mrs. MacOstrich, foiled for once in her usually successful attempts to intimidate unexpected visitors, fell back.

Lucy walked into the sitting-room feeling exhilarated. A small woman herself, she had all the small woman's determination and courage, and she now went from strength to strength. "Perhaps you would open a window for me?" she asked, finding it pleasant to be able to say what she liked to this disagreeable and malignant little person without wondering if she would take offence. "After the fresh air it is really very stuffy in here."

Muttering balefully but indistinguishably, Mrs. MacOstrich flung a window open far wider than she needed to, and tramped from the room.

Lucy shivered. She infinitely preferred the cold air to the now vanishing smell of dog, but it seemed to her unnecessary that she should shiver when a fire, ready laid, only asked for a match to be applied to it. Was the wretched Robin doomed to come back to this smelly, airless ice-house? She lighted the fire, and as it blazed up, piled coals and wood on it and sat down in front of the leaping flames to warm her toes.

Presently the housekeeper came slowly and heavily in again carrying a meagrely appointed tea-tray which she set on a table. She glared at the fire in speechless fury, and Lucy said: "You may shut the window now."

"And who may you be that's giving me orders?" demanded Mrs. MacOstrich.

"I am Mrs. Lockhart from Soonhope," Lucy said in pleasant, impersonal tones. "Though it is hardly your province, is it, to ask questions like that?"

"Never heed the provinces. It's my business to ken why married women comes here without their lawful husbands."

"It is your business to be polite to your master's visitors," Lucy told her. "By the way, do you dust this room yourself?"

"And what if I do?"

Lucy looked round with eyes that missed no speck of dust. "I thought so," she murmured. "Please shut the door as you go out."

Mrs. MacOstrich realized with helpless fury that she had been dismissed, and she was baffled. Never before had she met such composure, such calm certainty that an order given would be obeyed at once. "Brazen!" she muttered, tramping out once more and banging the door viciously behind her; but she felt defeated.

Lucy had time to wish more than once that Robin would come, before she saw him pass the window and enter the hall. Mrs. MacOstrich must have been lurking to waylay him, for her voice could be heard talking at length and violently, and then Lucy heard Robin say: "Very well. At once, if you like."

The sitting-room door was thrown open and he came in, kicking it shut as Henry might have done. "Lucy!" he cried, not waiting for greetings, but seizing her in his arms and kissing her heartily on each cheek. "You marvel, how did you manage it? Mrs. MacOstrich is leaving to-night. Thank God for it!"

"Well, I didn't look for quite such an easy victory," said Lucy with a faint smile. "One of the advantages of being a shrew, I suppose. Did she give notice just now?"

"Did she not? She's shocked at your coming here as if the place belonged to you, all alone, without either an invitation or your husband. And as she's not 'used with these loose-like ways' she's going. I can never thank you enough. What put it into your head?"

"Your aunt. And I'm glad I've done something to make you grateful to me," said Lucy nervously. "Because I know I am in your black books, and I'm sorry."

He shrugged his shoulders. "It was such a damned silly thing to think," he said. "I should have thought you'd have known Andrew— and Kate—better than that."

"Who told you?" she asked, flushing the unbecoming red which betokened anger or, as in this case, extreme embarrassment. "Andrew?"

"There you go again. Of course Andrew didn't, nor Kate. But I could see the whole thing boiling up, and I did nothing. I trusted that your own good sense would stop you from playing the fool. My mistake."

"No," said Lucy. "Mine. I admit it, Robin. I've admitted it to myself for weeks, but I don't know how to put things right. Perhaps Kate won't accept any apology I make now."

"Yes, she will. Kate's generous. She and Andrew are alike in that. And she won't want to punish him, or Grey and Anne, just to spite you. If I were you, Lucy, I'd apologize. Even if they don't take it, you'll be right with yourself again. But they will, of course. You'd never appeal to either of them in vain. And besides," he added with a laugh, "who are you to say anything? Look at us alone together, and Mrs. MacOstrich shocked to the core—if she has a core, which I doubt. I suspect her of being galvanized iron all the way through."

"But this is quite different," argued Lucy, showing a trace of her usual self.

"Not a bit, to other people's eyes and tongues. I dare say they were all at the kitchen window watching me kiss you just now. I always have thought that window directly opposite the side one in this room was a mistake. You'd better sing very small, Lucy. This little excursion of yours will be published all over Haystoun by to-morrow."

"I don't know that I mind so much," said Lucy. "No, Robin. I won't wait any longer. I am convinced that your MacOstrich isn't going to allow me any tea, and if she did it would probably be poisoned. I must go home." She stood pulling on her gloves, fitting them to her slim fingers with care. "Try to help Andrew not to mind too much," she said suddenly. "I don't want him to go away again."

"He won't go. I know Andrew. But look here, do have a drink if you won't have tea. You've come a long way—"

"What? Turn this illicit meeting into a debauch? It would never do. And I'm in a hurry now. I want to write to Kate before the last post goes this evening," said Lucy.

And at that he let her go, watching her car cross the bridge and turn out of sight. It was a very strange conversation to have had with Lucy, of all people. He had never seen her out of her protective shell of conscious rectitude before; and he had a feeling that he would always like her better now, however stupid she might be in the future. Then he fell to wondering when Kate would come again to Soonhope, and whether it would do him any good if she did.

2

It was on a still, cold December afternoon not long before Christmas that Kate sat in the slow train, once more travelling to Haystoun. There was a powdering of snow on Lammerlaw now, and it was too cold to have the carriage windows wide open. Kate was sitting with her back to the engine, looking westwards along the way she had come at the last sunlight gilding the sky.

After a great deal of consideration, she had made mind that not to see Robin at all was much less bearable than seeing him; it would have astonished and slightly annoyed Lucy if she had known how little her suspicion and her sincere apology for them really counted with Kate. She had used the awkwardness of meeting the Lockharts as her chief argument against going to Soonhope when she spoke about it to Grey, but nothing counted, when it came to the point, except seeing or not seeing Robin. And now she was going to spend Christmas in the country she loved better than any other. In the end, it had been decided for her. An old friend of Greystiel Heron's had asked him and his wife to stay over Christmas, and though the parents had demurred at leaving Kate and Grey, it was plain that they wanted to accept.

"So you see, Paw," Kate said to her father, as he wound the clock, a ceremony which had taken place in the dining-room every Sunday morning for as long as she could remember, "if you and Mother would only be pets and go, Grey and I could stay at Soonhope. Grey is dying to, poor boy, but we didn't want to desert you."

"Oh, well, if you're so keen on going to Soonhope," said Greystiel, his eyes brightening to an almost unbelievable blue in anticipation, "I don't see why your mother and I shouldn't accept George Buist's invitation. She would enjoy it." And after a pause, dreamily, his keen look wandering to the gun-case in the corner: "Wonderful pheasants he's got, Kate. If the weather's any good at all, we should have a couple of days' fine shooting."

Kate, in the train, laughed at the memory of this conversation, so exactly like a hundred others, so exactly like Greystiel that she could shut her eyes and see him there, the clock-key in his hand.

And her mother, too, saying resignedly: "Greystiel will love every minute of it, and I shall eat far too much rich food and put on weight, and be bored to death by George Buist's dull wife. I do wish that your father's friends hadn't all married such worthy women."

"But you and Paw are coming to Soonhope to bring in the New Year," Kate reminded her. "You'll have that to look forward to, darling."

"I shall need it," Mrs. Heron had said.

Starting that morning, early, with the stars not yet gone from a sky of polished steel, and the smell of frost making the nostrils prickle, Kate had thought it was a good sign that, as she got into the hired car to drive to the station, she had heard a harsh, angry cry far above her, and looked up to see two herons, dark, angular shapes with strongly flapping wings, fly slowly over the house towards the loch-side wood. It had cheered the first chilly bit of her journey, and she still liked to think of them now, when the stars were beginning to sparkle above the Lammermuirs, above the roofs of Haystoun and the leafless beeches round Soonhope. The train gave its last loud toot, gathered speed, and rushed noisily into the station, and Kate, fumbling with the carriage door, had it torn from her grasp, and almost fell into Henry's arms on the platform. It was difficult to recover her balance, as Virginia, attached to a lead which she most bitterly resented, instantly wound the slack of it round and round both Kate's and Henry's legs, so that they tottered unsteadily and were only saved from collapsing in a heap by Adam's timely support.

"Hullo, Kate, this is grand," he said. "Henry, you young ass, unwind your dog."

"She's so pleased to see Kate. So am I," Henry said, running round Kate in the opposite direction until she cried:

"Stop, Henry, you're making me giddy!"

Henry came to a standstill with a reproachful sigh, and Virginia promptly wound her lead round Kate again. "There, you see," said Henry. "Oh, I say, Kate, Father's come to meet you, too, only he's looking at the wrong end of the train. Hi, Father!" he raised his voice in full pitch, causing the few passengers and the entire rail-way stall, including the driver and fireman of the train, to look in his direction. "Father! Here she is!"

In the meantime Adam had quietly unfastened Virginia's lead, and Kate walked out of the coils of stout leather, leaving the end trailing on the ground.

"Well, Kate, I'm more than glad to see you," said Andrew, taking her hand in his warm and friendly clasp. "But I don't need to tell you that."

Kate looked at him by the dim oil-lamp flickering above them, and saw that his face, though worn and thin, had a more restful expression than she remembered in the autumn.

"I'm very glad to be here," she said, and the squeeze she gave his hand said everything that her tongue never would or could.

"Let's get out of here. There's lots to do at home— and mistle-toe to hang up, and all sorts," said Adam, and they moved towards the covered stair, Henry still trailing the dogless lead behind them. Only after luggage had been collected, as well as various Christmassy boxes and parcels did he discover his loss.

"Virginia! Where's Virginia!" he shouted. "Adam you fool, you untied her and she's gone!"

"Look in the cab of the engine," advised Andrew, and sure enough there was Virginia, happily sharing the fireman's tea.

"Now perhaps we can go home," said Adam, with an awful look at his younger brother, who, quite unmoved, was hugging Virginia under the very feet of the ticket-collector, to that official's great amusement.

The short run in the car along the lighted road, the plunge through the dark, tree-shadowed drive, was over, and Kate was walking into the hall where she and Lucy had parted to very unpleas-antly. She could forgive Lucy, if she did not try to make excuses for herself, but it would not he easy to forget: the hall at Soonhope would always have the effect on Kate of making her catch her breath when she first entered it. But it was not nearly so bad as she had expected. Lucy made no excuses at all, even her manner was calm and ordinary, her eyes betrayed no uneasiness. In fact, Kate thought with amusement, there was very little difference in her; and then she wondered what she had expected to find? The leopardess could

never change her spots, and Lucy would always be a little dicta-
torial, a little lacking in humour, a little too ready to find fault. . . .

"But she's kinder, I think," Kate said to herself as she dressed
for dinner with a pleasant fire to keep her company. "It may be only
Christmas, of course, but perhaps she'll get into the habit of it."

"Kate," said Henry suddenly, during a lull in the conversation
at table that evening. "Kate, can you sing?"

"Sometimes. Why?" said Kate, for he seemed disappointed.

"Because you and Father have got to sing for the District Nurse
at Charteris, and I thought if you didn't want to, I would sing instead
of you. I've got a new voice now. Bass."

"Heaven forbid!" said Anne, while Kate was still puzzling out
this strange need for music on the part of the District Nurse. "I've
heard as much of your new bass voice as I can bear, and I'm sure
nobody else wants to. It must be more than an octagon lower than
any other human voice, and it sounds like a streptococcus calling
to its young."

As this remark seemed even more impossible to construe, Kate
looked hopefully at Lucy, who was shaking her head at her younger
son. "It isn't exactly the way I should have chosen to ask you to do
it, Kate," she explained. "But as Henry has rushed in, will you sing
at Charteris next week? Vera Charteris is getting up a concert to
raise funds for the district nurse in their parish, and everyone has
taken tickets and promised to come. The trouble is collected nearly
enough performers."

"I don't think I sing well enough," Kate began doubtfully. "Really,
Lucy—"

"Andrew isn't so marvellous himself, but we thought that if you
and he could sing a duet it might be rather effective," said Lucy. "Do
say you will, Kate, and we can practise after dinner."

"Yes, Kate, come on. I don't mind making a fool of myself in
company," said Andrew cheerfully. "But I have flatly refused to
sing a solo."

"They should have asked me. I'd have sung them a solo, two or
three solos, if they liked," said Henry, with a disparaging glance at
those whose services had been requested.

"Shut up," said Adam, and added unkindly: "If you don't eat your
pudding pretty quickly you won't have time for a second helping."

Henry scraped all that was on his plate into one enormous spoonful, forced it into his mouth, and hurriedly helped himself from the dish which Nina was presenting at his left elbow. Then, swallowing with evident effort, he announced his intention of letting them all hear how he could sing *Here's A Health Unto His Majesty*.

"With a fa-la-la la-la la LA?" asked Kate, while Lucy said firmly, "Not at table, Henry."

"Father, *you'd* like to hear me, wouldn't you?" said Henry, turning his shoulder to his mother. "You know mother doesn't care about singing, but you—"

"Certainly not. Wait until we go to the drawing-room," said Andrew hastily. "I shall feel stronger after a glass of port."

"Port is very good for the vocal chords," suggested Henry. "Do you think I'd better have some? It's not that I *like* the stuff, but it's good for my voice, and I expect you want to hear my bass at its very best, don't you?"

"Best or worst makes very little difference," was Adam's brutal reply, while Anne was heard to murmur that really Henry gave himself airs enough for a *prima donnerina* or something.

Port being refused, the singer had to content himself with the grapes suggested by his mother as a substitute, of which he disdainfully ate the greater portion of a large bunch before leaving the dining-room.

After a suitable interval, Kate and Andrew proceeded to try various songs to Lucy's accompaniment, while Anne and Adam played double-dummy bridge and Henry, lying on the hearth-rug, tried to curl his long nose into a shape indicative of scorn.

"That's not *bad*," he said finally, when they had decided that they could sing *Leezie Lindsay* and *The Crookit Bawbee* quite creditably. "I dare say the people at the concert at Charteris won't mind it. And now I'll sing. Mother, will you play for me?"

When he had made several false starts, each time blaming his mother for playing in a key either too high or too low to suit his capricious vocal chords, he began in a voice of such astonishing profundity that it sounded like a Saint Bernard's growl, to wish *A Health Unto His Majesty*. In spite of manful efforts to remain bass, he emitted from time to time a shrill treble squeak very trying to the gravity of his audience, and Kate became really anxious for him as she watched his earnest youthful countenance slowly becoming more and more apoplectic in tint. However, he reached the end of his song without accident, and instantly demanded: "That's a good bass, isn't it?"

"Well, it's certainly bass in bits," said Adam with the air of one making a generous concession against his better judgment. "But I like the other bits better."

Anne had given way to disgraceful laughter in which the others did not dare to join, though their lips twitched and their eyes watered.

Henry shrugged his shoulders. "'The man that hath music in himself, nor is not moved with concord of sweet sounds,'" he began, when Adam placed a large hand over his mouth.

"Less Shakespeare," he said sternly, while from behind his hand came in incoherent mumble of 'treasons, stratagems and spoils.'

"It's time for bed, Henry," Lucy said hastily, and unfairly ended the evening as far as her younger son was concerned.

3

"Do you feel nervous, Father? I bet you feel nervous. You probably won't be able to sing a note," said Henry, in intervals of taking a fond farewell of Virginia and assuring her that he would not be away for long.

It was the night of the concert, and Andrew and the two boys were waiting in the billiard-room for Lucy, Kate, and Anne. Lady Charteris had invited them all to dinner, but, in response to the urgent pleas of the two performers, Lucy had refused, and they had had a light, early meal at Soonhope before starting for Charteris.

"I don't feel nervous yet, but if you go on like this I shall be a wreck before we get there," said Andrew, trying to convince himself that a curious dryness in his throat was pure imagination.

"When Wardlaw had to sing at the School Concert," pursued Henry agreeably, "he was in such a funk that he just stood there in front of everyone opening and shutting his mouth like a fish. Gosh, he did look a fool! I hope you won't look such a fool, Father."

Unable to bear his younger son's society any longer, Andrew went out into the hall. The front door was open, and Kate stood on the step, regardless of the frosty air.

"You'll get cold, Kate," said Andrew, joining her. "And as Henry has already prophesied in my case, you won't be able to sing." His voice sounded husky, and he cleared his throat.

"Will you, Andrew? You sound like a frog," said Kate, her own voice clear and composed.

"God knows. I used to have a habit of losing my voice entirely in times of stress, and it seems to me that it's going to happen again to-night."

"Splendid," said Kate cheerfully. "Then I shan't have to do my piece either. I won't sing alone, and though I'm sure Henry is burning to offer himself as a substitute, I don't propose to do it with him. You'd better go in. I want to look at the stars."

Orion was mounting the south-eastern sky, the Pleiades twinkled confusingly overhead, the Plough ruled in the north. "I can see the papoose on the old squaw's back. They are very clear to-night," said Kate, turning unwillingly from their splendour as Lucy and Anne came downstairs.

"You idiots. Are you both quite mad?" asked Lucy, hurrying to the door and shutting it quickly and decisively. "I've ordered coffee, and we'll have it now, just before we start. Andrew, I suppose you are driving Kate and Henry and me in the big car? Is Adam safe to take Anne in hers? She doesn't want to drive herself in her new dress."

"Perfectly safe," croaked Andrew; and Lucy, without a word, fetched him a large glass of port, which she made him drink.

It was a long drive to Charteris, and Kate occupied the time by thinking of the lovely sight of the wild geese which she and Andrew had seen the evening before at Crookedshaws Loch. Shivering with cold in spite of many coats, they had crouched behind one of the small hides in the gathering dusk, hearing duck quacking on the water and gulls calling overhead, straining their ears for the first sound of geese. . . . At last, after a long wait, there had come the far crying that might have been hounds in the distance, the sound that, with drum-beats and the thud of horses' hoofs coming up the straight and the maddening music of the pipes, is surely the most heart-stirring in all the world. Two geese appeared, black against the grey sky, honking to each other in turn, spying out the land for the rest. When they had settled on the water there was another pause, and then, faint but clear, the clamour of the flight approaching. That wild unceasing crying brought tears of excitement to Kate's eyes, she was clutching Andrew's sleeve to keep herself from calling out. Suddenly she had seen them, the black symmetrical wedge, the great wings beating, the sharp-eyed heads thrust forward on long necks. Skein after skein came in, blackening the evening sky, and to their loud music was added the steady, windy throb of thousands of powerful wings. They passed overhead, the air alive with their voices, and landed with a crash on the steely surface of the loch. Shortly after that Andrew had given her the sign to move softly away, and Kate remembered how surprising it was to hear the splashing of water, the low continuous contented gaggling murmur that issued from those same birds' throats. She smiled, sitting silent beside Lucy in her corner of the car, glad that she would always have it to think about. It was too beautiful to miss. And there had been more. As they had crossed the mile of bleak moor to the road where they had left the car, Andrew had quoted to her from a poem of Housman, something about a 'land of lost content,' and she had disagreed with him, saying that she thought that content belonged to childhood and inexperience, and that no one would really wish to be there again. "You know you wouldn't have kept that lost content at the expense of never having met your Elizabeth," she had told him.

"No, I wouldn't, Kate. And I have won to a different sort of content, after all," he said, adding, "Elizabeth's gone out to Rhodesia to some cousins. I don't expect she'll ever come back to this country. Did you know that Robin had asked her to marry him? He's a chivalrous old ass."

"Chivalrous? Why, he's in love with her." Kate could almost hear her own voice again, sharp with the pain brought by knowledge of that love.

"*Was* in love with her. I'm pretty sure he isn't now, you know. I think myself that he's been out of love—with her—for ages," Andrew had replied with a calm certainty which defied doubt. It had remained with Kate ever since, strangely comforting, though she told herself angrily that it really made no difference to Robin's feelings for her. If any: she doubted if he had any, or else why couldn't he have written or done something after she had gone home? No, the real truth was that all her attraction for him had been that supposed resemblance to Elizabeth Fardell. . . .

"Here we are at last," said Lucy. "I hope you aren't cold, Kate? It's such a long way on a dark night."

And Kate, who felt as if they had only left Soonhope a moment before, found that the car had stopped at a great doorway at the head of an imposing flight of wide stone steps. The whole front of the big palladian house was blazing with lights, cars were parked in rows at the edge of the wide gravelled sweep, and more were coming up behind them.

"Lucy," said Andrew in a hoarse whisper, pulling her aside as they entered a warm bright circular inner hall, delicately scented by great banks of hot-house flowers, gay with the crimson berries and glossy leaves of holly. "Do you hear? My voice has gone completely. For God's sake keep Henry away from me. If he offers me another throat pastille I'll fell him. Can they do without our turn? Kate's and mine, I mean?"

"Andrew, how tiresome. I don't think they can," Lucy said anxiously. "In fact I am sure they can't. I am so sorry about your voice, but how maddening of it to fail you now."

"I'm dashed glad!" whispered her husband. "Look here, Lucy, get hold of Robin and tell him to sing those songs with Kate, he can do it far better than me. Only don't let Kate know, or she'll get nervous. Just let her think I'm singing as arranged. Can do?"

"Leave it to me," said Lucy, a gleam of understanding in her eyes. "I'll see to it. Andrew, do you mean that Robin—and Kate—?"

He nodded. "Looked uncommonly like it in the autumn. This will be a chance for them," he croaked.

"I'm glad Kate is looking so well to-night," said Lucy with satisfaction. "All right, Andrew. You keep out of the way and I'll see to everything."

She flitted off to find Lady Charteris, and Kate, thankful to hear the last of Henry's tales about chaps who had forgotten the words of their songs as soon as they stepped to the platform, went to a small room where the other performers had been marshalled by Sybil Charteris, who was dressed for the Spanish dance she was to do presently. Anne, seizing the reluctant Henry by the arm, dragged him to the ballroom, which had been filled with a mixed collection of every chair in the house for the concert, while large curtains draped in front of the small orchestra platform had transformed it into a stage for the occasion.

Henry, provided with a supply of sweets bought from some of the younger Charteris's, who were selling them as a side-line, settled down to stern and critical enjoyment of the entertainment, after pointing out to Anne in his loudest whisper that the stage at school had footlights and was at least three times as big as the one here. A spirited performance of *The Bathroom Door* merely drew from him the comment that if he'd been taking part in it he could have showed them how to do it; and he then sat in silent but restless misery through a violin solo, the Spanish dance, and a great many songs and recitations.

As the moment approached for *The Crookit Bawbee*, he became alert and interested. "I bet Father'll be in too big a funk to sing," he hissed to Anne through a large mouthful of nougat. "He should have let *me* do it."

"Hsssh!" said Anne.

The curtains were pulled back to show Lucy at the piano.

"I told you so," said Henry. "They've both funked it."

He did not know, of course, that Lady Charteris, to spare the nervous duettists the ordeal of standing side by side on the platform facing their listeners while the opening chords were played, had arranged for them to enter from opposite doors to the first bars of the music. So it happened that the unsuspecting Kate came in and found herself face to face with, and already singing to, Robin Anstruther. She faltered and almost turned back, thinking that there had been some mistake in the programme, but fortunately, before she could move, Robin's excellent voice was asking her, without a tremor, to the familiar tune: "Oh, whereawa' got ye that auld crookit penny?"

"*Gosh*, Anne, do you see? There's been a mix-up," muttered Henry, squirming delightedly. "Robin's gatecrashed their song!"

"*Be quiet*," said Anne savagely.

Surprise and indignation did Kate a good turn by robbing her entirely of nervousness, and though she glared at Robin in a most unloverlike way, she sang so well that she astonished herself.

"Where's Andrew?" she asked him crossly, almost before the curtain had fallen on polite clapping and a burst of tumultuous applause raised by Henry in support of what he obviously considered the home team. "Have I got to sing the other song with you, too?"

"I'm afraid you have. Andrew's voice had packed up," said Robin. "Do you mind? How do you do, by the way?"

"Oh, no, I don't mind at all. Only I think I might have been warned. How do you do?" said Kate, all in the same chill, uninterested tone.

It had been bad enough to sing the song of love that had waited faithfully, with him, but she thought that *Leezie Lindsay* would probably be even more embarrassing, consisting as it did of a proposal, maidenly hesitation, and a coy acceptance. "Anyhow, I'm looking nice," she consoled herself, remembering how pleased she had been for once with her reflection in the long glass. She was wearing a stiff gown of green, watered silk lent her by Lucy, with long, tight sleeves, and on her head a wreath of holly berries and green leaves, which, Henry told her, made her look like Santa Claus, but suited her very well.

"I'll play up to him this time. He took me by surprise with *The Crookit Bawbee*, but I'll show him that he can't have it all his own way," she thought, and went on to the platform again, determined to do her best—or worst.

And when Robin, in the character of Lord Ronald MacDonald, besought her to 'gang tae the Hielands' with him, she gave a display of girlish surprise, tinged with the pleasure of conquest, which convulsed the watching Andrew and delighted the rest of the audience.

'Poor old Rob,' he thought. 'He's being put through the hoop now, all right. I never would have thought that Kate could be such an outrageous flirt.'

He teased her with it on the way home, but Kate took it very coolly. "I think you and I did it better together," she said. "Of course all that coquettishness was just part of the song. It would have been very dull if I hadn't done it."

"It wasn't half-bad, Kate," said Henry in a voice in which condescension strove with yawns. "Not that you wouldn't have been better off with me as Lord Ronald—" but here an indignant chorus cut him short, and he had to resort to growling: "Will ye gang tae the Hielands, Katy-Waty?" in his best bass, this transposing of names affording him exquisite pleasure at his own subtle wit.

Kate could have dispensed with this reminder of the words Robin had sung to her with such melting ardour, but they rang in her head even after she had gone to bed, and kept her awake for quite a long time. Nor was it helpful to a calm and disinterested frame of mind to be greeted next morning, as she went to her bath, by the same song rendered by Henry, who had stolen in ahead of her, and was now lustily carolling: "Will ye gang tae the Hielands, Katy Waty?" as he wallowed and splashed.

Deciding to do without a bath until later in the day, Kate beat a hasty retreat; but it was no better downstairs, where his offspring were assuring Andrew that Robin's voice was streets ahead of his, and that he would not have done nearly so well.

"I'm going for a walk, Lucy," she said, shortly after breakfast, putting her head round the parlour door. "Until luncheon, unless you want me. Any messages?"

"Oh, Kate, I've got some New Year presents for Mrs. Anstruther and those horrible Milligans. Would you hate to leave them at their doors, like an angel?" Lucy sprang up and found three neat parcels wrapped in white paper and girdled with coloured ribbon. "Tablet for Mrs. Anstruther, she's so fond of this special kind, and a pair of gloves for Miss Milligan as a hint not to wear those thread ones, and a really very ugly little hug-me-tight for 'Mamma' who doesn't deserve anything at all."

Kate laughed, took the parcels, and went out. It was the last day of the year, and the grey skies seemed to regret its passing, as they hung low above tree-tops and roots. She delivered Mrs. Anstruther's parcel to the grenadier, who actually achieved a smile as she announced that 'the mistress' was resting until midday. Kate was not sorry that she had not seen Mrs. Anstruther, she did not want to meet those sharp black eyes at the moment. But she had to endure a prolonged and searching examination when she reached Mrs. Milligan's house in Pettycraw Street, for Mima, without taking the presents from her, turned and ran to fetch Miss Milligan. Only too well did she know what a scolding she would get if neither of her mistresses saw Miss Heron.

"So *very* kind of dear Lucy," said Miss Milligan ecstatically, as she clasped the parcels to her meagre bosom. "Please tell her how much we appreciate her thought for us at this time, Kate."

"I will, with pleasure," said Kate. "I hope Mrs. Milligan is well?" ('And able to enjoy gossip as usual,' she added inwardly.)

"Mamma is quite wonderful, thank you," said her daughter with pride. "She is thinking of taking up contract bridge. At her age! She has a most alert and brilliant mind, and this, I hope, will be a real interest to her, though for my part, I shall continue to play whist. I find all that declaring of trumps so difficult to follow . . . Must you go? Well, I won't keep you. No doubt you are meeting someone?"

"No one. I'm going for a walk by myself," said Kate hastily, and went quickly along the street.

Miss Milligan stood in her doorway looking after her. So many odd things had been whispered about Kate Heron, it had been said that Lucy wouldn't have her at Soonhope because of Andrew. But that must be untrue, since there Kate was, and singing at a concert at Charteris last evening, and of course dear Lady Charteris would be the last woman to allow anyone about whom scandal had been talked to enter her house. So perhaps the story about Kate and Robin Anstruther walking about Haystoun in the middle of the night was all a fabrication also? 'I hope so, I am sure,' thought Miss Milligan, watching Kate's straight back, now almost out of sight at the end of the street. 'Such a pity when a girl gets talked about, and of course there could have been nothing in it, when Robin is still in love with that Mrs. Fardell.' She sighed, however, as she turned to go in and pour out a glass of Wincarnis for Mamma. It would be very dull if there was nothing and no one left to talk about!

4

Kate walked out of Haystoun by the bridge over Alewater, and took a road leading to the hills. It seemed to her, now that she had seen Robin again, that it would have been easier after all if she had not. The dull ache in her heart had quickened to a sharper pain, for she had had forgotten what he looked like, and now his picture was far too clear in her memory for peace. She was glad that, when her father and mother, who were arriving at Soonhope in time for tea, went home again in a few days, she would be going with them. It only made her restless to be here. . . . And yet, in spite of all this, the cool air soothed her to a vague dreamy happiness as she walked quickly up the deserted road, noticing the lovely shapes of the bare trees, the brilliant green of moss about their roots, where everything else was brown. All of a sudden she found that she was humming *Leezie Lindsay*, and her face flamed.

"Kate Heron, you're nothing but a fool," she said angrily. "A silly old song that doesn't mean a thing to you."

A robin, hopping close beside her, cocked his head to listen, decided that he did not care for the sound of her voice, and flew away in disgust; and Kate, who always noticed birds, did not even see him go. When she roused herself and saw where she was, she was astonished to find how far she had walked, for she was now on the track which the road had dwindled to, at the foot of the Lammermuirs. As if to compensate her for her energy, the sun suddenly came out from a wreath of cloud, and shed a pale, wintry light on the bare hillside, discovering a single blossom on a clump of whins growing at the side of the rough path. Kate realized that she was warm, that the day was unseasonably mild, and that she had walked far enough, and sat down on a large stone to look at the hills.

And there, after a few minutes more peaceful thought, she was disturbed by a footstep, quick and decided, and looked over her shoulder to see Robin Anstruther.

"Kate," he said at once, without any show of surprise. "I thought I'd find you here. I was in at the farm down the road and saw you pass, so I came after you. Will you marry me?"

Kate gasped, but quickly recovered herself, though the hills were jumping up and down in a most peculiar way. "Is this because you haven't a housekeeper—oh, yes, I've heard all about Mrs. MacOstrich and why she went away—or because I remind you of Mrs. Fardell?"

"Neither, oddly enough," he said. "You know, you ought to marry a man who will beat you when you're tiresome. I'm the man."

"Really?" said Kate, raising her eyebrows. "Is this romance? They do it better on the films."

"Kitty, don't torment me," said Robin, still looking down at her without coming any nearer. "Won't you come with me—not to the Hielands, but to Pennymuir?"

"Your—your bride and your darling to be?" asked Kate flippantly, but her voice stumbled over the words.

"Yes. Just that."

"Well, will you promise never to laugh at me any more?" asked Kate.

"Of course I won't make any such silly promise. I'll always laugh at you. Don't you rather like it, my funny dear?" said Robin, and now he did step forward. He put his arms round her, pulled her up off the stone, held her closely to him. "Don't you like it, Kate—darling?"

"You big stupid, I believe I do," said Kate quite angrily, and then had neither time nor breath to speak because of his long kisses.

At the touch of his lips all her doubts and unhappiness melted away. She did not care whether he had loved Elizabeth Fardell or not, for now he loved her, Kate Heron, and she would be his all the rest of her life, to love and quarrel with and make it up again. . . .

"Oh, Robin! Your eyes are *blue*!" she said rather breathlessly, when he had held her a little way from him and was looking at her slowly and carefully as if he had never seen her before.

"Sort of greyish, I thought. Is it important?"

"Frightfully. And not greyish. Quite blue, nice and dark, almost navy-blue. That's very satisfactory. I have always preferred blue-eyed men, and I thought yours were brown or something."

"Your own are brown with green bits."

"That's why I like yours to be blue," Kate explained patiently. Then she laughed. "I've thought of a much more suitable song than *Leezie Lindsay*," she said.

"What is it?"

"Kind Robin lo'es me," said Kate impudently.

"You hussy. And do you lo'e kind Robin?"

"Not at all. What an absurd idea. I'm marrying you for an establishment and because I've always wanted to live near Lammerlaw."

"Darling, I'll sell Yennymuir and take you to a nice little house in Haystoun, preferably next-door to Mrs. Milligan."

"Very well, Robin," said Kate meekly.

He shook her. "Don't dare to be meek with me. And—er—it's customary for a young woman to use a few endearments when addressing her fiancé."

Kate looked piteous, and to his horror he saw her eyes fill with tears. "I—I can't," she said. "I've always scattered 'darlings' and 'dears' over everyone I'm fond of, and now when I want to call you all of them I don't seem able to get it out. But, ok, Robin, Robin darling, I've always thought them about you!"

Robin laughed. "My absurd sweetheart, bless you for thinking them. But you've done very nicely for a start, you know. You called me darling just this minute."

"So I did. How clever of me," said Kate gaily. "I believe it's going to be rather fun being married to you, Robin. You're so *encouraging*!"

5

They were all gathered in the billiard-room at Soonhope, watching the minute-hand of the clock moving over the last minutes to midnight. Henry, wild with excitement and inflated with success, for he had sung straight through two songs without producing a single treble note, was assisting in the brewing of a huge bowl over which Andrew, Greystiel Heron, and Robin were all hanging "like the witches in *Macbeth*," said Kate.

"How now, you secret, black and midnight hags!" cried Henry instantly, overjoyed at the aptness of the quotation. "And you see, Mother, it *is* midnight, or very nearly, isn't it?"

"Not too much lemon, Drew," murmured Greystiel Heron, stirring the concoction with a large ladle and an air of happy absorption.

"Do you think Virginia would like a little drop of punch, as I helped to make it, Mother?" asked Henry. "I don't like her to be left out of things, it hurts her feelings, Mother."

"I doubt if she would enjoy it, Henry," said his mother, but she smiled at him. It seemed to Lucy that life was beginning to run smoothly again for them all at Soonhope, though she knew now that Andrew's heart was lost to her, if indeed she had ever really had it, yet she could rely always on his steady affection. It was as much as she deserved, she thought, with a humility which was good for her, though she would never let anyone else know that she had grown humbler than she used to be. . . . Anne and Grey sat side by side on a sofa, speechless, a dead loss to the party as far as other were concerned, they scarcely realized that there were other people in the room at all. . . . Mrs. Barlas was happy, her daughter, her nephew who was like her own son, and her old friend Mrs. Anstruther, all within sight, and the younger ones rushing in and out of the billiard-room marshalling the maids and the Pows at the doorway to bring in the New Year.

Perhaps Greystiel Heron and his wife were not looking forward so much to the New Year, when both their son and daughter would marry and leave the shabby old house that was still home to them; but they knew there was no help for it, and hid their feelings successfully, except from each other and Kate. Kate knew, and hovered about them in turn, neglecting Robin to such a degree that Anne was horrified and Adam said approvingly: "Thank goodness Kate's sensible. There's nothing of this sickly lovey-dovey business about her and Robin."

Kate, overhearing, and knowing just how little sensible she was, laughed and looked at Robin across the room. At once, as if she had touched him, he looked back, and she was content.

Henry began to carry the steaming glasses round, with one eye on the clock, the inevitable result being that he left a trail of punch behind him on the carpet.

"Be quick. Oh, do be quick!" he said in an agony of impatience. "Or it'll be New Year before everyone's got some!"

"This will be so good for my arthritis," murmured Mrs. Anstruther, accepting a slopping glass. "But I must drink to a happy and prosperous year for all, especially Robin and Kate."

Everyone in the room, and the servants clustered in the doorway, were served just as the clock began to strike.

"A good New Year to one and all!" cried Andrew, raising his glass, and they all drank with a sudden solemnity silencing them for the moment. Then an orgy of kissing broke out, interrupted by a shrill yell of outraged modesty from Florence, whose cheek had been gallantly saluted by Geordie Pow.

"Now *Auld Long Syne*! We must do the thing properly, so that I can tell the fellows next term how it's done," said Henry, seizing Mrs. Anstruther by one hand and Mrs. Pow's May by the other. Thus urged on, they all formed a circle and led by the celebrated bass voice, sang the time-honoured words.

Kate, between her father and Robin, sang mechanically, looking round her as if to fix the scene on her memory. There was Florence with her cap over one eye, Geordie Pow elated by punch, Mrs. Pow unmoved as ever. There was Mrs. Anstruther, her sharp eyes rather dim, dear Granny crying with a smiling face, her mother, so pretty, clutched by Grey's large hand, who had the love-dazed Anne on his other side, there were Adam and the loud-voiced Henry, with Virginia sitting in patient bewilderment at his feet, quietly chewing the red bow he had tied round her shrinking neck earlier in the evening. Kate did not need to look at the two men she loved most, for she held them tightly.... Last of all, her eyes roved to Lucy and Andrew. Lucy was to all appearance unchanged: the real difference was in Andrew. For he had lost his conciliatory manner towards his wife, his faint consciousness of inferiority. 'And what a good thing,' thought Kate. 'The superiority is in far better keeping when Andrew has it. It won't ever be obtrusive, but just sort of hanging over Lucy so that she doesn't forget she isn't perfect. She will always be yoked with a lamb—dear Andrew, such a nice lamb! But she'll never, never be quite so sure of the lamb's meekness again in her life!'

THE END

FURROWED MIDDLEBROW

CPSIA information can be obtained
at www.ICGtesting.com
Printed in the USA
LVHW031751170521
687666LV00006B/147

9 781914 150470